PRAISE FOR JULES WATSON

THE SWAN MAIDEN

"Wonderful. Watson does not tell the story, she lives it. Mystical and poetic; a tour de force. A magical and compelling recreation of the lost Celtic world."

—ROSALIND MILES, author of *Isolde, Queen of the Western Isle*

"Jules Watson has conjured up the mythic past, a land of Celtic legend and stark grandeur. Readers will find her world and characters fascinating and unforgettable."

—SHARON K. PENMAN, author of *Prince of Darkness*

"In this graceful retelling of the Irish legend of Deirdre of the Sorrows . . . Watson's characters have both a larger-than-life appeal and a commonality that emphasizes their human frailty as well as their dedication to life and love."   —*Library Journal*

"A Perfect 10 . . . The Celtic legend of Deirdre of the Sorrows is given a very human, yet enchanted retelling . . . both glorious and heartbreaking, and Jules Watson uses her beautiful prose and Celtic knowledge to weave a stunning novel that is both uplifting and magical. For a wonderful love story, and some unforgettable characters, I highly recommend *The Swan Maiden.*"

—*Romance Reviews Today*

"Watson weaves the story of Deirdre's deepening understanding of her druid side and her powers to bridge the human and spirit worlds together with history and a powerful love story in this page-turning retelling of one of the Ulster Cycle tales."

—*Historical Novels Review*

"The Irish legend of Deirdre and Naisi is retold in exquisite detail by Jules Watson. She brings to life every drop of rain, blade of grass, and scent of the forest for her readers. Her characters sway you with their heart-rending love for each other and their lands, but what really strikes a chord is how she digs deep into their souls and lays everything bare. Their pain and sorrow are as poetically described as their joy, and each page feels like lyrical prose. Such attention to detail and beautifully rendered dialogue is the mark of a true artist, and Jules Watson should be applauded, for this is a book to be read over and over. Five cups."

— Coffee Time Romance

THE WHITE MARE

"With nods to Marion Zimmer Bradley's *Mists of Avalon* and Diana Gabaldon's Outlander series, newcomer Watson presents an ancient Scotland tightly laced with romantic tension, treachery, and cliffhangers aplenty.... Mightily appealing."

—*Kirkus Reviews* (starred review)

"Watson deftly blends fact and fancy, action and romance in her splendid historical fantasy debut.... An appealing love story, well-researched settings, and an interesting take on goddess worship."

—*Publishers Weekly* (starred review)

"It requires a special sort of imagination to create a plausible vision of Britain at the time of the Roman conquest. Jules Watson rises effortlessly to the challenge."

—*Daily Express*

"In the grand tradition of the historical epic, this is a tale of heroic deeds, kinship and kingship. Truly sumptuous reading."

—*Lancashire Evening Post*

"A sweeping tale of the struggle for love, honor, freedom, and power."

—*Home and Country*

"Strong characters, a compelling story, and sound historical research make this a winner. A stunning debut novel."

—JULIET MARILLIER

"Lovers of all things Celtic will find much to satisfy in this incredible tome."

—*Good Book Guide*

"She breaks new ground targeting Roman incursions north of the border, a road few historical novelists dare to tread."

—*The Herald* (UK)

THE DAWN STAG

"Richly imagined . . . Watson brings first-century A.D. Britain to vivid life with just the right details at the right times, and successfully keeps the tension high, balancing violence and tragedy with romance and religious transcendence."

—*Publishers Weekly*

"Epic and spellbinding . . . The exploration of period gender roles and the intriguing diversions into pagan mythology enhance this enchanting tale. And while the tale is dense and leisurely paced, its emotional impact is significant. . . . If the components of a novel are a volley of arrows, then Watson hits her targets every time."

—*Kirkus Reviews* (starred review)

"A scorching read that will keep readers breathless."

—*Good Book Guide*

"The writing is smooth and pleasing. If you like your Celtic historical romance well written and constantly interesting, this book is for you."

—*Historical Novels Review*

ALSO BY JULES WATSON

The Swan Maiden

The White Mare

The Dawn Stag

Song of the North (U.S. edition)

The Boar Stone (UK edition)

The
Raven Queen

The
Raven Queen

JULES WATSON

 BALLANTINE BOOKS TRADE PAPERBACKS
NEW YORK

A Spectra Trade Paperback Original

Copyright © 2011 by Juality Ltd.

Published in the United States by Bantam Books,
an imprint of The Random House Publishing Group,
a division of Random House, Inc., New York.

SPECTRA and the portrayal of a boxed "s" are trademarks of Random House, Inc.

Map © 2011 by Daniel R. Lynch

Library of Congress Cataloging-in-Publication Data
Watson, Jules.
    The raven queen / Jules Watson. — A Spectra trade paperback ed.
       p. cm.
    ISBN 978-0-553-38465-9 (pbk. : alk. paper) — ISBN 978-0-345-52486-7
(ebook)
    1. Medb (Legendary character)—Fiction. 2. Women—Ireland—Fiction.
3. Mythology, Celtic—Fiction. I. Title.
    PR9619.4.W376R38 2011
    823'.92—dc22
    2010041449

Printed in the United States of America

www.ballantinebooks.com

9 8 7 6 5 4 3 2 1

*To Claire, for story-catching in Ireland,
and Alistair, for always*

ACKNOWLEDGMENTS

Thank you to Anne Groell at Bantam for being so clever and polishing my book, a treat after finally prizing it from my weary hands.

Thanks to Russell Galen—known in my household as Russ Superagent—for his soothing voice of reason, which floated over the Atlantic to calm a few writerly storms.

I could not have pulled this off without the generosity of Bella and Charlie Miller of Lerags House, who gifted to me a "room of my own" in the last months of writing when I foolishly managed to misplace my house. Without the brownie crusts, kitchen-stool philosophy sessions, and really bad movies...I would not have got there. Bella, I will always be grateful.

Claire Swinney was at my side in Ireland when this story was born, and we fished it from the waters and gathered it from the airs together. There are no words of thanks for that.

I am always grateful to my dearly beloved Alistair, who managed to squeeze in read-throughs while moving continents (not literally) and zipping about the world. People have had enough of me being soppy about you. Nevertheless...all my love, always.

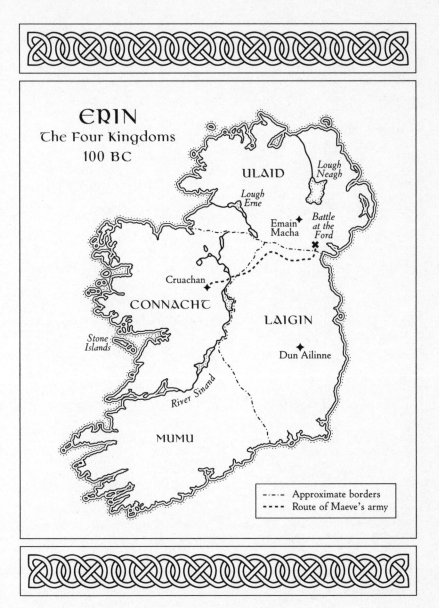

ERIN
The Four Kingdoms
100 BC

ULAID

Lough Neagh

Lough Erne

Emain Macha

Battle at the Ford

Cruachan

CONNACHT

LAIGIN

Stone Islands

Dun Ailinne

River Sinand

MUMU

- ·-·- Approximate borders
- - - - Route of Maeve's army

CHARACTER, PLACE, AND PRONUNCIATION GUIDE

THE FOUR ANCIENT PROVINCES OF ERIN

Ulaid	*Tribe who lived in and gave their name to Ulster*
Connacht	*Old name for Connaught*
Mumu	*Old name for Munster*
Laigin	*Old name for Leinster*

CHARACTERS

CONNACHT

Fort of Cruachan Aí:

Eochaid, *King of Connacht*

Innel, *his son*

Maeve, *Eochaid's daughter*

Garvan, *a young warrior*

Fraech, *Maeve's distant cousin*

Idath, *Fraech's father*

Felim, *Fraech's uncle*

Tiernan, *the chief druid*

Erna, *a female druid*

Lake

Ruán, *a wanderer*

LAIGIN
Fort of Dún Ailinne:

Ros Ruadh, *King of Laigin*

Ailill, *his son*

Finnabair, *Ros Ruadh's daughter*

ULAID
Fort of Emain Macha:

Conor, *King of the Ulaid*

Cormac, *his eldest son*

Fiacra, *his youngest son*

Fergus mac Roy, *former king and Conor's
stepfather*

Illan, *his youngest son*

Buinne, *his eldest son*

Warriors of the Red Branch:

Cúchulainn, *the King's Champion and
nephew*

Ferdia mac Daman, *his best friend*

Naisi, Ardan, and Ainnle, *the sons of
Usnech*

Conall Cearnach, *a Red Branch hero*

The forest:

Deirdre, *King Conor's betrothed*

Levarcham, *King Conor's druid, Deirdre's
teacher*

PRONUNCIATION OF NAMES
Places:

Connacht	KON-AKT
Cruachan	CROO-a-karn
The Ulaid	The OO-lee
Emain Macha	OW-en MAK-uh

Characters:

Ailill	AL-yil	
Cúchulainn	Koo-KULL-lin	*"Hound of Cullen"*
Dáire	DAW-re	*"fruitful, fertile"*
Deirdre	DEER-dra	
Eochaid	YO-khee	
Ferdia	FAIR-dee-ah	
Finn	FYUN	*Anglicized Fionn, male name, "bright/fair"*
Finnabair	FYUN-oor	*"fair spirit"*
Fraech	FRAYkh	*"heather"*
Garvan	GAHR-vawn	*Anglicized Garbhán, "little rough one"*
Levarcham	Lev-ARK-um	
Maeve	MAY-ve	*Anglicized Medb, "she who intoxicates"*
Meallán	MEL-awn	*"lightning"*
Miu	Mew	*Egyptian for "cat"*
Naisi	NEE-sha	
Nél	NYAY-uhl	*"cloud"*
Ros Ruadh	Ross ROO-ar	*"red promontory"*
Ruán	ROO-an	*Anglicized Rúadhán, "red one"*
Tiernan	TEE-ar-nan	*"lord"*

Spoken as written:

Conor	*Anglicized Conchobhar, "dog/wolf lover"*
Conall	*"strong wolf"*

Erna	Legendary maid of Maeve's, gave her name to Lough Erne	
Fergus	"man of strength"	
Innel		

OTHER WORDS:

Sídhe	shee	*Fairy folk, Otherworld beings*
A stór	AH store	*"beloved"*
Banshee	as written	*Ban "woman" and sídhe "fairy"*
Ceara	KYAR-a	*A name meaning "fiery red one"*
Derbfine		*The kin from which a new king can be chosen, descendants of one great-grandfather*
Fili		*A bard.*

FESTIVALS:

Samhain	SAH-win	*November 1. The ancient Celtic New Year; a feast of the dead. The veils to the Otherworld grow thin, allowing the sídhe to pass forth.*
Imbolc	IM-bulk	*February 1. The coming of spring and lactation of the ewes. Sacred to the fertility goddess Brid.*
Beltaine	Bee-YAWL-tinnuh	*May 1. May Day; the fertility festival heralding summer. Cattle are driven between bonfires to bless them.*
Lughnasa	LOO-nah-sah	*August 1. The harvest festival sacred to the god Lugh.*

The
Raven Queen

CHAPTER 1

LEAF-FALL

CONNACHT

Maeve risked a glance behind her. By now her husband would know she had run. Were the clouds darker already in the north? *Don't be a fool.* She heeled her horse over a ditch that cut between banks of yellowing trees.

The stallion's haunches plunged, his forelegs scrabbling. Maeve slammed into the saddle and clung on for all she was worth, rubbing her chin on her shoulder. She might herself throw everything away, but she wouldn't let a man—or a slip of the ground—take it from her.

Dusk veiled the west of Erin by the time Maeve's horse flew into her father's stronghold in Connacht. Ramparts of earth topped with rows of stakes closed about her. Smoke leaked from thatched roofs into the mist.

Cruachan.

At the stables, Maeve leaped from her mount, Meallán, and caught his foaming muzzle. Then she closed her eyes, her brow on his. "I am so sorry, *a stór.*" Woman and horse-breath mingled, and Meallán's hide trembled beneath her palms. "Rest now."

Maeve had been gone so long she didn't know the horse-boy who was gaping at her. "Water him, please," she instructed the lad.

"I must see the king." And she bolted outside, her windblown hair flying.

At once she caught herself. *Remember who you are.* Drawing straight, she picked her way along earthen paths between the little huts where the crafters lived, their mud walls damp with moss, their reed roofs sweeping the ground. People's chatter died as they stared at her mud-spattered trews and cloak, and the kilt of leather strips that covered her thighs, scored by branches and thorns.

Some of the crafters she knew, and their faces kindled when they recognized her. "Lady," they stammered.

One of the weavers reached out gnarled hands that had once braided Maeve's copper hair. Her eyes were milky. "Is that you, child, back with us again?"

Maeve touched her fingers, gentling her voice. "Yes, Meara. But I must get to my father."

The noble houses that jostled for rank around the royal hall— gaudy-painted, banners flying—were nearly empty. The warriors were no doubt huddled somewhere muttering about the king, Maeve guessed. The few older lords who were left stared at her with narrowed eyes.

Her appearance in her old home often coincided with some upheaval, and men muttered that she brought trouble with her. *Such troubles are not of my making.* Maeve thrust that fierce thought at them with her chin, until they looked away.

The king's hall of Cruachan stood at the heart of Connacht like a golden hill. A great ring of stone wall was topped by a vast thatch roof that almost touched the ground, sweeping up to a carved crest hung with banners.

A circle of stakes around the doors held shields, racks of antlers, and pennants of wolf-tails, now limp with rain. As Maeve approached she smoothed her wild red hair, shielding her eyes from the guards and sweeping past before they could stop her.

The hall swallowed her, a cavern of oak pillars and thick furs gleaming in the firelight. Flickering lamps picked out the glint of shields and swords on the walls. A hint of strange herbs made

Maeve's nostrils flare. Yes, there was sickness here. The rumors she had heard were right.

Her heart thumped as she fumbled her hair into a braid with chilled fingers and pushed through the servants about the fire-pit. She clambered up the ladder to the sleeping floor—a ledge of oak planks that ran inside the great roof. Beds nestled beneath the eaves, screened by wicker.

Hurrying to the king's chamber, Maeve charged into the back of her older brother Innel. Years of fighting and illness had thinned the ranks of siblings until only these two remained.

Whipping around, Innel caught hold of her.

Maeve stared over his shoulder at a spindly figure in a pool of lamplight. *Father?*

"What the gods are *you* doing here?" Innel's arms were iron bands, cutting off Maeve's breath. "Out, all of you!" he growled at the servants, who fled. Only then did he release her.

Maeve swayed. Her sire Eochaid had always been a stern oak tree looming over her. Now he was a fallen trunk, his branches withered. The fiery hair he'd bestowed upon her and Innel was now the hue of ash. And his face...The left side was melted like wax, and slack lips spun a thread of drool. One eye drooped, revealing a sliver of white.

Maeve had to make her throat move. "When were you going to tell me, brother?"

Innel's eyes were cold as he folded his brawny forearms. Sword scars webbed the corded muscles with silver. "You seem to have forgotten you are of the Ulaid now, sister—Conor's *queen*. You do not belong here."

Maeve got up. Her brother always stiffened his ruddy hair into spikes and wore his scars, broken nose, and butchered ears as battle spoils. She must be wary, but she was also trapped. Her husband King Conor's famous Red Branch warriors—the elite fighters of the Ulaid war-bands—could be coming already to drag her back to their fortress.

She curled her hand at her neck, hiding her pulse. For the

safety of her people, she could not stay silent. "I have run away from Conor."

Innel grimaced and grabbed her wrist, pushing her against the slope of thatch. His breath reeked of ale. "You stupid ... willful ... *bitch.*"

Maeve arched a brow, breathless. "Surely I cannot be all of those, brother. It takes sense to be willful, after all."

He growled, his grip biting. "Father sealed the Ulaid alliance with oaths—with *you.* You'll draw the wrath of Conor and his Red Branch upon us at the very moment he is weakened. Do you care nothing for our people?"

"I care only for them, which is why I've come back!" She dragged herself free, rubbing at the welts he had left. "I lived among the Ulaid for two years. I know their heroes, their war-bands. *I* know the mind of Conor the cunning."

Innel paced, plucking at his ruddy moustache. "We must hand you back to them without delay."

Maeve's nostrils flared as she sought for her only weapon. She cocked her head. "So already you make Father's decisions for him. You hover around his sickbed like a crow on a carcass."

Her brother clenched his fist.

Maeve watched it, readying herself to duck.

Just then King Eochaid groaned, and his body stirred beneath the coverlet of wolf fur. Fear darkened Innel's face.

Ah, Maeve thought. She traced the bedpost with a shaking finger. "If Father is ill, other kinsmen will be gathering, as hungry as you to rule. So you will send your thugs to drag me back to the Ulaid now, leaving you here alone?"

Innel scowled, knuckling his temple as if her words strained him. At last he stalked past her. "You will soon be begging my favor, sister—when I am king."

After he left, Maeve sank onto a stool at her father's side and rested her brow in her hands. Her jerkin of toughened hide dug into her ribs, making it hard to breathe. *What have you done?* But sometimes she had to act, or she felt she would burst open ...

A cracked wheeze. "You...broke...my alliance?"

Maeve sprang straight. Eochaid's good eye was blazing.

Her gaze flew to his hand, and out of habit Maeve flinched. Only then did she realize it still lay limp. "Yes, Father."

"Conor's warriors will fall upon us...battle and ruin..." Spittle gleamed on his lips. "Traitor!"

Maeve was on her feet. "Three times you married me off to kings and princes, Father, and *you* broke two of those alliances yourself." *Just as I finally scrounged some scraps of peace.* She gulped that down. Eochaid hated defiance but admired bravery. How to walk that line? She lifted her chin. "None of them made war once you returned their bride-gifts. They all had other women, and Conor does, too. He is already betrothed to someone else, an orphan girl he has raised as kin. He will soon have other wives..."

"*You* are his wife! You were given to him to seal our oaths, his and mine."

A cow to be bartered away. She swallowed that, too.

"You would not dare defy me if I was well," he slurred, withered fingers knotting the blanket. "A raven, you are, come now to pick over my bones."

Maeve's nails dented her palms. No, she was merely desperate. And this close to him—listening to his labored breath, seeing his helpless limbs—she could not think of anything save when *he* first made her feel this same way.

Paralyzed.

Maeve turned from him, trying to fill her lungs. But she was there again anyway, sixteen years ago...as if yesterday. The day her father first gave her body away.

The firelit lodge of the aging King of Laigin, Ros Ruadh. Once more she tasted the sting of vomit in her throat, felt the drag of robes too heavy for a twelve-year-old. She heard the bracken crackle as she cowered into the bed, too shocked to whimper; remembered the gleam of sweat on the Laigin king's brow as he labored over her, wheezing.

Maeve's will had long ago conquered the pain. It was the

invasion that was so hard to banish, the sense of her own bright self being ground away into nothing.

When she was sixteen, her father plucked her from the household of the stern and indifferent Ros Ruadh, only to marry her again to Diarmait, prince of Mumu. *He* pinned her with brute arms and a heavy belly, to make her writhe so he could strike her and stoke his lust.

She eventually found a way to make him leave her alone, though: claiming a say over her body by rutting with men of her choosing, and many of them. She had to endure worse beatings at first, but finally Diarmait's rage turned to repulsion, as she had hoped. He sought other wives and kept the alliance with Connacht in name only.

So again Maeve carved out a sliver of peace for herself, this time for ten years. It was then her father went after his greatest prize yet: kinship with the Ulaid, the most powerful kingdom in Erin. Two years ago Eochaid broke his oaths with Diarmait of Mumu and she was sent away for a third time, to be Conor's queen.

Of all her husbands, it turned out to be Conor, with his sardonic smile and opaque eyes, his stiff body and dry, cool hands, who alone sought Maeve's bed every night.

It was not *she*, though, that made him want to plow that field. At twenty-six when they wed, Maeve was already too old for his tastes. Though graying and wrinkled himself, he liked fresh maids who had never been broken by another.

No...Conor wanted an alliance with Connacht, so his western flanks would be protected. And more. In an ancient war, Connacht had taken the hill that was the sacred heart of Erin. Since then it was said that with their bodies, royal daughters of Connacht bestowed upon their mates the blessings of all the goddesses of Erin.

That was why Conor so fastidiously folded aside his embroidered robes and lined his rings up on the dresser while his guards tied her wrists, taking no chances. And why, as he thrust atop her, he stared at the wall with such fierce determination—not for her, but to possess Connacht's sacred blood for himself.

Now she knew why.

Maeve closed her eyes, blinked to clear them, and turning around, sat by the bed. The movement made the lamp flame dip, and shadows reached for her. "Father," she said in a low voice, "I came back because I heard you were sick, because I want to look after you."

So you will let me stay, and for once be Maeve alone. His little warrior, bold and fearless, who had once made Eochaid laugh with pride...before she grew breasts and he remembered that he could use her for better ends.

No more marriages. No more bodies crushing her. No one but her own self.

The king's good eye narrowed.

Maeve took a breath. "And I came back to bring you urgent news of Conor mac Nessa." Maeve covered her father's paralyzed hand with her strong one. "Conor does not want an alliance with Connacht. *He wants to take us over.*"

Eochaid gargled in the back of his throat.

Maeve's knuckles went white. "*That* is why I ran from him, to tell you before it is too late!"

Eochaid struggled to wipe away his spittle with his other hand. "You heard him say this? What proof?"

Maeve hesitated. "I heard...whispers, asides...remarks I did not at first understand. But they have built a certainty within me."

He hissed under his breath, one side of his mouth pulling down. "So you know nothing."

Maeve clung to this lifeline. She had thought that if she could lay some great triumph at his feet, he might free her and let her stay here at his right hand. Safe...at last. "I know that Conor wants to rule all of Erin."

"*Know?*"

She suppressed a shudder. "I...feel it. Sense it. He wants to rule everything." Her body had been conquered by Conor mac

Nessa. His bones had caged hers. Of course her instincts sensed more than anyone could ever know. And then, only days ago, she had heard his whisper in the night...she was sure it was not a dream...that he would wrench a son from her and use him to make Connacht his own.

Men might use her, but not *her child*.

Never again.

Maeve's belly cramped and she bit her lip. "We must gather fighters and attack before he does—"

"Bah." Eochaid struck her away. "The four kingdoms have stood for many ages; the gods hold this as sacred. We are well-defended, and Conor is powerful. It would be madness to attack him without proof or reason. Unless *you* have just given him one." His lip curled. "I did not ask you to *spy*, I sent you to be a queen to him, *to bind me to the Ulaid throne*. And instead you insult him and run away? I will pack you back off to him with no delay!"

Maeve endured this torrent, but she would not endure Conor mac Nessa again. One day he would come for Connacht—her people, free and proud—and she would be here to defend them when he did.

As Eochaid paused, wheezing, Maeve leaned her arms on the bed. She put her chin close to his on the pillow, like she did when he loved her like a son.

Before he sold her body to an old man.

She dropped her voice. "If you order me back, Father, I will make sure that all the bards of Erin sing of the heartless king who crushed his loyal daughter, and so was punished by the gods." Her finger shook as she pointed at his frozen legs. "Can you survive *that* with your hold already weakened?"

Wrath twisted Eochaid's body up, rucking the blanket as his face flushed. All at once his eyeball rolled back. "Ah! Dagda and Lugh...lords above..." His gaze wandered across the roof-beams, suddenly untethered from all sense.

The hairs on Maeve's neck rose.

Her father chuckled, his eyelid twitching. "*Aye ... my* strength ... my true blood. *The one to come after me ...*"

Maeve's shoulders went rigid. "What?"

Her father's head tossed on the pillow. "No ... I ..."

As Maeve gripped his arm, Eochaid's good eye flared and blinked. Sense gradually crept over it again, the pupil sharpening, the mists driven back.

"*I heard you.*" Maeve was breathing swiftly. "I am the only one with your courage, your strength! Set me in a place of honor beside you!"

A trusted adviser. Devoted daughter. Anything.

With a stony face, Eochaid gathered the blankets and stared at the roof. "You speak madness because you think me mad. You have no allies or sword-brothers. You are nothing, a woman. You have no power."

Maeve stood, a knot gathering in her chest. "You could give me that."

Give me my own, so no one can hurt me ever again.

Not even you.

Eochaid's bark of mirth turned to a coughing fit. Maeve did not stir, and eventually Eochaid thumped his breast, wiping more drool away. "If you were truly mine, you would not need me to give you anything." His lips thinned. "If Conor demands you back, I will tie you up and send you to him. If not ..." His eye darted aside, and Maeve read a fear there that, for now, was greater than Conor of the Ulaid. For Eochaid's seizure had struck a dangerous blow to his kingship.

"I will keep you, for now. My kinsmen circle, waiting to snap me in two; waiting for my mind to falter along with my body. *You* will tell me everything they say. And if you amuse me, and feed me my slops, and bathe away my filth, I may keep you here even longer."

The bitterness was so sharp Maeve could taste it. *Scraps, and never more.*

With heavy steps Maeve returned to the stable in the rain to un-
saddle Meallán and shoulder her baggage. The dusk shadows had
gathered inside the round thatch building, with its two wide
doors separated by a cluster of blackened oak posts. Her instincts flared when she saw her stallion's ears turned back, but it
was too late.

"So you've dragged yourself away from the old bastard at last?"

Maeve spun around, reaching for a blade she did not bear.
Conor never let her wear one ... but gods, her hand itched for a
sword.

Her brother Innel was astride a mounting stone beside the
other door, a dagger in his scarred hands. Frowning, he dug dirt
from his broken nails with the blade, then leaned over to sharpen
the edge on the stone again.

Maeve decided to leave, then return later with someone she
knew. Innel would not hurt her horse, of that she was sure.

Her brother was a heavy brute, but his warrior skills were
better-honed than that blade. Even as Maeve turned, his shoulder
knocked her against the stable wall. Before she could twist away,
his dagger hand thumped down beside her head, the other catching her wrist as she struck at his belly.

"Why are you here?" he hissed. "You think, after all this time,
you can be Father's favorite again?"

Maeve could not stop the flare of her eyes. A strand of wet hair
was caught across her mouth.

Innel laughed. His skin was ale-veined and thickened into
folds by the sun. Up close, the oil that curled his red hair smelled
rancid. They were both born to be tall, with strong, sharp bones,
but Innel's had been overlaid with flesh from too much rich food
and mead. "You stupid bitch."

"You really should think up some new curses, brother."

Innel's brows knitted, one dragged down by a ragged scar. He
had placed the knife along the wall, and now the cold tip brushed

Maeve's neck. She swallowed. Conor had kept a dagger like that beside her when he rutted, barely touching her throat, as if it was not really there.

"You endanger us with this habit of running from your husbands, sister. Father will not stand for it again."

"*He* broke my other marriage oaths himself."

"But you tried to run from Diarmait of Mumu once, I seem to remember. That nearly cost us dear at the time."

No one knew the reason for that flight but her father, Maeve, and Diarmait himself. "I went back to Diarmait," Maeve forced past the pain in her breast, "and was a wife to him for many years. It was Father who took me away for the Ulaid—"

"Then you should have stayed there! Instead, you risk our kingdom and think Father will love you for this? If you have come to lie, and plot, and take *anything* from me—"

"Have a care, brother." Maeve's voice was unsteady as she drew her heels together, pushing her back up the timber wall. "I bring Father important news of the Ulaid." She peeled the hair from her face, improvising wildly. "That is why he made me wed Conor—to spy on his Red Branch warriors."

Innel snorted, holes gaping in his grin where he'd lost two teeth. "You mean spread your thighs for the Red Branch."

She turned her flaming cheek aside. "It was our plan all along, mine and Father's. So you will not harm me or that plan will be ruined, and Father will blame *you* for it."

Innel's smile flickered, but though his lip remained curled beneath his long moustache, he drew the knife away and sheathed it. "Liar."

Her nostrils flared. "Try him, then. But remember you are not the only kinsman with a right to the throne. Others gather at his sickbed, lords with more allies than you." She bared her teeth. "So I wouldn't make any mistakes about my loyalties, and what powers *I* hold."

It was a desperate throw that seemed to work.

Innel's mouth spasmed and he swung his hand. Maeve held

rigid as he stopped short of her cheekbone, but he contented himself by pushing her temple with the heel of his palm, as if they were still children. "I will be watching, sister."

He lumbered away. Maeve did not move, though her blood was racing. Innel flexed his burly shoulders, his head swinging to either side as he searched the darkness that gathered between the squat houses, their roofs of thatch now dripping with rain.

He was afraid.

They all were, for what might come now that Eochaid's iron grip was weakening.

Maeve shouldered her pack and made her way to the women's lodge beside the king's hall. There she sought out an older serving maid who knew her from before. The little woman gripped her fingers with floury hands, touching her face and damp hair and marveling that she had not changed. No one had taken Maeve's bed-place yet, she told her.

Maeve climbed the stairs to the sleeping ledge beneath the roof, shifting aside the piles of furs and baskets tossed on her mattress. The lumpy pad of bracken and linen was musty, but she did not care.

Scraping a little hurdle of willow across for privacy, she threw deerskins over the bed and, climbing in, drew a beaver fur over her. She settled on her back, groping either side for the mattress as if she was in a boat on a stormy sea.

She was alone.

Her body could spread across the bed and meet no rigid flesh or clenched muscles. No harsh breath would stir the darkness that cradled her.

As her fingers reached the rails of the bed-box, and still the space was hers, Maeve's shoulders at last lowered. There, she let her breath out for the first time in days.

In years.

Later that night Maeve wrapped herself in furs and curled up on the earthen ramparts around the mound of the warriors.

Despite the frost, the hall doors behind her were slightly ajar. A sliver of firelight spilled across the turf, along with shouts and a ragged tune from bone flutes. The roar of warriors was pierced by the shrieks and laughter of women.

Maeve sat with a rod-straight back, clasping her knees. As a child she often pretended she was a shield, arms bound around legs like toughened hide to wood. One shield was not enough now, though, for Cruachan was a royal fort like no other in the four kingdoms.

Mumu in the south was safe behind its mountains. The rocks of the Ulaid, in the North, yielded so much iron and gold that Conor had built the strongest war-band. In the east, Laigin boasted rich fields of barley and wheat. Close to the sea-routes, Laigin exchanged grain, furs, and hides for wine and other treasures from Gaul and the Middle Sea, and the other kingdoms relied on that trade.

Connacht in contrast was all pasture, soaked with marshes and rivers, the meadows sprouting lush grass that fed the greatest cattle herds in Erin. It was rich in beef, hides, milk, butter, and honey. These lowlands, though, were vulnerable.

Cruachan itself was built on an undefended plain—a sacred place where hundreds of barrows of the sídhe and the ancestors were scattered over the turf. The ancient mounds were hallowed, and avoided by the living.

Tonight they were an ocean of darkness.

But around them blazed life. Her people's lives.

Fires picked out the temples, king's hall, and warrior mound, each surrounded by a ditch and bank with stakes marching along the top. The crafters and herders, however, lived in exposed huts dotting the plain. Now Maeve yearned for a great fort on a hill like Conor had at Emain Macha.

A place that was strong and high.

She strained north toward the Ulaid. The wind brought down a flutter of dried leaves, rasping along the oak planks beneath her. The long dark would soon scour Erin down to bare trees and hills. There would be nowhere to hide.

A complex web of alliances bound the four kingdoms, spun from fear and mistrust. Though the young warriors boasted their bravery with cattle-raids, there had been no great wars for many years. Conor's gold attracted the greatest warriors, but he knew that if Mumu, Laigin, and Connacht ever banded together, even the Ulaid would fall. Of course, the others would not risk that, for fear one of *them* would then become all-powerful.

Such fragile alliances...and Maeve had just snapped one. It was either that or break in two herself.

She jumped at a querulous mew as something curled about her legs. Her breath rushed out. "So you are still here, my beauty." At first sight Maeve had been entranced by this odd striped creature aboard a ship from the Middle Sea. Unlike hounds, Miu was aloof and utterly uncontrollable.

The cat had to be hers.

"At least you are happy to see me." Maeve caught the creature to her chest, savoring the rare sense of a heartbeat next to her own. When Miu stiffened and twisted free, Maeve also tensed. Belatedly, she recognized one of her father's warriors, Garvan, weaving along the rampart.

"Heard you were back." Garvan hunkered down and propped a jug between his feet. Grasping Maeve's head, he smacked their lips together.

Kissing him back, Maeve reached out and clouted him in the belly.

"Lugh's balls!" He rubbed his stomach. "Do that again and I'll empty my guts on your feet."

"Charming." Maeve left her hand on his chest. Beneath a thatch of black hair, Garvan had a blunt, kind face, with a snub nose— broken like that of most warriors—and a mouth always ready to laugh. Below that he was far more interesting. At twenty-three, his muscles were carved by swordplay, not slack like Conor's.

Maeve was older than Garvan, but as a royal lady she had bathed in milk, and plumped her skin with honey and Greek oils. The lines about her eyes were not deep, and her limbs were still lithe from riding. "I have not seen you for two years, and you think you can bed me just like that?" She prodded his chest.

"We've never shared soft words, spitfire." Garvan belched, his thumb drawing unsteady circles on her neck. "So living among the Ulaid has weakened you, eh?"

"Balls to that!" She smacked him again. Men always took from her: Conor, Ros Ruadh, Diarmait. Her father. Now *she* would take, because pleasure could burn even this darkness away.

She spread her fist into soft fingers, stroking up Garvan's neck. Encouraged, his hands dived inside her tunic and there paused. Maeve had always bound her breasts with linen to make it easy to ride and throw a spear.

Garvan snorted. "Still a battle to reach you, then, spitfire."

"I told you the Ulaid haven't weakened me."

Garvan clumsily unwound the strap, wafting freezing air across her chest. Over his shoulder, Maeve faced the night, eyes wide open. "Tell me which lords are circling, and what the men say of my brother and father. Tell me everything."

CHAPTER 2

LEAF-BUD

R uán stumbled into the hollow and fell in the mud. He crooked his chin over his shoulder; he could no longer feel the presence of the farm-lad who had led him here. His throat cramped in panic.

That sense of another's spirit was all he had, now that he was blind.

Ruán had felt the lad's fear like a throb in the darkness ahead of him, all the way along the fringes of the marsh. At last it got the better of the child, and he fled from this ragged druid with the blood-soaked cloth over his eyes. Far away...

Ruán groped the pebbles, his mind wandering.

The wisewomen on the islands used to whisper he was a stag, not a man. They traced their fingers over his lithe flanks, tangled his hair. *Russet as a deer*, they sang. The lords thought this fine form of his echoed a noble mind. They listened to him.

Ruán smiled, tasting fever-sweat. Now he made children run away.

Now the world was forever dark, the ground plunging with every step. Thorns and branches always grasping at him from that blackness, scoring his face and arms. Rocks striking his bones.

Ruán hung his head, water pooling between his fingers.

These are the mere-lands, the frightened lad had stammered. *Folk get lost here and don't come back.*

Swamps, lakes...yes, the heart of Connacht was wet. *There is water to sink into here.* Ruán was aflame, the wounds in his eyes burning.

He made himself crawl on, groping through the sludge, nose

thrust out to try and pierce the darkness. Yet every time he got his feet under him, he staggered and fell, until he gave up and could only belly his way over the mud. At last a vast quietness opened ahead.

Lake-water glinted in his mind.

There was no sound but the rustling of reeds. Ruán parted them and fell to a sandy shore. There he stripped off his ragged tunic, the sweat running from his skin. He groped along until he found some posts that arched a little jetty over the water.

His druid memories flared. People came here to give offerings to the lake.

Now he would be an offering.

When he reached the end of the jetty, the burning moved from his eyes into Ruán's heart, and on his hands and knees he gagged on bile. He spat it out, but the gnawing remained. Why could he not retch up guilt before he died?

I killed Lord Mulach's boy. I killed him.

The gods did not take him, though, when the burning poker seared his eyes, so he knew their punishment must have been for him to live. Could he force their hands now? *The fire…his head…*

His training could no longer control the pain.

Drawing himself up, Ruán wondered in a daze whether to say a prayer. But a gust of wind hit him, and he toppled. He plunged into the blessed water.

He was flying, at last.

Turning in darkness, he imagined sunlight shafting down and cradling him in gold. He curled up like a babe, letting go of life, the relief pulling him deeper. Surrender. Salvation…

Something touched him.

Fingers knotted his swirling hair, clasping his arms and legs. They dragged Ruán back as he feebly struggled against them. At last he broke into air and collapsed on the ground.

The world spun as Ruán retched up gouts of brackish water. The rest of his senses turned black as well, and then the void claimed him.

In the northern lands of the Ulaid, Levarcham hovered in the shadows of King Conor's hall.

As the king's druid, she sat by him when he feasted chieftains and traders. Tonight, though, the hall at Emain Macha had been given over to the Red Branch, the most highly skilled warriors in the Ulaid war-bands.

All young fighters coveted a place in their sacred brotherhood, and the Red Branch had gathered from all over the Ulaid now for a feast to initiate the new recruits. Elite they might be, but Red Branch bellowed, reeled about, and stunk of sweat and sword-grease like any other man. And still Levarcham couldn't seem to leave.

A foreboding kept her here in the darkness beyond firelight.

No one approached her. Her strange mingling of smooth, watchful face and prematurely gray hair unsettled people, though it was her limp they looked away from, this mark of the gods. At forty, her hip deformity was paining her more each day, and *that's* what scared these brawny warriors.

The hall doors creaked open with a gust of icy air. There was something familiar about the man shouldering his way through the throng, with a plump woman behind him. Huddled into himself, bowed head—he was no warrior. As the firelight caught them, Levarcham came to attention. It was Fintan and Aiveen, Deirdre's guardians.

Deirdre. An orphan maid betrothed to Conor since her birth, when the druids foretold that the girl would blossom into a rare beauty.

Conor's great desire. Conor's prisoner.

The king had taken the babe and hidden her in the woods to be groomed as his bride, with only Fintan and Aiveen to raise her—and Levarcham to teach her. She was nearly eighteen, but late-blooming, and Conor had not plucked her yet. No one was meant to ever leave her alone.

My chick. Levarcham flew around the shadows to Conor's carved chair. Fintan was stammering an explanation to the king, and Aiveen's eyes were terrified. Deirdre must be dead. Levarcham groped for the back of Conor's chair, winded.

"She has *disappeared*, my lord," Fintan babbled. "Run away." He wrung scarred fingers together.

Levarcham could only see the gray braids snaking over Conor's shoulders. He had frozen. The silence drew out, the air stretched thin. *"What?"*

All the boisterous warriors turned at the slice of the king's voice. Levarcham's mind hissed that this must not be revealed before the fighting men and nobles. Deirdre had run away from Conor, and after his wife Queen Maeve ran from him, too. But it was too late to stall Fintan's tongue. "She has been acting strangely for moons. And now she's just...gone."

No one noticed Aiveen scuttle to Levarcham in the shadows and press something into her palm. Aiveen's hand was icy.

"Where is that wife of yours?" The king's roar slammed into the rafters. "I want an account of this *now!*"

Levarcham could only squeeze Aiveen's arm. One of them was gray, lean and severe, one plump and plain, but both were Deirdre's mothers. The druid managed to slink out the door as the uproar grew behind her. The king's wrath turned into demands for horses, chariots, and weapons, and servants and warriors began scurrying around.

Levarcham let the ruckus fade as she hobbled to her own lodge and crouched by her fireside. She smoothed out the scrap of kidskin Aiveen had just given her. Deirdre had drawn upon it with charcoal.

It was a line of three blackbirds with a fourth hovering behind, wings spread. Levarcham had taught Deirdre to fashion birds with great skill, and these could not be mistaken for ravens or crows. They were blackbirds. Three singers with dark plumage... dark hair. Someone had ventured into the barren hills around Deirdre's hiding place and helped her escape from King Conor.

But who? Someone who could face down cold, storms, and wolves. *Warriors.* Three black-haired warriors. Famed singers.

There was only one family that fitted that description: Naisi, Ardan, and Ainnle, the three sons of Usnech. *The fourth following of her own will.* Deirdre had broken from Conor's cage after all.

She had run away with Naisi and his brothers.

Levarcham's sight clouded and her thumb caressed the charcoal, smearing it. Sense compelled her to throw the kidskin into the fire, but as she did, her heart reached to snatch it back. It was the last thing Deirdre had touched ...

Sense won. No one must know how the girl had fled Conor.

Levarcham knew him better than anyone. Last leaf-fall, after Queen Maeve ran from him, Conor had stormed to the little steading in the woods to see Deirdre, seeking a balm for his wrath. The blossoming beauty performed a swan dance for the broken king, and that night Levarcham had watched Conor's mask at last slip.

All these moons she had not been willing to face what she saw behind it, for it was primitive ... savage.

An obsession so intense it turned his mind away from Maeve of Connacht altogether and fixed it upon Deirdre, as if the possession of her—nay, her utter consumption—would right every wrong and make him stronger than ever.

Now Levarcham saw his hungry face in the flames of her fire, and clenched her fists in her lap. Deirdre must remain free, and never fall into Conor's hands again.

A few days later King Conor summoned Levarcham.

With leaden legs she climbed the stairs of his hall to his chamber, an alcove sheltered by wicker screens. The chamber was almost in shadow, a single lamp waving a feeble flame. The light was enough, though, to root Levarcham to the spot.

Conor possessed a proud, bony face, with arched cheekbones

and an elegant nose above thin lips. But his jowls and mouth were now haggard, his rigid back slumped. "The girl has taken refuge at Aed's dun, to sever a betrothal she says was not of her own consent. She wishes to be released from her childhood betrothal *to me*. So what do you think, Oh learned one, of such a claim? You know the laws." Conor swung to her with feral eyes. "Did you put her up to this?"

Levarcham tried moistening her lips, but her tongue was stuck. "You know I had no forewarning."

"Damn all that. Is what she says true?"

Levarcham was struggling to keep her wits afloat. Deirdre was *alive*. A darker rush followed. *Foolish maid! You wound such a king and think no blows will be returned?*

"Woman," Conor hissed, "answer me!"

Breathlessly, Levarcham relaxed her expression. "Given her unique birth, it's possible. Of course, it is the elder druids you must consult."

Her voice was calm, but Conor struck without warning. He crossed the room and gripped her jaw, forcing back her head. "Did you know," he whispered, "that she was stolen away by that black pup Naisi? Did you?"

Levarcham kept still. She had never seen Conor lose his wits and lay hands upon a druid. The force of his wrath loosed strands of graying hair that fell across his sunken cheek, and the sense in his pale eyes had been shattered by something she now recognized as humiliation—a force greater than anger. "You forget yourself," she gasped. He released her, and Levarcham rubbed her windpipe.

Conor spun about, gripping the edge of a low table. "You told me she would be pliant. Even if you were not there when the theft occurred, still you bear the blame for this!"

Hiding her wrath, Levarcham decided to divert him. As his druid and talking-woman, she was meant to skewer the king's follies, remind him of generosity and wisdom. "You say 'theft' and 'steal,' though everything points to Deirdre leaving of her own will." Even as she said it, Levarcham realized that Maeve of

Connacht had chosen the same thing. Two women had left Conor mac Nessa now, the most powerful king in Erin. And all his warriors knew it, and all the other kingdoms soon would, too.

At that moment the lamp-wick burned through and the reed fell in the oil, sending out a bright flare. Only then did Levarcham see what lay at Conor's feet.

An Aegyptian chair of cedar had been torn apart. The legs were ripped off, the cushions shredded, feathers speckling the wood like lichen. The pieces that were left had been stamped on until they splintered.

Levarcham's skin went cold.

⌘

The Red Branch warrior Ferdia glanced at his friend Cúchulainn's back.

The fort of the Ulaid chieftain Aed had fallen away behind the green haze of budding trees, and Ferdia and his sword-brother were alone on the muddy track. They were in the Ulaid borderlands near Connacht to the west, and these dangerous hills were almost deserted.

Clouds bore down on their heads, needling them with rain. Ferdia squinted through it, nudging his horse to catch up. Cúchulainn's own stallion was bound to his soul, and it was skittish now, picking up his master's tension and tossing his head.

Cúchulainn had not said anything since they left Aed's stronghold. Naisi, his two brothers, and King Conor's betrothed—the girl Deirdre—had all been sheltering with the old cattle-lord. Then someone tried to kill them on a deer-hunt, and one of Aed's nephews had died instead. Naisi and his brothers had fled with the girl before Cúchulainn and Ferdia could reach them.

Now Ferdia could see that Cúchulainn was chewing his cheek. Ferdia waited, walking his horse beside his friend.

Cúchulainn expelled a breath and struck his leather breastplate. "*We were too late.* We must get to Naisi and the boys before anyone else does. All these lies about their so-called betrayal—it's madness!"

Ferdia grimaced. It was Conor's greed in imprisoning the girl that started all this. And his long-standing—and unreasonable— jealousy of the three brothers that made them run as if guilty.

"We will not go home until we find them," Cúchulainn muttered, wiping rain from his face. "I will not sleep in a bed when they are lying on the ground, cold and afraid!"

His gray startled into a canter, and Ferdia kicked his own horse up, casting an eye about to see if there was anyone to overhear. There were no woods, only brown fields that spread toward the hills, the crops still slumbering beneath the wet soil.

It was vital that Cú gain his temper before facing the rest of the Red Branch. Not all the warriors loved the three brothers as Ferdia and Cúchulainn did. As for Conor...There was something strange about this whole thing, black and twisted.

At that moment, Cúchulainn bellowed and streaked ahead, his fair hair streaming out from his leather helmet. Ferdia forgot everything else, desperately heeling his horse. He and Cú had trained together, fought across Erin and Alba, and shared food, beds, and women. So Ferdia alone could feel the rise of Cúchulainn's sacred battle-rage as if it surged through his own body.

Cúchulainn was the Champion of the Ulaid, the Hound of Cullen, the greatest warrior in Erin. Most of the time his blue eyes were a calm sea, his bright, boyish face belying his twenty-five years. It was easy then to forget the divine rage he could summon, the violent storm he unleashed in battle.

And that when he was exhausted like this, his control of that frenzy could falter.

Ferdia caught up, hauling his horse before Cú to make him stop. "We don't know which way they went!" Ferdia panted. "We've been two days without sleep, and darkness falls. Let us camp. We can track them better in the morning."

Cúchulainn's scowl softened and gave way to a sigh. He scrubbed his wet face on his shoulder.

As they unpacked, the rain blew away. The dark was soon pushed back by glowing flames, a grove of oaks cocooning the two men. On the road, Ferdia did not have to share the Hound with the king, the Red Branch, the adoring crowds—or Emer, Cúchulainn's wife.

"Who did kill Aed's nephew, then?" Head down, Cúchulainn unrolled his bed of furs. "They all say Connacht raiders, but Naisi was their main target."

"Raiders from Connacht would spear the nearest man," Ferdia agreed, tugging a dry tunic over his head and ruffling his dark hair to dry it. Better they expunged this now, so neither betrayed themselves in other company.

"Hmm." Cúchulainn gulped from a flask of ale.

He didn't offer it to Ferdia, and Ferdia didn't reach for it. Name someone the supreme warrior and every man with a sword wanted to take you down, so by habit Ferdia stayed clear-headed to cover Cú's back.

The Hound swallowed, watching steam rising from their wet mantles. "Do you think the king...?"

"You saw his distress when he found out about the attack on Naisi." *The Red Branch must not falter.* Ferdia had been repeating that to himself every day. Doubts must never come between Red Branch warriors, rumors must not spread. "Conor wouldn't break the honor vows by killing his own fighters."

"But Conor is no warrior." The Hound picked at the wax cap of the flask. "He never took our oaths. And... how can we forget the rest?" Cúchulainn jumped to pace around the fire. The flames turned his hair red and reflected in his eyes, so he looked like the hound after which he was named. "At her birth, yes, the druids spoke a prophecy over Deirdre that 'Erin's greatest beauty would bring Erin's greatest woe.' But it was not the ruin only of the Ulaid they foretold, Fer. It is the ruin of the *Red Branch* itself."

A night breeze scraped the branches against each other, and Ferdia brushed his neck with irritation. Uttering such words made of them a spell, summoning the mischievous sídhe who roamed the dark woods. "We fight *that* by keeping our sense, brother."

"Tell that to Conor, who can halt this unraveling with one deed—by letting the girl go."

"*You* tell him; you're his bloody champion. And his kin."

Cúchulainn cast a withering glance at Ferdia. "I have. I may as well be talking to a rock."

Ferdia picked a stick from the pile, cracked it and threw it on the flames. "The fairest thing I can say about Conor is that he is clever. Clever men would not risk ruin by stooping to such a betrayal."

"Women make men lose their wits."

Cúchulainn would know; he had Emer. If the Champion of the Ulaid had a fabled sword-arm, in all good bard tales he had to have a fabled love as well. Ferdia looked down, his lip curling at the hollow drop in his breast. "Lugh's balls, Cú. Conor would not know love if it threw him to the ground, sat on him, and beat him about the head!" He flung a shard of wood at his friend.

It hit Cú's back and the Hound grinned, planting himself on his bedroll. He dug out some dried deer meat. "We need to find those boys and hammer sense back into them and into the king. *Make* it all fit together again."

Ferdia watched the Hound's battle-scarred fingers tearing the meat into shreds. Cú could forge anything he wanted with those hands.

They could bind or destroy with equal fervor.

⁂

Ruán wheeled through a great darkness. At its heart was a tiny flame, and his awareness was tied to it by a thread. He was exhausted by his endeavors to snap the thread so the flame could go out and he could be set free.

The light guttered. It was nearly gone.

He was nearly gone.

At once he was surrounded by an urgent whirl of *others*, vast and leaping flares of light, radiating white fire in all directions. These flames twisted themselves into intricate patterns, unwinding and then coiling up again, their movements too fast to follow. Living stars.

Their dance caught Ruán up and spun him away. And he forgot the little fire he had been trying to extinguish.

Then he was sinking through the lake again, the water now a luminous green.

A single star still hovered over him. It was formed of colored rays, as when sunlight shines through a crystal. Ruán stared into the water-star, and the star gazed back. For a moment it shimmered into an elongated face: ears, chin, eyes, head, and limbs formed of streaming fire.

Then that fire moved closer and engulfed Ruán, as if he was falling into the sun.

So the last of the darkness receded.

Ruán solidified again to bones and flesh. Feather-light touches bathed his ruined eyes. Those fingers were insubstantial, somewhere between warmth and breath. A band settled over his brow and a familiar scent tugged at him. Crushed herbs.

Waves of sound passed through him. *Singing?*

A sweetness dribbled onto his tongue. Herbs, petals, honey … the essence of earth soaking into his body. Its vitality spread through his wasted flesh like water through tree-roots.

Life coursed through him.

Ruán gasped, and drew in a deep breath of his own will.

❂

Time passed, the days growing warmer. Ruán was comforted by the cool weight of the poultice over his eyes. The nectar changed to berries, pressed between his cracked lips, followed by offerings of bread crumbs and dabs of milk.

And then came a day unlike any other.

Light filtered into Ruán's deadened mind. The poultice was gone. There were blurs of green and white that moved with the rustling above his head. He kept drifting through his haze, because he knew he must be dreaming. And in this dream, he seemed to have eyes again.

The rippling shapes slowly resolved into pale blobs with dark spots. Faces. Eyes.

People.

Ruán's druid mind stirred from slumber, for he was trained to seek meaning in dreams. The strangers were small and slight, and wore deerskins. Dark hair fell to their shoulders, framing narrow faces with eyes the brown of fallen leaves. Unintelligible sounds swirled about them, an echo of the music that had wound through his sleep for so long.

The brine of the lake prickled his nostrils, and Ruán shuddered. He did not smell in dreams. He sent his awareness along his limbs. He distinctly felt the uneven clumps of bracken under his back and thighs, and the furs brushing his naked chest. He was awake.

Awake.

Ruán's blood roared in his ears.

And he could see.

CHAPTER 3

LEAF-FALL

A t Cruachan, Maeve stood beside her dead father, chin down. From the corners of her lowered eyes, Eochaid's death-rites were a blur.

Lamplight flickered on damp mud walls. The king's bier was a scarlet pool of cloth in the dim hut, the ghostly figures of druids in pale robes chanting around it.

Maeve's gaze was on the floor-rushes, but her attention was elsewhere. On the other side of her father's body was a hole in the world that swallowed all light. Beneath the singsong voices and hiss of water on flame, she suffered its throb.

Innel.

For this past year her father had indeed kept her safe from her brother. She had stayed by Eochaid's bedside through the long dark, while Innel and his drunken men sprawled about the warriors' hall. Conor of the Ulaid never demanded her back, but as news traveled slowly, it was only when the leaves budded that she discovered why.

As soon as she left, Conor had turned his attentions to the maid, Deirdre, to whom he had been betrothed since she was a babe. The bards recited with relish that the girl had just reached breeding age and, hot for young blood, the old bull had been chasing after her instead all through the long dark. Maeve thought she understood. If this girl was the glory the druids had foretold, then Conor would want her at his side to shore up his power before he took any revenge.

Amid the last storms of leaf-bud, Maeve had thanked the unknown Deirdre fervently for this respite.

But her relief proved fleeting.

In sun-season, Maeve's father took a turn for the worse. As the sun waxed, Eochaid waned, and his words returned to haunt Maeve. *You have no allies. You are nothing.*

After all she had endured, Maeve would not bow down to that. Without any clear idea of what to do, she began to escape her father's bedside. As the barley sprouted, she rode from dun to dun scattering seeds of her own. She had not lived at Cruachan much since she was twelve, but as the days grew longer she sought out the noble lords and their wives, the druids, the young warriors, and little by little began to win their favor. She must find a way to be safe, somehow.

At last leaf-fall had wheeled about again.

Beside her father's dead body, in the cold of the funeral lodge, Maeve wondered if Innel knew what she'd been up to. Her eyes rose.

Innel's gaze bored into her, unblinking. He knew.

The chief druid, Tiernan, leaned across the body, his sleeves falling back from bony wrists as he sprinkled sacred water over the king's covered head. The gold beads in his gray hair flared in the lamplight, blotting out Innel's scowl.

The king had died close to Samhain, a dangerous time. At Samhain the veils drew aside and the dead and the sídhe flew back and forth from the Otherworld in chaos. If set adrift now, the king's spirit might lose its way. The druids would therefore hold vigil over his body, their songs binding his spirit until he was laid to rest.

People had already begun gathering for the Samhain fair. The warlords were riding from their forts across Connacht in milling streams of gold and furs, sharp eyes and the gleam of bared teeth. Maeve knew she had work to do with them—with the living.

"We will leave him now," Tiernan intoned.

Released, Maeve spun on her heel. She wanted to feel, but her muscles were coiled so tight that nothing could move. The neck-torc of twisted gold pressed on her collarbones, and the arm-rings, chiming anklets, and girdle of bronze encased her in a hard shell. She was only hung with these garlands of metal because she was Eochaid's daughter, and that was why Innel looked at her like he would kill her.

They could be nothing but cold and heavy.

Father.

"Damn that gray!" a voice roared. *"Move your rump!"*

The crowd bayed as the horses flew around the racetrack.

"Not fast enough," someone else crowed. "Who'll bet this on Daíre's bay instead?"

The glittering nobles sprawled on piles of cushions in painted chariots, high above the rest of the spectators. The cold, fine day was nearing dusk, and the mead and ale had been flowing since high-sun.

The thrill of Samhain and the uncertainty over the king's death had heightened the atmosphere. It would not be seemly to mourn, for the king was setting forth on a glorious journey to the Blessed Isles, to rest among the gods before he was born again. Sadness—if anyone felt it—would only keep Eochaid's spirit tied to Cruachan.

And they don't want that. Maeve glanced at the cattle-lords from beneath her lashes. For the real race was only just beginning— who would rule now? The lords decided, choosing a man from among the derbfine—the royal kin—just as they backed these horses.

A strong, fine, young new king. Maeve bit her lip as her brother's sneer filled her mind. *Surely not.*

Among the nobles the betting was furious. The fading sun flashed on finger-rings and armbands as warlords and their women tossed jewels between the piles whenever horses pulled ahead. The noblemen squinted as the racers thundered past, shouting in glee or disappointment, reaching for earthen jugs of foaming ale.

Maeve remained straight-backed, her hands in her lap. Her bets were not laid upon horses.

On one side of her a lord in a mangy wolf-fur cursed as his horse faltered, shaking his mead-horn in frustration and spilling liquid all over his trews. Maeve was surprised he had anything to bet, for his barley crop had been hit by blight in sun-season. She had taken cartloads of grain and food to his people—in her father's name, of course.

The chief's nose was webbed with spider-veins. "Lady Maeve!" He bellowed fumes over her. "Let me wager this ring for you— *Ach!* Blast my boy, he's broken stride again!"

Maeve's smile was bright. "It is a shame he does not have his master's grace."

The gaggle of nobles around her laughed, for the chief was squat with stumpy limbs, and the worst rider for leagues about. He grinned ruefully, patting his belly.

The lord on Maeve's other side plucked a pin of gold from his cloak. "Five-to-one Daíre's stallion wins—and the prize to the Lady Maeve in my name!" His wife elbowed her husband, muttering to him. He tore out a matching pin from his other shoulder. "Double the stake!" he slurred. The nobles exclaimed, shouting out new bets.

Maeve smiled at the chieftain, touching his arm. *His* fort had been struck by a terrible coughing sickness among the children. Maeve summoned healers and rode there herself in a bitter storm, working alongside the lord's wife for three days to tend the sick. "You are making me dizzy," she laughed. "I don't have enough limbs for all these jewels."

"Then borrow mine," someone crowed at the back. "Or just the one between my legs!"

"You'll have to pay *me* for that," Maeve returned, cocking her chin. The men dissolved in a wave of mirth. Maeve held her smile, her jaw aching from many moons of such banter.

"What about that black, Lady Maeve? I'll triple my stake if you back him."

"The black is mine," a smooth voice interrupted. A nobleman with slicked hair and oiled beard sauntered up, bowing to Maeve. His eyes swung toward her, brimming with heat. "I'd be honored to take you to see him once he's won." He smirked. "He loves a lady's touch."

Did he actually waggle his brows? Maeve glanced over his shoulder with dismay. "He might rather need a kick in the rump," she rejoined, "for he seems to be losing."

As the chieftain spun toward the horses, Maeve flipped her legs over the cart and leaped down. People were screaming and jumping about as the racers pounded down the last straight, and it was then Maeve made her escape.

The crafters had set up carts to show their wares to the nobles: tooled leather and wood, woven baskets, jewelry and wool. Slipping around the bronze-smith's stall, Maeve flopped against the yoke of his wagon, rolling her shoulders and letting her back slump.

Two swordsmen were skulking nearby—hairy wolves that ran with Innel's pack. One scowled at her. They'd been listening to her with the lords.

Maeve's hands tightened on her thighs, but all that came to hand was the flimsy green wool of her dress. The cold waft up her buttocks made her long for her trews, leather breastplate, and kilt. Her armor. She was supposed to look like a princess now, though.

Well, at least *appear* marriageable once more...

She caught a movement from the corner of her eye. The cart-box was draped with a tent of cowhides, and a small pair of eyes was shining at her from the shadows. At the other end, the smith's wife, Eithne, had her jewelry spread on a little table to attract the noble ladies.

Maeve held the child's eye, pressing her finger to her lips, and crooking her leg over the cart-box, clambered inside, slipping away from her brother's guards. "I am being chased by wolves, Líoch. Don't let them get me."

The little girl grinned, sucking her fingers. She had been a babe on Eithne's breast when Maeve left to marry Conor. It seemed hardly any longer since she herself had been the child, racing through wood and stream with Eithne and her siblings, piling at their mother's hearth like one of her own cubs. Maeve was always happiest playing among the crafters, getting dirty and hot, or sneaking out to hunt with the king's warriors, or following the herder-boys, swinging a switch and singing to the cattle as they did.

The child stared at the gold torc at Maeve's neck and put out a chubby hand to grasp it. Maeve hesitantly touched her soft hair. The crafters and farmers had never wanted anything of her but herself. She should have been born a child like this.

"Maeve!" Eithne was standing at the tent flap at the far end that faced the stall, her hands on her ample hips. Maeve scooted forward, waving Eithne to be quiet. A little peace, she needed, hidden from all those avid eyes.

It was too late.

"Lady Maeve...?" A richly dressed lord's wife was browsing the jewelry. She stretched her neck to peer into the cart, a festive ruffle of feathers perched atop the gray coil of her braids.

Maeve stared at Eithne in dismay. Lifting one shoulder, the smith's wife returned a rueful smile.

The noblewoman held up a string of amber beads. "Lady, you *must* try these on. Why, they match your hair!"

Maeve sighed, and in a manner that was not at all ladylike, slid out of the cart. Brushing straw from her dress, she straightened her back and stepped around the stall.

To make allies among the noblewomen, she had spun yards of lumpy thread, stabbed her fingers with embroidery needles, and hung cheeses in the dairy until her hands were milk-stung. She hoped it was worth it, for something.

The older woman slung the beads about Maeve's neck, fussing. Eithne held up a bronze mirror with a grin.

Maeve arched a brow at her. "Hmm." Instead of admiring the necklace, she fingered the frown between her brows. She needed to look better than *that* to keep the interest of men. This past year had hollowed her cheeks and pointed her narrow chin, and with her slanted blue eyes, she looked more than ever the vixen her father named her. Haunted.

Her breath caught. "Thank you, lady, but I...have enough amber." With a tight smile at Eithne, Maeve ducked out of the beads. The noblewoman was tutting behind her as she all but fled.

The smell of grease pulled Maeve up, and a different pang came in her belly. She had let herself get light-headed with hunger, just when she needed her wits about her. She changed tack toward the cookfires.

There, a harassed servant wiped sweat from her face and shaved flesh off a crackling pig. Smoke in her eyes, Maeve grabbed a bannock and retreated, colliding with someone behind her. "Lord Fraech," she coughed, burying her mouth in the meat-filled bun.

"Lady." Fraech's nostrils flared, as if he longed to charge in the other direction.

A distant cousin, Fraech was twenty; tall and lithe rather than brawny like Innel. He was of the derbfine, the royal kin from which rulers were chosen, and she had heard he was being prodded toward the kingship by a father and uncle of ravening ambition. They must be rubbing their hands now that Eochaid was dead.

Maeve chewed as Fraech flailed for something to say, giving her time to see him up close.

His brown hair was tied in a simple horse-tail and he wore only one arm-ring. He was no puffed-up cock, then. His green eyes were steady, his face fine-boned and calm. His skin was unscarred, so it must be true that he was an exceptional fighter, his quietness at odds with a swift sword-arm, she had heard.

"I am sorry . . . about your father," he managed. "Lugh bless him on his journey."

"Thank you." Maeve swallowed. "I am sure *your* father is dreadfully upset. I feel for him, I do."

Fraech clamped his lips together, but a small smile still escaped. "I will be sure to pass him your sympathies."

Self-control *and* wit. Ally? Enemy? She did not know. Maeve scanned the throng around her. "Oh, look," she said. "I've been wondering where she was." When a waft of smoke obscured them, Maeve slipped away, wiping meat-juice from her chin.

Deep in thought, she was nearly bowled over at the fighting ring when a pair of wrestlers toppled across the ropes and fell, spattering her with sweat. A horn blew. "Out of bounds!" the druid shouted in the ring.

Maeve was turning away when she spied an old chieftain

watching the match. She hesitated, then realized she couldn't wipe away the sensation of Innel's eyes boring into her over their father's body. All the stakes had been raised now.

She ducked beneath a slew of fists in the crowd, the warriors all screaming and cursing. "Lord Donagh," she murmured to the white-haired chief.

"Lady." Donagh did not glance at her, nursing a horn of ale.

The bloodied winner was circling, waving his arms. The unconscious loser was being carted off, his arm bent at an angle and his face bone-white. The ranks of warriors parted.

Maeve froze.

Innel was there, protesting to the druid, his face scarlet. He jabbed a finger at the downed fighter—one of his own men—and then at the priest.

Donagh hissed under his breath. "With the king gone, he thinks he cannot be touched. If I seek justice now, he will slaughter my people and blame it on Ulaid raiders." His eyes creased with pain. "How could you curse me with this secret, this shame?"

Maeve poked a fallen leaf on the grass with her toe, as if they weren't speaking. "If not for me, you would never know that it was because of Innel that your daughter died. *He killed her.*"

A shudder passed over Donagh. Across the grass, Maeve watched the tendons bulging in Innel's neck and arms, and her skin crawled. Did he hold Donagh's young daughter down like that as he forced his way into her?

Maeve remembered how it felt, that weight.

Some things only women could draw from other women. Following a trail of rumors, she had gleaned how Innel's babe had begun to grow in the girl. Of itself, that was a blessing...but it would have betrayed Innel's violence against a noble maid to the druids. He silenced her with threats against her family, and she resorted to a birch stick, and died of womb-fever.

Maeve blinked the dead girl away, her belly turning. "If I can deliver you justice, you said you would support me if I needed you." Two promises, and she had no idea how either would be fulfilled. Many seeds, though, had to be sown so that one might sprout.

Just one to give her some kind of safe haven, somewhere.

"I value my honor," Donagh sniffed, wiping his sleeve across his nose.

"So do I." Maeve made herself hold his eyes. Donagh commanded many warriors and was allied to many chiefs.

A bellow claimed their attention. Innel's ale-soaked cubs were brawling with the winner's friends, fists and kicks flying. As the druids called for order, Innel ripped out one of the posts and clouted the victor over the head.

"Sacrilege!" Donagh gasped. "His father lies dead ten paces away!"

Maeve bared her teeth. "That's my brother."

Dagger-hilts cracked skulls; noses shattered and more blood spattered the shadowed turf. Fraech appeared, plowing in to drag his warriors off. He plucked the victor up and hauled his men away, scowling and filthy. Innel was left grinning among his pack of fighters.

Maeve glanced around. A few old chieftains had been drawn from the ale kegs by the unseemly brawl. Their fingers glittered with gaudy rings, but as they lifted their cups, their mouths were grim behind them.

Here was the moment. The lords were on this side of the crowd, Innel on the other. Maeve moistened her tongue, heart hammering.

She knew only that her brother could not become king. If he did, she would not outlive the royal feast.

CHAPTER 4

"So it begins." Maeve's voice cracked and she cleared her throat. "Can such hot blood rule a kingdom? My father did not think so."

No one could dispute what her father thought now.

"Lord Cormac," Maeve addressed one of the lords by the wrestling ring. "You suffered when Connacht cubs raided Mumu without my father's say. The Mumu sought revenge, burning your people's steadings, we heard." She did not point out that the cubs were her brother's men, seeking cattle to bribe his supporters for the kingship. Everyone knew that.

Maeve ignored the hiss that came from somewhere at the back. No one spoke. The lords all looked away with brows and mouths drawn, before quickly dispersing. Donagh had already slipped away.

Maeve's knees went shaky and she crossed her arms to hold herself. She felt a prickling on the back of her neck but would not look toward Innel. Instead, she pretended to be watching some girls practicing their dancing in the next field. Gradually, her brother's braying grew fainter.

They had gone.

In the brief silence that fell, a youthful voice piped up. "Lady Maeve!"

Maeve plastered a bright smile on her face and swung about. Shadows were now stretching long fingers across the bronze grass. The brown and gold trees were fading into a mist that was curling up from the nearby stream.

A knot of young warriors had reclaimed the ring, throwing aside the broken stakes. They prodded the speaker, who stepped forward. "Will you join the last horse race before dark?"

Maeve walked toward them, sway-hipped. "Now, Lassar, I have been outracing you for moons. Do you really want to be beaten just before supper?"

The youths guffawed, strong teeth gleaming in the twilight.

"But I've been feeding up my stallion," a bold one drawled, waving at his groin. "If you sat *his* saddle, you'd be surprised at his brawn."

"I heard he bolts the start, Ruari, and spends himself too soon." Maeve grinned, a hand draped at her waist. "Not a good bet for a woman."

They all laughed, jostling closer as she brushed back her scented curls. To the young and fiery fighters, she had summoned the mask of a goddess of the woods: wild, untamed, and *almost* unreachable, riding out on their hunts and joining in their sword sparring. Around them, she left her hair unbound whenever she could stand the inconvenience. Married women wore theirs coiled, maids in long plaits. She was in-between now—and the only place hair ever tumbled about a woman's shoulders was in the bed-furs.

"What about the spear-feats?" another suggested.

"It is too dark," his friends argued.

Exhaustion was creeping over Maeve. She unclasped a bracelet. "I'll come see you race in a moment. The first home wins this." She lifted the ring so the sunset fired the bronze. "And I'll sit by the winner for the Samhain tales." They gawped at the promise in her smile. "Hurry up!"

Grinning and shoving each other, the youths raced to their horses.

Darkness had almost swamped the field now. People were drifting away from the games toward the flaring bonfires on the meadows and the trill of pipes. A drum began to beat. As the last of the boys leaped the ropes, Maeve saw a single man left, stretched out against a post that held up one of the leather awnings.

Garvan tucked his arms behind his dark head. "You must be bloody exhausted."

Maeve threw herself to the ground. "Can still outrace you."

"That's not what I meant." Garvan's eyes glinted. "Those boys can't decide whether to fight you or bed you—or both at once. Your sword skills impress them."

Maeve tensed. "I learned much in the years I was away."

In Laigin, the moment he got a child on her, Ros Ruadh had shoved Maeve aside like one of his hounds. By the time her shock and illness ebbed, he was hoarding the babe as his own treasure, his women nursing her. Bereft, Maeve had wandered, drawn again and again to the warriors with their fiery eyes and sharp blades. They radiated life, when the only thing that was ever hers had been taken.

Maeve's throat ached, and distractedly she rubbed it, turning her face to the cold dusk. In Mumu, when she was older, she sought out the warriors not just for her bed, but to teach her to fight. That was when she found she could expend sorrow in sword-blows and sweat.

No one knew it all, though.

"Your efforts are leaving you too weary for some things." Garvan scratched the black fuzz along his jawbone. "Why have you not come to me for so long?"

Maeve looked at the stars kindling over their heads. Because her favors were a currency now, and if her father used them, she must, too. Every lord must think he still had a chance to become her royal mate and sire a child of Eochaid's blood. It was a scrap of power she would hold onto.

"Stop griping." She poked a buckle on his belt. Garvan had been her guard on every foray this past sun-season, and many gifts had flowed his way. His battered face had never attracted many women, but his new array of bronzes did. "Girls are throwing themselves at you now like salmon up a stream. I bet you'll land a wealthy wife come Beltaine."

"She wouldn't be as understanding as you, spitfire."

"Probably not. She catches you wriggling another, and you'll get a tail in the face." She chuckled, dangerously light-headed as what she had just done hit her.

Garvan did not smile, picking at the damp grass. "I could marry you. You'd be safe then."

Maeve cleared her throat, her face burning. She touched his hand, the knuckles swollen from sword-fights. "You do me great honor, but what men value in me I must use for myself now. And Innel is already suspicious of you."

Garvan pulled at one scarred earlobe. "Don't you think I can handle him?"

She grinned. "You can't handle me."

His only answer was a snort.

Maeve let all the masks fall away, flopping on the turf and knuckling her eyes.

Garvan uncorked a goatskin and handed it to her. "Just be careful. Innel heard what you said to the lords."

"All the more reason to get them on my side." Maeve gulped mead and handed the skin back. *But to do…what?*

Garvan's eyes were suddenly uncertain. He ran a hand through his black hair, making it stick up in a crest. "Just what are you getting me into, spitfire?"

Gods, to have one person who did not look at her like that. She sprang straight, pulling her knees up. "Don't be like all the others," she burst out, knotting her hands about her legs. Then she caught herself and put a hand on Garvan's arm, the muscle ridged and hard. She breathed out, her smile crooked. "Treachery has been inflicted on me so many times, my friend. I would only ever bring a man down through his own weakness, I swear."

I will never be my father.

Garvan searched her face, and eventually his shoulders lowered. He reached out and pinched her chin.

The girl summoned Ruán awake once more without words.

Her particular scent drew him from sleep first: smoke-tanned hides and pungent herbs. When his sight cleared, her eyes were hovering over him, the irises shimmering through all the hues of moss and wood.

Girl, woman...his sense of her shifted like the watery light of the lake.

Her features were delicate, her chin pointed and neck long, framed by dark hair braided with shells and feathers. She was the only one of his rescuers to appear in daylight at the little shelter he slept in, a dome of reeds that seemed to have grown from the marsh itself. Only at night, lost in wanderings of the mind, did he glimpse the eyes of others shining around the fire.

The druids spoke of little, ancient hunters who lived in Erin before the tall lords came with their iron swords. There were rumors of their remnants clinging on in hidden places. Earth people. Tree people. It seemed impossible they could be so cut off from the tribes that they did not share a language, but they never spoke to him, or answered him. He only heard them singing— a burbling melody that always sent him back into slumber.

This day, the girl's eyes were more penetrating than usual. Belying her delicate appearance, she flashed a feral grin and poked him in the chest. That made him sit up.

She leaped up, twirling a foot to kick the furs off his legs. At the edge of camp she looked back, cocking her head with a challenge in her bright eyes. It was unmistakable. *Get up, and come along.*

Ruán clambered up, his limbs surging with a vitality that had become more intense with every passing day. Reveling in that rush, he bounded after the girl, down the slope.

The camp sat on a knoll of hazel and alder trees. Below was a sea of reeds, their bronze stalks gleaming, and beyond, the glitter of the lake. Behind the knoll, channels of water almost cut this spit of land into an island.

Ruán broke out of the shade and collided with sunlight. *He could see it.* He put his arms out and turned. It had been an endless sun-season. As he swung around, the warmth on his bare chest melted away the sense of his body, and he became pure light as well. The mud squelched between his toes. Moist air curled over his cheekbone.

He had always questioned, and craved answers—and had nearly died of that. Now he would question nothing, know nothing but the green haze of trees and the silver sky.

Ruán spun to a halt. The girl dangled a dripping bag of mussels before him.

But before he could reach for them, she danced away and, turning for the shore, raced off through the shoulder-high reeds. He plowed after her, leaping over channels of water that cut the reed-beds, the marsh-grasses tangling in his spread hands.

He came upon her at a hearth she had built on the lake beach. Fire-things were spread before her: flint, iron-stone, tinder. She pointed at his hand and gestured with her chin to the hearth.

Ruán sank to a squat. "I *can* do it, you know. You would not believe it to look at me, but I was a druid once." With a wry smile, he looked down at himself, poking a hole in his threadbare trews. His ruddy hair was tangled with leaf-litter, and they had given him a tunic of deerskin, crudely sewn. No, no one would believe him. *And, fool, you haven't made a fire for years.*

He was always given the honor-seat beside the hearths of great halls. Lord Mulach's hall ...

Ruán's smile died.

Startling him, the girl patted his cheek. She grabbed his hands and guided them to the fire-kit like he was a child. Ruán snorted under his breath, but gave in. She had saved his life. He would do anything for her.

Fingers tangled together, they shredded pieces of dried mushroom into tinder and struck the stone with the flint. When the spark caught, the girl wafted the smoke over him, sucking it in with an exaggerated flare of her nostrils.

Ruán chuckled. "Yes, I can smell it." He blew on the flame,

piled on grass and shards of wood. As he wrapped the mussels in leaves, the girl hopped up and walked to the shore.

Ruán tucked the mussels in the fire. The maiden was standing thigh-deep in the glittering lake, her hands hovering. Something about the spread of her palms made the hair stand up on Ruán's neck. She'd never done this before.

Without a sound, she sank beneath the lake. Ruán waited, but there were no ripples. His heart thumped loud in that silence. A gust of wind sent bright wavelets to shore, and with them Ruán caught a snatch of her song, faint and fleeting.

Come...come...

Without realizing, Ruán was on his feet, ankle-deep in water.

Come...come...

Ruán's body became untethered from his mind, swaying with a life of its own. At that moment the girl rose grasping a bream, the gleaming fish already limp in her hands. Dazed, Ruán looked between the girl and her catch. It struck him forcefully how the fish appeared *empty* rather than dead. The enlivening force in it had simply...gone.

The girl turned, her glance glinting with approval. She came ashore and left the fish, taking Ruán's wrists and spreading his palms over the water. Baffled, Ruán shut his eyes.

Ideas flowered within him. A great rush of life had filled him whenever he drank their nectar, and it surged through him now. He could also sense that charge in other living things—as a blind man he had always known when someone was near, even if they were silent.

The girl was singing. The vibrations of her voice tickled his skin. Then they were inside him. Ruán released his breath. The sun was dissolving his body, his awareness, and merging it with the watery light all around him.

Ruán's palms prickled. He felt...*bright-glowing-warm-darting* things below. Fish.

Come... His thoughts seemed to flow out on that rippling light. A fish swam into his hands. Beyond the glide of the scales,

Ruán's fingers tingled as if the creature was made of sparks. He saw and felt a bright burst—the flame of life in the fish and his own flaring together. Ruán laughed with a joy that blanked out all questions. *Incredible.*

His heart beat five times, and the body of the fish fell slack in his hands. But Ruán could have sworn that its essence swam on through finer, invisible currents, disappearing beyond him. He gasped, and spun around.

The girl was perched astride a branch of an old birch tree, swinging her legs. For a moment her skin glimmered with the silver he held in his fingers.

The sunlight dimmed, and Ruán waded to the sand.

Hands...she always grasped his hands, making him delve for roots in the soil and mussels in the water. When the girl wanted to show him plants to eat, she crushed them to his nose. Among the reeds, she bade him listen to the splashes of the ducks in order to find their eggs.

Feel. Smell. Hear. Taste. Nothing more.

"Who are you?" he cried. "What magic is this?"

With one graceful leap, she hopped off the branch.

Looking into her liquid eyes, Ruán knew she understood his speech and always had. He flung the fish down and blundered toward her. "What are you?" A terrible dread overcame all sense, and he groped for her shoulders. *"What am I?"*

Touching her was like plunging into a thundering river.

Memories poured over him. The sand of his island home between his fingers. A leaden sky; whitecaps on the sea. The faces of his family, pinched and thin, and hunger gnawing his belly. And gulls on the wing, always glimmering above him, far out of reach.

No. An old instinct crushed that surge. He had always summoned silence and stillness, the cold of stone. Only then was he empty enough to hear the voices of the gods.

The girl was not silent. She leaned forward, cupping her hand around his ear. "Why did you not save the lord's boy?"

That blow thrust Ruán back. His hands dropped away from her.

And then he was spinning around and stumbling back through the reeds. The glints of water were a blur now, as a growl of denial built in his throat. Past the little camp he staggered, falling on his knees in the pools of water and mud, before dragging himself back up.

The roaring grew louder around him. *Grope. Hear. Smell.* That is all she had ever bade him to do.

Ruán plunged through swamp-grass, farther than he had ever gone. The ground began to rise away from the lake as he neared the forest and, beyond, pasture.

Plunging through a scatter of trees, Ruán hit a wall of night. Everything went black, the glow of the water and sky snuffed out. He pitched forward and smacked into the mud, his body crumpling.

The truth burst from him in a great howl.

He was still blind, now and forever.

It was the second night of the Samhain feast.

The bonfires on the black plain of Cruachan were ringed by a whirl of carousing people. Boots thudded out spiral patterns on the frost as lines of dancers wove between the flames. Men slung arms around women, groping at breasts and nuzzling necks. Spilled ale gleamed in beards and stained tunics.

With darkness came the cold, and Maeve drew up the hood of her red mantle edged with stoat fur. On the way back to the women's lodge, she passed a little campfire in the lee of some bent rowan trees. The plunk of a harp-string caught her ear. The listeners around the bard were hushed, and his voice carried to her on the clear air.

"... Conor mac Nessa ..."

The night breathed ice over her, and Maeve halted.

"...the king's wrath spreads over Emain Macha like a storm-cloud," the bard intoned. "The maiden of dawn has taken the sun from him. His face is frost and twilight, his hair gray mist. His eyes are as black as stones of the hills beneath rain. And no one knows when the sun will return, for the maiden is gone into the dark woods."

Maeve peered at the bard. Judging by his shabby clothes and inexpert playing, he was one of the traveling poets who plied their trade between cattle-lords, looking for a hearth for the long dark. She fancied she had seen this one before.

The moment the little group around him went in search of ale, Maeve swept in and dragged the harper aside. Before he could protest, she pressed a ring into his palm and folded his callused fingers over it. "What is this news of Conor mac Nessa?"

Bleary-eyed, the bard blinked at the iron ring.

"And make it to the point," Maeve growled. "What 'dawn maiden'?"

"The girl Deirdre, Conor's betrothed. She has escaped her woodland prison, run away with Naisi and his brothers. They have been fleeing Conor's wrath all sun-season, racing across the Ulaid from lake to hill, forest to sea."

Naisi. Maeve could not easily forget those three Red Branch brothers: tall and blue-eyed, with a startling coloring of black hair and fair skin. *And Deirdre...* Maeve searched her memories once more. There had been another rumor of the girl at Emain Macha, something dark. The Red Branch would not speak of it, clamming up when it was breached. Something of this Deirdre affected the Red Branch...and Naisi and his brothers were Red Branch. "Why have I not heard this before?"

"Ah, the Ulaid hide their troubles, lady. It has taken me moons to root out a bed at their fires, and as for getting them to speak—Lugh's breath and fire! The servants know little, for though their masters glower, their tongues are bound." He lowered his voice, glancing over his shoulder. "They are afraid of Conor, see. They say grief has twisted his mind. One lord harboring the fugitives was attacked by raiders, another stripped of his lands. The Red Branch have been chasing all over the North after the girl and the boys, and then..." His small eyes gleamed. "Some of them did run them to earth, and Naisi dueled with Leary, Winner of Battles, and *killed him.*"

Maeve's mind was a storm. Red Branch warriors did not kill each other. They prided themselves on their unique fighting skills and their secret, mystical bond—the nature of which she'd never discerned. Now Red Branch not only stalked other Red Branch, but slayed each other?

The deadly heart of Conor's war-bands was fracturing.

She nodded at the bard, uncramping her hand from her hood as she turned. Only then did it hit her. Another woman besides Maeve had scorned Conor—and this one had taken off with the most beautiful youth in the Ulaid.

Maeve stumbled as the king's hollow eyes appeared in the ground mist at her feet. She was one of the few who knew what his coldness masked: an intense flame of jealousy and pride. She kneaded her temple. She had been so relieved when Deirdre turned Conor's wrath from her. But instead the foolish chit had merely wounded him, and then unleashed him upon them all again.

Belly-sick, Maeve realized she was facing the dark mounds of Cruachan. Across a river of blackness, only the bonfire at the temple of Lugh flamed.

Maeve had decided long ago that the gods and the sídhe did not trouble themselves much over her—she fancied they had a mutual understanding to leave each other alone. Yet tonight, with the druids holding vigil over her father, the shrine was the one place she could find some quiet to think. And perhaps... some sign of what she should do?

She strode across the crackling grass and onto the track that wound between the houses outside the ramparts of the king's hall, the stakes outlined against the glittering sky. Wind funneled along empty paths, for everyone was at the fires. She reached the last lodges before the temples. The thatch roofs were coated with crystals of frost, turning them gray under the stars. Maeve buried her chin in her cloak, head down.

The shadows came alive behind her.

Hard fingers bit into her arms, flinging her off her feet and onto her belly.

CHAPTER 5

M aeve kicked out, struggling to breathe.

She'd been thrown on a midden, her nose pressed into dung, rotting straw, and gnawed bones. Geese honked and dogs broke into a frenzy of barking.

Hands caught at her flailing arms, and knees ground them into the filth. She felt a needle of cold—they'd slit her layered skirts with a blade, baring her rump to the air. Maeve gagged, writhing, as harsh laughter broke out over her head.

The knife was replaced by something warm and muscular that jabbed the groove of her naked back. Her gargle of fury was lost amid the jeers.

"We hear you beg for this," someone hissed. "So this is where you'll have it, in muck and piss."

She tried to scream but her throat cramped, and then she thought she heard a distant thud of feet. "It's that black-haired bastard," one of her attackers spat. The knee holding her arm shifted, freeing her hand. Maeve's mind gibbered, but some instinct of her body reached down for the knife in her boot.

"Come on!" When her attackers leaped and ran, one lagged behind. Maeve yowled and stabbed her dagger into his foot. The man cried out, hopping. She jumped up and blindly barreled into his belly, head down. They hit the ground in a tangle, his dagger flung from his grip onto a broken millstone outside someone's door, striking with a clang.

Maeve bucked, dragging her fingers free and jabbing at his balls, and he cursed and rolled off her. The distant footfalls sped up, and when her attacker was distracted, she stuck his thigh again, savoring the snap of skin and muscle. The man roared and clouted her, sending her reeling before staggering away.

The footsteps charged up to her. Dizzied, Maeve lunged at this new torment.

"Whoa!" Garvan curved away from her blade. "It's me, spitfire!"

Maeve swiped at the shadows instead, and plunged the knife into the midden. She pushed a scream out before it choked her, stabbing the filthy straw until she could move no more, before lying there panting. After a moment she got to her knees, clenching her fist. She had grabbed her own knife awkwardly, and blood oozed between her fingers.

"Maeve."

As her head cleared she became aware of the cold air playing over her bare buttocks. She tasted copper on her split lip. When Garvan tried to take her arm, she threw him off.

"By the gods, woman." He scraped back his hair with both hands. "Innel heard everything you said, and knows everyone you've courted, thinking yourself so clever." When a shiver wracked Maeve's shoulders, he took hold of them. "Your father can no longer protect you."

Maeve broke away and clambered up. "I thought...Innel was stupid..." Her brother knew she'd never reveal this outrage to the druids, for then everyone would see he had bettered her, that she was weak...a woman the lords could ignore. It was meant to silence her, and if she would not be silenced, then who would miss her if she disappeared one day in the woods? Everyone knew how wildly she rode. She coughed, picking straw from her bruised mouth. "I am the foolish one."

"I'm glad you've figured that out, at last." Garvan stepped closer. "I'll take you back to the women's lodge."

Maeve limped in front of him with head up, cheeks burning. Garvan tailed her as they passed between the ramparts that encircled the mound of the royal hall and the small women's lodge beside it.

When Garvan pulled open the oak door, Maeve turned. "Leave me," she croaked.

"I'll stay here on guard."

Avoiding his eyes, she lifted the deerskins that covered the entrance. A murmur of women's voices floated out—the servants who'd come back to stoke the fire. "Innel will never attack here. He prefers the dark for his games." Her dead voice was someone else's. She could not feel her body.

"I will stay."

"If he finds out you guard me, you will be more than beaten." When he still hesitated, she pushed him with the heel of her hand. "Now who's foolish?"

"Then stay here. *Promise me.* I will see what I can find out."

Head down, Maeve swept past the chattering servants, and climbing to her bed, tore off her dress. With shaking fingers she pulled on buckskins, her jerkin, and kilt. She splashed water from a jug and scrubbed her filthy face, swilling her mouth out before sinking on the bed. There, she thrust her hands between her thighs, rocking. Innel wanted her to be cowed. Each day he would have her followed, so his men could lie in wait for her again.

How could she protect herself against that?

She tucked wet strands of hair behind her ears, glaze-eyed. The next moment all sense fled, the need to get away overwhelmed her, and she was on her feet.

She had to find somewhere safe, away from here.

At the hearth, the women's faces were a blur, no matter how

she blinked her eyes. "Áine," she addressed one of the younger servants. "Walk with me from the lodge, as if I am one of the maids and we are going back to the fires."

Goggle-eyed, Áine and her friends leaped up. "Of course, lady."

While they donned their cloaks, Maeve took from the porch one of the battered mantles of oiled leather the servants used to run errands on rainy days. It was hooded, dark and voluminous, and she disappeared into its depths with relief.

The little group emerged from the house, the girls giggling about the cold. Maeve kept her head down to hide her height and eventually peeled away from them among the narrow paths between the crafters' houses, hiding until she knew she had not been followed.

She crept along dark lanes, then snuck to the stables for Meallán. All the horse-boys were at the fires, and the guards at the gates were used to maids slipping out to meet their lovers at Samhain, so paid her no heed.

Maeve lead her horse by deserted trails away from the ramparts. Only when she disappeared into the woods along the river did she break into a wild run, hauling Meallán along the path. The stars spun above her as if tossed by the wind, and her breath joined them in gusts.

She emerged far upstream. A track led over the fields, the edges marked with white pebbles for the messengers that rode to Cruachan. The moon had blanched all color from the land but made the stones glow, and when she was sure of the footing, Maeve mounted up.

Ruán lay in a ditch of water, the rain battering his cheeks where before there had been sun. *He was blind.*

He knew now that they were not ancient people. They were the magical sídhe.

He sank facedown in the puddle, curling on his side. He was

not saved by the gods—he was not forgiven. They had just been taunting him. He opened his mouth and the foul water rushed in.

Bubbles brushed his cheek, and he remembered swimming in the lake with the sun streaming through a trail of them. The memory ached. Had it even happened? Against his will, a yearning flared to feel the sun drying the water on his skin just once more, to feel that life soaking into him. Instead, all he had ever been came down to a lonely death in a filthy mire.

This would be all he left behind.

Pride flared in Ruán, maddening pride. He grappled with it, but suddenly he was clawing his way out of the ditch. His back spasmed, and his belly clenched as he retched the foulness back up. He curled there shivering, his hands tucked beneath his arms.

Dry ground, high ground… The feeble flame in him flickered, unwilling even now to let go into death. *Get warm.*

Afterward, Ruán barely remembered that nightmare of sucking mud and icy water. He slithered into stagnant pools and hollows of rotting weed, enduring the sting of nettles and brambles all over his face and hands. Rain hammered his head. Up he crawled, the ground growing harder beneath him.

At last his hands grasped the roots of a wizened oak tree, and he knew he was free of the mire. It had stopped raining. On the other side, the ground fell away without warning, and he tumbled down the slope and came to rest. The first birdsong pierced the still of dawn.

Ruán's head went up, his nostrils flaring as he strained with all the senses left to him.

He reached out a shaking hand and it met a flat rock surface. He placed his palm on it. A low vibration came through it, a pulse. It was a standing stone, tall and upright, hewn and smoothed by human hands. The ancestors had raised them long ago to mark sacred ground.

Ruán clung to the rock. This was a better place to die.

As his fingers reached around the shoulder of the stone, they slid over a carving on its flank. His breath caught, and he traced it. A spiral. There were other symbols carved below it: diamonds within diamonds, and lines of ripples like sea-waves. Collapsing against the rock, he shivered as he caught the faint throb of more uprights all around him.

A circle of stones.

As the mud dried on his skin, he crawled to each stone in turn, reaching up to stroke the carvings, trying to picture them. His mind was sluggish from the cold and the pain of the night, but he discovered more spirals, layers of rings, and starbursts of spreading rays inside circles.

He turned his head toward the heart of the stones. The ground seemed to keep sloping down toward the center, and inside that ring a vast stillness opened up.

Ruán hesitated, shame sweeping over him. He could not break the sacred boundary…surely he must be cursed. Yet as he wavered there on his knees, the ground gave beneath him again and he tumbled over before he could stop himself. He slid and came to rest once more, the fall jolting him out of his daze.

The symbols on the stones burst alight inside him. *He knew them.*

These carvings filled the tombs of the ancestors. He had lain beside them in trances, beating the drum as they swam around inside his head. He always thought they were keys to unlock some mystery of the gods that only *he* was meant to discover.

And so he had turned away from sunlight and the rush of life in the forests and seas, burying himself in dark caves where there was cold and silence. Banishing all bodily senses, he sought to force his way out of his flesh, out of Thisworld. He confined himself to his mind, hoping he could use it to pierce the veils of the Otherworld. Though he never gained more than glimpses, he pronounced to his people what he thought the visions meant as if it was truth.

Another jolt arrested Ruán.

When he nearly died in the lake, he remembered floating

and...something hovering over him. A water-star. *Sídhe.* In those fever-dreams, as they healed him, he had glimpsed their true forms of radiating lights, crystal flames and sun-rays.

Rays in circles. Diamonds within diamonds.

The stone carvings.

The ancestors were carving the sídhe all along. They saw them for what they were: vast stars dancing between the veils of the worlds.

Ruán's laugh was no more than a croak. He had spent all that time thinking he knew everything, but it seemed he had always been blind. He panted, smiling, as something hard left his heart.

He flailed to sit upright, and as he did his arm hit another stone at the heart of the circle. It was a low, crouching thing. Ruán hauled himself up and laid his head back on it, his face turned to the sky. There he smiled again as the strength bled from him.

The sídhe had not taunted him. They sang for him in his illness, rocking him with song, and their rays of fire, their brilliant light, had given him a last glimpse of sun on the water.

So...let him rot away now and feed the land and its creatures in return for that. He was no more than mud and water anyway, and always had been—and suddenly that was a wonderful thing. *He was only ever made of earth.* How could he not have seen it? Let him melt into it now, for the Mother was earth and water, too...

As his pulse slowed, Ruán heard a humming. What tune was it? He realized that something was stirring into life in his belly. A growing pressure, a pain. Heat. It moved up to his breast and pushed on him from the inside. At last it crested, and something in him tore open. He gasped.

His memories burst into life all around him, as if he walked through them again.

A girl came whirling through a sunlit glade. *Orla.* Without hesitation, Ruán dived back into that day when he hovered between boy and manhood. Before he ever sought for anything.

"Blow!" Orla demanded as she spun in a cloud of dandelion seeds. "Harder, Ru!"

"I've got no more breath left, I swear." The boy Ruán collapsed, strewing the empty dandelion stalks on the ground. Orla's brown hair had become a crown speckled with seeds, and her frayed dress whirled as if woven of fine wool. He could not breathe. "You look like a princess."

She giggled, bounding up and sitting on his belly. "A princess of the cows, of the porridge pot!" She stroked his face, her fingers callused from the flour-stone at her father's fire.

Ruán caught her red hand. "You are *my* royal lady."

"You talk too much." She kissed him with berry-stained lips.

Ruán drank her in as she pressed her fresh young body into his. Though his shoulders had not filled out, one part of him was fast flowering into manhood. The blood rushed to his groin, and he could not stop it.

Orla raised her head. "Can't lie on you with that poking me." She leaped up and streaked off.

His face flaming, Ruán scrambled after her.

Through the lush woods they ran, splashing through streams and jumping up to touch each tree bough as they passed. At last Ruán pinned Orla against an oak. The beat of his pulse made everything vivid—the leaves brushing his cheeks, Orla's eyes, the smell of the rich earth.

"Ru." Orla's breast fluttered. Turning from his lips, she began to sing against his cheek. "Marry me, my strong one, my dark one, my fine one. Marry me at Samhain when the frosts are in the air." She trailed her fingers through the ruddy hair over Ruán's shoulders. "Marry me, my deep one, my *red* one, my sweet one, marry me at Beltaine when the blooms are in my hair..."

The adult Ruán thudded back into awareness among the stones, the song trailing from his lips. His voice cracked and faded, but the singing carried on.

He went still. The singing became deeper, more resonant, until it echoed off all the stones, rebounding back on itself and growing louder. It vibrated through his heart, and the stone beneath him rang like an anvil.

Spires of flame kindled all around him, their crests radiating flares of light.

Sídhe.

Their brilliance seared into his mind, as if they moved through layers of the worlds that had nothing to do with his scarred, useless eyes. As they came closer, their light blinded him for a moment, and when it cleared again the night sky of Thisworld spread once more above him. A round moon swam through shredded clouds. The stones were black against the stars.

They made him see.

The sídhe girl was once again kneeling beside him in human form. The moonlight shone from her skin, setting her aglow. *To gain what you seek, you must surrender, not strive.*

Ruán did not see her mouth move: her meaning rose inside him as if it was a thought of his own.

So stubborn you are! But now you glimpse it at last.

At the moment he gave up, willing to melt into water, rot away into soil ... so at last they came to him.

With a smile, the sídhe leaned in and breathed over him. It was not breath, though, it was light. It rushed through Ruán and ignited, low in his groin. *Orla.* He recoiled from that dangerous surge, that old desire of the boy in the glade.

No, the sídhe said. *This is a good place you have gone. Live in your body, not your thoughts—feel all the life of the world!* Her smile flashed and she laid a hand on his chest. Her true self was flame ... towering, streaming flame ... and now her fire entered him and Ruán was back there once more.

His body sank into Orla's, and in delight she reached up and spread her hands to the sky, drawing the grasses through her hair. As if she was earth and he the sun ... He poured himself into her.

In the stones, the same quickening went through the adult Ruán, but instead of pleasure, the burning in his body grew more intense. The fireball in his groin began to surge up his body. As it did, it forced out old, buried things.

Hidden things.

He stood on a sea-rock with Orla, the pleasure of the forest forgotten. The boat was waiting below, tossed on whitecaps. Orla's crying was pitiful. "What happened to you?"

The spray stiffened Ruán's face. He had to force his cold lips open. "It is a rare chance for one like me, Orla, to study under the druids."

"You want to run from me—from all of us!"

"No. I have to be pure for my studies. I have to be able to think." His voice cracked. "I try to bind my body to my will, but I cannot when you are near."

"You are so cold," she wailed, clutching his arms. "Kiss me the way you used to!"

Ruán fixed his gaze on the gray sea. The other novice druid, a youth from a neighboring island called Áedán, was beckoning to him from the little boat. *Hurry,* his wave said. *Here is the way out of it all.* The hungry farmers and fishermen, scratching a living from thin soils. His mother's face, pinched and white.

"The training will take all of me, Orla. I'm going to the Big Island. It is a great honor that Lord Mulach will have me." He gritted his teeth. "You will marry a fisherman, someone who will sit by the hearth with you."

Orla shook her head as she wept. She bent over with arms crossed, as if he was pushing his feelings out of his heart and into her.

Guilt, the edges jagged.

On the muddy ground between the stones, the fire in his body flared again and Ruán began to shake. His pores ran with sweat, wetting his hair. His belly burned, the pain making him cry out. The singing of the sídhe peaked, the resonance of their voices at last shattering the guilt into sparks that blew away, purging him.

But there was no relief; the molten heat only moved higher.

Now Ruán saw Lord Mulach's face, carved with grief for his dying son. The boy tossed in a delirium, his skin running with the same fever that gripped Ruán now.

Save him, Mulach had begged Ruán. *You have said you see all.*

Ruán had tried, with all the powers of his training, mind, and willpower. But not his heart. He could not go there. And so, he had failed.

The boy died.

The fiery column now reached Ruán's heart. It was shame... hot and bitter.

Ruán gasped and arched his back as, again, he felt callused fingers holding him down—Lord Mulach's men—and he watched the glowing fire-iron coming toward his eyes.

So now, the lord said, *you will see nothing.*

Ruán's great cry of agony was lost among the singing of the sídhe, as the fire burst from the crown of his head, his whole body a spire of flame like theirs. Ruán's awareness of himself—limbs, mind, pulse—was burned away.

His life-force fountained up. For one glimpse, a single heartbeat, that power flared all over the land, and he saw himself as Erin itself. His bones became the rocks, his flesh the living soil, his blood the streams and seas. His hair wove the grass and trees, and his pulse fired the life that ran through everything.

He was the king-in-the-land.

Then the sunburst was gone, and Ruán fell back into his own body with a shock that woke him to his human shape, and the moon, and the night wind.

The sídhe girl's laugh still held the ecstasy of that rush, that great flame of life.

So you burn away what was! Now you can become something else.

⁂

The day was sinking to dusk when Maeve reached the great hill that stood alone on the west shore of Connacht, looking over the sea. It was crowned by an enormous cairn of tumbled stones. Others thought it haunted by the sídhe of the Otherworld, but Maeve had always craved being scoured clean by wind.

The sea was copper beneath a red-streaked sky, the trees down the slopes burnished with the same shades of ocher. All the green was gone. There was only the rust of iron, of blood.

Many times Maeve had stood, chin stretched to the west as if this hill was the prow of a ship that would bear her away. It had never gone further than fantasy. If she had ever defied her father, she would have ended up with nothing. No one would have harbored her in Erin, and over the sea she'd have been an exile without rank, prey to men who did not know her gods.

Though it was already encased in tough leather, she caged her breast with her arms. A faint sound escaped her throat. *I endured you, Father, and you leave me to be raped in filth?*

Maeve ground her chin into her shoulder, her gaze dropping toward the southern foot of the hill. There sat a cluster of stone tombs, gray humps with gaping mouths. They had been built by the ancestors, but it was said the sídhe guarded the mounds now, the beings of the Otherworld.

Maeve's eyes burned. Once, hardly more than a girl herself, she had cast herself upon those tombs. Railing at Ros Ruadh, at her father, she had wept for her lost child as if torn in two again by her birthing.

When she still had tears for that pain.

The farmers always left little carvings of the goddesses there, and she had clasped them to her, their swollen bellies and breasts promising the fruitfulness of the Great Mother. *The favor of the Mother.* But though she pleaded, their eyes had remained blank to her. No help had come from the magical sídhe then.

And no help would come from them now. The mounds must be long dead, after all.

Maeve turned her head, but still that memory rose within her in a silent howl. At last she sank to her knees, as she had here on this hill every time the losses became too great to bear.

Her children, gone.

The moments of peace she had carved out in Laigin and Mumu, torn away by the whims of kings.

A knife on her bare skin…death in her brother's eyes…vile curses spat into her ear…

Leaning over, she buried her mouth in the carpet of heather so she could bellow into the earth and no one could hear. Her lips open, Maeve let each cry be swallowed by soil and rock.

Hidden, secret—dark disgorged to dark.

Ruán knelt by the lake, staring across the water. The glints on the waves danced. Within the orbit of the sídhe, it appeared he possessed the sight in his eyes, both in Thisworld as well as the Other.

You must mark your body, they had said in the stones.

Drained, he had not questioned that, walking back on trembling legs through the meadows of marsh-grass touched by dawn. There he plunged into the lake, scouring away all the mud and blood. When he emerged, he took up the stone blade by the hearth.

Mark the journey in your flesh, so you always remember.

Ruán carved nicks in his skin, tracing the slabs of muscle across his chest, the dip of his breastbone, and the flat of his belly. He was as clear as the water, as calm as the dawn.

The blade trailed fire, and when his palm grew slick he paused to wipe it and carried on. Once it was done he smeared the wound with the sacred matters: fire-ash, earth ocher, and plant juice. The offering of blood was his own, and the water already coated his skin. Slowly, he worked it all into the cuts.

Branding himself, he had scored the great spiral that continues curving forever inward, and forever outward. All druids knew that symbol.

The journey in seeks the heart of the One truth that joins All together. The journey outward, the growth and expansion of a soul.

When the sun ignited the frost on the grass, Maeve opened her eyes. Wrapped in her leather mantle, she had fallen into an exhausted stupor and lost the night.

She was lying among the heather, her knife in her hands. The cut had opened in her palm again, and blood gleamed in the dawn. Unrolling, she knelt. The sun spread down her side from the east, and her head instinctively swung toward it. She stopped herself. East was her brother, at Cruachan.

West was exile over the sea. There, without kin, she would be enslaved.

South was barred to the likes of her, a pit of heart-sorrow among the sídhe mounds.

Maeve's gaze rose higher. She got her legs beneath her, took a few steps up a rise and at last faced the north.

The Ulaid.

She could almost feel Conor's eyes upon her now, baleful amid curtains of gray hair and beard. She had wounded the King of the Ulaid. But now he had lost both her *and* Deirdre, and had been utterly unmanned before his Red Branch warriors.

Her father's doubts over Conor's intentions—and her own denial—had bound up Maeve's fear over this past year and hidden it away. Now it broke free again, sharp in the clear air. She wiped dew from her cheek with a shaking hand.

Warriors flocked to the Ulaid to vie for its gold and iron, making it strong in spears and swords. But cattle were the true, *sacred* wealth. A king could not be all-powerful without vast herds of cattle, and the Ulaid was too mountainous for this. It was Connacht that possessed the meadows and pastures, the cows growing fat on lush grass.

And now this kingdom Conor mac Nessa had always coveted—her kingdom—was about to be riven by a fight over the kingship.

Maeve knew all about warriors. They clashed like stags at leaf-fall, obsessed with who was strongest and boldest. They were ruled by pride and oaths, slights and humiliations. They vied for gold to hang on their limbs, swaggering about and wallowing in ale, roast boar, and women.

With shallow breaths she looked into the mist and saw old Meara's wrinkled face and Eithne's wry smile. Maeve felt the tenderness of Líoch's neck when she touched her hair in the shadowed cart. As the derbfine squabbled over the kingship, their eyes lit by greed, who would give a thought to the herders, tillers, and fisherfolk? Her brother? He cared only for fighting and rutting.

The whims of lords had wrought too much destruction in her life. How could she stand by as the same happened to her people—the only ones who had ever made her feel in brief, precious moments that she belonged?

Fate hung like the last stars over the sea. The echo of her father was already fading, but something surfaced now that Maeve had forgotten in her scramble to stay alive.

The one to come after me.

At that moment the sun lifted above the mist and flooded the hilltop, lighting up the frost on the stones. Maeve looked around her in a daze. Her skin was as white as that rime of ice, her mane as red as the dawn. Her bones were the stones beneath her feet. The blood coursed through her, roaring like the streams down the hill.

As a mother of babes, she must be cursed, yes. But was it because...she was meant to protect *all* her people? The priestesses on the sacred hill said women had greater hearts than men, and wiser heads.

A mother of all.

Maeve put a hand over her eyes, unable to let the words take form in her mind. Instead, a fierceness swept her that was pure instinct.

Hardly realizing what she did, she raised and then stabbed her dagger into a mound of sedge on the cliff top that faced north.

Her own blood was on the hilt. "I will not let you destroy them!" she cried to Conor of the Ulaid.

As that cry left her, Maeve shuddered, the ripples spreading out into the land. In its wake a faint echo. *I will not let you destroy me.* To her brother, her cousins; to any man.

If she ruled herself, no one could hurt her again.

Maeve brushed that whisper aside, and panting, drew back her aching shoulders. The colors of dawn had blurred into one brightness all around her. Only then did she remember the oldest name for the mount on which she stood.

Cnoc na Rí. The Hill of the King.

CHAPTER 6

Great bonfires roared on the frosted plains of Emain Macha in the north of Erin.

People clustered around the spits strung with boar and sides of beef, driving away the Samhain ghosts with singing, dancing, and barrels of ale. Music threaded through slurred laughter, and drums beat out the rhythm of thudding feet.

Cúchulainn and Ferdia stood alone to one side of the Hound's fire, heads bent over their cups.

Cúchulainn glanced at his wife Emer, bouncing another woman's babe on her hip. Her smile held a promise. The Hound sighed. It wasn't safe to try for a sacred babe of their own amid furs on the meadow. The Ulaid was seething with dissent.

At least the kingdom of Connacht was quiet.

Cúchulainn still simmered with frustration that King Conor would not command an attack while Connacht was recovering from Eochaid's death. But Conor was obsessed with finding Naisi and Deirdre, sending Red Branch warriors after them instead of after Connacht. Cúchulainn made sure the kingdom's defenses were still manned, and spent what time he could away from Emer and the rule of his clan riding Connacht's borders, but it was not enough. Ferdia, with no wife or family ties, had been in the saddle for moons, gathering news.

"The mutterings of the border lords grow louder." Ferdia swilled water in his beaker. "Everything Conor fears is being said ... that he's an old fool with a withered prick."

Cúchulainn grunted, shaking his head. Above, shreds of cloud shrouded the gold of the low moon.

Ferdia dropped his voice. "The warriors admire Naisi and think this is just the jealousy of an old stag for a daring younger one. The chiefs see the king's behavior as indulgence."

Drunken voices broke through the music. Their sense of danger heightened, Cúchulainn and Ferdia glanced at each other and, without a word, sought out the source of the trouble.

King Conor's youngest son, Fiacra, was staggering before his best friend Illan. "You *dare* say that about my father?" Fiacra bawled. His breaths were explosions of vapor.

Illan was in turn the son of the great warrior Fergus mac Roy, who had been king before Conor. Illan and Fiacra had been raised as brothers—almost twins, they were so close.

Illan jutted out his jaw, his eyes glazed. "No one can tear Naisi from our hearts! *You* are Red Branch. We are your first loyalty!"

"Naisi betrayed us by stealing my father's bride! Why can't you see it?"

"He didn't do any such thing," Illan slurred, teetering on his heels. "And tonight's for honoring the dead, isn't it? Because they may as well be dead!"

Other youths weighed in on both sides, bellowing over each other, and it swiftly descended into a brawl. Cúchulainn dragged Illan off, and another Red Branch hero, Conall Cearnach, took hold of the struggling Fiacra.

At that point King Conor strode into the firelight, his appearance cutting off both the baying and the flailing of fists.

A hush settled, punctured by the crackle of a bonfire and the wail of a babe. Conor gazed around, marking every young brawler's face. His eyes were bloodshot from drink. He swung toward Illan. "It is treason to take the side of a traitor like Naisi."

Cúchulainn's nostrils flared. He was about to speak up when a deep voice boomed out behind him.

"Treason, Nessa's son?"

It was Fergus. The old battle-horse shouldered men aside to stand by his son Illan. His mane of silver hair crowned his great bulk, his craggy face wrathful. "Illan did nothing but repeat a song your own bard once wrote for the sons of Usnech."

Conor knotted his thin lips. "Nevertheless, I forbid it."

Cúchulainn glanced between them, his heart pounding a warning. The Ulaid could not afford to have this old wound broken open. Not now.

Thirty-five years had passed since Conor's mother Nessa had seduced and wed Fergus, then king of the Ulaid. Conor had been fifteen. Boisterous and hearty, Fergus soon tired of the onerous duties of ruling a kingdom and set off adventuring, feasting and fighting his way across Erin and Alba.

Nessa convinced Fergus to let her son Conor rule while he was gone.

The cunning young man proved so able, however, that when Fergus returned, the lords of the Ulaid voted to give the kingship to his stepson, ousting the older warrior. Used to battle-blows, Fergus declared himself relieved and soon moved on to other wives, who bore him braces of sons and daughters.

Sons he would defend to the death.

Fergus's eyes nested in wrinkles but still held the power of a great lord who commanded many men and the loyalty of every Red Branch warrior. "Words and thoughts are free." Fergus's thunderous voice carried over the hushed crowd. "By honoring the

comrades with whom he shed blood, my son fulfills his Red
Branch oaths."

His expression held another message: that Conor wouldn't
know about those warrior vows because he had never taken them.

Conor tilted up his long nose. Their gazes locked. "Naisi gave
up that honor when he betrayed me. And that is why *no man* will
sing of him or his brothers, for they are traitors, all of them." Unsteadily, he turned on his heel and strode away with his guards
about him. Fergus led his drunken son in the opposite direction.

"They stir up a pit of coals," Cúchulainn murmured to Ferdia.
"Soon we won't be able to quench them."

Ferdia gripped his shoulder, his hand resting there as if they
were one flesh. No other man dared touch the Hound like that.

Cúchulainn could not look away from the bonfire as it roared
through the wood, logs breaking apart with a gush of sparks. "We
must leave no stone unturned to find Naisi and his brothers."
Cúchulainn forced out bitter words. "Not all those who seek
them want to save them."

"Who trained Naisi not just in sword-skill, but in tracking,
woodcraft, hunting, *running*? You did. What you gave him, he will
use to escape Conor's clutches."

Cúchulainn's thought was bleak. *But how will that bind anything
together again?*

Emer slipped to Cúchulainn's side, winding her hands in his
fair curls. "This is a night for laughter," she scolded, her voice
husky. "And here I see you two with faces as long as spears." Cúchulainn pulled her in to smell soap and bread, women's herbs and
wool, on her skin. She batted his lips away. "Not before Ferdia!"

Ferdia's smile was strained. "I think I need to seek other company anyway." He had rumors to uncover.

When he had gone, Cúchulainn let out a deep sigh.

Emer went on tiptoe to kiss his nose. "I am forced into finding
some way to bring your smile back, husband." She tapped her
teeth. "Now ... what could that be?"

Cúchulainn gazed down into her beloved face, blessing it for its quirky flaws: the untamable black curls, snub nose, and wry smile. Emer did not possess the beauty to set warriors at odds, and he was grateful for it.

She pouted at him. "You are far away."

He buried his face in her neck, lifting her off the ground. "I'm right here," he said, breathing her in.

※

A line of torches snaked away from the Connacht marsh like a vein of molten copper in the darkness.

The men holding the flaming brands reached dry ground again. Now that they had made their offering, they turned their backs on the sacred place, crossing their breasts with an arm, touching their brows.

The spit of land that reached into the lake behind them was only tenuously attached to the living realms, almost cut off by channels of dark water and reed-beds that exhaled mist.

An island of the sídhe.

At last the torches disappeared over the hills and the chanting of the druids faded. The body of Eochaid, king of Connacht, lay at rest on a bier by the water. He had been honored with the triple death. First, he was laid out naked for his flesh to be consumed by the creatures of the land. Then, his weapons would be sacrificed to the sídhe in the lake. Finally, his bones would be interred in the mounds of Cruachan with his ancestors.

Pitch brands still flamed at his feet and head, until at length they guttered out and the world sank into blackness.

For a time all was still, until a full moon broke over the hills. The lake-water flared into life. The reeds were tipped with silver, dipping and whispering. The streams and pools ignited into sheets of brightness. What had been clear in the day and empty in the dark now became something blurred. Gray. Silver. Indistinct. An in-between place.

Maeve emerged from the woods.

She approached the silent bier by the water, her legs leaden. The breeze chilled her palms, and only then did she realize they were damp. *The sídhe cannot hurt me,* she repeated. *They never answered my prayers; they don't care what I do. I exist alone.*

Something splashed in the shallows and she whirled toward it. A duck. Maeve wiped her mouth with the back of her hand. Unlike the tombs, this place was not dead. Goose bumps rose over her arms; she could feel something. She reminded herself that royalty could pass from Thisworld to Otherworld—and back.

And yet in that moment she was also a child again, her pulse galloping as her old nurse Brenna whispered of what happened to mortals who strayed into the lands of the sídhe.

But nothing had struck her down by the time she reached her father. A deerskin covered his legs, his naked torso gray and cold in the half-light. The druids had rested a jug of milk next to him, and a basket of bread—an offering of food for the sídhe while they waited for his jewels. She was glad his eyes were covered with bronze disks, for it took away the humanity of his withered face, and a childish part of her realized he couldn't hurt her now. His shade was gone; the druids had sung it away.

A breeze must have scythed across the reed-beds, for their murmuring grew louder. Maeve's nose wrinkled at a waft of decay and she fixed her eyes on his ankles. Across them lay the king's sword.

She drew toward it. If she was to be felled by an invisible blow, it would come now. No one had ever taken a king's sword from a funeral bier. No one had ever dared.

No one but me.

The sword was unsheathed, and light played over the blade—and for a moment she was sure it breathed in time with her. Then she realized it was just the shaking of her body. The hilt was deer-bone shaped into a stag, its muzzle the grip, its antlers flaring into the guard. The carved eyes of the stag were impassive—or challenging?

As she reached for it, Maeve's thoughts disintegrated. *I seek not to dishonor. I will gift something of greater value, I swear. See how I will protect my people...better than any man!*

Her fingertips met a wave of pressure above the sword and she faltered. The next moment one hand was about the hilt, one cradling the blade. Filling her lungs, Maeve swung the sword around, stepping back and spinning faster until she staggered to a stop. Nothing felled her, nothing struck her down.

She stabbed the blade into the spangled sky with a disbelieving laugh.

The sword flashed back the moonlight, and it was alive. *Her* life had entered it. The stag fit her palm, the bone already warmed by her blood. She went down on one knee to thank her father, backing away with platitudes to the sídhe.

Maeve flew across the grass, her chest bursting. She splashed through puddles and wove between the trees, paying no mind to where she was going as long as it was far away from the druids and their torches. Skirting the lake, she drank in the shine of the moonlight on water, then raced through another bank of woodland.

At last she broke out into a clearing and shuddered to a halt.

A man was rising from his knees at a forest pool.

Dazzled, Maeve stared at him, every thought driven from her head. He was bare-chested, his body made of moonlight... a gleaming carving of flared shoulders and narrow waist. The light gathered in his face and she could see nothing but that blinding glow.

He was a sídhe. One of them had come to her in man-form, after all. She had summoned him with her bravery!

Maeve was too dizzied for sense. There was no love lost between her and the sídhe. She had always respected them, though never prayed to them or left offerings at their springs. She was outside their favor...but she knew they revered courage. Were the Shining Ones testing her, for Connacht's sake?

Every fear she had crushed, every frustration, and all the loneliness she had ever borne, came rushing up. She needed something wild and glorious now to sweep them all away. She needed magic.

She stumbled forward, insane with daring. Curving her hand around his neck, Maeve of Connacht closed her eyes and kissed the sídhe.

Their flesh met—and Maeve fell.

A deep roaring sucked at her, as of water rushing underground. Gasping for air, she clawed her way back to some sense of the solid world, her hand dropping away.

The moonlight blinded her to everything but the sídhe's mouth, parted in what looked like shock. Only then did he come to life, gripping her wrists and pushing her from him.

Maeve's craving instantly tipped into something darker and utterly senseless. *The sídhe rejected her again.* Shaking with fury, her body took over, lifting the sword.

As if in a trance, the sídhe tilted his head toward her blade. Maeve had never seen anyone look to their own death with that graceful lift of the chin, as if he did not care. But he was immortal; he could scorn her petty threats.

Her arms went nerveless and the sword lowered. With a growl, Maeve gripped the hilt tight and, spinning about, fled with the blade trailing behind her.

Garvan crouched in the ferns by a stream as Maeve scooped water into her mouth.

"What is this about, spitfire?"

Maeve wiped her chin, unable to meet his eyes. Her sight was still dazzled by the afterglare of moonlight and luminous skin. She contained a shudder. "Where is my brother? And Fraech?"

Garvan plucked a dead leaf from her braid, eyeing her filthy clothes and mud-streaked leather.

For three days a storm had covered the brown and yellow

woods with sleet. She didn't want to risk the lives of the herders she knew by seeking shelter with them, so she had huddled in her oilskin under the evergreen boughs of yew trees, nursing a feeble fire.

At last the clouds had cleared, the sun warming her frigid face again. It had also melted the remnants of frost into a mire.

"Fraech, his uncle, and his father all left the funeral feasts straight after the storm. Innel rode west, to the sea-lords who have not come out to support anyone for king yet." Garvan looked hard at Maeve. He had accompanied her to those western forts in sun-season, where she'd drunk mead with those sea-chiefs. Innel would soon discover her efforts there, too.

Maeve glanced over her shoulder. She had wrapped the sword in sheepskin and tucked it in the roots of a gilt-leafed oak tree. Now she felt the pull of the hidden blade, like a glowing fire on a cold night.

A path to safety...? But so desperate, so foolish! She wavered, wanting to cling to the sword—wanting to throw it from her. And if she did, she would always be running, from her brother, from Conor, until they hunted her down.

"Spitfire?"

Maeve dropped her chin, shook her head. It was too late to back out now, for with this theft she had just invited the wrath of not only her brother's men, but other lords and the druids. "Have the rest of the nobles gone home?" she asked Garvan, her voice husky.

"Not while there are bones to gnaw and kegs to drain. They want to argue about the kingship without Fraech or Innel to hear them."

Maeve placed her hands on her knees, the gleam of melted frost on the branches blurring around her. She remembered barreling into the man who attacked her, her instincts always to throw herself at danger before it had a chance to leap at her.

"Then first," she said, "ask the lords to linger, for they must witness something important. Second, take one of the druids with you and track Innel down." She looked at Garvan. "Issue him my challenge: single combat, here at Cruachan."

Garvan snorted. "Oh, aye." When she did not smile, his face fell. "He will slit your throat before you've taken your first swing."

He will find a way to do that anyway, if I do not stop him now. Somehow. "Innel sent men to silence me. Now he gets his chance to kill me, if he is brave enough." Garvan's mouth dropped open, and now Maeve did smile. "They are the words I want you to use before his men. Alone with him, tell him if he does not face me, I will reveal the death of Donagh's daughter and his own treachery against me."

"Spitfire, he'll only send someone to finish you off in secret."

"If they can find me. The duel will be at high-sun in four days. Tell the chiefs to gather at the fighting green."

She braced to rise, but Garvan grabbed her wrist. His black brows were drawn together like lowering clouds. "You are skilled with sword and spear, more than any woman I have known. But Innel is twice your size, and a hardened warrior. How in Lugh's name are you ever going to win, Maeve? You're mad."

She regarded him with a strange calmness. She had set her feet on a clear road at last, and either way, she would be free. "Too many people call me that." She rose, smiled, and flicked a dark curl off Garvan's forehead. He still retained the faint brown of sun-season across his crooked nose. "You do not know all of me," she said softly.

"The woman is dangerous. If I have been discovered, I must leave. Disappear through the veils as you do."

The radiance of the sídhe girl washed over Ruán. Her hands were beside his in the water. They both stared down into the crystal depths. A fish brushed his fingertips.

We said your time in your world is not over. Your fate calls you.

"Then tell me what it is! Should I escape...hide? Her touch brought foreboding into my heart..."

The girl's amusement rippled through his senses like the water against his legs. *I cannot speak your fate, for it is not made real until you reach it yourself.* She waved an airy hand. *Perhaps I don't know.*

I doubt that. He forgot to guard this thought.

She grinned. *Your will is free, not bound to ours. You might choose to wander along another path. And if you do...* A shrug.

His choice. His path. Why, then, did they save his life? Ruán chewed his lip, peering into the glints below the lake surface. He was determined he would ask no questions, demand nothing of the sídhe-maid, nor do anything to bar himself from these glimpses of sight at her side.

Now that he was physically well, more and more they bade him to cross the boundary of the veils back to the world of men. There, he was on the same shores of the same lake, only the skies poured rain and it was cold, and he had to hunt for food with touch and hearing.

There, he was blind, and wore a strip of deerskin over his eyes, padded with leaves to stop his scars from twisting.

In the forests, he bathed in moonlight to sense it on his skin; to help him to remember the glow of the sídhe. But sometimes, when he still wept for his blindness, the girl woke him on a dawn like this and the world flowered around him again. And peace returned to him once more.

A peace that had been shattered by the woman with the sword.

The sídhe-maiden's eyes flashed sidelong. *She has her own purpose, and her will is also free. It is not for man or sídhe to turn someone away when they hear the call of the lake.*

※

Maeve left the horse tied up and crept through the rushes.

The dank mists were lifting off the lake, and cold sunlight

glimmered on a flock of ducks that rose in a cacophony of squawks.

The whiff of decay from her father's body pushed her toward the north shore of the little island, almost cut off from land by the water. Her pulse skittered. Perhaps she had only been lucky; this trespass might rouse the wrath of the sídhe in earnest.

Maeve saw a movement through a thicket of bare blackthorns. She froze and dropped. It was him, walking along the shore as if he had just come from the water.

His deerskin trews were soaked, and stuck to his thighs. A great tattoo curled over his chest—a spiral that traced from his heart to belly to breastbone. It moved as he breathed. Maeve dragged her gaze from it. His long hair was a dark auburn, trailing about his face. He did not swagger like a warrior, with flexed shoulders and brawny arms. He was taller and more lithe, his chest proud and lifted high. His graceful steps appeared to flow with the land, as if the air parted to let him by.

It was disconcerting, and she did not like the sensation.

A strip of deerskin hid his eyes. Maeve searched her memory of tales about the sídhe. Was this a mark of sacred sight?

The sídhe was gliding along the sand, smiling at something in the water. As he drew close to Maeve, he squatted and unfurled a hand toward the lake. The muscles along his shoulder blade rippled, the hollows between his ribs glistening.

A snub head appeared, pushing through the water-grass. Maeve glimpsed a humped back and the flick of a tail.

The sídhe was murmuring. To her astonishment, the otter clambered out of the water and put its paws on his knee. The sídhe held still, then lay back on the sand. The otter climbed his thigh before curling up on his belly, grooming its whiskers.

Maeve's mouth fell open.

The sídhe stroked the otter's flank, and when the creature chittered, he laughed. That made his belly shake, which prompted the otter to hop off, flashing a look of injury at him before diving again into the water.

The sídhe lay then with face lifted to the weak sun, as if drinking it in. The pleasure in his expression … the absorption … it cast a spell over Maeve. For a moment she forgot why she was there, drawn to sink into the warm sand the way he did …

He scrambled up then, turning toward the blackthorns where she hid.

Maeve's legs were trembling but she made herself stand. She stepped into the open, whipped out her father's blade and knelt with it across her palms. "Forgive me for my mistake in the forest. I … was not in my right mind." She paused to steal a glance.

The sídhe's graceful shoulders had tensed. "So this time you give me a chance to run before striking me down." His voice was hoarse, but beneath that, the resonance reminded her of the chief druid, Tiernan.

Maeve blinked. "I … ah … have come to beg the forgiveness of the Shining Ones. I took the sword to protect my people." She had come to make sure they would not curse her for her daring, for now she must face Innel—or die. "I can give you much in return."

His expressive mouth quirked. "You think you can *bargain* with the sídhe?"

"Everything is a bargain."

An ungodly snort startled her.

The sword slipped to Maeve's knee, and she frowned. "As Queen of Connacht, I will ensure my people avoid your lakes and hills and leave you in peace."

His ruddy brows arched above the blindfold; his full mouth drew into a thin line.

Maeve thought it must be scornful, that look. She tensed as the old hurt surfaced from the past. Twice she had prayed to them, and twice was met with silence. "The sídhe owe me."

He turned on his heel and flowed back along the shore. "I lost my sight." He sounded distracted now. "Do they owe me?"

Gods, he was not a sídhe. *Stupid … stupid …* Maeve's limbs sprang to life and she ran after him. "Who are you?" She reached to halt him, and only then saw that the blindfold had slipped, and between his brows, an older mark—the horned spiral borne by druid-kind.

Maeve clasped his arm, but did not get anything else out.

This time something poured from him *into* her. First a flood of heat that loosened muscle and bone, then a rippling of her body, as if she was no longer solid. The air around her shimmered, a silver corona sheathing her in a different form.

She was sinuous…curling through sunlit water in a spiral of lithe muscles.

Her hand dropped away.

Glimmering bubbles all about her…

Maeve spun, sheathing the sword. She stumbled into a run, expecting that shining wave of water and light to crash over her, fill her nose and throat until she drowned as a punishment for her daring.

She threw herself onto Meallán's back. "Fly," she gasped to him, her knees prodding him into a gallop.

All the way home that potent tide surged and ebbed through Maeve. She could not feel the shape of her own body—and she had never been more afraid.

⁂

Ruán slipped on his belly in the shallows. The reeds murmured above his head. The ache of the icy water was shut out by the turmoil of his mind. He kept his mouth under the surface, nostrils flaring, so he didn't scare away the birds.

Queen of Connacht! They didn't tell me that. They didn't tell me anything.

Then he realized the sídhe could hear his mental wrath, so trying to drown it somewhat defeated the purpose. Ruán drew his legs under him and crouched on the lake-bed, swiping drips from his face. Dancing out of reach, capricious, fleeting…aye, the sídhe were just like the glints he remembered of sunlight on water.

He had accidentally dislodged the blindfold, and after a struggle with his temper, pulled it back down and bound the ties. He had now discovered the best reason for wearing it—the pressure on the sockets stopped him straining his empty eyes.

To truly see, you must seek the light that flows through all things, the girl had urged him. *The creatures and plants, but also water, soil, and air all glow with their own hue. Human eyes cannot perceive it, only your spirit sense, so you must practice.* She had grinned at him. *You have the time.*

Ruán breathed out, letting his discomfort flow into the cold water. He had just begun to catch flickers of light behind his own eyes now, which was all that mattered: to perhaps one day actually see again in Thisworld. No one was scaring him away from *that*—he would stand his ground before any so-called Queen of Connacht.

And anyway, the woman had crept in secret to a place that held a funeral bier, hiding herself from her own people. These were not the actions of the ruler of a kingdom. She must be lying.

Ruán sank up to his nose, drawing the memory of the otter to inhabit him once more. A few drops of rain spattered his brow, and a frigid wind stirred his wet hair. Gliding along, he made himself forget everything but the water clothing his skin and the scent of weed and brine. He emptied himself, imagining that he dissolved into the lake like a handful of earth.

There. A glimmer, a pulse of light. He followed it. There was a flap of wings and a squawk as the duck flew away.

Ruán reached into the reeds, tenderly tracing the little nest. Seven globes, warm and smooth. A great bounty, so late in the season. He took two, wrapping them in a bag of nettle rope at his waist. *I give thanks for your strength that will fill my body. For I, too, am a child of the Mother.*

He did not forget the humbling of the stones, and how ready he'd been to give his substance up to Her and feed the other life of the land. But not yet.

Not yet, they said.

CHAPTER 7

A voice cut the darkness. "Chief druid."

Tiernan halted, snapping out of his reverie. Few people dared the oak groves at night, and not in this deepening cold, the sky now empty of cloud. His brethren carried on down the path to Cruachan, their robes glowing under the waning moon.

Whoever interrupted him was covered in a cloak from head to foot. Under the trees he saw only a pale blur and a cloud of breath that billowed out into moonlight.

"It is Maeve. I must speak with you."

Tiernan had not seen the king's daughter since the Samhain feast. She had always caused a slight disturbance in the ether around her, and he only now realized it had been absent for many days.

Immediately, he turned back for the sacred grove. The thatched temples were comforting to ordinary people, with their lamps and wooden idols, but druids preferred to worship among the oaks in the night. Maeve would speak to him on his ground.

Within a clearing ringed by gnarled trees, Maeve put her hood back, her flaming hair now turned dark gray. "I have challenged my brother to a duel. I want you to make sure he fights me."

Tiernan merely stared, for these words made no sense. In the icy moonlight her features were as sharp and hungry as ever. Her gaze was fixed beyond him, though, and for a moment he thought he glimpsed a bright flicker around her. He reminded himself that the oaks tricked the eyes at night. "Why would I do that, lady?"

"Because he has already tried to silence me, and now I must kill him before he kills me. But even if you don't care for that, care for this." Maeve thrust herself closer, making Tiernan draw back. Her words tumbled out, her eyes flaring, the pupils wide and black. "The men, including Innel, are going to fight for the kingship. You will soon have a war on your hands between kin, and Connacht will be weakened and vulnerable to attack. I, though, stand outside those factions. I know how to bring a new king to power, in peace."

Tiernan blinked to clear his head of chants and incense. Was she plotting to snare herself another husband? He stroked his beard, fingering the gold beads woven through the gray. "You think killing a man will bring peace?"

Her brows arched, bringing her cold face to life. "Do not play with me, chief druid. Men often die to win peace. But if you'd rather, think of it as me removing a problem we both share."

Age had stooped Tiernan, and he leaned on his staff to pull his spine to match her height. "These are druid matters."

"The nobles choose the king," she cut in. "The druids only bless that choice. And you could not, in all conscience, bless Innel. His bloodlust and greed will make him a terrible king! He raided Mumu to win support for his kingship, and the Mumu took revenge on innocent herders—"

"The warriors raid cattle. Your father did."

"But that is *all* Innel has to hold his warriors—brawls and raids. He does not command true loyalty of the heart. With him as king, we will be endlessly at war. Kings must be wiser than that, know who to provoke and placate. Raiding should not be used to preen, but for protection and strategy." She caught herself, turning to face the fading oaks. "We need a ruler who strengthens the people, who *is* the people." Her voice trembled. "Someone who will be wedded to the land, and not to their own greed."

Tiernan realized then that what he always felt radiating from her was heat. Like any flame, it drew a man in—even him. He pounced on that human weakness, crushing it. "Your cousin Fraech enjoys the support of many men."

"My brother and cousins splinter the men's loyalties, each with too small a following alone and too many enemies. None of them can unite our people as one."

Tiernan cocked his head, drawing the silence out and changing tack to assert his authority. "You were named well—'she who intoxicates.' Even when young, you had a way of making men do your will."

She snorted. "And even then, I never got what I wanted."

"And that was?"

"Wouldn't you like to know, chief druid?"

Now he saw that her array of wry smiles and blunt manner formed her own kind of armor.

She spread a hand. "Pray, do go on. I never tire of hearing my own faults flung back at me."

His lip curled. "You are unmarried once more, and have ways of making men cleave to you. That makes you dangerous." *She seeks power through a man.*

Her chuckle was harsh. "That is all men see when they look at me."

"Not all men."

She caught her breath, and moonlight moved within her eyes. "Then use one danger to rid yourself of a far greater danger. My brother."

Tiernan's spirit senses probed her. She was unpredictable, his mind hissed, her loyalties uncertain. On the other hand, she would probably die on Innel's blade, and then Eochaid's cubs would stir no more trouble at Cruachan. "You have considered this well."

"As a dove among foxes, I must always stay a flap ahead of their jaws."

"A dove," he mused, his gaze traveling over her strong shoulders and hard thighs beneath her leather trews.

He then discovered Maeve of Connacht also knew how to unbalance her opponent. She flashed a feral grin that lit her face. "All you have to do is let me fight him."

Garvan met Maeve in a little-used stable far from the king's lodge. With the help of the crafters, she had managed to slip back into Cruachan, bundled in their farm-carts among the women and children, her stained cloak hiding her hair.

"Innel has returned," he reported.

Squatting in one of the stalls, Maeve coughed on chaff and old horse-dung. "What did he say?"

"Fury brought him charging back, but then he calmed down, saying he would not demean himself by fighting a woman. And then—you won't believe this—Tiernan stood before all the warriors and said every person who could fight had the right to issue a challenge, and that he had to meet you or be named coward!"

So you play your own games, chief druid. "Innel cannot afford this accusation."

"No, by the gods, he cannot. He flew into another rage, ordering his servants to grease his weapons, and polish armor, and cut the green so the turf is flat." Garvan chewed his lip, eyeing her. "And here you are, spitfire. The druids agreed on first blood."

That law ensured that few men died in duels. Once a wound was taken, the fighting stopped. It also meant there was little time to win.

Before he finds some other way to kill me.

Maeve leaned her head against the timber stall and the world shimmered again. Ever since she had touched the man at the lake, she was aware of a current running through her. The air glimmered like a reflection of water, the ground rippling like waves. She had considered delaying the combat until she shook off this strange trance, but every time she thought it, her body throbbed. *The rush of the tide…the light…*

Garvan gripped her wrist. "We have sparred together, Maeve, and I know you can fight. But you cannot beat him."

She smiled. His face was washed with streams of bubbles. "I have to." Though deep inside she trembled, there was no other way but this. She would not be hunted. She would not be violated. And with nothing else to grasp for, the only way to triumph against Innel and his cubs was to be a warrior like them.

"You are a damn fool!" Garvan leaped up. His cheerful face was haggard with something Maeve dimly recognized as grief. "Start listening to me, spitfire—or I won't be part of any of your idiot plans, ever again!"

"If I die, you won't anyway."

He grunted in disgust and vaulted over the stall, kicking up muddy straw as he strode out.

There was no need to hide anymore.

Ignoring the whispers of the servants, Maeve went to her bed-nest in the women's lodge to dress herself. She could not bear any men arming her, with their cold iron, callused hands, and heavy tread. She did not want any touch upon her, dragging her back to shore.

Here she floated, as if it was not really happening; and yet at the same time she was drawn along like a leaf on a tide. An end had to be made now, of some kind.

The morning mists melted, pouring a faded, leaf-fall warmth over Cruachan. The day climbed to high-sun, clear and still.

The gossips had done their jobs well. People were gathering at the fighting green, the throng speckled with the sheen of furs and glint of bronze that picked out the noble folk. Women flocked the rutted paths between the huts, bundled babies strapped to backs and children dragged along by the hand.

Maeve was barely aware of them on her way through the king's ramparts and scattered thatch lodges of the crafters. She reached the fighting green before the mound of the warriors—a square of turf marked out by spears laid on the ground.

A stillness descended. Everyone was staring because Maeve wore only a breast-band and breechclout beneath her hide armor, her legs and arms left naked. She was also barefoot and bare-headed, her hair tight-bound.

No shield. No iron but the sword she carried on her back, wrapped in linen.

A desire had seized her to capture every current of air on her skin—the scent of the wind, the give of the turf—unimpeded by a shell of metal. Her breastplate and kilt had been molded to her body when the hides were wet—they were a second skin. She padded along on bare soles, sleek and graceful as Miu.

A gust of wind blew through the gold and brown trees along the stream, showering leaves across the flock of people. Children put their chubby fingers to them, laughing in their mother's arms. Maeve unfurled her palm without breaking stride, daring the gods. *Would she live?* A withered leaf caught in her hand and she folded her fingers around it. Was it death, or a sign of life to come?

The faces and bodies of the enormous horde soon merged into a sea of luminescence through which Maeve swam. Innel was a dark weight at its heart, his body clanking with mail-shirt, helmet, sword-belt, and shield. His hatred was in his sneer as he swung toward her, but she felt nothing.

She floated, rocked on invisible currents.

Dreamily, she drew her sword-bundle into her arms.

Just then Garvan thrust the knots of spectators aside and bounded over the spears to her side. "Aye, I'm back." He held her elbow, his breath spiked with ale. His black hair stuck up as if he'd been plucking at it. "Spitfire, the men know you're good. You don't have to be so stubborn. Let it go, and come away."

The sea of light bound by the spears beckoned Maeve, radiant waves lapping through her body. She met his eyes. "Each time Father married me off, did you think I was content to be hearth-bound? Do you think I gave away the freedom of my thighs for nothing? Endured, for nothing?" She tilted her head, dazzled by the glow about him. "I sought out the best warriors in Mumu, and some among the Ulaid. And in the glades, they gave up their fighting secrets to me."

Garvan's eyes bulged. "What...?"

"My skills are untried. But I hid those I had, wondering if one day I might need them." Her breath gusted out. "This day."

"But...I've fought with you..."

"My friend, you fought a part of me. For the rest, I sparred alone. It is not the same as warrior training...but it will have to be enough." Her sight unfocused, she saw that utterance ripple out through the silver sea.

"Balls to that." Garvan's green eyes were too bright, his mouth screwed up like a dried cherry. "I've dug up something for you." He put his lips against her ear. "Innel's knee was sliced on a raid many years ago, and though he keeps it a secret, he still bears the weakness." At last he managed a smile. "Target the left, spitfire."

Maeve nodded, and turned toward Innel, the wrapped blade still clasped to her breast. She strode to Tiernan, who stood between her and her brother at the heart of the sea.

Tiernan raised his stave.

"You will pay for your treachery," Innel hissed beneath the druid's prayers to the gods. Her brother held his shield over his chin. "My sword will rip open your bowels, and you'll burn on a pyre I build with my own hands."

A slow, knowing smile spread over Maeve's face. Innel faltered. At the last moment she yanked the last wrappings from the bundle and clasped her father's hilt. Innel's eyes widened, a curse leaping to his lips, but no one else was close enough to see what blade she bore.

Tiernan's staff plunged between them.

Maeve dived into the depths of light, and was freed.

Innel stabbed in with the weight of muscle and thick bone. Maeve twirled out of his way, lithe and swift. The delight of that weightlessness, the thrill of that glide, lifted her heart. *It was true...* she swam through air. She laughed with delight.

Her brother roared and swung, unable to twist at the waist because of his bulk and armor. His feet churned up mud, splattering Maeve as she darted out of reach.

Over the years, Maeve had sought out not the brutish fighters, but the swift and skilled. She'd coaxed from them the sword-edge flips, tumbling runs, salmon leaps, somersaults, and spear-springs, practicing until she wove those patterns into the very fibers of her muscles, honing nerves and sinew.

Now the aura that had trailed her from the lake gathered into a glowing nimbus about her. It was a sleek creature, its quicksilver grace added to her own litheness. Pulses of alien instincts wound through her own reflexes. Her mind was not hers; it was liquid, flowing.

She gave herself up to that alchemy, and was Maeve alone no more.

Innel saw her delight, and his fury crushed all his remaining sense. It made him swing wildly, losing control so his shield dropped. Maeve spun through radiant seas, leaping to his side behind the shield's arc and trailing her blade across his mail-shirt. Innel cried out at the metallic ring and lunged over his left knee to reach her. Maeve heard his breathless grunt of pain, saw his face spasm.

Innel sliced in again, and Maeve sent herself into a high vault at dizzying speed, digging her sword-tip into the earth. She landed behind Innel, making him shake his head like a baffled bear. Warriors did not skulk *behind* their opponents. The honor code made them charge at each other face-to-face.

But Maeve had been barred from taking warrior oaths.

She darted around again while Innel was still turning, forcing him to lunge left once more. Her blade nicked his elbow before glancing off his mail-shirt. Innel's angry yelp echoed off the trees.

"First blood, first blood!" Garvan shouted.

Innel growled in denial, tossing the shield away. Shock passed over the crowd, the exclamations appalled and thrilled. Panting, Maeve nodded. She knew this would not end at first blood, for if they both lived, the fear would never die.

She smiled, weaving their father's sword before Innel with the same undulations of the creature who inhabited her. *Come*, that smile said. Innel's features contorted as his eyes followed the blade, blood running down his arm.

And something unexpected came.

The currents around Maeve rippled. A brilliant arc swept through the watery veils a heartbeat before Innel actually moved. *She saw his intent, his thought, as if it was made of light.*

Maeve had already ducked by the time Innel's sword passed over her skull, missing her by a hairbreadth.

Innel swept his blade back on its return swipe. With a sinuous twist, Maeve undulated onto the back side of his sword. While he was still lumbering to turn, she finished her spin with a cut across the side of Innel's neck. A seam of blood opened up, and Innel gargled his fury.

Maeve was going to wear him down.

For what seemed like an age she ebbed and surged with the silver tides, making Innel's bad leg thump down over and then again, the knee twisting. His pudgy face soon streamed with sweat, his chest working like a bellows.

At last he surprised her by contracting his body halfway through a swing, changing direction to slice across her bare thigh. Innel's men let out a great cheer, and Maeve looked down in a daze as blood trickled over her knee. The pain was distant, its fire quenched by the silky waters.

In defiance, the glowing wave swept her up with renewed force.

She sprang from her injured leg and spiraled around Innel, stirring the currents with the speed of her leaps. He was limping, his movements labored. Soon his arms, neck, and jaw were crisscrossed with glancing wounds. He never managed to land a blow on her with all his weight behind it.

Mumu's champion had shown Maeve a daring feat. If Innel's knee slowed him, she could do it and unbalance him further. She flung her sword in an arc and dived beneath it, cleaving the silvery sea.

A twist under Innel's grasping arms, a tumble past his feet. He lunged for her, and then suddenly his leg spasmed and gave out. Innel collapsed, crashing to the ground with his bad knee bent beneath him. Plucking up her sword, Maeve bounded onto his back, pinning him down. She curved her bare toes to grip the wings of his shoulder blades.

He will kill me.

Nothing existed but that primal terror, a savage flood that drowned all else.

She kicked up the flare of the neck-guard on his helmet. There was a place below the dip in the skull...

He will kill me.

Innel bucked, trying to twist her off. If she'd been shod, he would have managed it, but she clung on with toes and the arches of her feet. Sucking in a breath, Maeve lifted the sword and stabbed down two-handed, throwing her whole weight on its length so the stag hilt dug into her belly.

The tip drove between the gaps in Innel's spine.

His scream pierced the air, his limbs thrashing. Senseless, Maeve straddled Innel's head and hacked his neck again, and then again.

She didn't know when he died. Only when his stillness was complete did she halt. Blood was dripping down her chin, the taint of copper spreading over her tongue.

The bating of the audience had died out. Maeve was now enveloped by a great silence. The silvery tide drained from her, rushing out to sea, and she began to sway. Garvan's arms were about her when she sagged to the ground.

Maeve returned to herself. The cut on her thigh throbbed, and her muscles burned.

Innel's men were bellowing their anger, others roaring to release pent-up bloodlust. Garvan's pleas for help were drowned out by the clamor of the warriors as they broke the sacred bounds of the ring, swarming over the blood-soaked ground.

Maeve stared at her dead brother. Someone had turned him over, and now they lay in the same pose, arms out. His eyes were glazed, though, his coarse skin smeared with gore.

Maeve's throat bobbed, then spasmed. "Water…" she gasped. "Wash it all away…"

Garvan barked orders, and cool liquid poured into her parched mouth. She beckoned with a feeble hand until Garvan sluiced it over her face, arms, and legs, too. He was mumbling incoherently, stroking her wet hair. Shouting warriors were milling about. A druid bent over her wound, prodding it until she batted him away. She groped for Garvan's arm. "Get me…up."

"We have to stanch this bleeding."

"The show of the sword," she croaked.

"Spitfire—"

"*Help me up!*" It had to be now. Garvan looped an arm under her and hauled her back up. The pain made the daylight flicker, but she shook it away. Blood trickled down her shin; water dripped from her face.

As the press of men drew back, Maeve stabbed her father's sword into the sky. The lowering sun kindled it into a flame in her hands. A hush fell again, so that only her scream of triumph echoed over the plain of Cruachan.

At last the warriors recognized the stag on the blade, and their shouts crashed in upon her. *Eochaid. The king's sword!*

Garvan yelped and, taking her wrist, shoved her sword-arm higher. Dazed, Maeve's knees buckled again, Garvan's grip alone holding her up. Perhaps it was all over, after all. Innel was dead. She was safe. It could end now; she could turn from this path, find somewhere quiet and still.

Jostled by warriors, her eyes fell upon Eithne, her hand over her mouth as she stared at Maeve's dead brother. And little Líoch, gazing wide-eyed as Innel's supporters stormed around, howling with wrath.

Maeve's pulse drummed in her ears. It was not over. Fraech and his kin would see her as an enemy now, as would others. They would come after her.

*And Conor…*The rest of her people could not run and hide from him.

Tiernan strode to Maeve's side, making the yelling warriors fall silent and peel back. "*You* took this blade from your father's body?"

With his shaven hairline pushing his gray mane back to his crown, there was nothing to distract from the high arches of the druid's brows or blade of his nose. His domed eyelids gave him the look of a temple idol, except that at this moment his eyes blazed with a very human wrath.

Panting, Maeve nodded.

"Why?"

She had to force her trembling legs around, lifting the sword across her palms. Still she wavered, her belly sinking with an unknown dread. She yearned to curl up in a hidden den now that no one would ever find, but there would be no peace for her people while Conor stalked the land, and Idath and Fraech brooded in their mountain fort.

And there was only one true way for her to be safe from them all—and that was to be stronger.

Maeve breathed in, looked over all the fighting men, the lords, the crafters, women and children. "Because I would be Queen of Connacht, if you will have me."

The world fell quiet.

"My father was struck down before he could announce me his heir. He said I was the most like him, the only one who would do what is best for *you*." It wasn't a lie, she told herself fiercely. He meant that; it was truth.

"You have dishonored the sídhe," a druid stammered.

"Sacrilege! You will bring calamity on us all!" others babbled.

Tiernan's gaze had turned glassy, as if he sought an answer inside himself.

Maeve leaped in. "I am a royal daughter, sacred consort of

kings. Only *I* had the courage to brave the sídhe, to prove my worth." Her sight wavered as she remembered touching the strange druid, the rush of it.

She blinked, her gaze seeking out the warriors and noblemen one by one. *Now* she must touch a burning brand to the tinder she had been gathering for so many moons. "I defeated my brother in combat—a man whose folly would have led us to disaster. *I* am the ruler my father wanted you to have!"

The crowd was thunderstruck once more into silence. She had this one chance. Maeve ignored the pain, taking a deep breath. Her words flowed from her on the last wave of light.

Every man of the derbfine had as many enemies as allies, but she was above these old feuds. She wouldn't turn warrior against warrior, or put her own greed or pride first. She had worked beside them for moons; she understood the concerns of the lords, crafters, and herders in a way no one else could.

Finally she loosed the specter of Conor—a humiliated king who would soon seek to prove his strength to his men again. She argued the need for a ruler who could forge all of Connacht into *one* blade to lift against him, rather than those who would weaken the kingdom with the battles of clan against clan.

At last Maeve paused, panting, her bare foot slick with blood.

"No woman will rule us!" one of Innel's warrior's shouted. "Abomination!" others cried. "Shameful!"

Maeve's gaze pierced the throng to seek for one man. The chieftain, Donagh.

Your promise, her eyes demanded. The murderer of his daughter lay dead at her feet, by her hand.

Donagh's cheeks grew florid above his beard and he hesitated. Glowering, he at last made his way through the ranks of sword and spearmen. He was a powerful lord, and the men fell silent as he limped to the front. "The Lady Maeve has been steadfast when we needed her, unlike her brother. Innocent people lost their lives because of his hot blood; flocks and herds were stolen. She is not too proud to realize the strength of Connacht lies in its cattle-lords." He stared about him, defiant.

"The lady brought us grain when our harvest failed," one of the bolder noblewomen put in. And so on they came, a tide of all those Maeve had exhausted herself to court over sun-season.

"We have many strong warriors who could be king," an older chief argued. "The lords will choose one, as we always have."

"Fraech is an honorable man," Maeve agreed, hoarse with strain, "but his uncle and father have many enemies among you. How will you fare under their rule? They only want to possess the king's hall and the king's cattle!"

Fear clouded their faces, and Maeve rested the sword on her shoulder. "I married into Laigin, Mumu, *and* the Ulaid. I lived among them, watched their warriors train, know their lords, their lands, their trade routes, their wealth. Does Fraech know so much of these kingdoms? No."

More arguments broke out, the din rising until another of Innel's swordmates stormed, "A queen of Connacht is impossible!"

"Why?"

People peered around to see who had answered. It was a dark-haired young female druid called Erna, one of those Maeve had sent to heal the babes with the coughing sickness. "The tales speak of ruling queens, do they not?" Erna gazed up at her chief druid with opaque brown eyes.

Tiernan's mouth was pursed, his knuckles white as they clutched his staff. "There were queens of the Tuatha de Danann, when our gods walked this land. Other tales speak of queens among our ancestors, yes."

One of the boisterous young warriors who had been trailing after Maeve for moons now jabbed the air. His face was alight with the thought dawning over many of them: that when she became queen, they would be favored. "There are queens among the Britons *and* Albans, and they are strong peoples. We need the best ruler. That is all that matters!"

"The goddess Macha was also once a human queen, I believe." Erna added a respectful bow in Tiernan's direction. "Is there not another tale of her as queen among the Ulaid?"

With a scowl, one of Innel's cubs gestured toward King Eochaid's aged bard. The old man was sitting on cushions beside the ring. "*You* tell us this Ulaid tale, honored brother. We would hear it from you."

The bard unwound his wiry body and stood, white hair stirring in the wind. He bowed to Tiernan, draping his cloak over his arm in the bardic stance. "It is called Macha Mong Ruad; Macha of the Red Mane."

People exclaimed, swinging toward Maeve and her own fiery hair, now stiff with blood. Her heart skipped. This she had not foreseen. She wiped sweat from her lip, taking the weight off her leg. Garvan went to help her but she shook her head, and frowning, he folded his arms.

"Macha's father was a great king of the Ulaid," the bard intoned. "After he died, Macha sought the throne. Her cousins would not let a woman rule, and so battle ensued." The bard closed his eyes. "Macha killed one of her cousins with her own sword so she could be queen."

Eyes darted toward Innel's body, forgotten in the chaos. Maeve's mouth went dry again.

"She married the second cousin and built the great fort of Emain Macha with her own hands. Afterward, she ruled well for many years—a blessed age for the Ulaid when their streams ran with gold. Their herds multiplied, and when she passed back through the veils she left a land richer than it had ever been." The bard bowed his head, his aged, swollen fingers clutching his cloak. "The Ulaid have revered her in song ever since."

Maeve's throat closed up. A rustle of wonder ran over the crowd. *The Ulaid had a red-haired queen, and see how strong they became! The Tuatha de Danann had many queens. We have all heard the stories.*

Breaking through the crowd, Garvan strode forward, waving

his own sword before stabbing it into the turf. "Have your wits deserted you? No one has ever braved the veils of the sídhe for a king's sword. *And they did not strike her down!* They chose her, for she is a hero from the old tales. Imagine this story of *Connacht's queen* being told at every fireside in Erin. The Ulaid will think her this Macha Red Mane come back, but to *us.* They will think we are favored now, and *that* will put the fear upon them!"

Maeve's supporters among the warriors began to echo Garvan. As one pack, they whipped up the people's blood with everlouder whoops. They brandished swords and spears over their heads, and the children shrieked, goggle-eyed.

Tiernan pierced the racket, striking his staff on Innel's discarded shield. "Enough!" he roared. "All you say may be true, but she has dishonored the sídhe. The Shining Ones are the spirits of rain, the seeds, the forest, and seas." He pointed at Maeve, his hand shaking. "Their wrath may not have fallen upon you, lady, but it might descend upon *us* and the land be laid waste—grain withering, cattle sickening!"

Maeve lowered her father's sword, her mind racing. There was no other way, lest the chance slip away all together. "I *am* chosen, but if you doubt, let us see what the long dark brings. The land slumbers then, and the raiders of the Ulaid, too. If the sídhe are wrathful, the land will show it at leaf-bud. If I am blessed, we will also know it. For now, Conor's troubles keep him close to home... We have a little time for the nobles to choose the best ruler for Connacht."

This raised murmurs of approval from the chieftains. It was better to choose the right person to lead them rather than rush to elect someone who would falter and bring ruin to Connacht.

Tiernan went to protest, his eyes narrowing.

Maeve cut him off, throwing herself on her good knee before him. Pain shot along her damaged thigh, and more blood welled. "And if I do not have the blessing of the sídhe, I swear now that I will offer myself as a royal sacrifice—for the sacred triple death." She would be dealt a blow to the skull, then strangled, then staked in a bog, one of the watery doorways to the Otherworld. Maeve struggled to fill her lungs as she said it. "I will go to the gods and beg them to favor our people with the same courage I have shown this day."

This invocation of sacrifice and magic at last made the storm break. People cheered and stamped, gabbling with the release of tension.

The chief druid stared down at Maeve, inscrutable. "The offer is accepted." He lifted a hand to the milling crowd. "And we hereby lay a sacred peace upon the men of the derbfine until leaf-bud. We must stay strong and united under druid rule, to defend our land if need be."

As the clamor went on, Tiernan's eyes glinted at Maeve with something that could have been admiration. "I will tell the sídhe they can have you themselves come leaf-bud."

"I meant it." A humming was growing in Maeve's ears, her vision narrowing. "You can kill me with your own hand."

And then she fainted.

CHAPTER 8

"It is foolish," the druid Mahon growled, grinding herbs in a mortar by his fire. "That woman is a banshee."

Tiernan was collapsed in one of Mahon's willow-branch chairs, exhausted. He had been placating his fellow druids for days, soothing their fears and outrage.

The wisps of Mahon's white hair trembled as he worked the pestle in agitation. "Why did you agree to put off the king-making?"

Tiernan stared into the flames, which danced in a draft that crept under the doorskin. The fumes from Mahon's various bubbling pots on their little tripods caught at his throat. "She has won many lords to her cause. And with the sword, and her victory in the duel, the warriors see her as the goddess Macha returned to us. If we crush her, we risk the very war breaking out we wish to avoid."

Mahon scraped the pestle against the mortar and sniffed the crushed herbs. "You don't sound angry."

"I'm not. I'm … intrigued." Eochaid had enjoyed a long reign, and it had been many years since Tiernan was required to deal with such an upheaval. "Fraech and Innel won the support of some lords, but many are their sworn rivals. You know how warriors collect slights along with the enemy skulls on their doors. The Lady Maeve does stand *outside* these feuds, as she says. It is possible she can bring us peace."

Tiernan watched Mahon's hands as he rose and felt among the bunches of herbs hanging from antler tines on the low roof. Mahon used another sense in his healing, an instinct. Then Tiernan went still. He was using his *mind* as chief druid, and not his own gifts. He clambered up, throwing his wool cloak about his bony shoulders. "We need to pierce the mists that are obscuring this matter, for all our sakes. I must seek more visions until I see true."

Without speaking, Mahon reached to his shelves, nudging aside bundles of roots, jars with wax lids, and sheaves of speckled feathers, until he withdrew a hidden leather flask and slipped it into the chief druid's hands. The dreaming potion. The older druid bowed toward the little shrine of the healer god Dianket in the corner, and its wooden idol with eyes of pale quartz. Tiernan joined him.

It was the Dark One he truly invoked, however. The god who hovered in the murk, the mists, veiling truths. Tiernan needed sight, as he had rarely needed it before.

It was just past dawn, a week later. The hills to the north and east of Cruachan were the dark rust of dead bracken and the last brown leaves. The scatter of pools and marshland in the valleys below were shrouded in a pale mist, the sky streaked with rosy cloud.

"Spitfire?" Garvan nudged his horse behind Meallán.

Maeve did not turn. "I've changed my mind about journeying to Lord Ardal today. I have somewhere I need to go first, alone." She did need to shore up support among the chiefs, but every night since the fight, her dreams twisted into visions of her death—a noose around her neck, her blood drifting through water like smoke.

"We agreed you need guards now, Maeve. We must come everywhere with you."

"Not this place." Maeve blew into her frigid hands, trying to pierce the banks of mist with her sight. The rising sun was now burning off some of the vapor, and every now and then a glimpse came of shining water etched with slow currents.

The lake.

Hidden at his side, one of the warriors spread his fingers to ward against enchantment. They thought she had the power to summon the armies of the sídhe. They thought her blessed by the Shining Ones, but she wasn't. She couldn't be.

They must have let her have the sword for their own reasons. They were tricksters, after all.

Maeve kneaded the knitting wound on her thigh. The druids had sewn and poulticed it, and it was healing well, but it only reminded her that the threat of Fraech and his kin still hovered.

And beneath that, her vow to Tiernan was ice in her veins, not the glorious rush such dedications were meant to be.

She had promised a divine blessing. Fertility. Fruitfulness. Bounty. She was declaring herself a *mother of the land*. Maeve worried her lip between her teeth. She had always thought herself cursed as a mother. Long ago she took that pain and hid it in a fold of her heart, and it made that a numb place, and that had brought relief.

But for Connacht to be strong now—to save her very life—

she must seek what she had once spurned. "I do not know how long I will be."

"Forever?" one of the men muttered. Mortals could be captured by the Shining Ones and not returned for many years.

Maeve bent a stern look upon him. "Do you think I cannot part the veils?"

Garvan was still cocking a doubtful brow when Maeve spun her horse, slashing her hand between them to cut the ties to the world of men. "Wait for me," she snapped. "No one is to venture to this lake of the sídhe. It is for the queen alone."

And she kicked her stallion down the slope.

Maeve slid from Meallán's back at the lakeshore, hopping on her undamaged leg.

Since the fight, her mind kept swimming back and forth between light and dark. She should feel invincible after such a victory, but she felt insubstantial instead, her pulse erratic.

There could only be one cure.

Leading her stallion, she ducked beneath barren ash trees, their brown seeds hanging in clusters. She limped across the cold, purple marsh to a hearth of rocks and spread her hand over it. Warm. He was close. She tied Meallán's reins and left him, crouching instead behind a fallen trunk.

The weak sun had broken fully over the lake now, lighting up the mist and painting the tips of the reeds.

This time the man was thigh-deep in the wetlands, his back to her, his buckhide tunic and trews water-stained. He stood with hands spread as if beckoning the surface to rise toward him.

Maeve craned her neck until her wound cramped and she fell on her buttocks. She could have sworn something rippled from the stranger's palms into the water. He dipped his arms in and then lifted up a gleaming fish that appeared to already be dead, bent over his palms.

How did he catch it with that blindfold?

The man glided out of the lake and past Maeve's hiding place with that curious, flowing stride. His full mouth was soft with wonder. He was transported, unaware of her.

Maeve was arrested by that glimpse of private ecstasy, as if he looked upon something *beyond* this place. His face was tender and aglow with it, and for some reason her heart contracted. Did she look like that when she was caught in that silver tide?

He trod on light feet to the fire and curled up, seeking for his stone blade by touch alone. His fingers traced the curves of the hearth as if savoring them, shaping the rocks and trailing across the spangled grass until they found what they were looking for, and then cradled the blade.

Mesmerized, Maeve found her cheeks growing hot. She started as Meallán's ears twitched at the stranger's presence and the stallion stamped. The man paused in scaling the fish but did not look up. Only then did she notice all of the scratches that webbed his hands.

Blast. Maeve shook off her daze and limped toward him. "You're a priest."

The stone hovered over the sheen of scales.

"I saw the mark on your brow. You are a druid, not sídhe. And if you are one of their priests, then I have come to ask you to pray to them for me."

The man began scaling the fish. Close up, the dance of his fingers was even more unnerving. His dark russet hair fell in a tail down a perfectly straight back. Like his scarred hands, though, this grace was marred by a ragged forelock that looked as if he often stuck his hand through it, and copper stubble over his jaw that was roughly shaved by stone, not steel. Baffling.

"What must I do for this blessing?" Maeve's mouth had gone dry. "I need the power of the Shining Ones to make the land fruitful. I will offer the gifts, and you can perform the rites."

The blade came to rest on the druid's knee. He lifted his face and the sun caught it, and for the first time she looked at *him* and not his tattoos or blindfold.

His full mouth bore defined peaks, the corners curving up a little, as if he once had been inclined to laugh. His jaw flared out like a square shield, though his nose was prominent enough to anchor it, a little dip at its tip echoing the obvious cleft in his chin. It was a warrior's face, not that of a pale, thin druid who spent all his time at studies.

His voice was still low and rich, but with a hint of exasperation. "You cannot speak to them through someone else any more than you can bargain with them." As if that was enough, he returned his attention to his blade.

Maeve, though, saw he had caught his lip in his teeth. Not so calm, then. "I hold the safety of many people in my hands." She tried to rein in her desperation. "You will help me, or—"

"You'll risk the ire of druid-kind as well as the sídhe?"

Maeve tensed, making her wound protest. She kneaded it again. "I will risk anything for my people. I have already risked my life."

"If you have that much courage, put yourself in their hands and surrender your heart. That is what they ask." Frowning, he dipped his chin, rubbing his stubbled jaw on his shoulder. "Or so I was taught."

Surrender...? If she had done that, she would be a cowering thing in Conor's bed, a broken bird. Or dead by her brother's hand.

"Where are they? I will prove to them that I deserve this." Maeve charged away from him through the blackthorn thicket, ignoring the scratches on her arms and face. "I beg you to show yourselves," she pleaded. "You have seen I am brave, and worthy." She swept the grasses aside and broke out into the marsh. Scores of ducks took wing in a flurry. Dizzied, Maeve flung her arms to the sky. "I will honor you, if you will help me!"

The feathered reeds closed about her. The splashes of the

ducks settled. The pale sky was empty. *Come to me.* Maeve squeezed it out of her heart. *Please come, as you never did before. There is more than me at stake now.*

Nothing.

With heavy steps she limped from the marsh. Panting, she sank on the grass by the stone hearth and stretched her sore leg. *Lugh's balls.* She stared at the glinting water, surprised when her eyes blurred, shattering the reflection. If she failed, what would happen to Connacht? The derbfine would tear the land to pieces, and Conor would gobble them up.

The druid blew on the little fire he'd conjured. "Your steps sound lame."

Her head snapped toward him, a cramp in her breast. "A queen cannot be lame! I took a wound, that is all."

He couldn't see her glare, and so continued gutting the fish. He did not so much tear the flesh as stroke it clean. Maeve dragged her gaze from his maddening hands. "I know the druids for leagues around Cruachan, so I would like to know why you are here alone..." She hesitated. "Without your sight."

The rhythm of his hands faltered. "I took a wound, that is all."

A stab of amusement severed Maeve's frustration. It took effort to push and bear up all the time, and she was exhausted.

"I am a wanderer," the man went on. "I hold no allegiance to anyone anymore, least of all the druid brotherhood. In fact..." His brows showed over the blindfold. "You'd best ignore me altogether." He spitted the fish on hazel sticks and propped it near the flames, wiping his hands on the grass.

"So I have not 'risked the ire of druid-kind' at all."

He snorted, the curves at the corners of his mouth deepening. "Not because of me."

This exchange was interrupted by a growl from Maeve's belly. She rubbed it, frowning. "But when I touched you, something crossed between us." She sat upright. "You *did* place an enchantment on me. It made me fight like I never have before, diving, twirling...I felt weightless." Her breath caught. "You lie when you claim you know nothing of the Shining Ones!"

The man went perfectly still. "*You* felt that?"

"After I saw you with the otter. It seemed to be ..." She shook her head. "...all around me, like nothing I have ever known. But what did I *feel?*"

The man leaped up as if she had bitten him. He turned toward the lake, his fists curling. "A glimpse of the otter's anam, it seems. It is ...something sacred to me."

Anam? Maeve rarely gave thought to souls, either her own or others. "How is that possible? Unless you do have the blessing of the sídhe ..."

He scraped back his russet hair. Maeve stared at the rigid line of his back, his muscles pushing out against his wet tunic as his breath grew swifter.

At last he lowered his shoulders and felt his way to the fire. "Every journey to them is made by one alone." He prodded the spitted fish. "They are not mine to command, and I have no blessing to give you." But he sounded as if it was an effort to speak so coolly.

A waft of smoke stung Maeve's eyes, and when she blinked it away, the man was holding out some cooked fish on a flattened shard of wood. He was not smiling now, the dips beneath his cheekbones more hollow. "I did use to be a druid. Fire and food must be shared with guests—that is the oldest law of all."

Maeve took the food. If he was not threatened by her, she could not assert any authority over him. "Then you will also know you trespass on sacred lands at your peril."

"Is that why *you* keep coming back with the fear of the gods upon you?"

Maeve trapped a disbelieving laugh. "You are dangerously bold for a landless wanderer."

He shrugged and folded roast fish in his mouth. "I have nothing to lose."

So he did not need anything, either. Troubling. Maeve peered at his blindfold. Why would he cover his eyes if he lived here alone? *Pride.* He must be a man, after all. "Well! You built this hearth, and I cannot eat without the name of my host."

He hesitated. "Call me Ruán."

"I am Maeve, daughter of King Eochaid. And...wait, I have some food as well." She limped to Meallán's saddle-pack, digging out barley and honey cakes and a flask of mead.

They ate in silence. When Ruán washed his hands, he remained crouched by the lake as if seeking for something in its glittering expanse, his elbows on his knees, his fingers dripping. Maeve glanced between him and the sheet of sunlit water, wondering what he saw. A brackish scent rose from the reeds, striking her with a curious pang.

Freedom. Silence. The timeless water that every day captured the sun soaring and then sinking into night.

Ruán began to hum. Lulled by the haunting tune, Maeve leaned back, her thighs relaxing as the warmth of food and mead sank through her. Her mind sent out a feeble warning. *Danger.* But her instincts did not agree, for against all her efforts her eyelids began to droop, though her hand remained on her sword.

The singing wound through her descent into blackness, and Maeve could do nothing but let go into a child's sleep she had resisted for too long. She drifted in and out of wakefulness, like a fish swimming from sunlight through shadow.

The singing became a murmur. *If your heart strains, lay it down and your weariness will be cleansed. The strength in your back is great, but be soft now, for all creatures find rest here...*

Maeve fought against the tender voice. She could not be soft. She jolted awake, her hilt in her palm. Moistening her sticky tongue, she turned her head.

Ruán was holding Meallán's bridle, his graceful head bent upon the stallion's muzzle so that their breath mingled. He was singing to him...no, *saying* those things to Meallán in some strange druid-speech. And her fiery stallion, who bore no touch but her own, nudged Ruán's chest with his brow.

Maeve grasped for the sword, forcing herself up. She never let her guard down, and neither did Meallán. Now was not the time to falter, not with so much at stake. Furious at herself, she barely noticed the pain as she hobbled to the horse.

At the last moment she stumbled, and unerringly, Ruán's hand reached to catch her.

She plucked herself free. "I must go. My guards will think I have come to harm." She tried to clamber into the saddle, but her wound cramped and she sank back, head swimming.

"Here." Ruán cupped his hands.

She had no choice, placing a foot in his palm. Once up, she scrubbed the creases of sleep from her cheeks. "Thank you for the food."

A little, crooked smile. "I am merely placating you, so this does not come flying at me again." He gestured toward her scabbard on her belt.

Maeve stared down at him. "I do not make mistakes twice," she said faintly. "Farewell." She kneed her stallion and set him into a canter across the turf.

I am always running from him. Her face burning, she slowed Meallán. Only then did she remember that the man could not see her. She stopped her horse and looked back.

This Ruán had not moved, his arms by his sides. Yet Maeve recognized his relief that she was leaving, even from afar. A calmness flowed all about him now, as if he was gathering in the vast stillness of the lake and sky and holding it within his own body.

She was seized by a craving to plunge back through the long grass and sink into that nameless well of peace that pooled around him. She would never have to summon forceful words again, never have to struggle, to fear. She would let the constant heaviness she bore fall to earth and simply breathe in the great silence.

Her hand unconsciously reached for it, the movement startling her from that baffling trance. Her breast thumping, she dragged Meallán around instead.

This time the horse absorbed the leap of tension in Maeve's body. Once he lurched up the slope onto the track, he broke into a run of his own.

CHAPTER 9

As the long dark tightened its icy jaws about the land, Tiernan at last caught a glimpse of what he sought. In the bare oak grove, he lay so still for so long that his breath coated his hair in frost. A glittering film covered the cowhide enveloping his body. His heart slowed and he wheeled with its beat, far from the shell of flesh he knew.

His own murmur accompanied him, a strain of music beyond the stars. *Show me the king.*

Cold and hunger helped the spirit fly free, for suffering made the body an uncomfortable home. The pinprick of silver that was his own essence now rushed up and out into the void, bound to his flesh by only a thin cord. Clouds of sparkling dust swirled about him, slowly condensing into things he recognized: sights, sounds, and feelings.

And now, after so many weeks of searching, it burst upon him like the sun breaking through cloud.

The Lady Maeve...

...in a watery place of marsh and lake. Silver surrounded her like the moon's crown on a frosted night. He glimpsed something else—a flare that was centered in the middle of her body. Was it...a sword she brandished before her? Did this mean she was the warrior-lord they needed?

Tiernan's awareness circled, seeking more. Power radiated from her like the ring of a struck blade, resonating through tree, rock, grass, and stream in the land around her. And they all began to vibrate, as if they were made of a substance as fine as air, and she was the source of that resonance, that song...

The sickness of the seeing herbs sucked Tiernan back to himself.

He retched on the ground, belly cramping and hands burning as he cursed his human frailty. At last he wiped his numb mouth, groping for meaning. His thoughts were too fragmented to grasp, though, and when he began to shudder he knew he could not stay here. Wrapping the cowhide about himself, he leaned on his staff to hobble down the frosted path away from the starlit oaks.

With a flick of his hand, he summoned an image of Maeve so vivid she hovered before him. She was lean-muscled, clothed like a warrior, her hair stiffened into a wild mane that drew all the men's eyes. He had to acknowledge that her proud bearing, bluntness, and vibrant laugh disturbed the man in him. Was it some primitive awareness telling him to fear her?

He had always thought it strange that she was so willful, yet went obediently to every new husband at Eochaid's order. *She knew she needed to be bound to her father, or die,* his instincts whispered. Eochaid would have had no hesitation in tossing her out of Erin if she had not obeyed him. Or worse.

Now there was no father, or king—only a woman who sought to rule alone, bear the wounds and fears on her own. Die alone.

Tiernan left the grove more troubled than he'd entered it. The moonless night steeped the barrows of the ancients in gloom. There was no light to guide him here.

Cruachan waited, caught in the endless time of the long dark.

⁂

"I have never known a druid sift mud for his supper," Maeve said, squatting on the sandy shore of the lake.

Ruán was digging mussels from the silt with his fingers, his nose just above the water. "As you see, there is no one else to feed me," he gasped, straining to reach the lake-bed. With a curse, he suddenly took a breath and sank completely beneath the brown water.

Maeve saw his hair waving like dark weed, and shivered.

It was an iron-gray day, the tracery of branches in the woods behind bending in a bitter wind. Clouds crowded the sky. Maeve huddled in her thick oilskin, her hood up, her hands tucked beneath her arms.

Ridiculous, she thought, and did not mean Ruán being in the water on such a day. That was merely mad. She was the one who kept coming back to this cold place, bearing gifts of tools, blankets, bowls, and pots. It was she who trailed after him like a supplicant as he fished and gathered berries, trying to tease scraps of information from him that might help her, so far to no avail.

With her father and husbands, she had adorned many shrines with royal gold, and placated many druids. She knew exactly what was required.

She thought.

Ruán surfaced in a rush of foam, blowing water from his nose. His skin had gone red, his fingers white-tipped as he placed the muddy handful of mussels into his net bag and flung it to shore.

"*So*," Maeve said, dogged as ever. "If there is no one with you, then you must be in some kind of priestly seclusion."

"Which does not appear to be working," Ruán remarked, wading out bare-chested.

At first Maeve had gaped when he said such things; now she had to bite her rebellious lip when it threatened to twitch. She must keep her mind sharp. She suspected he wielded some magical tricks, the way her thoughts so often lost focus. *Be careful.*

She summoned a frown. "And lakes and springs are where the sídhe live...so...you have taken a sacred vow to serve them, have you not?" If she shot questions at him, one day she might catch him off guard.

That lift of his lips was always maddening, as if she privately amused him. He slicked his dripping hair back with both hands. His chest and arms were puckered with gooseflesh, and the spiral tattoo seemed to pulse as he panted from the cold, strands of dark red clinging to it.

Her own heart quickened in sympathy. Annoyed, Maeve grabbed the wool mantle she had brought and flung it at him.

Ruán caught it, then hesitated, as he did when accepting any of her gifts. But a deeper shudder seized him, and reluctantly he wrapped it around his wet shoulders. "I was terrible at being a druid," he said, his jaw outlined against the gray clouds. He shrugged. "I could never reach the sídhe, though I nearly killed myself trying. I did not come here to seek them."

With narrowed eyes, Maeve strained to detect the lie. But there was only truth in those words. Sighing, she crooked her chin in her hand. *Get up, and go.*

She had many important things to be doing. Winning more lords to her side. Salting meat and pickling berries with the noblewomen—a chance to dig up news of the derbfine over cups of hot mead. Sparring with the young warriors in the weapons hall.

Her days pressed upon her, full to the brim. And yet here she was.

Though Ruán all but ignored her, she would not let him beat her, even though it was excruciating to sit so still while he set out his careful snares, or walk so slowly behind him while he found his way with hearing and touch. She would not give up. He must know something.

A squall blew in over the lake, pecking at the water with raindrops. They began to patter upon Maeve's leather hood and drip down her cheeks, and she huddled even tighter. Ruán, though, put his head back and drank up the droplets, washing the brine from his face.

Maeve's skin prickled as she watched him. Somehow the rain joined him to this place, as did the cold and wind. The waters seeped through him, binding him to the land. The wind buffeted his body, roaring like a wordless song.

It was Maeve's turn to shiver. Gods. This was an exposed, barren place with no cozy hut and no roaring fire—she had not even discovered where he slept. No thatch sheltering her, no thick walls.

All of this waited for her back at Cruachan.

Yet as if spellbound, she tilted her chin, and the rain began to blow straight in her face, running down her neck, freezing and clean. Here at the edge of the wild there were no voices arguing in her head, no fears whispering. The squalls and wind drove them all away.

Maeve did not get up to seek a fire. She did not move.

Cúchulainn wiped flecks of snow from his numb mouth and cheeks. It was not a good day for hunting, with threatening clouds and sleet showers blowing in from the east of the Ulaid.

King Conor, though, had ordered a few Red Branch out for a boar hunt, perhaps to lift his head from the vat of ale in which he was trying to drown. Cúchulainn, Conall, and the king's eldest son Cormac had tracked the boar through bare forests close by Emain Macha, plunging through snow-slush and thorns in the thickets.

The boar was wounded now, trailing Cúchulainn's spear, and the dogs had brought it to bay among the roots of a dead oak tree. The king's huntsman deftly roped its tusks and tied them to smaller saplings to either side. Only then did the king ride up, dismount, and heft a spear.

Cúchulainn kept his attention on the boar's murderous eyes. Even at rest, the Source was a subtle flame joining him to the fiery webs of other living creatures. The boar's light was guttering now. The other men were silent, resting on their spears after the long trek through the cold.

King Conor was still bracing his lance, hesitating.

The Hound glanced at him. The spear-tip was wavering, and at that moment Conor swayed off balance and stumbled.

The boar grunted and lunged—and one of the ropes snapped.

Before Conor could react, Cúchulainn barreled into him, knocking him out of the way. Three more spears thunked into the boar's chest and neck, from Conall, Cormac, and the huntsman. The boar squealed, tottered a few steps and collapsed, its snout blood-flecked.

Conor's face was as pale as the snow, his eyes dazed. Cúchulainn knew better than to help him up, though, for the king was sensitive to such humiliations. Even his son Cormac did not start forward.

Scooping up the king's spear, Cúchulainn turned, glancing at red-haired Conall. The Red Branch warrior swiftly dispatched the boar with a sword-cut to the throat. The huntsman released the hounds to yap and mill about, and the men broke into banter that was forced and brittle.

While the others began butchering the carcass, King Conor wove away through the trees, clods of snow clinging to his red wool cloak edged in fox fur. Cúchulainn found him by a little stream, scooping water into his mouth with a trembling hand. "Watch that pup of Fergus's for me," the king slurred.

Cúchulainn peered at him. Conor was far drunker than before they set out, which means he had been slugging ale in the saddle. "Buinne?" The Hound named the former king Fergus's eldest son, hoping to turn Conor's mind.

"Ach, he is as dim as his father! No, the little pup."

Illan.

"He has a loose tongue—and looser loyalties." His beard dripping, Conor groped his way around an oak tree and Cúchulainn heard his piss trickling on the snow. "He was practically raised at *my* hearth with Fiacra, and now he whispers insults behind my back."

"Illan was in his cups at Samhain." The Hound quelled his

wrath, twisting the spear-butt into the snow. In his war-frenzy, he lost himself to the Source, so away from battle he never even raised his voice lest it take him over.

"I want you to watch him." Conor slumped against the trunk and waggled a finger. "I don't trust him. He wants his father as king again."

"He does not. He is loyal to you and the Ulaid."

"Watch them all. They hate me, and they want to unseat me." Conor thumped the trunk of the oak tree. "Any man that defends Naisi wants to unseat me!"

Fergus on one side, Conor the other—and Cúchulainn caught in the middle. He had sworn to protect the kingship *and* the people.

Despite the nearby laughter of the men, Cúchulainn was swamped by bleakness. It was as if he stood in the shield-wall in battle, and his sword-brothers on either side were falling, disappearing into the bloody mire beneath his feet. Naisi. Illan. Fergus. *The Red Branch...splintering.* Who would be next?

Conor was staring at his fist on the mottled bark, his mouth slack. "That bitch thought she could shame me, but she will find out how I deal with traitors. She will see that Conor mac Nessa's wrath never fades!" He struck the tree with greater force.

Cúchulainn frowned. Deirdre—or Maeve of Connacht? It must be Maeve, for the king only ever spoke of her with hate.

"I will show every warrior in Erin I am a stronger king than Fergus ever was." Conor hissed it under his breath.

Heartsick, Cúchulainn spun and stalked away from him. Behind the king's back, he coiled up his whole body and drove the iron-tipped spear through a thornbush, and left it there.

⚍

The sídhe appeared rarely now, and always unbidden.

Ruán had only their words to cling to.

He must open the eye inside him to see the *light-song* that flowed through all things. Each day he sought to surrender, letting the lushness of the lake world soak into him, letting himself melt into it. Then the ecstasy filled his whole body in a way it had not since he was a boy.

One morning Ruán waded through the reeds, caught in his trance. A smile touched his mouth. For a heartbeat a glimmer of light sheathed his body, coating him like the lake-water. Everything was vivid. A flap of wings came from the distance and he lifted his face. There...a bright streak as a swan flew away. Another shimmer; he turned toward it. For a moment there were silver sparks among the trees, and then they were gone.

The life of the lake was coursing through Ruán when he stepped ashore, the rich scent of mud in his nostrils, the wind stirring his hair. Wild as he was becoming, there was no need to think.

So his instincts immediately knew that Maeve of Cruachan had come.

Every time she appeared, he had no choice but to seat her at his fire, though when she spoke he barely answered, going about his business as if she was not there. He could not reject her outright, or give her insult. She did command warriors, after all, and could expel him from the lakeside.

He would not be beaten, though. This was his place, his doorway to the light of the sídhe.

Only he had since discovered that Maeve of Cruachan burned through his new senses like a falling star.

Ruán had endeavored to be repulsed by it, but every time she came, that vivid flame enlivened the ether around her, charging it like lightning and pushing back the black. He was a man who walked in darkness, and so for some reason his legs did not turn now and take him far away from her, as they should have done.

Maeve bounded down the trail from the woods toward him. "I have been waiting for you all morning! I should have left long ago."

Ruán pulled up. "Since you say these are your lands, I assume you come and go at your will."

She was silent a moment, a pulse in that flame he was beginning to recognize.

"Meallán and I brought you a proper shelter." Her voice held a smile. "It has sides and roof sewn of layered cowhides, and lashings, and poles."

Ruán had kept his sleeping place secret so far. The little dome of reeds existed in Thisworld, but it let in the heavy rains of the long dark, and it was cold.

"I found the perfect spot—there. Those yews will shelter you from the winds and leave you open to the sun."

Ruán had no idea what to say. He opened his mouth, his mind working. A spatter of rain hit his face.

"Thank me later." Maeve was brisk. "Those clouds up there... by their color they are bringing us heavy hail, and I don't want to be stuck in it. We can throw this up over the trees and protect Meallán as well." A growl of thunder interrupted her. "Hurry!"

Maeve began unrolling and flinging things at Ruán's feet as the wind shook the bare branches around them.

Ruán let out his breath, spreading his hands by his sides and flexing them. This was merely a challenge to learn from—to let go into his senses while distracted by her.

They lashed poles and spread the heavy folds of oiled hides over an oak branch. Maeve fell into a rhythm that seemed familiar to her, and to Ruán's surprise it was soothing. They flowed around each other. She spoke only to direct him, and he was able to focus and feel his way as he always did, with a delicate touch that drew the world about him into vivid relief.

"How does a queen learn such a skill?" Ruán knelt, binding the hides to the ground.

"Hunting. I was out all sun-season with the warriors, sometimes for days."

The relish in her voice confused him. A royal lady who enjoyed sleeping on the ground, and plowing through damp woods...

Ruán tightened the last thongs as a bellow of thunder broke

over their heads. Maeve cursed, trying to coax Meallán under the awning of hides. "I trained him to do this. The noise has unsettled him."

Ruán took over, gentling the horse's head until he backed in, Maeve and Ruán ducking after.

With another crack of thunder came a shower of icy projectiles that struck the hard sides of the tent, as lethal as sling-stones. Ruán tilted his head. "You were right." He had never heard hail like it.

"I smelled it." She sounded proud. "And recognized the color of the cloud. I've seen men bloodied by hail as large as that."

They were both crushed near the front, giving Meallán room. "Ow!" Maeve cried.

A hailstone bounced onto Ruán's feet. The air smelled of ice.

"When I packed the tent," Maeve muttered, rubbing her arm, "I did not think the gods would take it as a dare."

They squatted next to each other, shivering as the temperature of the air plunged. The hailstones hammered down, flung wildly at the shelter by the wrathful wind. In the midst of that tempest, Ruán was conscious of the strained stillness between him and this king's daughter.

He turned his head. The flare that was Maeve writhed with a turmoil she was struggling to contain. The intensity of it made the hairs lift on his arms.

Maeve cleared her throat. "A timely gift."

Wary, he nodded. "So it seems."

She hesitated, breathing hard. Without warning, a gout of flame spilled from her. "And in return for all this, you *have* to help me with the sídhe."

Ruán went cold. Every time she came, that vivid fire reached for him, but in his fascination he had forgotten it held danger.

The moment he drew away, Maeve gripped his wrist. "This is not for me." Her desperation engulfed him. "I took the sword to defeat a man who would have killed me. But the druids are afraid the sídhe are angry now, and I had to promise they would bless me, that the land would bloom. Without that blessing, I cannot protect those who need me, and I am running out of time!"

This torrent pressed Ruán back against the taut slope of the tent.

Her temper snapped. "Gods, I will not harm you! I have honored you with many gifts. What else do you need to trust me?"

Ruán stiffened, his nostrils flaring. "I am not *afraid* of you! And if you think my eyes make me weak..."

"Oh, stop it, *stop it*! I do not pity you—you know this land better blind than most with their sight."

He stared at her. All he could see was twisting flame, red and black.

She flung herself to her knees before him, blocking the exit from the tent. "I understand why you cannot trust me. I can watch and absorb all you do, but you do not know *me*. You cannot look in my eyes, at my truth, and tell just how much I *need* this, that I want only what is good for my people." She clutched at his sleeve. "So you have to see me *somehow*—to know for yourself that what I say is real!"

At that, Maeve of Connacht grabbed Ruán's hands and crushed them to her face.

Shock blanked Ruán.

For the first time in many moons he touched human skin. Though he wanted to recoil, his body was held there by the gusts of her warm breath on his palm.

This is foolish. But Ruán's fingers ignored him.

He had been training them to capture every new touch, to summon light from darkness—and now they held a great wildfire that roared through his flesh. And he could not forget that, without even trying, this brazen woman had drawn a glimmer of the otter anam into *her body*.

Gods, but how? He needed to know.

With a life of their own, Ruán's fingers began to move over her face. Maeve had placed them on her eyes, and her lashes brushed his palms. They were slanted, and he was surprised by the image that came to mind of a dusky glance, heavy-lidded.

"Blue." Maeve cleared her throat. "They are blue."

Her nose was long, her cheekbones prominent. Her jaw was delicate, considering she fought with a sword, though he could see how that pointed chin would thrust the world away.

"My father called me vixen, and I'm red-haired like a fox."

It was curiosity at first, like molding clay, until Ruán's fingers brushed Maeve's mouth. At his touch, her breath escaped.

Ruán's pulse was loud in his ears. This close, the charge of her presence became heat. Every cool thought of his slipped away, overtaken by a picture of lush, parted lips pressed to his skin. Surely that could not be *her* full mouth, with that sharp blade of a voice.

His fingers sprang away, his face on fire.

There was a rustle as Maeve sat back on her heels and put her hand over her mouth. Ruán felt the change in her, the flare wavering, then drawing back and growing darker.

When she spoke, her voice was unsteady. "As for the rest of me, I am lean like a deerhound, not plump or womanly. Men cannot better me that way."

The hail-shower had blown away now, and an eerie silence fell over the clearing. Ruán stood. "I do not have a blessing to give you." He spoke slowly, each word distinct. Any more and he would have to lie.

She could not know the truth, for whether her fire consumed the veils or her blade tore them, she wanted power—and the power here was not his to give.

His light, his sight.

Maeve was silent now, her light dimmed. Ruán caught her faint exhalation. "I brought food for you," she said, getting up.

In a tiny alcove beside her bedchamber, Maeve glanced up to the thatch as another fist of wind slammed into it, tearing at the straw. Outside, the heavy clouds brought an early twilight to Cruachan.

She poured a drink for the shabby bard on the bench facing her. She last saw him at Samhain, and again his trews were muddy, his tunic stained and threadbare. His gray hair straggled to his shoulders; no one would give him a second look. Good. She rested down the ale-jug, nudging the plate of sausages toward him. "You've been gone for weeks."

Miu sat on the arm of Maeve's chair, her unblinking gaze fixed on the intruder. The bard eyed her, licking his lips. "Lady, if I rush back here people will know who rules me, heart and soul."

"Spare me. It is my bronze you want, and no more."

That snuffed out his oily smile. He scratched his beard. "It takes *time*. I do not *enjoy* sleeping on cold floors. And the Ulaid are so afraid of each other now they let nothing slip!"

Maeve's gaze joined Miu's, both pinning him down. The harper stopped whining and blurted out everything.

Deirdre's flight with the three sons of Usnech had torn rents in the Red Branch. At Samhain, a fight broke out between Illan, son of Fergus, and Fiacra, son of King Conor. Cúchulainn took Illan's side, other heroes defended Fiacra. The king arrived and shamed Illan, and Fergus jumped in to defend his son. "And then, before all the people," the bard whispered, "Fergus and Conor spoke of *traitors* and *treason*."

The hearth-flames wavered.

Gods. The Ulaid were cracking, and Maeve could not muster warriors to strike Conor and weaken him further because she had tied her own hands. The Connacht druids ruled until leaf-bud— her only way to delay Fraech being acclaimed as king.

She dismissed the bard, and when he had gone, she leaned her head on her chair and exhaled. Now it was not the Ulaid that crowded her.

The strange druid said he was a no one, and wielded no power, but she didn't believe him. She would never forget the otter's anam turning Innel's sword away, so she *lived*. This druid commanded something, of that she was certain.

And she needed it.

She had toyed with taking warriors to the lake and forcing Ruán to beg the sídhe for help. This was a druid, though. Blind, living in seclusion...a mystery that required a delicate touch. He could easily disappear, or worse—turn the sídhe against her, so that everything of her was cursed, not just her womb.

So why did she lose all her sense and touch him? *Damn, damn, damn.*

Despite this, Maeve's hand drifted up now to trace her brows. She could still smell the blackberries on his breath. *Over her nose and cheekbones, across her lips.*

He did not possess the massive muscles that joined neck to shoulder as swordsmen did, the slabs of flesh and tendon that gave fighters a hulking stance. Muscled, he was, but finely molded, with flaring shoulders sweeping to a lithe waist. And he was straight-backed and light on his feet, his head drawn high... as graceful as a stag poised to leap away through the woods.

She must follow him down that path, for it led somewhere. A lake of light...? Maeve came back to herself, her fingers tingling at her throat.

These last weeks she had found it far too easy to slip into that trance of quiet water and glowing sky. There, peace kept seeping into her, as the mud crept over her bare toes and the damp soaked her wool trews. Her questions would disappear on gusts of wind, her muscles softening, her mind emptying.

A druid spell, it was—to make her forget.

Maeve's hand sprang away from her throat. She tucked her fingers beneath her thigh. And now, this day, her desperation had got all tangled up with lust. She had gone too long without the release of rutting, that was all; the only time she could push all frustrations, furies, and hurts out of her body.

She had always had that release...only now, she did not, for the competition among the men for her favor was too important.

She could not set one in the lead in case the others abandoned the race.

Neither could she continue to waste her time with a priest who refused to satisfy her over the matter of the sídhe. She had chiefs to win, so she could strike at Conor before his Red Branch grew strong again. For she knew that before long he would seek to strike at *her*.

Maeve withdrew her dagger in the firelight. The thud of her heart made it waver, and set off glints along the blade. The gleam of Conor's eyes, they were fixed upon her belly every time she ate in his hall.

She had thwarted his plans for Connacht. She had humiliated him. In his twisted thoughts, she and Deirdre bore the blame for his troubles. Whatever he did to Deirdre when he found her, he would want to do to her as well.

Maeve swallowed, lowered the dagger to her lap. She needed more than druid words—she must put her trust in swords now.

But whose? She searched the flames before her, hoping that there she would find the answer she sought.

CHAPTER 10

Maeve knelt before the eternal flame of the god Lugh, burning in its great iron brazier.

At last the temple was silent and empty, the druids having taken their songs to the oak groves. Lugh was the bright one, the many-skilled, the great light. On the longest night of the year the druids chanted all through the darkness, beseeching Lugh to swing the sun north once more and warm the land.

A hint of herb smoke still lingered from their prayer bowls.

Their dancing had churned the earth floor of the little hut, leaving the fresh scent of wet soil.

Maeve never used to come here, for Lugh was sacred to the sword-wielders and the crafters who laid their work at his flame. Women left offerings at the shrines of the mother goddesses, Bríd and Danu, Eriu and Fodla.

Maeve never ventured to those, either. She had no claim on them; her woman's heart had failed that test. And the tender places in it were long gone.

Something *had* changed, though. She was now a blooded warrior. She needed great daring for the plan that was forming, and forcing down her fear of what the gods thought of her, she had come to beg Lugh's strength at last.

The mud walls pressed in, the oiled roof-beams reflecting the flame, and she gulped down the lump in her throat. *Never let me be so desperate again,* was her hasty prayer. Then, unbidden, her heart spoke, a feeling without words. *And let me find peace.*

A strange thing, in a warriors' shrine.

She unclasped an arm-ring of her father's and placed it on the worn stone below the brazier. Above the fire a great shield hung, dipped in gold so the flame was caught in the glossy surface, bringing the sun to life in darkness.

Maeve was unsheathing her sword to bless it when there was a commotion outside, a thump and ring of steel. She'd left Garvan and her guards out there, warding the door.

She swung to her feet as two burly men swept in, sword-belts jingling. Fraech's father Idath and his uncle Felim. "No one will be hurt," Idath growled to Garvan's men, "unless you keep struggling."

Fraech appeared behind them, hovering near the door.

Maeve threw her fur cloak back to rest her hand on her sword. At least she had belted it over the blue dress she'd donned for the longest night feast. The sheath of thin wool was only lightly fastened on each shoulder by spindly brooches, the shift beneath flimsy linen. She felt vulnerable in that finery, her legs bare, her breasts outlined by the soft drapes. "Why are you here if not to hurt me?"

"We would not taint a holy place." The stocky Idath's hair and beard were entirely gray. He sneered at her sword. "Despite your grip on that blade, lady, you take refuge in the women's hall when you want to. It is hard to run you to ground."

"To get me alone and undefended, you mean."

Idath smiled.

Maeve glanced at Fraech. Though his face was guarded, she detected discomfort in his steady green eyes. He folded his arms, as if keeping himself separate.

"We come to warn you." Felim was thinner, with a stoat's narrow face. His cold glance sought to slice her in two, up and down. "You will abandon this foolish attempt to rule Connacht. Some may indulge your whims, but the other kingdoms will think our wits have deserted us!"

Maeve wanted her voice to be strong, but it cracked. "You heard me acclaimed before all the people—and the chief druid. Lords are on my side, and many warriors are loyal to me." She curled her lip. "You are afraid because I killed my brother."

Felim limped forward, his red nose thrusting through pallid curtains of salt-white hair. "You've proven only that you are versed in treachery."

Maeve had vowed to Garvan she would only down a man through his own weakness. She would never be known as a betrayer, never. "I won through my own strength and skill, like any warrior of worth." She forced it through gritted teeth.

"Gods' balls, you are dreaming!" Grizzled Idath brandished his fist at her. "Only *this* is real! Your greed cannot triumph over this, no matter how many dribbling old fools you trick. Everyone knows the enchantments you weave with your tongue."

Maeve went to speak, but was silenced by that memory of ecstasy, of leaping around Innel so weightless and lithe. Utterly free. It *had* to be right, for her and her people. Now Idath tried to take that from her. She stared at him, her eyes burning. Her people would suffer *these men* if she faltered now.

"It is not her tongue," Felim hissed, "unless she used it on a prick or two. The only way she's ever won a man is by opening her thighs. Anyone can sheath it in there as long as he pledges his sword after!"

A low rumble came from Fraech's throat. "Father—"

Idath ignored his son, his gaze lingering on the Aegyptian paint Maeve had used to play up her face for the feast. The black kohl and green powders elongated her eyes, and she had reddened her lips, too. A diadem of fine gold wire sat on her copper curls, and delicate balls swung at her ears. She must show her wares to suitors—it was shrewd to do so, the mark of a ruler.

Idath's smile, though, held contempt, as if she was no more than a gilded plaything. It made an old part of Maeve shrink into a child once more.

No. She was herself, a woman. She wobbled as she drew straight.

"Come leaf-bud, the warriors will ache to draw their swords among men once more, making *my son* the greatest king Connacht has known." Idath snorted, flicking a hand to dismiss her. "When their seed dries on you, they will all see you for what you are."

Maeve had to move or explode, and she would not let them turn their backs on *her*. She swept past the old men but paused beside Fraech, trembling with fury. "If you were truly noble, cousin, you would have nothing to fear from me. The people will choose their ruler."

Fraech towered over her, yet there was regret in his eyes. "Let it go, lady, and I will ensure no harm comes to you. You are not strong enough on your own. The men will not cleave to you when it counts." When she moved, he caught her wrist, and she balked at the youthful strength in that grip, the iron of a sword-hand. "Wake from this fool dream before it kills you!"

Maeve reclaimed her arm and folded it to herself with a show of dignity. But beneath the surface, all the pressure of these weeks of waiting, and fearing, were boiling up inside her.

Outside, the warriors holding Garvan and his men let them go, and Garvan raced after her. "Forgive me. They rushed us—"

He crowded her—another male voice, the reek of male sweat. The heel of Maeve's palm struck his chest. "Enough," she gasped, and stumbled away.

Rend something. Tear herself apart to release this.

Maeve staggered to the stables, where she fumbled to saddle her horse. Beneath that turmoil, a different yearning reared up. *Her bones traced by soft hands, fingers cradling her brow and cheeks.* Gentleness.

No, she could not break now. She must cling to rage, and nothing more.

At dawn she woke from a ride she barely remembered. She let Meallán have his head in the night and he came here. Or did she drive him? The bitter wind chewed the lake into gray and white waves, slapping the sand. The sun was low and red.

Maeve shuddered. She was dressed only in her feast clothes— that long flimsy dress—and the air had turned her bare legs to ice. Her face itched, and when her hand went to it she discovered the Aegyptian paint had cracked, melting in tracks. She did not remember that, either.

The reeds were snapping, drawing her eye to something that stirred in the ruddy haze of lake and sky.

Ruán emerged from the purple shadows farther down the shore, cocking his head, a net of some kind over his shoulder. He placed the bag down and let out a high whistle.

Meallán lurched to life.

As her horse broke into a gallop, Maeve lost his reins and could only grip his mane. He thundered right along the water's edge, his hooves drenching her in spray. She could have hauled him back but she didn't, the undulation and wind at last tearing a growl free of her breast. *Father!*

He had left her to men like Idath, and Felim.

The moment Meallán drew level with Ruán's outstretched hand, he dug in his hooves, plunging to a halt with head down.

Maeve sailed over his neck, hitting the shallows of the lake in an explosion of water. The cold snatched her breath, filled her nose and throat. She got her legs under her and staggered up, coughing and yanking down her dress.

"I did not know you were on him." Ruán was smiling as he rubbed Meallán's ears. "You are not hurt, I hope."

Maeve stared at him, a band tightening about her chest. He thought her a fool—all men did. But *this one* would not give her what she needed of the sídhe to save her life. A desperation seized her to wrench him open . . . to expel this terrible pressure inside herself.

She clambered out of the lake. The force of the fall had plucked a brooch free, dragging her dress off one shoulder and unraveling the clout at her loins. The sodden folds of the undergarment clung to her legs, and she kicked it away as she emerged. At the sound of her broken steps, Ruán's smile faded.

All of Maeve's remaining sense bled out into blinding white.

She craved anything that could release her—anyone. Winding her elbows about Ruán's head, she pressed her mouth to his windchapped lips. For a moment Ruán froze.

And then that cold statue came to life in Maeve's arms.

She caught a noise of surrender in the back of his throat, and his mouth opened beneath hers. Cold, rough skin gave way to heat and sweetness.

Maeve drank in his lips and tongue, pulling his groin in to wrap a thigh around his hip. She buried her hands in his tangled hair, grinding his mouth to hers.

Her urgency toppled them to the sand, and Ruán thudded onto his back.

Maeve straddled him, lifting his neck again to claim his lips.

Her dripping cloak and hair enveloped them, as if she were a goddess of death drinking life from a fallen warrior. Her fingers dug under his tunic to brush the ridges of the spiral scar, then slid beneath his arm to where the flesh softened.

She pressed herself into the hardness he could not hide, however unwilling the rest of him. He hesitated again, and then something gave way in Ruán and his hands were tangling with hers to unlace his trews and crumple up her dress.

Maeve rammed herself onto him, and after that became nothing more than a wrathful ocean battering its rage on a rock in a storm. She did not have to look into a man's eyes or hear a harsh voice. Her hands dug into faceless flesh as her desperation grew.

The friction of bodies was so violent that was all it took to ignite her. And when Ruán growled, that thunder of the storm broke the remnants of her shattered control. Maeve threw back her head to fling away her agony, and the pressure poured out and up into the impassive sky.

With one cry, she soared.

When the fall came, it was like plunging from a great height, and it jarred her back to cold awareness.

Wet sand.

Panting breath.

A man's ribs pushing against her hand.

Maeve unclenched her fists and crawled off the body beneath her. The world tilted, her hips aching. Nausea swamped her—that she would lose control with *him*, that he would see inside her. She dragged herself to the bushes and after a moment of swaying on hands and knees retched into the dead leaves.

A bird took wing among the reeds, making the stems grate together. Maeve unsteadily got to her feet, smoothing down the wet folds of her dress in a daze.

There was no sound behind as she wove her way to Meallán, quietly grazing on the turf. She fumbled for the horse's reins. *She would not look.*

Maeve put one shaky foot before the other, pulling Meallán behind her. Far away.

She did not glance back.

At the healing lodge, the young druid Erna was at an oak table, boiling bitter-scented leaves and roots over a brazier. Her dark, solemn eyes took in Maeve's bedraggled state.

The ride had dried the brine on Maeve's skin, stiffening her hair. The Aegyptian paint must be trailing down her cheeks in runnels of black now. She tried to summon her authority, but she had shredded her voice.

The scream, into the sky.

"I never thanked you for speaking for me after the fight," Maeve croaked. "Now I need someone I can trust. Keep your silence, and you will be rewarded."

Erna shifted the bubbling pot off the coals with tongs. "I can only do as my conscience allows, lady."

Maeve folded her arms. The trembling in them would not subside, though the day was nearly over—this day she must blot from her memory. "I am not asking you to poison someone. I need a potion for myself."

Erna's frown cleared. "Certainly, lady."

"To stop a child in the belly."

The druid's calmness did not falter. She wiped her hands on a cloth in her belt and smoothed her dark hair back. "To prevent a seed taking root, or to rid yourself of a seedling already grown? That causes great sickness in the body."

"To prevent one." Maeve was glad to find someone who spoke crisply. She could never have feelings for such things again, lest they weaken her enough for the wolves to bring down.

Among the Ulaid, she had found her own source for the women's herbs, which had now run out. In recent moons she had not needed more. "Children must come at the right time, you understand," she added.

They must not come at all, for then they can be taken. Maeve fixed her gaze on the bubbling pot and without thinking tucked one strand of hair behind her ear.

She saw Erna's brows rise.

Maeve understood. The herders bore children to mind cattle, and no one cared much how they were sired. But perhaps Erna, young as she was, did not know that the wife of a lord must be more careful. She had to guard her husband's pride in his virility, for that was bound up with the strength of his sword-arm and how many men would follow him.

The first time Conor saw her after the marriage oaths, he murmured in her ear that if she dallied with other men, he would kill her and any child she carried. She believed him, and risked it only with warriors she hoped might give her information to sway her father to bring her home.

The herbs did not always work, though, and for a few weeks she had suspected that she was with child. The day after she overheard Conor hint he would use a son to gain Connacht, she began bleeding. Soon after that she fled the Ulaid.

"A tea is best," Erna at last ventured. "Drunk in the morning."

Maeve nodded, her thoughts colliding as she clutched the back of Mahon's chair. "You saw me fight my brother. I believe a mother of the tribe will protect our people better than a boastful man ever could. I might need you again."

Erna came around the table and leaned on her folded hands. "I am sworn to serve the people and the gods. When you asked us to heal the babies from the seal cough, I saw you also serve them. And I believe what you said the day of the fight, and ..." At last she betrayed her youth, a stain creeping up her cheeks. "I know what it is like to struggle to be heard."

"By men, you mean."

Erna bit her lip, and Maeve nodded and forced her unsteady legs toward the door. "Prepare the tea for me so I can travel with it. And one more thing. I know you are not brethim, but I want you to verse yourself in the laws for me." She paused. "Marriage laws."

Before Erna could reply, Maeve swung beneath the doorskin. She halted in the porch and sank against the wall, her mouth crumpling. She had lost her mind. The lake druid would hate her now, any hope of his help destroyed. She had lost her chance.

So she had to find another one.

She dug her knuckles under her hollow ribs, where Fraech's words still echoed.

You are not strong enough on your own.

☒

Alone by her bed, Maeve filled a basin and washed the paint and the male scent from her body. She was drying her hair by the fire when Garvan burst in.

"Riders have come," he panted. "Being taken to Tiernan in the king's hall. The messenger wore a wolfskin, and the guards bore red pennants on their spears."

The linen towel fell to Maeve's lap. Wolves were mountain creatures, numerous in the Ulaid. And red was Conor's color.

On her feet, she cast a glance down at her old tunic and trews. She dashed back and dug her sealskin mantle from her dresser, tying it around her throat as she and Garvan hastened to the king's mound.

People were milling about the hearth-fire in the great hall, servants bustling past crafters and warriors who had come to see Tiernan for judgments or advice. Tiernan was standing near Eochaid's great chair, frowning at strangers before him—two spearmen flanking a third man in the wolfskin.

Maeve shouldered through the throng. Tiernan glanced up and waved everyone back. "Lady Maeve," the druid said when she reached him. "You may want to hear this."

She did not recognize the dark-haired messenger, though he

started when he heard her name. He rearranged his wolfskin, flinging back his shoulders. "I am sent by Conor mac Nessa, King of the Ulaid, who demands that he receives his due under the terms of the marriage contract with Maeve, daughter of Eochaid, King of Connacht."

Maeve's thoughts deserted her. "I... I left Conor," she blurted.

The man's brows arched. "Which is why he demands what he was promised."

Maeve's hackles rose, as if Conor himself was taking hold of her. She remembered the shackle of his hand, his thumb pressing her windpipe while he smiled at her. She licked her lips. "What does he want?"

The messenger's smile was haughty. "He claims Finnbennach, fabled bull of Connacht."

The people nearby gasped, and Tiernan's eyes narrowed beneath his domed brow. The royal bull was an enormous beast, white of hide and therefore sacred—the greatest of all Erin's cattle.

Maeve turned on the Ulaid man. "He cannot claim that!"

"In the alliance with your father, King Conor paid a bride-price of iron, gold, furs, and grain, and in return was promised a tie to Connacht's royal bloodline, and binding kinship thereafter, support from Connacht war-bands if he was attacked, and, of course... you, Lady Maeve."

The scorn in his eyes was like a slap.

The man spread his hands. "My generous king is willing to abandon all these claims, in light of your... difficulties. But only if Connacht gives him Finnbennach."

Maeve's head reared. The Ulaid already possessed the Donn Cuailgne, the other great bull of Erin. With their glossy haunches, fiery loins, and abundant offspring, such sacred beasts boasted a king's potency across his kingdom and far beyond.

Coveting both could be seen as the act of a madman, or...

Fury drove out the last of Maeve's sense, and before Tiernan could reply, she whipped her sword from its sheath and held it upright. "How many times have Conor's raiders slain our people? *He* respects an alliance only as long as it suits him, then tosses it away to spear us where we stand. Finnbennach belongs to Connacht. Tell Conor he will *never* have him, never rule us! The West will stand against him, free and defiant, for as long as we breathe!"

The Ulaid messenger gaped at the sword waving before his face.

Tiernan stepped in with a flurry of white robes. "That is the *essence* of our reply…." He spoke through gritted teeth. "However, we have bards here who will couch it to King Conor in more *polite* terms." He beckoned to other druids behind him, nudged the Ulaid man's shoulder. "Pray, go aside with them, take a cup of our finest mead, and rest."

Red-faced, the Ulaid rider was still looking at Maeve in astonishment as he was led away.

Tiernan pulled up his hood and stalked out of the hall. Maeve sheathed her blade and followed, her blood high. Along an empty pathway he turned, the shadows of dusk mercifully veiling his face.

"I know what you are going to say." Maeve glanced over her shoulder.

"That you have no authority to deal with royal messengers since you are not, yourself, yet queen?"

"Yes, yes." Maeve waved that away. "But don't you see what this means? Conor did not believe we would hand over Finnbennach. This was a message, but not what it appears to be." She stepped closer, shivering. "The man who possesses *both* the Donn Cuailgne and Finnbennach will command the greatest herd in Erin—a sacred herd. He will become *the* greatest cattle-lord. Every kingdom in Erin, Alba, and Britain will see him as blessed by the gods, a supreme ruler. Conor wants to be *ard-rí*!"

A high king of all Erin. No one had claimed that title since the ancient days of the Tuatha dé Danaan.

Tiernan was no longer angry, his pale eyes piercing the red haze of sunset behind her.

Maeve cut her hand across her palm. "*This* is but the first spear thrown over our heads. With all this business of his betrothed, Conor has been weakened before his men." She couldn't help herself, clutching the druid's pale sleeve. "I lived with him. He is ruled by such a pride! Perhaps he cannot rally all of the Ulaid right now, but he will look for other ways to make himself powerful in their eyes."

Tiernan bent his head to look at her hand.

She released his robe. "Chief druid, I strongly advise that we conceal Finnbennach." She was struck by inspiration. "His white hide makes him stand out from afar. We must quarter him in hidden valleys, not the river pastures, and move him from place to place. And the herdsmen should rub charcoal and mud into his hide."

Tiernan blinked, and she thought that in the blurring of dusk his long, enigmatic face held respect.

She stood back, drawing straight. "I think like a queen." The cold was invading her even beneath the sealskin. Idath, Felim... now Conor. The aches in her body, from loins to shoulders... it was like they had attacked her already.

It was coming. Maeve tried not to shudder as she held Tiernan's eyes.

At last he nodded.

Maeve's anger must have been a poison, for it grew in Ruán until he could feel nothing but that. She had scored a victory over him at last. She had stolen his peace.

He had vowed to protect the lake and its wonders, but she made him forget himself, forced him inside her so they were joined. She made him *know* her, so he was savage and desperate like her...

Ruán paced around the fire, scrubbing his palms to rid himself of her touch. But the afterburn of her flame was inside him, and that he could not expel. Just as he discovered this great truth of the sídhe, would he lose it again?

At last he crawled back into his tent, and when a knife came to hand, he stabbed it through the hides Maeve had given him and shoved his arms behind his head, breath bouncing off the slope of leather above him.

Eventually, Ruán slipped away into a strange state between waking and slumber. Time spun about him and he lost track of how it flowed. One moment he was asleep and the next he was standing under the moon.

The Shining Ones had at last pulled him from his dark dreams.

The illumination in their faces returned his full sight to him, moonlight pouring from their skin. They surrounded him in a crescent, the five who sung around the campfire when he was ill, and held him with their voices in the stones. Dark hair, shining eyes.

The sídhe maiden said, "Why do you hide?"

"She made me into someone like her."

"Perhaps you already are."

He caught his breath, his head snapping toward her.

The maiden's eye gleamed. "You are not angry, brother. It is shame that has you in its jaws."

He went to deny it, but a wave of heat took his speech. It was one thing to remember the sweetness of Orla. After all, it was that tender memory in the stones that had coaxed him into this great unfurling—until now he soaked up tree-sounds and water-scents, the sun's warmth, the taste of fish, with every moment of being.

But rutting with Maeve, he had entirely forgotten the sparks of light in the darkness.

The maiden tutted, and her teeth flashed as she shoved him in the chest. "It is about time you found the *wild* in you. Not some of it—all of it. Be abandoned!" She spun on her heel, braids flying. "Humans are such fools," she cried to the others, who all laughed. "The sun swings north again. Tonight, we dance!"

Baffled, Ruán glanced between them. Their somber manner had disappeared, in its place fiery eyes and restless limbs. The air almost crackled.

As they went to go, surrounding him and pulling him with them, a man with an ageless face leaned in to Ruán. "You think her so black," he whispered, "but even in battle a heart beats behind every shield."

Ruán passed across Connacht in the train of the Shining Ones. They were soon joined by other beings of light who flowed to them like silver rivers from all over the dark land. The streams of sídhe fed into the burgeoning flood, until a glowing wave poured over the hills.

Swept along with them, Ruán discovered it was Thisworld through which they journeyed. As in the stones, if he was within the aura of the sídhe he could see. Every now and then he glimpsed the far-off fires of his own people. On this night of frost and deep cold, they clustered around flames that were red and flickering, not silver.

The sídhe poured through gullies and leaped across ridges, ducking branches and bounding over rocks.

One moment Ruán thought he was with people, their long braids blowing in the wind, their deerskins flapping. Then, from the corner of his eye he would glimpse something different, vast plumes of fire forming elongated bodies and heads, their hair streamers of flame. Long dark eyes opened to rafts of stars.

What were they?

An eddy of the dance hurled Ruán free, and he staggered and fell to the wet ground. He was lying by a copse of leafless trees growing from a cleft of rock. Hidden water trickled through a carpet of ferns, their leaves brown and curled.

A group of sídhe left the dance with him, settling like a flock of glimmering birds. They twined along branches, curling into the hollows of rocks and molding themselves to the earth. He sensed their cascades of laughter as ripples on his skin.

We are the gatherers.

They were answering him in song.

We are the light-bearers.

His sídhe maiden was standing by the stream. She gazed at him with fathomless eyes. *We are the Bridge between Worlds.* Twirling, she circled him and he turned to follow, making him dizzy. *The Otherworlds lie alongside your own, all of them woven through each other like threads. But we are the bridge. We bring the light-song of the Otherworlds into Thisworld.*

"Light-song...?"

There is no word. It is the fire of all. Source of life. Spirit undying, which joins everything. We call it from the Otherworlds into this, make it flow freely, strongly. Look!

She swept her arms out and danced along the stream-bank. With a motion of her hand, the hidden spring ignited into fire and gushed from the ground as molten silver. It was not just water, but Source. The sidhe on the trees seemed to merge into the bark, until every branch and twig glowed. The rocks flared into light.

The stream of Source they summoned spread, gilding the ferns, the dormant leaves and trailing stalks. It seeped into the ground, curling around the grains of soil and seeds, making them glow. It rushed up the trees and down to their roots, washed over the forest beyond.

Ruán saw it all.

The maiden breathed in his ear. *Life comes from Source. We bear it from the worlds of spirit to this world of yours...strengthening, summoning, and warding it. For you humans possess will and choice, but the wild things have no guardians but us!*

All the sidhe leaped up, and their dance became frenzied. Faster they spun, and to Ruán's dazed eyes they were each growing smaller as the trees and rocks loomed larger. Finally the sídhe were just tiny sparks, reams of them. They shot off in different directions, plunging into the stream, the trees, and the earth.

Now you will be sídhe, the maiden cried, and yanking Ruán's arm, drew him with her, the air rushing past.

The tree in front of them grew enormous, for Ruán and the sídhe appeared to be shrinking as they flew closer. And then what Ruán thought was solid trunk and bark disintegrated into a cloud of sparkling dust.

He plunged in. Nothing was solid.

Streams of tiny motes made up the substance of the tree. The rafts of sparks were denser where they formed wood, and raced more swiftly where water ran through the tree-veins. Now Ruán was no more than a minute star diving through these clouds of tree-sparks, and also a swirl of other stars—the sídhe.

Their singing grew louder, the harmonies ringing out.

Their song shimmered through the motes of tree-bark, wood, and sap, making each spark dance faster, glowing more brightly. So the sídhe drew more Source from the veils of spirit to fill the tree.

Bridge between Worlds.

The next thing he knew, Ruán was flung out. He came back to himself sprawling on the wet grass, in his own body. He rolled on his side and pushed up on his arms, gulping air. "Everything is... made of... sparks!"

The maiden leaned her palms on his ribs, her hair a black tangle. *All the sparks of Source stream together. There are no boundaries. There are no veils, no death, no end. There is no before, or to come, no here and there, for all moments and places are but threads woven through each other.*

Ruán struggled to absorb that. The maiden appeared on the shore of his world, but with a wave of her hand he was on the same shore in *her* world. They made his past with Orla flower around him. The worlds lay close. *Moments* lay close, wound together.

She jumped up, cocking her head. *And if you can shape the sparks of Source, Ruán of the lake, what might you do?*

He sat up, swaying. "What..." he panted, "do you do?"

The maiden pulled him to his feet, swinging him around. *I make eyes for you to see,* she cried, tickling her fingers across his eyelids. She cupped her face, sticking out her tongue. *And a girl-shape, so a sick man is not scared all the way to death.*

The night in the standing stones filled him. "You burn away what rots a man."

Not unless the man lets it free. She thumped his belly. *So now, do it again.* And she grabbed his hand and began to run across the frosted grass. The air roared past and he could hardly feel his feet. At the lip of the ridge she did not slow, flinging him by the wrist out into night.

Ruán plunged through blackness, flailing. The world reeled. He was nothing, no one—only a spirit soaring through a void.

At last he landed with a crash in peaty water, sodden marsh beneath.

Sounds rushed over him. Another life, as another man.

Shouts and screams rolled over him. He heard the clang of iron. Water splashed his face as feet thudded past his head. Memory returned.

Fool! He tripped—him, the champion of his people! He heard a swish as his opponent lunged in, and with a roar he forced himself up and skewered the man on his sword. He stared at his quivering arm, ridged with tendons. Blood spattered his wrist. He looked into his enemy's fading eyes. "Honor me to Her," he muttered. The other warrior fell into the reddened stream, and the victor thrust his blade into the sun. "Great Mother of All!" he screamed, and leaped toward the rest of the enemy, clustered beneath a torn, stained banner that cracked in the wind.

A savage face swam before him and he hammered his hilt in and crunched bone. As his sword-brothers fought on either side, he threw back his head with a howl of life, of freedom. There was nothing in that moment but the marsh-water on his lips, the sting of sweat and fire of sunlight on iron and bronze. The battle-rage flowed up his body and out his blade, burning him with ecstasy.

For the Goddess.

She cushioned his feet, watered his tongue, filled his belly. He would not let Her be overrun by these cowardly bastards from Alba. His glee tipped over into madness as he swung his sword. He was filled with the hunger to tear the world apart just to know his own strength; shatter himself into pieces so he could *be* wind and water, sun and blood, mud and rock...

A blow caught his side. He stumbled and fell.

It seemed distant, that pain. Dazed, he turned his head so the peaty water could flow into his mouth and bring him the taste of mud and salt, crushing shreds of grass to his nose with a bloody hand.

He sank in the mire, and it cradled him.

Ruán surfaced with a gasp.

The sídhe sat in a circle, beating little skin drums. Stars spun above. The fire was moving up his body as it did before, from belly, to heart, to throat.

The maiden's cool hand was upon his brow. *You are not here to fight anymore, so let the swordsman go. But remember how life was sweet to him and cherish his joy in his body. Find the wild in you!*

Only then did Ruán realize the heat was shame, for abandoning himself to desire with Maeve. It was an old folly. On the island, he had also cut himself off from that flood of earth-sense, to seek the gods. And that is what made him fail, and that is why the boy died...

The fire kept roaring, rising up through Ruán. At last he shouted a battle-cry of release, the shame burning away.

As the flame burst from his crown, Ruán saw Maeve as if with his own eyes.

A mane of red hair framed a face that was not hard, but lit with yearning, her eyes seeking for something she longed for...*beyond it all.* He saw she stood in a battle line, bracing a shield before her.

But just as the sídhe said, her body was swaying with the beat of a wild and lonely heart, her soul lost to feeling.

Not a maid of iron after all.

So the priest is gone, the warrior is gone, the maiden whispered. *Perhaps now you can find another way to be a man.*

Ruán's lips were numb, body spent. "Tell me."

She laughed, throwing a piece of wood on what he realized was his own fire. *You have to be it, not hear it!* She poked a finger between his eyes, and the lights went out.

Ruán woke to a blind world in the morning.

But the wood was fragrant as he fed the fire, and he drank in the loamy scents of the swamp and realized that the quiet of the lake had crept into his heart again. He traced the scar on his chest, baffled at what was dream and what was real. If he was nothing that he had been before, what was he now?

There was no answer from the lake but the chuckle of the birds as they woke.

CHAPTER 11

The darkness in the abandoned hay-store was thick with the must of straw and the rustle of field mice. Maeve crouched in the loft, not for the first time questioning her sanity. Crossing Erin in the depths of the cold, deep into enemy territory ... many would think it mad.

Coward, she said to herself, huddling into her cloak. Laigin and Connacht were not true enemies, though their fragile peace was rooted only in fear. Both bordered the Ulaid, and if they weakened each other, Conor could march through and take all of Erin, just as he craved.

The air nipped Maeve's nose, and she cupped her hands over

it. Her father had severed her marriage to Ros Ruadh, Laigin's king, so many years ago that she prayed with everything in her that he was not still bitter. When she was sixteen he threw her out, enraged at her father's actions—and here she was, thirteen years later, creeping back *into* his fort near Dun Ailinne.

Another shiver overcame her, rising from those mists of memory. She *would not* give in to them.

For it was not Ros Ruadh she had come to see.

Maeve had left Garvan and her guards at the Laigin border. There were some advantages to being an unarmed woman, it seemed. No one challenged a lady, hooded for the cold, traveling alone with a female druid. A flirtatious smile, some banter, and the bored guards at the ramparts around Ros Ruadh's stronghold—too young to know who she was—let her send Erna inside with a message. Soon after, they let Maeve in herself.

Up in the hayloft, she uncurled her frozen hand and spanned a hole hewn in the wall. Her fingers broke the moonlight into rays. Her pulse skipped. She remembered this. She jumped at the scrape of the door, and smoothing all fear from her face, she turned.

The loft creaked as a man swung up. "By the gods, Maeve. Is this a new game of yours?"

Maeve took a breath. "Ailill."

One of Ros Ruadh's sons, a prince of Laigin. She had last seen him when they were both sixteen. Maeve scrutinized Ailill in the ray of moonlight. He'd developed a brawny build, with bull shoulders. His hair was still a lush brown mane, the lime he stiffened it with speckling the ends.

Ailill peered at her. "Why did you not announce yourself to my father? Where are your guards?"

She painted an inviting smile on her lips. "You are the only one I came to see, Ailill, and it had to be in secret." She brushed her loose hair over her shoulder. "Don't be afraid."

Ailill stiffened. She'd always said just that when urging their horses over precarious jumps, or sneaking with him over the ramparts at night. Nevertheless, he crouched beside her.

Maeve raised her chin, baring the length of her neck to the light. "Do you remember when you did this?"

Ailill shuffled over and prodded the cleft in the wood with thick fingers. "Gods, I forgot this..." He chuckled. "I can still feel the mark of my axe! No wonder it's always so damn wet in here. We gave it up for grain years ago."

Maeve glanced at him sidelong. His forearm looked like a bundle of ropes, and his thighs strained against his trews. His belly pouched over his belt, though, and his cheeks were heavy, with mottling around the nose. Apart from the torc of twisted gold, he wore no other adornments. He still reveled in base pleasures, then—fighting, food, and ale. Her desperate gamble was strengthening.

She let down her guard, her smile wry. "We lay in this moonlight once, drinking it in. Things were simple then."

Ailill studied her. "The years have treated you well, firebrand, but you've never been simple. You are tangled as a thorn-brake." He cocked a brow. "You have been Mumu princess and Ulaid queen since last you were here. So who are you now?"

"*That* you may be interested in." She patted the hay.

Hesitating, Ailill dug a knuckle in his ear and skewed it around. At last he folded up and sat down. "I'm too old for this," he grumbled.

Maeve placed a hand on his forearm. "You have aged well. I see you still fight."

"My appetites are great for all things, as I'm sure you remember." His lazy eyes glinted. "Except flattery. Spit it out."

Maeve summoned her childhood smile, full of secrets. "I *have* seen more of Erin now, and I found myself thinking of you. I mean, with your father living to such an age it must be frustrating to wait, unable to indulge your desires—to live freely—wondering when you get your chance to be king."

A frown had lowered over his brow. "I do what I want, mostly."

"Except you are subject to your father's will." She traced the coarse hairs over his battle-swollen hand. "You love women and food, and Laigin enjoys trade with the Middle Sea. But you do not get the pick of Greek wine, do you, Ailill? Your own herds are not enough to gain you all the slave-girls you want, the rich cloth on your limbs."

Ailill crossed his burly arms into a barrier between them. "What are you up to, Maeve? Trying to trap me into betraying my father?"

In one movement she was on her knees, her belly crushed against his arms, her hands on his thick shoulders. The moonlight cut Ailill's face into craggy lines, axe-hewn. She blinked as the light shimmered into someone else.

A jaw carved by a finer blade. Streams of ruddy hair caught in her fingers. A swollen mouth bruised by her teeth.

"I have come to offer you marriage," she barely managed. "With me." *She had no choice.*

The prince of Laigin gaped.

"You will be king, Ailill, not a prince-in-waiting. You can *rule now*, with me."

His eyes glazed over and his arms broke apart. Maeve wriggled into his body, leaning on his knee. She forced it out, past the heaviness in her heart. All the wealth he craved, the power, the ease and beautiful things—*now.*

At last he focused on her. "I lost two wives in birthing, but I have one left. I doubt she'd enjoy being second to you."

"Then give her back her dowry ... unless you love her."

"I am content with her."

"Oh!" Maeve made herself smile. "Content, lazy, *bored.*" She poked him in the chest. "I bet you have been slowly falling asleep for years, Ailill. Don't you want to wake up?"

Something began to light in his face, but then his mouth pursed, eyes slitting. "What do you get out of this? If you really wanted *me*, you could have come years ago."

Maeve realized she had to share the truth with him, for them to be able to trust each other. An equal bargain. "Your father's bride price, and the power of an alliance with Laigin, will drown the last ambitions of my cousin's kin. Then I will be named queen, and can protect my people from warrior-lords that will bleed them dry."

And no one can ever threaten me again.

He laughed at her bluntness, and rubbed his jaw. "Life with you would not be boring, firebrand."

"It would be powerful. And rich, and satisfying."

Their gazes locked. "If you want gold, Maeve, my father would have to agree. What are you offering him?"

"His son on our throne, and a new alliance with Connacht." She lifted her chin to breathe. "For I heard that Conor tricked Ros Ruadh out of valuable land as part of the Ulaid's so-called treaty with Laigin. I heard that Conor treated you badly." She prayed he would not remember her own father's treachery. So many years had passed.

Ailill looked up to the spill of moonlight, torn. Maeve was overcome by pure survival; she had no other safe harbor to seek but this. Innel might be dead, but Idath's and Felim's wrath would be brewing even now, ready to fall upon her in earnest. "So we must forge an alliance now to keep us both strong against the Ulaid." Desperate, she pressed her parted lips to Ailill's wrist. It tasted of the wool-grease from his sword.

Instead, she drank lake-water from a man's clear skin, the mist rising from his pores.

She squeezed her eyes shut. "And a final thing. Though you will be our king, when your father dies I will use Connacht's power to also win Laigin's throne for you."

Ailill betrayed himself with an exclamation. He was so close to saying yes.

Maeve knelt once more, burying her fingers in his hair. *She had to.* "You enjoy many women, Ailill, but I was the first to make you feel this." She touched her lips to his, her breath hot upon them.

"And this..." She reached down to stroke him, bringing old memories to life.

Again, they were two youngsters creeping away from the king's hall, their blood catching alight for the first time. It had become the only defiance left to Maeve, the only thing that was hers after Ros Ruadh took her child. And Ailill had looked at her as if he actually *saw* her, and adored her. His touch had been gentle... young, soft skin against hers...

Now, as they shared that caress once more, Ailill moaned.

Maeve braced herself, this time willing her muscles and mind to harden. She stared into the moonlight so it blinded her. *And still she felt the heat of the red stag, as she buried him within her.*

Her voice was strangled. "Give me my freedom, and I'll give you yours."

Ros Ruadh told her bluntly the next day that he was much happier without her than he would have been with her all these years. All things considered, Maeve accepted that with good grace.

Nestled on cushions close to his hall-fire, the old king banished his son and servants out of earshot. He was white-haired and mottle-skinned now, though still wiry from swordplay. His blue eyes were also just as shrewd.

Trying not to look at his veined hands, Maeve set out what she was giving Laigin: a valuable alliance, and if she bore Ailill's child, a blood tie with Connacht's rulers.

"We had an alliance with you." Ros Ruadh's tone was bone-dry. "It was severed, I believe."

Maeve's cheeks grew warm. "That was with my father." She held his eyes. "*I* keep my oaths. You will see me prove more honorable than any man of my kin."

The king's white brows rose.

She sat forward, dangling the bait she had been keeping just

for him. If he agreed to the marriage, for the first time in generations Laigin's druids would be allowed to worship at the sacred
Hill of Uisneach—land won by Connacht in a battle long ago.

Ros Ruadh's expression gave nothing away, but she was not
fooled. He was old. Soon his priests must sacrifice to the gods for
an easy journey for him through the veils. A chance for them to
do this at the most sacred place in Erin, the heart of the four kingdoms, was too tempting to reject.

He surprised her, clearing his throat. "And what else do you
want as part of this bargain?" He tapped a ringed finger on his
chair, staring at it.

In that quiet, the invisible presence rose between them. Her
own words were still echoing in her heart. *A blood-tie to Connacht's
rulers.* There was a blood-tie, once.

A question trembled on Maeve's tongue, but at the last moment she swallowed it. He did not speak of their child because
she was gone. Long gone. If he would not set the ghost free, she
would not—it would only give him power over her.

She moistened her mouth. "I want a troop of the Galeóin to
train our men, and an oath that we can call on the rest if we get attacked." The Galeóin were an old tribe of Laigin. Small, dark-
haired, and deadly silent, they were known for their skill with
spears and rigorous training.

Relieved, Ros Ruadh nodded, and she moved the conversation
to bride-price: gold, cattle, servants, grain, and mead. The wariness
left the king's stooped shoulders. "What if your bid to rule fails?"

Maeve sat erect in her chair. "Then both your son and bride-
gifts will be returned. I make this offer as a free woman, and
Fraech will not hold it against you. I alone will lose." Flinging it
out released some pressure in her chest. "I, alone."

Ros Ruadh thought for a moment, then crooked his finger to
summon his servant with the jug of mead and two cups.

A roar went up from the men around the downed stag.

Maeve lowered her spear and uncramped her hand, her body still quivering. It was good that Ailill's barb had hit the deer's heart.

Her Connacht guards released their hackles now and smoothed stiff backs, congratulating Ailill with hearty slaps. Hounds crowded their legs, tails waving. Laigin and Connacht men laughed together, reaching to ruffle the dogs' ears. One of the huntsmen slit the stag's throat to let it bleed out.

The season had broken very early, and on their way home through Connacht, frosts gave way to rains. Now Maeve plucked her feet from the mud beneath the oak trees, scraping her boots on the roots as she made her way back to her horse.

Garvan glanced over, his face cold. He had barely spoken to her since she chose a Laigin prince over him, but she was too tired to coax him out of it. He would understand, soon.

She dug a flask from her saddle and slurped ale as she leaned on Meallán's flank. Below in the sunlit clearing spread the traveling camp furnished by Ros Ruadh. Outside the jumble of tents, lances had been stuck into the ground—a forest of pale shafts and glinting spear-tips against the leafless, mossy trees. Painted shields hung on tent poles.

Maeve drank in that view with more pleasure than the ale. Laigin was famed for its lowlands of barley and wheat, and its protected coast that drew rich trade ships from eastern lands.

Behind the tents, therefore, sat rows of carts holding jars of Greek wine, Laigin ale, and sacks of grain. There were costly cedarwoods and fragrant oils from the Middle Sea, and silver, tin, and gold guarded by Laigin swordsmen. It was the greatest bride-price ever assembled in Erin.

Maeve squinted at it, wondering if it would banish the frowns of her lords when they found she'd bought a Laigin king for Connacht.

Something caught her eye—a person struggling in the grasp of two of the Laigin warriors. She slipped the flask away, wiping

clammy sweat from her brow as she shaded her eyes. The Laigin
guards were dragging a slight figure up the slope between the
trees, a youth in costly if battered war-attire: a dented helmet that
was too big and a mail-shirt that reached past his knees.

"What is this?" Maeve demanded when they reached her.

Exchanging fearful glances, the warriors gave their prisoner a
nudge and let him go. The boy stumbled. The helmet slipped
over his eyes, and he tilted his head to see Maeve, blowing away
wisps of ruddy hair.

Not a boy, a girl, with a pointed chin and slanted cheekbones.
Maeve's mind stalled and went blank.

The girl's eyes flashed, and the look pierced Maeve's belly.
"Hello, Mother."

CHAPTER 12

All color bled from the woodland, as if it was still under frost.
Maeve only saw the girl, her hair a light shade of amber,
freckles scattered across a snub nose. Her features were cast from
the same mold Maeve saw in her own mirror every day—except
this girl boasted the large eyes and round face of the fox-cub,
not the vixen.

Ros Ruadh's child.

Maeve couldn't face those eyes again. She stared instead at the
challenging twist of the girl's sweet mouth, so jarring against all
that creamy skin. She heard steps behind her. Her mind was a
trapped bird fluttering against the cage, and she could only grasp
for the one thing she knew: Ailill.

Unseeing, Maeve turned to him. "Bring her to my tent." And
then she walked away.

Ailill delivered his half sister less gently than the Laigin guards had, elbowing up the flap of Maeve's tent, dragging her in and giving her a shove.

The girl rubbed her arm. "Easy, brother!"

Ailill grunted, striding to the trestle table laid out with honey bread and a haunch of beef boiled over a campfire. One of Maeve's servants had swiftly lit a stone lamp, and the little rush wick now burned with a feeble glow.

Maeve had used those snatched moments to pull off her filthy tunic and drag on a clean one. To smooth her hair with shaking fingers.

Now she stared into a cup of Erna's herb brew. Shadows moved in the beaker as the lamp flickered. The part of her heart that could make sense of this had been hollow a long time, and she poured this brew into it every day, deadening it further.

Dead was easier. It let her breathe.

But there was a hole just the same in the world, a sliver cut out where the babe once existed. Now that emptiness was crowded with something warm and alive, that breathed behind her in the same rhythm as she did.

Maeve blanched and set the cup down. "Finnabair." She turned to the child. *Child…she is nearly sixteen.*

Maeve had been three years younger when the birthing nearly killed her. By the time she was well, Ros Ruadh had given the babe to a flock of Laigin women who guarded her jealously.

But there were moments together, snatched ones that seemed timeless, where she felt…*No.* Maeve stared into the girl's eyes. *Gods.* As blue as her own, and as bright as when they followed the little seal Maeve cobbled together from scraps of fur, diving it back and forth, back and forth, through the air…

No.

Maeve's lips parted again but nothing more came out.

"Finn," the girl stated. "I am called Finn."

"You know Father hates that." Ailill drained a cup of ale, throwing his wet cloak on the cowhide rug, where one of his servants scooped it up. "It is a boy's name, unbecoming to a royal lady. As is stealing away from home without leave."

"You did it all the time when you were young." Finn rocked on her toes. "And anyway, if I was as fat as you, no one would know I *was* a girl."

Ailill fought down a smile. "Vixen," he growled.

A shudder nipped the back of Maeve's neck. She turned to Ailill as he flopped onto a pile of fur cushions. "Why did you not tell me she was at Dun Ailinne?" Her voice cracked, and she pulled at the heavy neck-torc. "I...thought she had been sent away years ago."

She had been able to tear no word out of Laigin about the child. No word at all.

Ailill shrugged, gesturing to his serving girl to pull off his sodden boots. "You didn't ask."

"And why did Ros Ruadh not tell me—" Her voice was rising too high. She cut herself off, resting her knuckles over her mouth as the servant unlaced Ailill's boots.

Ailill cocked a rueful eye at his sister. "She has always been his favorite. He probably didn't want you knowing she was still around."

Blunt Ailill shot very straight barbs. Maeve remembered that flicker of fear in the king's eyes. Did he think she had come to demand this girl as part of the bargain? *Daughter.* Maeve could hardly even conjure the word.

"Which is why he will be livid when he finds you gone, little sister." Ailill flexed his wet foot, wrinkled and white. "And just how did you manage it?"

"It amused some of your men to keep me secret—until that stuffy old Lonan found out." Finn pulled off her battered helmet with a flourish and dropped it. "And I left Father a message with my women. He'll understand. He *always* understands me."

His treasure. His own. Maeve had heard him whisper it into Finn's ear as he rocked her.

This was foolish; she had to force herself to turn around once more. "Why are you here?" Her voice was unsteady, and there was nothing she could do about it.

The tips of Finn's teeth showed between her lips. "I am a marriage gift, Mother. From me."

"Don't be ridiculous." Ailill tossed roasted hazelnuts into his mouth. "You will have to go back."

"Why?" Finn returned. "It is time I visited my *other* kin, especially now that my brother will be king. I cannot think of a better time, can you?"

Maeve stared. When she spoke to her own father like that, her only reward was a blow to the cheek. Yet beneath the girl's haughty chin and flaring nostrils, Maeve thought she saw a tremor go through her.

The world must stay as it was; it was all Maeve knew. "We *are* sending you back," she stammered.

"If you try, I will scream and kick all the way back to Dun Ailinne. People will laugh, and from what I heard, Maeve of Cruachan would hate that." Finn's eyes widened, the surface opaque.

"Lugh's balls, let her stay." Ailill looked his sister over. "She is passing pretty when she's clean. She can be part of this great spectacle you are weaving."

Maeve grasped for that, clinging to those thoughts that had now become ingrained. Many eyes would be upon her when she returned home, and a spurned daughter would not be viewed with favor by the chiefs and their wives.

"I can ride at the back with the women," Finn chimed in, watching Maeve carefully. "I brought my horse, Nél. You won't have to see me again."

The relief that caught Maeve up was so strong it blotted out all else. She needed the cold of the woodland, hares to set the dogs after . . . something to do with her useless hands and limbs. With a nod to Ailill and his sister, she grabbed her cloak.

In moments she was once more surrounded by yapping dogs, gripping a rowan spear in a sweaty palm. The sensation that crept over her the rest of that day was not the looseness of freedom and tired limbs, however, or the numbness of cold air.

Had she been broken on *his* body after all? For it seemed she was fragmented, and could not bind herself back together again.

Try as she might, she could not summon the Maeve she once was.

Maeve sent a messenger to Tiernan that the column of horses, carts, and fighting men came in peace, and that she led them.

She said no more.

The rain cleared to a sunny, cold day, and she ordered the covers of the carts to be rolled back. Some things were more powerful than words. The fine weather had drawn everyone out. Tillers were sowing beans between the barley. Cruachan's houses were bustling, men up ladders mending the thatch, women and children slapping mud on wattles to fix fences and doors after the long dark storms.

Everyone stopped what they were doing to gawp at Maeve's arrival.

Laigin warriors pranced on their ponies; bridle bits, buckles, and hilts all polished. Shields decorated the carts, drawing the eye to the gleaming spill of grain in open sacks and the vivid hue of real gold piled among them. The brightly dressed women who accompanied the warriors thronged the carts, hair braided with ribbon and limbs wound with bronze.

The stern Galeóin trotted at the rear in perfect rows, crowned by carved spears, and trailed by Connacht lads who exclaimed at their weapons.

Settling Ailill in the best guest lodge, Maeve perched near the hearth as his servants scurried about storing away furs and platters, piling cedar tables and cushions against the walls.

Ailill sprawled with his feet on a bench, nursing yet another horn of ale.

"Set out ten of the Greek wine-jugs at the feast," Maeve ordered one of the maids, her bracelets jingling as she waved her away. During their passage through Connacht, she had sent messages to all the nobles nearby to attend. They would already be on their way.

Ailill sat up, scowling. "That wine is mine. You can't waste it like that."

"You bought me with it. It is mine."

When his lip jutted, Maeve slid on the bench beside him and focused on him long enough to pat his hand. Her mind kept roaming far away—and she kept wrenching it back. "The nobles have to see what they can gain from an alliance with you...and trade with Laigin."

Grudgingly, he folded his arms and swung his feet back up. "Then buy me more wine with your own cattle."

"Soon I will possess the king's herd, and enough calves to buy a ship of fine wine." The words were tasteless and empty, but they made Ailill smile.

That night, Maeve sat by until the lords and their women had drunk their fill. The pig baked in a salt crust—valuable British salt, from Laigin—was now stripped to bone. They smeared Connacht butter on soft white bread ground from Laigin's wheat, and used it to mop up the drizzles of Greek oil that glazed the salmon, exclaiming at the taste.

She had sent Finn to the women's lodge, guessing that the girl would detest being paraded for Maeve's nobles. She could not bring herself to demand it of Finn even though it would have been shrewd. Ailill was her prize—he had agreed to it. An equal bargain.

The meal became a blur about Maeve, though, for she could not rid her mind of that pale face with the blazing eyes.

Eventually she rose, waiting for the lords to fall silent. As she went to speak, she swayed with exhaustion, and realized she had lost all willpower to embroider her words. It was so hard to fight, to keep fighting, when sometimes it all wavered and she could not grasp what she fought for anymore...

Maeve straightened her neck. Power made a shield. The shield kept the blades away. *Conor. Idath. Felim.* "I have offered myself to the prince of Laigin as his wife."

Scandalized, the guests began muttering to each other.

Maeve spread her fingers. "This war-band is not a threat, it is a gift. Such a treaty with Laigin will bind us closer than either kingdom can ever bind to the Ulaid." She placed her palms on the long, low table, meeting the eyes of the great cattle-chiefs one by one. "*And this makes us stronger than we can be alone.* Conor mac Nessa wants to be ard-rí, that is why he demanded Finnbennach. We need all the strength we can muster against him."

Gruff bearded men nodded, others fiddling with their wooden beakers, deep in thought.

Tiernan placed a sparse slice of bread on his platter with elegant fingers. "And you did not think to consult us on this matter?"

"I am a free woman. If I am to rule, chief druid, I must trust my own judgment."

This was dangerous ground, for the cattle-chiefs wanted to think they were in charge. Sensing the mood, Maeve swung back to them. "I will never, though, be subject to my Laigin husband. In all matters of Connacht, I will rule alone." She smiled. "With the advice of my most loyal nobles, of course."

Ailill was glaring at her. She had left that part out.

Remember what you get in return, her eyes replied.

He looked impressive, at least. His shoulders were broadened by lush folds of stoat fur, brown as his hair, and leather belt and boots tooled into intricate designs. Ros Ruadh had emptied his coffers to adorn his son, wreathing him in enamel-studded bronze and twisted gold rings.

Well-fed and glossy as a bull.

"No man of the derbfine can match this," Maeve added. "A marriage with the next king of Laigin, and a treaty with the ruling king. I have added their wealth and power to our own. You've seen the riches I won for us, the wheat, the *gold*." Maeve drank in the avid expressions of the lords and warriors. "Can Fraech give you all this, *or* weave such alliances to hold us strong against the Ulaid storm? No! His kin have spent all their gold trying to buy the goodwill of their enemies!"

There was a ripple of laughter. Taking a breath, Maeve let it out, lowering her shoulders. "Enjoy this bounty, and remember that with me as queen you will only enjoy more."

As soon as they were chattering, she slipped to the oaken doors of the hall, which someone upon exiting had left open a crack. In the shadows of the porch, she drew in the cold draft to clear her head.

Tiernan appeared at her elbow.

Maeve hastily straightened. "The pieces are nearly in place," she murmured. "Fraech cannot command such power, and you know it."

"Not all the pieces."

A flickering lamp hooked beside the door cast a sheen over Tiernan's unblinking gaze. Maeve had a moment of clarity: her knees on damp grass as she offered him up her naked sword. And soon after, curls of swamp-mist rising over her own watery grave.

"You cannot command everything," the druid said.

"No." Her eyes saw nothing now, her fingers curled at her throat. "We must both trust to faith for a time yet, chief druid."

***

After a night without sleep, Maeve rose at dawn and, rubbing her gritty eyes, went directly to the stables. Outside, the biting air would blow away the fog of wine, though her temples pounded with every strike of Meallán's hooves as they cantered out through the gates into gray and blue shadows, and a low sun slanting across the bronze grasses.

She headed for a ridge to the north and east of Cruachan.

There, she could ride in peace, avoiding the busy cart-tracks among the steadings and fields. Meallán lurched up the crest and the rising sun blinded her, so when he suddenly shied she was almost thrown from the saddle.

She did not at first recognize the other horse and rider coming down. Shading her eyes, she saw it was Finnabair, dressed in riding trews and a shaggy sheepskin cloak.

Why was she out here unguarded? Sharp words rose to Maeve's tongue, but they died away as she was arrested by Finn's stricken expression, her eyes enormous in her pale face, her mouth pursed tight, drawing in her cheeks. The girl's knuckles showed white and red on the reins.

"Sorry to startle you," was all Maeve could mumble, urging Meallán to flat ground.

"I heard you coming." Finn wiped her face smooth of emotion. "Your horse has a heavy tread."

Maeve stroked her stallion's dark mane. "He is a big lad," she agreed. "And headstrong. When he was young he scared most of the boys off. That's why I wanted him."

"Of course. I heard that somewhere."

It was disturbing to hear that clipped voice emanating from such a sweet mouth. *What did I expect?* Maeve expected nothing, because the sliver had been cut out of the world . . . her heart . . . as if it did not exist anymore. Unable to think, she blurted, "I can outrace all the warriors with him."

Talking about horses seemed to soothe Finn. "He looks too heavy to be fast."

"Not fast? He's the swiftest racer in Cruachan." The stallion's ears turned back. "Yes, *a stór*," Maeve murmured, stroking his neck. "Or perhaps it's just the love for your mistress that gives you wings."

Finn was staring at Maeve's hand with an odd expression. She flushed, tossing her copper crown of coiled braids. "Nél is the one to beat. Father got him from a Greek trader from Massalia. He's so light, he'll outpace any mount as stocky as yours."

"Ah," Maeve returned with a smile. "Meallán's legs are powerful, but also long. Look at the arch in his neck! He was bred from a Roman horse whose sire came from Parthia in the east. That's why his coat is red."

That trumped Greece. Finn's eyes kindled, the sullenness in her face burned off by excitement. In that moment, she looked like a little girl. "Race me, then."

Maeve recognized that thrilling mix of defiance and terror very well.

"Come on," Finn cried. "If you think he's unbeatable!"

With that impertinence, she wheeled her horse and trotted to a rowan tree that clung to the windswept hill, its withered berries picked out by the early sun. Maeve considered for a moment, then nudged Meallán to her side. A long pale track cut through the emerald turf of the ridge. "We cannot race up here," Maeve argued. "It's too dangerous."

Finn's flushed cheek was averted, her hands smoothing her horse's dappled gray coat. "Surely *you* are not afraid?" Her voice was muffled by the wind. "Tales are told of your bravery all over Laigin."

Maeve sighed and squinted along the ridge. "Very well, but don't venture off that path. At the end, before the ground falls to the plain, two rowans have grown together. That is where we finish."

Maeve gathered her reins. Meallán pawed the ground; Finn's mount shook his head and pranced. With a startling whoop, Finn was off, and Maeve let her stallion have his head. The two horses streaked side by side, plunging up and down the hollows and rises as if sailing over green sea-waves.

They soared and thudded across foaming streams, dodging bare, bent trees as the riders lurched in the saddle. Maeve's heart was in her mouth, though she had never been afraid on horseback before, her gaze locked to the perilous progress of Finn's mount. Eventually, she had to drag it away to focus on her own ride. The freezing wind pulled her braids apart and flung her hair into her open mouth.

Only when she felt Meallán pulling ahead did she dare another glance, and was surprised by a savage look on Finn's face. The girl was bent over, clenching the reins to her chin, and her mutters in her stallion's ear now looked like pleading. Desperation.

The blow winded Maeve, and her knees fell slack. Meallán's stride began to slow.

Finn saw him falter and cried out again. "Nél! Faster, *a chuisle,* faster!"

Finn reached the rowans first in a shower of mud-clods and threw her head back with a shout, galloping in a circle. Her stallion was pacing by the time Maeve walked Meallán up. Maeve's horse was snorting, and flecks of foam from his mouth coated her hands.

She was about to speak when Finn hauled Nél around. The wind had also torn Finn's hair free, and it whipped across her, the red-gold mingling with the stallion's gray. Finn flicked it from her face and her eyes blazed out—the mask stripped away. Her cheeks were crimson slashes, her mouth awry. *"Why did you leave me there?"*

Undefended, Maeve vainly shielded her breast with one hand. "You just threw me away, like you do your *lovers*..." With every word, Finn flung out her arms, making Nél prance on his back hooves, shaking his mane. "Aye, I heard the whispers of you in Mumu and the Ulaid—as did everyone who laughed behind my back. When you left, you made Father look an old fool, and *me* nothing more than a pup you kicked away when you got bored. *My kin* called me the spawn of Cruachan." Her mouth crumpled and she yanked her hands so violently Nél reared and slammed down again, nearly unseating her. "You made me a stranger in my own home!"

The dead place in Maeve beckoned. She knew how to curl up

in its dark and cold, blessedly numb. For if she faced *this child*, these memories, it would bring back the other lost one as well.

Her voice emerged without her will. "Did they wed you to anyone?"

Panting, Finn scowled.

"Then you are lucky to escape such enslavement. Insults mean nothing; that is the least of what happens to women. You have been..." She swallowed. "You have been blessed."

Finn gasped and spurred her stallion forward. "How dare you say my pain is naught, when I have been waiting years to lay it at your feet!" She crowded her horse into Meallán and grabbed Maeve's wrist, dragging them both off balance, her eyes senseless. "You will not baffle me with words or run from me again. Tell me why you left and never looked back!"

That touch was the thrust of a spear, instantly shattering Maeve's numbness.

Despite herself, she ignited.

"Why *I* left?" She flung off Finn's hand. "I was twelve when my father sold me to yours, Finn; a man five times my years! I almost died birthing you when I was younger than you are now! My father dragged me away, but you belonged to Ros Ruadh and he would not let you go." She choked on it. "You were Laigin's... always Laigin's."

Finn was gulping at the storm she'd unleashed. "Why did you not defy your father, then—or mine? You are fearless and willful—they all say that about you!"

Guilt was a fist sunk into Maeve's belly, and all the fighting she had done, and all the tears, suddenly meant nothing. "If he had let me live, my father would have named me traitor; cursed my name and banished me from Erin forever. Would you defy your father to spend your life cursed and alone?"

Finn's eyes streamed in the wind. "With me, you would not have been alone."

A pained silence fell. "You cannot judge me." Maeve's voice

shook. "Your father protects you. *He loves you.* Count yourself lucky for that."

"Lucky?" Finn barked a laugh, dashing tears from her cheeks. "Everyone was suspicious, thinking I would turn out like you. No one wanted to be close to me but Father. No one wanted to know what I thought, or felt!"

There was only the sound of their harsh breathing, mingling together. Maeve scrubbed her face with the heels of her palms, resting them over her throbbing brow. *Find the cold, the dark.* "Be glad, then, you were not ground down by some grunting man, until you could barely remember yourself."

Finn gasped again, dragged her stallion about and spurred him away. She rode straight into the rising sun, until when Maeve raised her head she could not see her anymore.

The women were still avoiding Maeve's glowers at her bath the next day. The wooden tub sat at the rear of the women's lodge on flagstones, near a hearth to heat the stones. This day the water bore a slick of oil of lavender, one of Maeve's Roman treasures, and some of the tight buds bobbed around her shoulders.

Her wedding day. Again.

Knees up, Maeve drank in the steam, trying to let it warm her inside. The brethim laws meant no one could stop her—she was a freewoman, not a queen yet. Messages would still be flying south to Fraech's kin like poisoned barbs, though, for this was not about marriage alone, as Idath and Felim would know.

Afterward, servants rubbed her with linen towels and applied honey balm to her skin, another working at the snarls in her hair with an antler comb. Maeve closed her eyes. This primping was familiar...having her glossy mane brushed out, being prodded toward an old man who would slap her rump and cackle, "A fine filly!" to her father.

It is different now. She just had to get through it. Her throat was parched. How would she speak loud enough for all the people to hear? "Wine," she croaked. A maid held a cup to her lips and she gulped.

Her eyes flickered open. At high-sun she would hold the mead cup to Ailill's lips like this. She imagined a horde of people all staring, and she standing distant from it all.

Finnabair, her thoughts whispered. Fair spirit, it meant. White ghost.

Unwillingly, a glimpse came of Finn haunting Laigin's halls as a lonely wraith. Maeve batted the comb away. "There isn't time, Niamh, you know what my hair is like. Pile it up and curl the ends, and no one will know it's a bramble-patch." Some of the women tittered nervously, but no one was fooled by her hollow voice.

That girl on the horse was no wraith, Maeve said to herself. Finn smoldered.

And I lit that flame. I lit it.

The wedding was held outside the temple of Lugh, with the lords who supported her in attendance, and restless masses of people on the churned-up meadow below. As befit the worship of Lugh, everything was chosen to dazzle, and capture the god's light.

The audience was a muddy river of brown workaday clothes, worn leather, red cheeks, and windblown hair. The wedding party blazed. Rich things glinted and gleamed, their furs, their glossy woolens, and their jewelry.

The daunting Galeóin formed a glittering arbor of spears along the steps. Every part of Maeve was braced by unyielding metal and stiff robes of felted wool and heavy embroidery. She was a husk that moved and smiled beneath the dome of cold, blue sky, vacant-eyed as she lifted the sacred cup of mead, Tiernan's voice droning in her ear.

When the battle horns blared and people cheered, Maeve realized with clarity that *nothing* made this different. Her father had trapped her with duty, necessity ... and now she did it to herself.

Inside, her heart began racing, longing to sweep her out the gates. *To fly after him over the silver lake to a distant shore that glimmered, far beyond the world ...*

She bit her lip and lowered her lashes to blot out Ailill's smirk. Afterward, she fled to her bedchamber to disrobe.

A servant lifted off the gold headdress of scrolled leaves and bird-heads, and Maeve began pulling out pins. She didn't care that her hair would be a mess for yet another feast—her skull ached. "That's better." She turned, massaging her scalp.

Finn had followed the servants up the stairs into the alcove off the sleeping floor. Maeve had not seen her since their ride—indeed, she wondered if she would ever see her again. Maeve was baffled as to why she was here now, after they had flung such hurt at each other.

Finn leaned on the wicker hurdle that screened Maeve's bed, huddling into her arms. Her bold demeanor had been stripped away.

Maeve dismissed the maids. She glanced warily at Finn as she placed her bracelets in a dish on her wooden dresser. "Shouldn't you be eating, or dancing, or having some fun in the hall?" *Someone should.*

Finn ignored the question, staring at the headdress on the beaver-fur blanket with a frown. "You didn't look afraid."

So she was in the crowd. Maeve held up a bronze mirror to hook a ring from her earlobe. There, she could watch Finn in its polished surface.

"Everyone looking at you, and you just stand there untouched." Finn sounded frustrated. "How ...?"

The glow from the little lamp made Finn's pale face float amid shadows. Maeve was struck again by its familiarity. The clean sharp bones had yet to fully emerge from those plump cheeks, but the hints were there in Finn's chin and the tilt of her eyes. It could almost have been her...before the etching of pain. At that moment Finn lifted her gaze.

She didn't look young anymore.

The mirror clattered to the dresser. Maeve's smile was tight. "I was raised to take part in such rites." She took out the other ear-bob. "To help the people feel safe. I have been goddess, warrior, doting daughter." Her lashes lowered. "Whatever is needed."

Finn touched the embroidered mantle hanging over the screen. "And I suppose you have performed *this* ceremony before—more than once."

"Well, there is that."

Finn swung to her. "You were not afraid, but you were not happy," she blurted. "You were thinking of something else."

Heat flooded Maeve's cheeks. Was that intuition some trick of shared blood? She rose, ducking to avoid the slope of thatch roof, and tossed a rope of amber beads to the bed. "For once this was my choice, so I am happy."

"Your choice, and you pick *Ailill*?"

Maeve fumbled with the chain around her waist, an ache in her chest she could not ward away. What if Finn harbored dreams of a mother who would nestle her in plump arms, cook her tidbits, bathe her fevers? What if Finn were hoping she was not as the tales painted her?

When I am many things worse than that.

She could not stir up what was buried and still stay strong enough to survive. *This* was the Maeve who had endured, and this was all she could be: for her sake, for her people's sake.

There was nothing left of anything else.

Still, she knew all about yearning, and hoping, and how bitter it was when a dream was shattered. She could not inflict that on Finn. Let her know about Maeve now, when Finn's defenses were still braced like a shield.

"It is a rare sister who thinks highly of her brother." Maeve's hands dropped away, and she turned to her daughter. "I killed mine."

The horror in Finn's eyes was eclipsed by a slower darkness, which descended like the bleak fall of night.

CHAPTER 13

Maeve was trapped inside a bard's tale, nothing but a listener in the audience as some other person's story played out around her. *There was a woman at her wedding feast, a bride to a rich prince of Laigin...*

In the king's hall, chattering people leaned past to grab roast beef, crisp-skinned pig, and honey-cakes from the low, carved tables. Laughter pierced warm air thickened with sweat, perfume, and charred meat. A drumbeat rumbled off to one side as a whirl of dancers blurred the flames of the fires. Lamps had been hung from the thick rafters, all of them blazing.

Maeve was surprised by the unconscious movement of her own hand as she poured more ale for Ailill. Her sleeve fell back, baring her wrist, and she stared at the stark veins. Her blood *was* beating.

Ailill gulped the ale in one swallow and slumped on her shoulder. "Need...sleep..." he slurred, wreathing her in fumes. "Wake for you...t'night." His paw reached around to squeeze her breast.

Maeve snatched up a different jug, sloshing mead into his empty beaker. Blearily, he threw it down his throat. A chieftain on his other side shouted in his ear, and Ailill lurched toward him, letting Maeve go.

She sank back on the cushions and sheepskin throws and

fixed her gaze on a bronze lamp before her, fashioned in the shape of a boat.

Her sight went out of focus and the flame wavered. Flickering, sinuous, it gradually blotted out the noise and stink of the feast, the rush of color and movement.

It was done now, for the children and women, the druids and fighting men. She had a husband, and an alliance with Laigin. She had riches to feast many warriors. A girl who already hated her now hated her more, but Finn must know what she was or suffer a greater hurt.

It was done. She would make them all safe from the clouds in the North.

This vow brought no relief, though, only a rawness that gnawed deeper the longer Maeve sat still. She topped up Ailill's cup again, and he planted a wet kiss on her cheek and clapped the chieftain next to him on the shoulder, both roaring with laughter.

Maeve winced and leaned the jug on the table, which was stained with spilled ale and meat juices, the empty earthen platters scattered with bones. People flocked about their bench, bodies crushed on top of each other. Hidden from everyone's eyes, her fingers drifted slowly to her lips and rested there.

A memory of his touch. The only thing of hers this day.

Ailill's men could not carry him to bed, so Maeve asked them to cover him with furs and leave him snoring on one of the cushioned benches. Other warriors simply slid to the floor in untidy piles. The hounds sniffed about beneath the tables, crunching bones.

When everyone was beyond sense, she slipped away.

The feast had begun not long after high-sun, and she made her way along the last league of the trail to the lake as night fell. There she stood among the trees as the glow of dusk faded. She had to wait for daylight—and real life—to disappear before she could walk into the dream.

Step by step Maeve crept closer, until she saw the flame flickering through the ground-mist that rose from damp pools among the black woods. His campfire. She wove toward it.

Ruán was already on his feet by the time she stumbled from the trees. He did not lunge for his knife, though.

He knows me.

He recognized her without sight, when people's eyes had been following her all day and seeing nothing of her. The throb of that was like a tide, pulling her over the dark grass toward him.

Ruán had dragged his nest of furs from the hide shelter to the fireside. Her blood coursing, her heart too full, Maeve glanced up to the spangled sky to steady herself, wondering why he lay under the stars when he could not see them.

He feels them... Hadn't she watched him, drinking in the world?

Ruán wore a wolf-pelt she had given him. The shaggy folds were bulky, but she would recognize from afar the poise of the body beneath. His head was lifted high, chest proud, as he turned toward her. The firelight turned his hair copper. Maeve's lips parted, trailing puffs of mist. She knew him, too.

"I thought you had no need of this place now." His voice was soft, considering the violence she had last meted out to him.

Maeve halted. The world was so cold its frozen air seemed to have splintered, jagged on her raw skin. "I thought so too, but..." She faltered. *But sitting there I couldn't breathe, and now she is here and I cannot think, or feel...and there is Ailill...and Fraech's kin...they will know by now, they'll come...*

Conor will come for me.

It all rushed out of Maeve's mouth as she stared at the fire. "And I *never* forget him, never! But they are all around me, watching, *wanting*, and how can I sense what Conor will do next? He will come for *me*..."

"Maeve, stop." Ruán was gripping her arms.

The heat from his fingers melted that cold. He was holding her *up*. She did not remember the last time someone touched her without grasping. She clutched the fur at Ruán's waist.

His muscles tightened, but he lowered his voice like he was soothing a horse. "Conor mac Nessa is a king. He thinks only of lands, warriors, people—"

"I am my people." It slipped from her, her eyes glazed, and then Maeve dropped her head to rest it on his forearm. There she paused, panting.

She did not know what movement he made then, or how she slid into the crook of his shoulder ... or why his hand held the back of her head.

Only then did she realize she had not collapsed into him after all. Their bodies were fused along thighs, bellies, and chests, her temple on his jawbone. They braced each other.

"I married the prince of Laigin," she said into the wolf-pelt.

There was a pause. "You keep interesting secrets."

"I did not have enough power on my own. There are lords who will fight to stop me being queen. And Conor of the Ulaid, he *will* try to kill me, to kill all of us ..."

"Take a breath."

She could not believe his fingers were at the nape of her neck like this. She bent her chin up. Beneath the blindfold and its secrets, his smile was oddly gentle, as if in her absence he had seen something of her even she did not know.

"I am so sorry for what I did to you."

He snorted, wry once more. "I was hardly unwilling."

"I was angry, though, and not at you. By the gods ..." Maeve's laugh was strained. "My apologies are rare enough. I would make the most of it, if I were you."

Neither seemed willing to step away. At last Maeve softened against him, allowing herself to absorb the warmth and shape of this body she had watched for so long. Her brow on his chest, she held her breath and let her hands slide down his waist and over the hard curve of his buttocks, instinctively molding him to her, too entranced to wonder at what she did.

His breath escaped, stirring her hair.

She shuddered.

"Come, you need to get warm," he said, his voice husky. He prodded her toward the fire. Maeve crept into the pile of deerskins and curled up, and Ruán sat and lifted one of the hides around her shoulders.

His arm hovered, uncertain, the heat of his skin raising the hairs on her neck. Maeve swallowed. The gnawing pain, the restlessness—surely it could not have been this...craving?

In all she had done that day to secure her people's safety, she had kept only one thing for herself, and that was a memory of his touch. But she needed more than memory now.

Ruán dropped his arm, but Maeve stopped him from pulling away, curving her fingers about his jaw to draw it toward her. She kissed him.

This time she kept her eyes open, savoring the shape of him against the stars, the firelight tracing his cheekbone. She drank in the natural ebb and flow of the kiss, gentle and tentative to start. Soon it deepened, however, and her thirst came alive.

Too many arid nights had passed for her, holding herself still before others, veiling her eyes, masking her thoughts. She needed...*abandon*.

Maeve knelt up, holding Ruán's cheeks to crush his mouth to hers, then tugging his tunic over his head and fumbling to unlace his trews.

At first he raced along with her, kissing the hollow of her throat as she untangled their clothes and tossed them aside. She was used to wrestling men in the bed-furs, and it was habit to try to drag him on top of her now. Such need...desperate...

"No." Ruán held himself from her, braced on his elbows. The firelight set his hair aflame.

Maeve panted, trying to read his face below the blindfold. Only then did she recognize his smile was sad now. Baffled, she arched her body again.

Ruán grabbed her wrists. "You will let me see my way." The low force in his voice silenced her as he trapped her with one forearm.

Her instinct was to writhe beneath him, enjoying the fight. But instead, Ruán took his other hand and trailed a caress so soft down her flank that Maeve was stunned and could not move.

Ruán's touch swept from her shoulders across her belly, from her hips to her collarbone. Over and over he bathed each curve with the tingling warmth of his finger-pads—the dip of her waist, the hollows beneath her arms, around the swell of each breast.

His expression betrayed an intense focus, as if he was utterly absorbing her. Maeve bent back her head and exhaled the last of her struggle into the sky.

Ruán cradled her thighs and calves, then her arms and hands, as if sculpting her with his palms. She lay still, savoring the heat of his skin hovering just above hers, focusing on every tiny gust that brushed her lips, her belly, as he tasted her, and shaped her with breath.

He flowed around her, turning her in his arms until the front of her body was pressed into the fur. Then his lips came down upon the nape of her neck. Their bodies fitted together, each curve nestled into a hollow. With a thundering pulse, she thought he might bite her there, like two foxes mating. But Ruán's mouth trailed down between her shoulder blades instead, and there he paused and breathed into her back, the heat spreading into her heart.

Drunk on touch, Maeve loosened, until all sense of her flesh melted away. Only then did Ruán stretch alongside her, turning her chin over her shoulder to kiss her. "*Now* you can move."

"So I wait for your leave?" she mumbled, spellbound.

He smiled, and she kept her eyes on those sensuous hands as they traced the curve of her buttock...just as she had watched them for weeks.

"The thrill of the new," he said.

She would not answer with words. Trembling, she turned over and reached for him. Only then did his mouth lower to one breast. Maeve crushed him to her, her awareness wrapped around that one sensation as it shot along her nerves.

Ruán pulled her with him and their bodies flowed upright, limbs entwined. He was murmuring something in a language she did not know, but she heard her name. *Maeve...Maeve...* And they were rocking together, him rooted within her, and she did not remember how they joined.

She could not control her shuddering breaths now. Each brought a stronger throb between her legs, and Ruán stoked it higher by rousing her with his fingers.

She knew only one way to rut—in a frenzy with eyes closed—and her body kept trying to twist into that habitual pattern as the pleasure took her over.

Ruán, though, had one last surprise.

Just as the cry kindled in her throat he cradled her jaw, as if staring into her. "Breathe slow," he whispered. "Draw each one up from the root of you, and open."

Maeve had never felt so exposed. The blindfold was irrelevant. His invisible gaze could still reach for her, binding them together.

They began to flow once more, each long indrawn breath roaring up them like a fire drawn by wind. The flame formed a spiral with their bodies, the pleasure gradually rising until at last Maeve's crown seemed to burst alight.

Her bellow came from the very cradle of her bones, Ruán's cry merging with hers. Out into the wilds they flung that howl, reaching for something beyond them.

For life.

Dizzied, Maeve waited for the plunge, and the collapse into blessed release. But she did not return to her senses.

Her awareness kept rushing outward, until stars were falling in a hail of light all about her. Then the black sky became the rapids of a dark river, and she was dragged along and sucked into a whirl of confusion.

※

Ruán stared down at Maeve, his pulse thundering. When the wild rose in him this time he abandoned himself to it, as the sídhe said he must. His body was aflame, the fire of that pleasure still licking about him.

But Maeve's undulations of pleasure had turned to shudders.

Ruán lowered her, feeling along her limbs. She was burning up, coated with moisture as she moaned and tossed her head. He knew that sweat, that shaking. Could it happen to her, too?

His instinct was to salve her pain, and without thinking he leaned over her. Placed on her flesh, his palms prickled. Maeve's anam did not feel like light now, but like a dark river pouring through her body, as if pushing something *out*.

At that moment she arched her back, and before he could pull away she let go a scream between his lips. Her breath rushed into him, and the spark of his awareness was pulled along in her wake. Down a tunnel of light and color they plunged together.

Into her memory.

The darkness around Ruán opened into the gray light of a cold day.

He looked out from Maeve's eyes, his spark of self hovering in a corner of her body. Around them humps of rock rose from green turf, tumbled cairns of stones and barrow-mounds with gaping doorways. The tombs of the ancestors. Above the tombs reared a great hill facing the sea. The Hill of the King.

The wind dragged Maeve's red hair over her eyes. She stumbled, and wept. "Come to me now." She hit her foot on a stone and fell to her knees. "Save me from this, I beg of you!"

The Shining Ones.

Ruán heard that cry in her heart. These stones were shaped by human hands, though. He knew now they were not the sídhe's halls of living wood, or earth carved by water and wind. The sídhe were not here ... but she didn't know that.

This Maeve from the past was rocking on her knees, pictures all jumbled up inside her. Ruán saw a babe snatched from her outstretched fingers, the fraught image gouged into her heart. Her babe ...? He felt the panic as Maeve lifted her head again. *"Give her back to me!"*

It was the cry of a lost child. Her arms were soft and unmarked, as were her bare thighs below her crumpled dress. She was just a girl herself, then.

Maeve hugged her waist and bent over, her agony searing Ruán. "Give her back to me, or let me stay ... Speak, so I know you will help me. I will pledge anything ..." She gulped a breath. *"Just stay my father's hand."*

There was silence but for the wind moaning between the tombs. The heavy-bellied clouds began to fragment into needles of rain, and Maeve slowly drew straight, her hands in her lap.

Ruán was conscious of the two threads of time. He felt the pain in this young girl of long ago, and where he held Maeve by his own fireside, he knew this wound was being cut afresh.

The young Maeve came alive, clawing on the ground for a stone. With it she began to gouge her arms until blood ran between her fingers. At last she wiped it along her cheekbones like war paint, and screamed at the silent sídhe. "Then I will never be yours ... and hatred shall lie between us *forever!*"

The force of her loathing flung Ruán out of the between-place.

He was only himself again beside the fire, the Maeve he knew a weight in his arms.

Her back was arched, her heels digging into the furs, and the same scream to the sídhe was echoing around the trees. As it faded she crumpled, breaking into sobs that shook her body.

Ruán touched her face and found her eyelids fluttering. She wasn't conscious; she wouldn't weep like this if she was. Her howls were almost animal.

Stunned, he crushed her face to his shoulder. Her agony was a wound in the Source around them, and he could not help but live it with her. Yet still her cry rang through him, her hatred.

Eventually, Maeve's shudders ceased. A jolt went through her, as if she'd only just come awake. Ruán laid her down, leaving his hand over her heart.

"Wh...what...?"

He swallowed to ease his chest. "You are safe, Maeve. Memories come alive in this place, that is all. To be burned away."

Her shoulders were still heaving, her teeth chattering. Gradually, her breaths slowed, her rigid body softening beneath his palm. He felt her wipe her face.

"Not all things can be burned away." Her voice was muffled, the tears thick in her nose, her throat. "Some prayers go unanswered."

The battle in Ruán bound his tongue. She wanted to be queen at any cost, that much was clear. So the very blaze that drew him was also his greatest threat. If she hated them so much, she would try to force the sídhe to help her, demand something from them.

She would drive them away, and with it his only chance for true sight.

Maeve sat up, turning to him. "There *is* magic here—druid magic. You wouldn't be able to live without your eyes if not. I've seen it in your hands. I've also seen priests go into fevered trances like this." She gripped his wrist. "That's what it is, isn't it? *You did it.*"

"No." He withdrew his hands and placed them on the ground, trying to still their tremor. "It comes from within *you*, Maeve, when you are brave enough to face it."

He felt her stiffen beside him.

"It happened to me," he said more softly, "when my despair broke me."

She wiped her face once more, breathing hard. "When I crumbled, and wept, I gained nothing. I *will not* do it again."

Trembling, Maeve rose into a crouch. Ruán sensed her poised there, as if torn by an impulse to flee.

"I understand that druids have their mysteries," she said, "and...that our bodies just needed release."

Ruán let out his breath. *Yes, that was all this must be.*

"But still I would know, Ruán of the marsh—what was burned from you?"

Now her voice was that of a child, terrified that her pain set her apart from others, forever. Ruán had felt the very same thing, and pity stirred in him. *Damn.*

He jumped up, hauling a deerskin around his bare shoulders as he tossed branches on the fire. At last he turned, caught by an inexplicable need to fling something free, too. "I served the lord of the Stone Islands, and thought I knew everything. The chief's eldest son fell ill, and I would let no one touch him but me. I fasted him, sweated him, beat the drum until he got no rest. I spent night after night in the tombs, thinking that if I could *force* myself from my body, I would glimpse his salvation among the stars. If I could resist the cries of the flesh, then my spirit would be free to find his and bring it back." Ruán lowered his shoulders, clearing the catch in his throat. He felt Maeve's eyes on him and tilted his face away. "When we both weakened, the boy and I, the chief begged me to seek the wisewomen and their herbs, and chant their prayers to the Mother. To join with the Goddess, in water, in earth. In life."

To honor the fleshly body, and thereby heal the body.

Sweat prickled Ruán's lip. "But I thought I knew best. The boy died, and the chief put out my eyes. The men threw me ashore on the coast and I stumbled across Connacht until I ended up here."

There was no sound but Maeve's breathing. "And...have you forgiven yourself? And how do you, if not?"

That took him by surprise. "I do not know." He answered without thinking. "By making amends someday, perhaps."

The fire hissed in the silence, sap cracking and popping in the wood.

When Ruán woke in the night, he and Maeve had burrowed away from each other in the furs. The warmth of her body outlined her shape for him. That heat was almost a touch on his skin... until a blade of wind crept in and sliced through it.

Ruán wrapped a fold of deerskin tight about himself and rolled on his back, his hand behind his head.

Alone beneath the silent sky.

CHAPTER 14

M aeve rode Meallán all the way to the guest lodge, seeking news of Finn from the Laigin women. Then she turned her horse around. In the wake of this night with Ruán, the pull to the ridge overwhelmed even her fear.

Something had cracked in her since she gave herself to him. That wondrous abandonment that she had never experienced before... Such a surrender meant something of her contained self had passed into him. Her instincts knew it. The alchemy could work no other way. And the nightmare that came afterward was still alive in her, piercing with every breath. Her heart pounded. Had his spell shattered her will, then, her control?

Passing a hand over her eyes, Maeve forced all thoughts of Ruán aside as Meallán climbed the hill. *Amends.*

The winds on the ridge could scour anyone clean, surely.

Finn was sitting on Nél beneath the twin rowans, staring into the sun as it lowered. She did not appear to hear Maeve's approach until Meallán whinnied and Nél snorted in reply.

Finn did not even look at her, wheeling her horse along the ridge. Maeve swung Meallán to follow. She did not try to gain on Finn this time, keeping pace just behind, close and steady as they cantered. The only thing that broke the silence was the drumming of hooves, though Maeve recognized the tension gradually bleeding from Finn until she sat looser in the saddle.

Eventually, Finn took a muddy trail down the ridge to a stream hidden among a tangled scrub of alder and hazel trees. Maeve parted the last bare branches and dropped Meallán's reins, letting him wade in and dip his head to drink. On the bank, Finn was regarding the tumbling water with a frown, arms folded.

Maeve squatted, shredding fern fronds and tossing them into the foam. Sometimes, more than silence was needed. "When you were three, my father decided he needed an alliance with Mumu more than with Laigin. He broke my marriage oath with Ros Ruadh and took me away to be wed to the Mumu prince Diarmait, brother of Niall, who is now Mumu's king. But your father would not allow me to take you with me." Her chin dropped and she closed her eyes. "I want you to know I did fight them. I tried, very hard." She'd seen Miu writhe and spit when she was teased— she had fought like that. The blows returned by her father must still be imprinted on her flesh, somewhere.

Finn had not moved.

Maeve made herself breathe in. "Your father was so angry he would not let me back to Laigin to see you. And then I was told you had been betrothed to a distant king and sent away."

"What?"

"Sent to Alba, as a child. That is why I never came back. I know now it was a lie to keep me away, but I believed it. There was no news of you afterward. It was as if…" She could not finish that. The hollow place in her throbbed.

Maeve watched the last stalk be swept away by the current.

Surprising her, Finn snorted and caught her stallion's reins, rubbing her chin on his pale shoulder. She had blanched to the same hue as his coat. "You heard wrong. I was almost betrothed, many times, but…men changed their minds when they found out who my mother was."

Maeve stared at her. "You are of royal blood."

Finn wound Nél's creamy mane about her finger. "I suppose they were afraid I would be wild, cause trouble among the men… I do not know."

Maeve rose from her haunches, light-headed. "Are you telling me I actually saved you from being wed?"

"If you would have it like that."

The corner of Maeve's mouth lifted, and she covered it with her fingers. *She* had somehow won Finn the freedom she craved for herself.

Finn's fists balled up, her chin jutting. "Are you mocking me?"

Maeve bent her head. "No, daughter, only myself." *The gods show me for a fool!* In spite of all her scheming, they stirred the pot their own way. "I'll tell you a secret: I mock myself heartily, but only on the inside. Do it aloud and you give people power over you."

Finn blinked, color rushing over her face. "I will...remember that."

Maeve tried to pull Meallán out of the stream. He yanked his head and stomped, drenching her in freezing water. She cursed.

Finn stifled a smile. "He is not just heavy, but also badly behaved."

"Sometimes." Maeve wiped her dripping face. "But I never wanted to crush his spirit." She gently thumped her stallion's shoulder.

A strained silence fell. Finn turned, digging out a clutch of bannocks from her saddle-pack. Then she straightened, looking into the woods as if casting about for something to say. "Windflowers...already?" Beneath an ash tree, white blooms starred the dark loam. "They are early." Avoiding Maeve's eyes, Finn stuck out her arm, a bannock in her palm. Her hand shook.

Maeve took the barley bun, peering at the flowers as she broke it. A spill of sunlight deeper into the trees picked out more windflowers and primroses.

Maeve's pulse skipped.

The recent days had been unseasonably fine. The catkins on the hazels were already drooping fat lobes of pollen, as if about to burst. It had been a mild winter—and short.

"The bluebells will follow soon." Rocking on her toes, Finn betrayed the instinctive excitement that all people felt at first sign of leaf-bud. "I used to pretend to swim through them, to make my eyes bluer." As soon as she blurted that out she stopped herself, tucking her chin on her shoulder.

Maeve stared at that tremor in Finn's jaw, the copper wisps of hair at her brow, still soft as a babe's. Swallowing hard, Maeve crouched beside a butterfly that was flexing in the sun. "It was I who said your eyes would turn blue from the flowers."

Finn stopped chewing.

"You were so tiny, only three or so..." Maeve rested her chin in her hand. "One of my stories."

"You told me stories?"

"Yes. And they were all..." Maeve shook her head with a smile. "...very silly." She coaxed the orange butterfly onto a twig. "I did not know if you would remember, but it was just as I left, and I hoped...you might." She brought the twig to her face.

They both peered at the insect as it fanned its spotted wings.

Slowly, Finn lifted a hand toward Meallán. "Then tell me more of what I heard about *him*—how you beat off all the boys to be first to ride him. How you tamed him."

Maeve rested the butterfly on the ground. "I'll tell you while we ride back."

⁂

They were barely at the huddle of crafters' houses near the warrior hall when Garvan came flying out of the gate of the mound and raced across the grass to head them off. "I've been looking everywhere for you," he gasped.

"Out of breath?" Maeve teased. "You should be fighting more and trailing after me less. See? Finn and I are perfectly safe."

Garvan's eyes rose and held hers, no answering glint there at all.

Maeve's smile died. "You can speak before Finn."

Garvan grasped Meallán's bridle, holding him steady. "Idath and Felim are gathering a war-band. They have been raising men in the south, Maeve. To attack you."

"But...the sacred peace..."

"They have broken the peace! Ardal has joined with Felim and Idath. We gained the news from some of Ardal's warriors, who are unhappy about the company their lord now keeps. Their war-band was waiting for the weather to turn. And now, damn it, it has. We'd have had more time if ice and snow trapped them in their duns."

Maeve had just been rejoicing that the long dark had broken early. She rubbed blood into her lips with the back of her hand. For all her fine words to Fraech about betrayal...*and now his kin had actually dared*...

She hooked a leg over Meallán and slid to the ground. Her thighs buckled and she held to his flank.

"It was Laigin, Maeve." Garvan glanced at Finn from beneath knitted brows. "When you bought a Laigin king for Connacht, and a Laigin war-band, Felim and Idath began muttering that you'd betrayed Connacht—that *you* had broken the peace. They call you a traitor."

That hated word cleaved Maeve's shock. Fury cleared her mind. "Who else knows of this?"

"No one at Cruachan but me and Ardal's man."

"Then come." Maeve looked up at her daughter. The sunlit halo of Finn's hair now blurred the fear in the girl's stricken face. "Finn, take Meallán and stable him for me. Would you do that?"

Finn nodded, searching her mother's eyes.

Maeve felt compelled to offer her something else, however small. "You are the only one who will handle him from now on— in fact, you are skilled enough to take over the care of all the royal horses." With effort, she drew up the corners of her mouth. "That is one *good* gift that you get from me."

Finn returned a weak smile. "So you won't condemn me to sew and spin at the fire after all?"

Maeve blew out her breath. "I do not think there will be any spinning for some time."

Conor of the Ulaid called to him a group of young warriors who guarded his mother's lands in the North. They were eager to please, hot for blood, and swift riders.

And they were not Red Branch.

He drove his chariot from Emain Macha on the heels of a rainstorm, alone but for two bodyguards on horses. He met the pack of youths in a glade of dripping branches and rotten leaf-litter. Down through the woods, the great lake of the Ulaid stretched to the horizon, its gray surface broken by white crests.

Conor looked around at these young ones, wild-haired and bright-eyed, and smiled. They had never triumphed in the difficult battle-feats that would admit them into the Ulaid Red Branch. They had not risen to the ranks of those hallowed fighters, which meant their loyalty was given to him alone. They did not care about traitors such as Naisi and his brothers, or the sly manipulations of Fergus and his spawn. Right now, Conor did not trust his Red Branch to do what he commanded.

The damp wind blew his ruff of foxtails over his chin and made his nose run. "I will arm you with swords as sharp as wolf teeth, and put the swiftest mounts beneath you. And then you will cross the border into Connacht."

The men's eyes blazed in the dim light of that bleak day, their smiles glinting.

The king paced before them, his head beginning to pound. "And you will find me Finnbennach, the great white bull, his hooves and ears painted red, and you will drive him and his herd back to me."

Then his lords would see he would not be defied by anyone, least of all the treacherous whore of Connacht. She had scorned him for the last time.

He had just discovered that Connacht still had no ruler, and that bull held the very essence of its kingship, the blessings of the gods. Parading that potent beast before his men would prove he was still in his strength and that Connacht was faltering.

Then would the Red Branch and his cattle-lords put their squabbling aside and rally behind him once more. And then they would take not just Connacht's heart, but the entire kingdom.

And all of Erin.

Maeve paced around the hearth in Ailill's guest-lodge, sumptuously hung now with woolen blankets and rugs, and gleaming with every variety of vessel that held mead, wine, and ale. Bronze, oiled wood, glass, and carved antler and bone cups and jugs were everywhere.

She slept here when she could not avoid it, though it was clear that the older Ailill liked drink more than rutting, and on the rare nights he was sober, she found she could bear her wifely duties by retreating into a great many thoughts.

In light of this news of Idath and Felim, she had now banished everyone else from the lodge but her husband and Garvan.

"We can muster more men than Idath." By the glow of the fire, Garvan clenched his fist as if it already hefted his sword. "Gods' balls, Maeve, why won't you let me give the order?"

Maeve clutched her horn beaker, looking at the reflection of one eye in the mead. It was almost all black, the pupil stark. Inside, she was endlessly falling, as if she could find no solid ground.

Memories of Ruán kept flashing through her: his hand over her breast, claiming her; his lips at her throat as she flung back her head. Most of all, the heat of him cradling her in the furs as the fire died. To stay there...to never have to face this betrayal...
"There is more to think about."

"There's no time for thinking!"

"Watch yourself, mac Aed." Ailill sprawled in a carved and cushioned chair he had brought from Laigin. His eyes were veined after another long night, and his thatch of brown hair was uncombed.

"With respect, my lord..." Garvan chewed the courtesy with distaste, "you could be readying your own men. The Galeóin could be training the others—"

"No." Maeve set the cup upon a dresser and gripped the oak top, looking at her feet. She welcomed the constriction of the hide breastplate, the laces holding her tight. Armor made her remember there was no room for anything else. Not memory. *Not him.* "This rebellion of Idath's has to be put down without any Laigin warriors at all."

Garvan halted his pacing. Ailill's hand hovered with the ale jug.

"I cannot give strength to the charge of Fraech's kin. I cannot use Laigin warriors to subdue Connacht-men. The people will turn against me, see me as a tyrant who sacrifices her own warriors for power. Or, worse, a weakling who will let Laigin overrun Connacht."

"This is madness!" Garvan thrust a hand through his dark hair. "Many lords support your cause and will be enraged that Idath broke a sacred peace. It will take time to gather their men, though, and if we wait here—"

"We won't wait here," Maeve said.

"But if we march to confront Idath..."

"Our war-band will be too small." Maeve's voice held the ice that was in her veins. They were coming to kill her. They would trap her here, as Innel sought to do.

Fighting a mounting panic, she lifted her face to them both. "Still I must do this. If we take the warriors from Cruachan, we might reach Idath's forces before they are ready. After all, they do not know that we know. We could at least hold them in the mountains until the other lords send for more men."

Garvan poked a finger at Ailill, forgetting himself. "How can you let her do this? You have hundreds of warriors with you!"

His eyes bleary in the firelight, Ailill took another glug of ale.

"My men did not come to die on Connacht swords." He wiped his beard. "If her bid to rule fails, I return to Laigin with my bride-price and my men. She knows that."

Garvan glared at them both. He did not possess that princely skill of looking to his own needs above all else.

Maeve turned so only Garvan could see her face, her eyes softening. "This alliance with Laigin was made to protect us against the Ulaid. I will not be blessed if I use it to subdue my own people."

"Blessed?" Garvan's face cleared and his voice dropped. "You do not mean this dream of the sídhe? Maeve, they are tricksters; you cannot buy their favor. And that is druid business. *You* are a warrior."

"I have to be more than that; I have to be a queen." She arched one eyebrow. "I have you to think like a warrior."

"Only to ignore me!"

It came to Maeve then that the fierce surge on the hilltop that made her take the sword—all racing blood, no thought at all— had set in motion something that was now out of her control.

Slowly, she touched her blade where it lay on the dresser. The stag on the hilt was poised to leap over streams and charge across hills. That was how it stayed ahead of the hunters, how it led its herd far away. "Some things are simple after all. The gods reward bravery and strength. This is all I can show them now."

"What . . . right before you die?" Garvan retorted.

Ailill choked on his ale. "Enough! You forget yourself."

Garvan sucked his lips in, nostrils flaring.

Maeve stepped up and clapped him on his solid shoulder. "Send messengers out for the muster. We leave at dawn in two days, no later. Turn out the stables. Every man must be mounted."

With a sigh, Garvan nodded.

"And send a man to Lord Donagh."

Garvan checked, peering at her. "Donagh has many warriors . . ."

"And holds sway over many lords. He's been keeping men ready for me for a long time."

Garvan's mouth quirked, and he touched his scarred brow

with grudging respect. "Glad to see you've not completely lost your wits, spitfire." He bounded down the stairs.

"You shouldn't let him be so cocky," Ailill grumbled.

Maeve's legs were unsteady now, and she sank onto a thick sheepskin rug, huddling by the fire. Miu scooted from beneath a nearby bed and rubbed about her shins. Her hand fell upon the cat's soft back. "I like straight talking."

"Yet you spun me a tale that was *not* entirely true, firebrand— about your hold over your people." Ailill leaned his cup against his ruddy cheek, his eyes hard. "I could have waited to unpack my carts, eh?"

Maeve pushed her wrists on her knees, drawing her back straight. "No," she said. "Your bet is not lost yet."

Before that day ended, Maeve walked the dark paths to the little cluster of huts where the iron- and bronze-smiths lived, set by the rushing stream. There, in the darkened forge, she picked up her new war-helm, turning it in the glow of the coals.

The iron dome was crested by a bronze raven with spread wings, the sign of the triple war goddesses Morrígan, Nemain... and Macha. She had asked Eithne's husband to begin work on it after Idath and Felim scorned her in the temple. Now she would wear it before them.

If only it did not hang so heavy in her hands.

Maeve appeared to Ruán without warning, his senses for once not picking up the blaze of her spirit approaching over the marsh.

He had been finding it hard to concentrate since their joining. This day he was endeavoring to net fish in a stream channel, unable to call them to his hands.

"I came to say farewell," she said.

Ruán pulled the empty net out and leaped over the channel to solid ground. She stood in the shelter of a brake of thorns and alders, their mass of stems providing a barrier against the cold breeze. Where it was still, he caught the faint scent of may blossoms.

Only then did he realize that Maeve's wildfire was no more than a glimmer.

He replied without thinking, his trews dripping over his bare feet. "I suppose you still have many lords to win to your cause." A stray thought darted in, wondering only now how she had won the prince Ailill. The sinking feeling was a surprise, as was his hollow voice, but it was hard to feel his own self clearly through his confusion.

Was she here to demand his secrets again? Or was she the Maeve who wrapped him in fire and then wept in his arms?

"I have ... a problem to deal with. Something I cannot avoid. I might be gone for ... some time."

Ruán grew still. Instead of a blaze, she was a guttering flame. The tremor in her voice brought her alive in his mind: her shoulders in a huddle, one hand beneath her lowered chin. *Did he see her?*

His fingers flexed, the softness of her skin still imprinted on them. His hand stirred toward her, then halted. With her sword, and bloody duels, and savage talk of Conor of the Ulaid, she summoned a world he no longer wanted to even imagine: the world of battle-lords that took his eyes.

He wiped his wet palm down his trews, his voice low. "You do not have to struggle and fight, Maeve. You could choose not to." He thought of her in the sídhe vision, heart beating fast behind the shield-line. And what was in her face when she looked beyond, away from death. The depths in her eyes that drew words from him now. "There is so much more—"

"There is certainly *less*," she snapped. "Like being ruled by warlords and their bloodlusts. *I will do anything to be free of that.*"

Her fierceness was a blow to his chest, and it stopped Ruán's tongue.

Maeve expelled her breath, taking a faltering step toward him. "This is not about you. I came to thank you. I just ... I had to come. To you."

Her light was wavering. So she feared his touch, in case it summoned more memories, and yet still drew closer to him. She was brave, that was certain, for he would not willingly expose *his* pain again. "Thank me for what?"

He felt her searching his face. "For the pleasure we both enjoyed, of course." Her laugh was strained. "It seems we did strike a bargain, druid."

Of all the things to pierce him, it was that catch in her voice— the swagger that was cracked beneath. He knew those cracks now, for he had felt them echo through his own flesh.

Her hands hesitated, then came to rest on his waist, sending a jolt through him. In a rush, Maeve pressed her body up against Ruán, and at last he was eclipsed by her familiar heat. It flowed around him until he could feel nothing else.

Words were stilted things between them. Strangely, it was in the melding of their flesh that he touched an essence of her that was greater than her body or mind.

Ruán cupped Maeve's cheek, frowning as he moved his thumb over the corner of her mouth. Her lips parted, and he tensed, torn. Draw forward; pull back.

Maeve broke the barrier of his thought, kissing the curve of his neck, then trailing her lips into the hollow at his throat. Ruán's shoulders lowered, his sigh almost silent. Perhaps he should see her only as flesh and pleasure, after all. That must be all she saw of him.

This time Maeve's body rose up to meet Ruán's, and she did not fall into darkness. Buried within her, he was engulfed by the scent of crushed grass from their bodies, sheltered in the lee of the thorns. Tiny blossoms were caught in her hair; he imagined them starring her red tresses.

With the cool sun on his bare back, Ruán let himself sink into her lushness. Leaf-bud was barely unfolding, but for the first time he felt the faint stirrings of life around him.

When Maeve gasped and bent back her chin, and he cried out as he tasted the salt at her throat, Ruán's sight was flooded with a light he had never seen before. A brilliant wave washed away from his body...their bodies...as if borne on their wild shouts.

Maeve lay catching her breath, a hand over her eyes. But, astonished, Ruán propped himself up on his wrists. That light...an intense silver...continued rushing away from them, lapping at the trees and rises in the ground like bright water. Eventually it disappeared, draining back into the pool from where it came.

Dazed, Ruán gazed around at the glimmers left on branch and leaf.

"Farewell," Maeve said in a whisper.

CHAPTER 15

LEAF-BUD

Four nights later, in the southern hills of Connacht, the leaders of the warrior bands sent to Cruachan by Maeve's supporters gathered about her. She had three hundred men, but she knew Idath and Felim would have at least double that.

She had ordered that there be no fires, so they broke bread and cold mutton in a damp glade just before dusk. The rest of the fighting men were invisible now, scattered through muddy woods at the foot of a steep ridge, sheltering under yew branches or patched leather and sleeping off the day on horseback.

Among a scatter of granite boulders, Garvan had scrawled a mess of lines in the soil at his feet, showing the rivers and hills that threaded Idath and Felim's territory where it bordered Mumu.

Maeve stood nearby, looking out as purple shadows flowed down from the sun-reddened hills far above and lapped the trees. Arguments rumbled on behind her.

"They will scout us out," one of the battle-leaders growled. "We can't conceal this many men."

"We can hide our trail among the trees along this river," Garvan replied. "Look."

"That way will take too long!"

"What does that matter?" someone else put in. "If we dance close to them and then away, we draw them out. As long as we cut them off from Cruachan, we can keep them busy. They won't turn their backs on us."

"Idath's and Felim's people have steadings high up the ridges; they will see us from far away. And we don't know where they are mustering, anyway."

Maeve stood with her hand on the pale birch tree beside her, straining for the answer in the grating of the branches above her head. She could not seem to turn around, her feet stuck in the loam as if her body longed to melt into the earth.

She should have told Ruán where she was going and asked to be filled with the otter anam—with any power at all.

Now, here in the gathering dark, she felt the urge to voice to him what she could not to anyone else. *I am afraid.* Her body responded with another cramp of loosened bowels. *Blast*, she answered herself. *Would you rather die?*

Sheer bloody-mindedness was all she had left.

Maeve loped back to the fire and snatched the birch stick from Garvan. When she looked down at the map, however, all the lines broke into meaningless shards. She cleared her throat. "We discovered their plans before they were ready, and they will also have to break cover when they come down from high ground. Wherever they muster, they can only approach Cruachan along one of these three valleys...one, two, or three...between these ridges."

"We are marching blind," one man grunted, squinting at the map.

Maeve leaned both hands on the stick. The eyes of the warriors were hard in the shadows, like wet stones. "We will know more when the scouts return."

Their doubt was clear. Turning away, Maeve fought to rein in her pulse. She was a woman, which meant she always had to win against two sides—the enemy and her own men.

The Source that welled through the trees had a different flavor from the lake. The oaks were ponderous, unlike the quicksilver dance of water. Slow-creeping roots spread into loam. Gnarled branches lifted themselves to sun and moon, bearing witness to long wheels of time.

Ruán spread his arms about a vast trunk, his cheek pressed to the bark. There must be a pulse of life force in the tree he would not hear, but could feel. The glimmers behind his eyes were growing more vivid, and starting to hint at shapes, as he had seen in the sídhe dance.

He had to hone that skill for himself now.

He breathed out. If he could slow his heart to the same pulse, then something of his essence—the little sparks that made him—might pass into the tree. And if they joined for a heartbeat and the tree opened to him...could *he* summon a trickle of Source through the veils? Stir the currents of sparks in the oak, make them resonate as one so the tree drew in Otherworld light as well as water?

His chest barely moved. The swift rush of his spirit must slow into a welling river...

A stick cracked, and Ruán's hand slipped. No humans came here for fear of the sídhe—except one. He spun about, blood rushing up his body. Then he tensed. It was not her.

The flame before him was bright white, where Maeve was always fiery. Ruán pressed against the oak. He was clad in brown deerskins, and the hazel trees were already putting out their buds. Surely he was well hidden.

He heard the intruder fall to his knees.

"Forest Lord, I see your shining light...*at last*..." The man's cracked voice held wonder. "I left offerings, and pray you will overlook my boldness in seeking you. It is only driven by desperation to protect my people."

Ruán struggled to understand. He was still dazed by the touch of the Source, not yet fully returned to his own flesh.

"I know Eochaid's daughter seeks your wisdom, and you do not harm her for this. Now I come. With my inner sight I have sought a godly spirit such as yours, this great brightness I now behold. Forgive that I dared leave the groves to tread the sacred ground that you have claimed. Hail, King of Trees, lord over this humble shoot of the oak!"

A druid. Ruán only now recognized his manner of speech, for he'd lived strange lives since he himself bore the oak staff. This man also thought him sídhe. No matter how hard a druid sought, few ever saw a Shining One, let alone spoke to them.

He was about to set this to rest when the old man made some violent movement, his robes flapping. "I would not break your peace, but that my own is broken. If she must be queen, I cannot decide this alone!"

Ruán's mouth closed.

"*Help me.* The visions grow more powerful but less clear. And now...the stag and hind are going to clash, and spill blood. But whose blood? Fraech would be a fine king, but dreams of *her* hammer on me and I do not understand the warning. If she dies, have I betrayed us? Is she tyrant or goddess? Tell me, that I may be a true seer for my people!"

I have come to say farewell.

She had tried to tell him, and Ruán had not heard her.

Blood will be spilled.

Ruán braced his hand on the oak, forcing his words to flow as once trained. This druid was god-touched, and knew more of Maeve than he himself could fathom. "What did you dream of her?"

"Ah...so much." The druid spoke aloud his visions, which had grown from baffling glimpses into more vivid pictures. "But it was the dream last night...*this one*..."

It spilled from the old man in a torrent.

The druid beheld Erin from above, as if he was an eagle. Below, what looked at first like a green island then changed into a great mound encircled by a rampart of stakes. Four enormous spears were set around its edge, as large as oaks, and on each was a vast shield, brightly painted and streaming pennants. Each shield bore the design of one of the four kingdoms: Mumu, Connacht, the Ulaid, and Laigin.

"And then I saw her...Maeve...galloping on a black horse around the outside of the rampart. Her red hair streamed from beneath a crested helm. Four times she circled the mound, and she struck every shield in turn with her great sword, and screamed a war-cry, and the shields rang as they do in battle."

Ruán was so immersed, he did not realize he was moving forward, step by step, to where the druid knelt.

Inside the ramparts, the druid recounted, he saw people. At first he thought it was a few hundred, but as he looked they became thousands—countless masses stretching back into the mist. All were enclosed in the rampart, and Maeve kept up her fierce war-cries, striking the shields.

"Are they her prisoners?" the druid demanded. "Her victims? I see them all glowing white, as the ghosts of the slain appear when they pass through my visions!"

The panic in the old man stirred Ruán's pity. He knew what it was like to bear this responsibility. Without realizing it, his hand landed upon the druid's shoulder.

Ruán's spirit had not yet returned to his body—the motes inside him had been flowing *out* to join with the tree—and so with that touch he left himself again without conscious volition. He spiraled down through the vision held in the druid's own stream of Source.

At last Ruán saw the vast shields, the flashing sword.

The countless souls of people flamed like torches below. And now, at the heart of the fort, he spied something else. A spring gushed from a rocky cleft on the highest point of the mount. He thought of the well the sídhe showed him on the hill, a doorway to the Otherworld. To Source.

It was then he saw Maeve.

She was inside the mound now, a towering figure on the crest beside the spring. Her armor was gone. Her hair was so long the red tendrils tangled in the bubbling water. The folds of her green dress pooled among the ferns at her bare feet. She held a gold cup in both hands.

As Ruán watched, Maeve dipped it into the spring and held the brimming cup above her head in triumph. Her blue eyes blazed straight at Ruán as if she could see him, and at that same moment she tipped the cup and spilled the contents out.

A waterfall poured all over the ground, igniting into a silver so brilliant Ruán could see nothing but that. It flooded the mound, and the people, grass, spears, and shields were all swept up by the glowing wave. It spread over the land before settling into a vast lake ringed by green shores. A pool of light at the heart of Erin— the same light he had seen in the hands of the sídhe.

The Source, gathered by Maeve. *She is blessed by the Otherworld?*

"She is blessed by the Otherworld." He spoke aloud without thinking, so faint it did not sound like a question anymore.

The druid exclaimed and clambered up. *"I knew it."* The old man's breath was labored. "I thank you. I saw it in the land, but was unsure. The long dark so gentle, leaf-bud unfurling early... I sensed it in the land!"

Ruán was mute. Gods, he had felt it, too, though he did not realize. A quickening in the woods, a surge through the earth. His heart skipped. What made this? He saw his limbs entwined with hers, their heads thrown back. The silver wave, rushing away. He was paralyzed. *Maeve.* His heart spoke it.

The druid was retreating. "I must return and await the out-come," the old man stammered. "But if this is meant to be, my lord, I pray she prevails."

Once he was gone, Ruán stormed back to his campfire and spread his arms to the sky. "*Now* you will tell me what I see! Is she a killer...or a life-bearer? *Tell me.*" His voice rebounded off the trees and collided with itself.

Outside that, silence.

Ruán stalked around the fire, kicking aside anything that met his feet, breaking branches and scattering coals. In his wrath, the glimpses of light and flickers of flame disappeared—he was blind again. "You told me her fate was her own, that if she heard the call of the lake I must not stop her. But now...I spoke out of turn... and I wove her fate with mine!"

His shoulders heaved as he faced the colder air away from the fire. He needed to know his heart clearly so he could find out how to turn it from her. Maeve, the dangerous queen; Maeve the ruthless ruler.

But that wasn't what he felt the night they let go all barriers be-tween them, and something of his spirit wound with hers. And now he had seen the Source in her *hands*. "And," he panted to the sídhe, "you have me talking to myself."

No answer came.

The sídhe told him that they did not rule people, that they had their own purpose in bringing forth the Source. This was not about them—it was about him. And that made him more afraid.

Ruán gnawed on it into the night, flinging sticks into the fire with great force, but in the face of their silence, he at last curled up in his deerskins beside the coals. As he dipped for a moment into unconsciousness, he glimpsed a young girl, her back slumped. Small and defeated, with tears falling on her hands.

Instinctively, Ruán reached for her, the movement startling him awake. He rolled on his back and then came bolt upright.

The druid's vision...Maeve was *protecting* all those souls as she raced around the mound. The sídhe showed her to him as a queen of blades, shields, and blood—despise it or not, there it was. And her people needed her.

At that moment all those hard thoughts fled. With a growl, Ruán buried his head in one hand and ground his fingers into his scalp. *Maeve.*

She was going to die.

Maeve ducked into her dark tent, waiting as the footsteps of her other warriors faded. Grasping the pole, she let her shoulders sag and her brow rest upon it.

Garvan slipped in behind, his hands brushing her hips. "Your nerves are getting the better of you, spitfire. You cannot break now. We are so close."

Though she could not see them, the high ridges of the hills out there still prickled her senses. Black buttresses rearing against the sky ... closing in on her. They were deep within Idath's and Felim's lands now—the scouts had finally spied the warriors that were coming to take Cruachan.

To kill her.

Garvan's breath was on her neck. "Your blood is battle-high, that's all. And we know the way to soothe *that.*" Cupping her belly, he drew her against him. "You have ignored me for too long, but a tumble is as good as a wrestle for cleansing the blood. You can fight me if you want to!"

Maeve stopped breathing. *You will not fight me*, Ruán had said.

She wrenched herself from Garvan's grip, backing against the leather. "The scouts have sighted Idath's men—*Connacht-men.* How can you be eager for this battle?"

Garvan cocked his head, the starlight falling through the tent flap tracing his puzzlement. "Because this is how it can be laid to rest, at last." He reached to drag her into a kiss. "*Now* you will triumph."

Maeve instinctively shied away, pulling against his hand.

Garvan's arm fell away. "You used to wrap those thighs about a different man every night and were the better for it," he muttered. "You get no relief, and you're a woman who needs it. Do you have some notion that to be queen you must hoard your strength? Lugh's balls, woman, what else are you saving yourself for?"

The words hung there, but Garvan could not miss the coiling up of Maeve's shoulders. *Sleep with him and be done with it,* she cried to herself. It would loosen her, settle her mind.

Garvan was peering at her. "Oh ..." He trailed off. "*No.* Not you."

She stared at him, eyes wide, her own thought echoing his. *No.* It could not be so. And yet she could bear no touch, not even Garvan's. At night, dreams conjured a tangible sense of Ruán's body fitting hers, curve to hollow. And she sank into him and there was no hardness, no control.

Garvan tugged a hand through his matted hair, his laugh strained. "Well well. I didn't know you were so fond of that thick-headed bull of yours."

He couldn't think she wanted ... Ailill?

Only then did Maeve see Garvan's bleak smile. He didn't believe that, but knew better than to press her. "If you are going soft at last, spitfire, I'd wait until the battle is over."

Maeve smiled back, unsteadily clapping his shoulder. "You are greater than a friend, closer than a bedmate." She gripped his bones. "You are my *kin.*"

Garvan looked at his feet. After a moment he shook his head and snorted as if amused at himself. "Damn you, Maeve."

"Now *that* is a brother speaking." She ruffled his forelock and filled her lungs. "And I know a better way to rid myself of nerves. We'll fly up the valley and take them by surprise."

Garvan's face fell. "We just agreed to dig in and hold them until the other lords send more men." He waved his finger near his ear. "Or am I hearing things?"

Maeve went to the tent flap and looked out, flexing her fingers. She was sick of grasping at nothing but fear. She hungered to grip a hilt instead, just so she could move—strike, run, ride. "Idath has committed to a path down the western ravine. We cannot let him change his mind."

"He won't! Remember Lugh's temple. His contempt for you makes him foolhardy. The moment the bastards see our barricade, they will become so enraged they will storm us straightaway. They hunger to rid themselves of you."

"Thank you for reminding me," Maeve said over her shoulder.

"So we hide our spearmen up the slopes as agreed, draw them into that narrow throat and then hit them as they charge."

Maeve lifted her head, tracing the black ridges up to a cleft of glittering sky. It was before moonrise, and the stars were bright. "I've changed my mind. Higher up, the valley spreads out again. We can march overnight to get there first, form up, and charge them as they sleep."

"Maeve, we don't have enough men! We must wait for the lords behind us."

"And what if they don't come?" She whirled to face him. *What if they abandon me, as all have before?* "Idath's men will pile upon us, climb the slopes and surround us. I *cannot* be trapped by them—never again!"

"Ach, enough!" Garvan swept past her out of the tent. "Perhaps daylight will return not just the scouts, but your senses." He stomped a few steps and turned, glowering. "You would have done better to couple with me, Maeve, because tomorrow this fool plan will kill us both!"

After he left, Maeve threw herself on her bedroll, an arm across her eyes.

Maeve dreamed of lips hovering above her own. She arched her neck to lift her mouth to his.

"Come." He did not touch her, his breath tantalizing. "You must come."

She reached to wind her fingers in the ruddy hair at his nape, to pull him down, anchor him to her.

"No. You have to let go, and *see*."

Let go? She thought he took hold of her hand, the urgency in his voice rousing her. "Now, Maeve." A tug came that was not flesh but an invisible hook in her chest and belly. The hook pulled, and she was lifted up and *out*. She floated.

The world outside the tent should be black, outlining the looming hills that were now imprinted on her mind. Those shadows hid men who breathed mist, readying themselves to kill her.

It was not dark, but glowing. She drifted through iridescent veils, currents of radiant air. His hand around her wrist pulled her skyward. He was also made of silver—a bright, soaring bird, his face hidden by streaming hair.

"Where do we go?" She was lifted by exhilaration.

"Higher."

She flew, weightless and free. Nothing was hurtful or heavy anymore. Shackles fell away—duty... fear. She could *be* this light forever, soar through it and feel it inside her. *It was real.* This was what she glimpsed past all of her darkness and pain. Ruán would fly with her, far over the swells of glowing sea and on past the stars. *Peace...*

"That is death, Maeve, and not your path yet. By the gods, open your eyes!"

Maeve was caught by the desperation in his voice. Only then did she remember her name. It brought back to her the density of her own body, her pulse. She was Maeve of Connacht. Here, now.

She and Ruán were treading on the earth again, then, climbing the spur of a hill. Where their feet tore the undergrowth, a familiar scent rose, musty and wet. Dark slopes fell away around them; the spangled sky spread above. Ruán's hair blew in the wind, its warm hue turned black by night.

He dragged her to the crest and turned. She already knew the dips beneath his cheekbones, the little tilt at the corner of his lips.

Her fingers touched the familiar sweep of tendons between neck and shoulder, and traced the dark scar below his throat.

But for the first time, she now looked into his eyes. They were long, the lower lid straight across, the arch a narrowed sweep, as if they peered intently, saw deeply. They had gathered the moonlight, the irises glowing so she could see no other color.

"You came," she breathed. "My hurt brought you." Every nerve and muscle reached for him, and she clung to his solid-seeming body and claimed his mouth as if she was starving.

He broke away, pushing her from him. "*Look up,*" he demanded. "I cannot stay long. I am already drawn back…"

Forcing her attention to sharpen, Maeve bent back her head and gasped. Where stars had swung like steady lamps, they were now falling, a shower of them streaking across the sky. And then more came, trailing threads of fire before winking out.

They arced down to the dark horizon, and took her gaze with them.

Three ridges reached out from higher mountains beyond, the ravines between threaded by silver streams. Maeve remembered the scratches in the ground: three valleys.

The western ravine in which her men now camped was speckled with light, as if the falling stars had come to rest there. *Campfires?* She had forbidden all fires.

Ruán breathed into her ear. "They are men, each one a soul-light."

Source, burning in a human spirit. The druids spoke of it.

There were two whirlpools of stars in that valley, one Maeve's own camp of Connacht-men, the other farther up—Idath's and Felim's warriors, who waited for her.

"There is no time!" Ruán cried. "Have courage and seek farther!" His arm stretched black against the rising moon.

Maeve's head lifted to the east, and her sight cleared. *There.* A tide of flame swept down the deserted eastern valley. Hidden men, hundreds more.

"It is not brightness, but death, Maeve!"

Shock shivered through her, and she was falling. She spun like a broken bird and plunged into that far river of stars. And it was not light but *black*, filled with the stealthy creep of bodies and the hiss of harsh voices. She heard the jingle of weapons and glimpsed men crouching, shoulders swathed in shaggy furs.

Maeve jolted awake.

All the hairs on her neck and arms had lifted, and her pulse thundered. She flipped onto hands and knees, clawing open the tent flap and throwing herself outside. She got to her feet, shaking her head to rid herself of that terrible dream. A nightmare, that's all it was.

Panting, she gazed at the stars. *Are you so desperate for his body that you would conjure this?* She paced, gulping the icy air, then stopped. Not his body. Gods, not his body alone. The twist in her breast was unfamiliar. She put her hand to it...and then something caught her eye.

Maeve glanced up.

Where all had before been still, streaks of light now filled the whole sky—a hail of stars falling all across the horizon.

She stopped breathing and forgot all else.

CHAPTER 16

"Idath and Felim have split their men." Maeve pressed her tongue against her teeth to moisten her parched mouth. "They field two forces, not one."

Her commanders had been dragged from their beds, some still yawning, others scowling blearily.

Maeve shifted on her haunches among the wet ferns by a tumbling stream, chosen to cover their voices in the clear night air.

"The first war-band was to tempt us up the valley. While they hold us, the second is circling to fall upon us from behind."

A voice rumbled from the dark beneath the overhanging trees. "The scouts did not report this."

"They didn't go far enough. Idath has been clever. He must have sent the others out days ago along a hidden path. He knew we would chase after the first battle-group, giving the second time to outflank us. We have to be clever now, too." She peered into the shadows, picking out each man in turn. "We must strike camp, tonight, and head *across* the ridges. Then we fall upon their larger force at dawn."

Mutters and curses. "It is madness to risk this in the dark!"

"The moon has just risen," she replied, "and the hills are bare heather higher up. We have the light. There are deer-paths everywhere."

"We cannot make exhausted men fight after scrambling over the hills."

Maeve licked her cracked lips. "We have the advantage of surprise—and we'll be charging down from higher ground." She arched a brow with a cold smile. "Are your men really such weaklings, Lonan? Their blood should be tinder, easily set alight. Is that not so?"

Lonan pursed his lips. "Of course that is so. My lord will not have it said his warriors shirk from battle or hardship."

The rumbling voice broke in. "But how do you *know* any of this?"

Maeve uncurled to her feet, lifting her chin. She had donned her war-helm, the raven outlined by moonlight. "The sídhe sent me a dream. They showed me these stars that fly across the sky and burn with fire. I dreamed them, and now they come. They are the sign!" She flung up her hand, and another scatter of stars streaked across the black, as they had been doing on and off since she roused her men.

Their mouths hung open, and there was awe in their eyes when they lowered from the sky to her face.

"I took my sword from the sídhe veils. They made me strong enough to kill a man twice my size and win over many chiefs, including your own. So will *you* now question *me*—and the sacred message of the Shining Ones?"

Garvan broke the silence. "She is Macha of the Red Hair," he said softly. "She is the strength the Ulaid once possessed, now reborn to us. If the war goddess speaks in dreams, do we not listen?"

In the end they did.

⊠

The cold shadows of the night lightened to gray.

Her hands spread on the rocks, Maeve gazed down into the eastern valley. *There.*

Stray glints of metal, as dull light combed the forest. A murmuring like wind, though the budding leaves hung still and dripping on the branches in the dawn. Hundreds of men were bedded down in the undergrowth.

"All the gods above," Garvan breathed next to her.

Maeve caught the eyes of the two warriors who had argued against her. One bent his dark whiskers in a respectful nod. Lonan's smile was feral as he gestured to his warriors crouched behind them in the rocks. In silence, they reached for their packs.

Maeve's men had stowed away every piece of metal—buckles, brooches, and armbands—and muffled spear-tips, sword-fittings, and daggers in torn cloaks. Now, they unwrapped their weapons with knuckles bloodied by that cold scramble up and down stony paths in the night. A small group had been left to hold the western valley behind a barrier of felled trees, throwing spears in all directions to convince the enemy they were still there in force.

Beside Maeve, Garvan laid his sword along his knee and smoothed the edge. All the humor had fled his battered face. His features hardened, the warrior-self turning inward to gather strength. Maeve watched the transformation of the Garvan she knew into one she did not. Before her the hound who scrapped playfully with her became a lean dark wolf, his eyes intense and glowing.

Dry-mouthed, she glanced along the line of warriors as they stealthily armed up. It did not matter they had gained no sleep. Facing death, their blood quickened anyway, hearts pumping. They strapped and laced their clothes tight, bound their hair and muttered prayers.

Soon they would be diving into chaos. For some those moments would carry them through the barrier of Thisworld into the Otherworld and they would barely notice, charging on through a timeless place, spears flying through a colorless sky.

They would either live, or feast at the table of the gods. There was no reason for them to fear. *Utter freedom.*

Maeve tasted it, envied it. For her belly still gurgled, and she placed a fist on it, breathing out. She feared not only fighting, but the gods themselves. She knew they would not welcome her to the Blessed Isles—how could they know her, when she had closed her heart against the sídhe years ago, turned her face from the goddesses in the temples?

But Ruán came for her.

"Come," she ordered through cold lips, clinging to that hope.

As the dull light washed into gold, a flock of spears took flight. Iron beaks glittered, wood shafts hissed.

The deadly lances struck sleeping bodies rolled in hides, slashed through tents and skewered the men rising from their beds, yawning. Screams and shouts floated up from the valley bottom as Maeve's war-band all rose to their feet.

A sliver of bloody sun broke over the rim of the hills. Maeve thrust her sword into the air along with all the warriors around her. "Connacht! Connacht!" the men began shrieking.

Guilt wove a dark thread through Maeve—they were all of Connacht. Then she reminded herself that these warriors below had broken a sacred peace to betray fellow tribesmen. This was not about her alone, for Idath knew that many Connacht warriors supported her and would be drawn here to fight.

The guilt remained.

She had to force her way past it now. Live, or die. As she prepared to charge, however, Garvan slammed an arm across her chest. "*You stay back.*" Those wild eyes were not the Garvan she knew. His face was high-blooded, sweat already beading his lip and wetting his dark mane.

Another volley of spears staked scores of Idath's men as they scrambled for cover among the trees and rocks. Maeve's swordsmen were beating a storm on their shields, opening their throats to the dawn sky as they worked themselves into a frenzy before they ran.

Maeve swung her sword up so it locked on Garvan's hilt.

"If you die, this is for nothing," he snarled.

If I do not show bravery, I deserve to. She had to do something before she retched all over his feet. She forced Garvan's blade down and dragged the raven helmet from her head, raking her hair out.

"They will crawl over each other to get to you." Garvan's horror was clear. "*You* are their ultimate prize!"

Yes. She could not forget the cold trail of the knife that slit her dress. But Idath would do worse—give her as a slave to men. A stab of fury thrust the guilt aside and made her at last catch alight. "You called me Macha of the Red Hair, brother. How can the men believe it if they don't see me fight?" Her grin was savage, her blood now racing. "You can cover me, though."

Turning her back on Garvan, she danced out before her warriors, flinging her unbound hair into a flurry, sword aloft. "Connacht! Connacht!" They must catch alight with her or they would die.

Everywhere the men paused in the grip of their own battle-fury, staring at her with white eyes. Instantly, the battle-chant changed, rising and falling in waves. "Macha! Macha!"

The cry pounded Maeve's body, broke her down, possessed her. Garvan hesitated and then gave in to his madness, swinging his sword about his head with a feral grin, his shout merging with all the others.

Maeve put her head back with eyes closed, the flame of the battle-frenzy licking at the edges of awareness. Her sword-arm was on fire, and finally something was pure and bright.

Live, or die.

And so the war-goddess charged down the slope, her hair a flying banner to lead the way. The hillside seemed to collapse around her as men flung themselves into a shrieking tide, and she was caught in the flood and there was no going back.

Remember who you are. As she ran, Maeve's heart screamed the warning.

Surrounded by the churning limbs of men, it was easy to feel she *was* them, arms bundled with sinew, muscled thighs pumping. But that way, she would die.

You are something else. Maeve tried to summon it, until the charge broke upon the enemy with a crash, and she was flung into a dark world that stank of blood and she forgot.

She was sucked into a maelstrom. Shrieks and bellows hammered her ears. Bright iron flashed through a morass of dark hair and fur, leather and bloodied flesh. Spears reared and plunged all around her, the claws of a many-headed beast.

Wildly, Maeve jabbed beneath the tangle of arms, bumping Garvan as he fought to shield her. Reflexes made her duck whenever anything came at her, her feet sliding in mud. The roars of fury and pain were deafening. Her blade met metal and toughened leather, and sometimes the give of flesh or bite of bone, but she was snarling to survive and had no room to absorb it.

A mist of blood thickened the air. It coated her, until she felt she was seeping into that stink, ankle-deep in filth. A hilt cracked her skull and she staggered, blinded by agony. Garvan shrieked and hacked her attacker down. "Around her!" he cried to the men nearby. "Back-to-back!"

They clustered in, heaving and grunting as they sought room to wield their blades. Maeve saw a dripping axe descending and jabbed up in panic, snapping the tendons of the wrist that braced it. Unable to bring her sword about in the crush, she dragged her dagger from her belt and stuck the howling axeman in the belly.

Blows were being turned from her neck and back by the men around her. "No," she panted. She could not die here, crushed by male bodies.

Let go, Maeve. She heard Ruán's voice again.

Light. Breathe light...surrender. She had to melt outward and expand her senses, not coil up in panic. She closed her eyes, imagining. There...the glow of her dream-flight with Ruán. The shining currents that held her when she fought Innel. *She remembered.* All went silent as she slipped under bright water.

Time slowed.

The trees over the men's heads flickered with silver fire. The movements of the warriors were waves of radiance, breaking into crests. Her men needed her to fill them, lift them.

Maeve darted from Garvan's side, twirling beneath the blows of these lumbering men, the clumsy bludgeon of blades. Ahead was a barrow topped by a crumbling cairn, a grim tomb all the men were avoiding.

Sweeping up a lance, she bounded up the cairn. "To me!" she shrieked. "Me!" Holding the spear two-handed, she thrust it above her head, her hair tangled around the shaft like a scarlet battle-banner.

Her men raised their faces and saw their goddess rallying them to victory, and a brilliant tide of light washed over them. "Macha!" they screamed.

Yowling in fury, the enemy warriors also saw her and came running, but Garvan and his swordmates were there before them.

The two tides met, and molten waves crashed about Maeve's feet. She leaped down into that flood, every nerve exquisitely alive.

From the corner of her eye she glimpsed an enemy warrior, his intent to strike somehow sending out a flare of light before he even moved. She saw him coming and was already turning. His arm was only just bracing itself when Maeve stuck him in the hollow of his throat, and he fell at her feet.

Panting, she realized the chants of her war-band had changed again. They were now screaming her own name. "Maeve of the Red Hair! Maeve!" Their frenzy filled her, and her scalp rippled, the hairs on her neck standing up.

Just then a distant sound caught her attention—a baying like hounds at the hunt. The wonder spread among her men. Knee-deep in gore, the warriors of Cruachan lifted faces painted with blood, gulping the clearer air above the slaughter.

"The other lords are come!"

It sheared like a wind across the valley.

"Donagh's men, and Cormac's! They come in their hundreds!"

Maeve hobbled through the remains of Idath's camp, stepping around bodies with spears sticking out of them. The muscles in her back and thighs cramped. She nudged someone's pack over and dug out a water-flask. The stream nearby was choked with bodies, the muddy waters red in the sunlight that now shafted into the valley.

Maeve held the flask, making herself gaze at them. The victory was hollow, for the slaying of men could never be a triumph. Men who would not come back to their families now, their eyes empty. How could this be triumph?

Warriors were going to die in any battle for the kingship, she reminded herself, her hands shaking as she lifted the flask to drink.

But I vowed to bring peace.

And she would have sought it, proving herself through other strengths, if Idath had not betrayed her.

Back and forth her thoughts went as she drank with unseeing eyes and wiped her mouth. She felt sick. If she had not taken the sword...

"Maeve." Garvan was making his way across the piles of shredded tents.

All around him warriors dug through abandoned belongings for weapons. Others were hacking off enemy heads. Dead warriors must be honored, their skulls staked outside the houses to gift their strength to those brave enough to kill them.

Garvan's face was a mask of gore, his hair twined into stiff hanks. "Felim and Ardal are dead." He was battle-hoarse. Maeve handed him the flask and he splashed his face. "We captured Idath—and Fraech."

Maeve rubbed her gritty eyes, her ears still ringing from so many shouts and the clang of iron. She could not rid her tongue of the taste of copper. "I will deal with them now." She winced as she fingered the cut on her scalp.

Garvan had bound a wound on his forearm, but another on his thigh streaked his torn trews with blood. "Rest first. I'll bring Idath to you tomorrow—"

"No. Our men are still chasing the ones who ran. The battle goes on."

"So?"

"The brethim laws. Warriors can only kill in battle—druids alone take the lives of undefended men." There was a deadness in her voice. "If I take Idath home alive, he might only be banished, and so remain a danger to us all."

She limped away, and Garvan fell into step beside her. "The men won't like to see a defeated lord killed in cold blood, spitfire—no matter how traitorous."

Her gaze roamed over the twisted figures of the dead. *Idath did this*, she tried to hammer into herself. If he lived, it would happen again, and more men would continue to die, until the whole kingdom was drawn into that fight. An end had to be made this day— it had to. "The only oath I took was to protect my people from greedy bastards like him. I will give him his chance, but if he doesn't take it, the warriors have to know I am stronger than any man."

Amid a pack of filthy, blood-streaked warriors, Maeve watched as Idath and Fraech were forced to their knees. Their hands were deliberately left unbound, for she would not shame them and thereby stir pity among the men. Hefty fighters pinned each one with a hand on the shoulder instead.

Idath had put aside his rich furs and embroidered robes. His rotund belly was squeezed into a mail-shirt, the greased rings dark with blood. Gray hair straggled from a balding pate. Beneath a cut on the brow and a black eye, he was still scowling.

Fraech's brown hair had escaped its braids and hung lank with sweat. His back was proud, though, and he folded his arms behind him, staring through all the baying warriors into the distance, green eyes showing nothing.

Maeve nodded at Garvan, who stepped before Idath and raised his voice to carry. "You broke a sacred peace, coming to attack Connacht-men joined as brothers under druid rule. You will now swear allegiance to the victor of this field—Maeve, daughter of Eochaid, King of Connacht—and accept her as your overlord."

Idath sneered. "By Manannán's breath I will not." Fraech's gaze slid toward his father. "Did you not hear me?" Idath hissed at Garvan, avoiding Maeve's eyes. "I will never serve that lying, thieving *bitch*. She might have cast her enchantments over you, but she'll never enslave *me*."

Fraech colored and kept his attention on the trees by the river.

Maeve was distracted by the swiftness of his breathing, which his stony face did not betray. Was he afraid, or did his father's behavior disturb him that much?

She withdrew her sword and approached Idath. "I gained this blade by the favor of the sídhe and my father's spirit. He chose me." She gestured at the guards to release Idath, and extended her sword toward him. "You have one last chance to swear on it."

Idath's mouth twisted, and he hawked and spat at her. His phlegm dribbled down Maeve's trews, mixing with the crust of blood as he struggled to his feet. "I am Idath, son of Gabran! I will never subject myself to this traitorous, kin-slaying whore!"

Maeve's back stiffened. Her gaze rose to his face.

The invisible armor she summoned before the battle must still cloak her, for she felt no fear now, only a burning will to never be subject to a man like him again.

Idath was clenching his hands, ready to snap. She must goad him. She curled her lip. "The only traitor I see is the one who murdered his own clan, not just out of greed, but utter stupidity."

Idath spluttered and began to turn purple. The slightest gesture to strike was enough, and so it came. Idath curled a fist and braced his legs, then lunged.

A jolt went through Maeve, and with a final spurt of energy she strained her leg once more to throw herself unexpectedly to the side. Taken by surprise, Idath unbalanced, flailing. Maeve gritted her teeth past the pain, flicking her wrist back on itself in a clever sword-feat she learned among the Ulaid. It used up the dregs of her strength, but with a sudden pivot her blade nicked the vein in Idath's neck.

He toppled to his knees, his hand clapped to his throat, his eyes wide.

Fraech choked back a cry and caught his father, lowering him to the ground. Idath groped the wound, blood pouring between his fingers. His fading gasps were drowned out by the mutters of the warriors. No one moved until those faint noises stopped and Fraech's murmurs ceased.

Maeve faced the men with head up, hiding her trembling, her palm slick around her hilt. "I swore to make our kingdom strong by forging us as *one*. This is the vow Idath broke." Her voice cracked and she had to swallow again. "Every man of his still alive will be spared. Those who swear to me will be forgiven, and those who refuse will be subject to druid judgment. That is all."

Fraech's head was bent over his father, who was now motionless in his arms.

Exhaustion descended over Maeve as she forced her legs to limp to a lone ash tree beside Idath's camp. The mutters of her men behind her turned into exclamations and it was a tense few moments as some of them argued among themselves.

Maeve did not look over. After a while the tone lightened, the few voices of dissent silenced. They remembered the taste of glory, that they lived to feast and drink, and bed their women again. The banter resumed as they drifted away, seeking more spoils.

Garvan slipped to her side. "Fraech?"

Maeve kneaded her cramping thigh where the old wound had weakened the muscle. "I will see him when I have cleaned myself up. At sunset—but this time bind his hands."

Maeve and Fraech walked along the stream, trailed by Garvan a step behind with a drawn sword.

Trails of fire-smoke now blended with the haze of dusk. Maeve took a breath of churned ferns and the fresh scent of water rushing over rocks to clear her nostrils of blood. She still hobbled from the leap that killed Idath, her brow pummeled by the aftershock of the hilt-strike. No one spoke of the pains that dogged a warrior *after* battle.

Perhaps because relief lightened everything—for them.

She stole a glance at Fraech. He was tall and graceful, walking with such nobility he didn't look as if his hands were bound behind him at all. Whenever his face sagged into grief, he firmed his mouth, head up.

She blinked and tried to straighten her aching neck, too. Her promise to her people was to heal Connacht rifts. Dazed, she prized her cracked lips apart. "Most of your warriors surrendered. And . . . a hundred deaths do not fracture a people."

Fraech came to a halt, and Maeve faced him. "Everything your father and uncle said about me was a lie, and before Lugh in his temple, you knew it. I would not have attacked you. I would have been true. But the sword god bore witness to their treachery, and this was his punishment."

Fraech searched her raw, bruised face. There was no fury in his eyes; perhaps he possessed the wisdom his sire lacked. "My instincts believe you." He was red-eyed from smoke and hoarse from battle. "This way was not my choice, but my father owned my loyalty."

Maeve nodded, kicking pebbles from the stream-bank to dislodge them. She bent and gathered the stones, intently rubbing the mud away and splitting them between her fists. "I have the loyalty of many lords." She lifted one hand. "You have the rest. If we fight, we break Connacht apart." She flung both handfuls into a pool in the stream beside them. They pocked the surface, the rings shattering the reflection. "Or . . . we stay one." She looked up at him. "Swear allegiance to me now and I'll make you my war-leader."

Fraech's breath hissed out. *"What?"*

Maeve squinted at him through her headache. "You fought honorably, and I spared you. I can rise above this for the good of the people." She pushed back her matted hair with a wry smile.

Something kindled in his young face, smoothing the etchings of pain. "You toy with me." His voice was unsteady.

"I don't have that in me right now." She scrubbed her palms on her thighs, resuming their walk. "I cannot kill you, for you are a brilliant fighter and well loved. People will say you had no choice but to follow your father. I can't let you go, either, for men will rally to you, and we'll be mired in the same problem." She cocked her head, loosing a smile that startled him. "So what can *you* rise to, cousin?"

His face went still for a moment, before his nose cut the air. "Peace, yes. I have my father's honor to renew."

"Good, but that is still not enough. I do not want men whispering that I cheated your clan of the kingship." Flipping her dagger out, Maeve stepped behind him and with one swipe cut his leather bonds.

Garvan looked at Fraech's unbound hands and sighed through his nose, leaning his sword over his shoulder.

Maeve glanced at him, then faced Fraech. "So, cousin, I will also name you my heir, to rule after me."

As the words left her, Maeve was surprised by a pang of yearning, to let go now of something that already lay so heavy upon her. *Only when they are safe; when we are all safe.*

Fraech's teeth showed between his lips, half smile, half snarl of disbelief. "You will give me everything we fought for?"

"To rule *after* me. Either endure a momentary defeat, or a total defeat—though I sense you have a wisdom lacking in all those old war-lords put together." She reached out in the fashion of a warrior hand-clasp.

Fraech stared at her arm, then gripped her wrist. Relief washed across his features, making him look even younger, his green eyes vivid. "If we'd known you were mad, cousin, we would have challenged you long ago."

That was too raw. They dropped the clasp, and Maeve pointed to the barrow of stones. "Before your ancestors and every man on this field, you will now swear allegiance to me on your clan, your honor, and your place beside the gods on the Blessed Isles. If you break this, you lose the glory of your *own* name now." She appraised him, her head pounding more urgently. "I hazard a guess you treasure that rather dearly, cousin Fraech." She needed her bedroll. She needed to collapse.

Fraech loped straight to the barrow and began to climb the stones.

By the time darkness fell that night, Maeve's tent had become a safe womb, not a trap. She listened to the soaring sounds of the warrior laments. Sometimes the songs were mournful, like wolf howls...indeed she wondered if the wolves joined in, far away.

Beyond that came snatches of revelry. The victors had built enormous bonfires to spew out plumes of sparks, forcing back death and darkness. Their shouts soon became drunk with relief, and the reek of burned bodies was overlaid by the homely scents of roast deer and juniper smoke.

Garvan crawled in and flopped on his back beside her, stinking of burned wood and ale. "They will curse my name when I turf them out of their bedrolls at dawn."

"Why dawn?" Maeve mumbled, her eyes drooping. She thought she might never move again.

Garvan's reply wound into Maeve's dream as she began to fall. "Because you have a king's hall to claim."

CHAPTER 17

The wind whipped up the eastern sea, slapping spray over Cúchulainn and Ferdia where they clung to the rocks. The wild gusts tore at their cloaks and tried to push them over. Out on the ocean, the iron-gray of the clouds merged with the water.

"You cannot go in this weather," the Hound growled, eyeing the boat bobbing in a cleft in the low cliffs. It was a long, leaf-shaped curragh of tarred hides and hazel frame—light enough to fly over swells but still seeming fragile against those broken waves.

Fishermen were packing Ferdia's belongings between the oar-benches; another lashed the sail to the mast. Cúchulainn's war-spoils had bought these men to deliver Ferdia alive to the stronghold of Skatha on an island off the coast of Alba, across the straits.

"We've got one excuse to explain my disappearance, and a flimsy one at that. If we back out now, we'll only rouse the king's suspicions." Ferdia stretched his mouth in a grin that would not fool Cúchulainn. "First a sore saddle-arse, now I have days of puking to look forward to, before being tossed into that den of cubs all stinking of grease and trying to shave my eyebrows off with a sword. Oh, the joy."

Skatha, a warrior-queen, ran a famous battle school on her island. Warriors traveled there from the Amber Coast, Britain, and Gaul, and even Roman lands. Like an armored spider, Skatha sat at the heart of this web. She might have news of the sons of Usnech if they had surfaced in Alba.

"I should go to Skatha," the Hound argued. "You've been scouring Erin for Naisi and his brothers for moons. You haven't slept in one place for more than a few nights."

Ferdia handed a bundle of spears to one of the fishermen. "If you go, Cú, those bloodthirsty pups will be falling all over themselves to take the head of the great Champion of the Ulaid."

Cúchulainn stared at the waves, nostrils flexing. What he could smell on this wind, Ferdia did not know, but the Hound's body unconsciously strained toward the east across the ocean. It was unbearable, Ferdia knew: the loyal sons of Usnech—*Red Branch heroes*—exiled in Alba among hostile tribes. Ferdia saw in Cúchulainn's face the longing to take wing, swoop down, and bear them to safety. But even the great Hound of Cullen did not possess that power.

A stray thought darted through Ferdia. *But I can. I can bring them back in glory.* Face hot, he crushed that. "We were so close to disaster at Samhain," he reminded Cúchulainn. "You have to stay and keep the peace. If Illan and Fiacra can come to blows over Naisi, the rot *is* weakening us. Gods, that's like you and me fighting each other!"

Cúchulainn frowned as a surge knocked the boat against the rocks. "Do not say such things, even in jest. You tempt the gods to mischief."

Ferdia tossed the last pack into the hull, his stomach already beginning to churn. "If the king has sent so many trackers onto trade ships now, he also believes the brothers have abandoned Erin."

"Then we must get to them before he does!" Cúchulainn's outburst made all the fishermen look up. Cúchulainn turned Ferdia a few steps away over the rocks, his blue eyes dulled by the low, racing clouds. "I have never seen Conor's mind fracture like this," he whispered, shaking his golden head. "How is it possible this danger can be wrought by a maiden, a child?"

It was wrought by Conor.

Not for the first time, another thought rose in Ferdia—a rebellion to topple the king. Yet whenever he let it in, he saw fire over the hills of Emain Macha, a great blaze reflecting on the clouds.

Many chiefs supported Conor because of the cunning web of obligations he had woven over the years. Under him, they retained their petty powers, even if it meant turning a blind eye to his excesses. Unseat Conor, and war would break out in the Ulaid. The other three kingdoms would watch hungrily while the most powerful in Erin tore itself apart, and then dart in to gobble up the scraps.

There was a pale line about Cúchulainn's mouth. He was unshaven, the stubble pale, and there were rings beneath his eyes. Such fears could tarnish even the gold of the great Hound. "And if we think this is bad, brother, what calamity will befall us if he manages to kill them?"

Grazing nearby, the Hound's gray stallion raised its head and whinnied, tied into Cúchulainn's heart as always. It was a bugle of alarm, and Ferdia's tender belly flipped over once more.

Cúchulainn glanced at his horse, his forehead plowed with furrows. "For thirty years Conor was a good king. Selfish and wily, yes, but he built up the Ulaid, our wealth and strength. *He was a builder.* Now . . ." His gaze sharpened on his friend. "Now, you must go, and outrun this wind." He drew Ferdia into a hard embrace. "Take care of you as you would of me," he murmured.

That was always their farewell.

⚬

Maeve heard the cheering from afar.

Scouts had gone ahead to Cruachan, and as she trotted through the fields on Meallán's back she could see that the ramparts around all the mounds were lined with people. Vivid cloaks and blankets fluttered from the walls as makeshift banners.

She glimpsed the royal standard of Connacht, a white eagle on blue, hanging from the gate-towers of the warrior and king's hall, and her heart soared with its outstretched wings. Horns blared, their bronze throats singing the war-band home.

Maeve had kept herself at the rear of the column. She wanted to be among the men—they had won this day, and she felt reluctant to take any glory. It was enough to be jostled by smelly horses and even smellier fighters, her stained clothes blending with everyone else's. Her hair was tucked beneath her grimy helmet, her face obscured by filth.

The bolder warriors teased her, their horses shouldering Meallán. The shy ones watched her with awe in their eyes. She felt almost like a child again, riding back with the hunters, dirty and tired from her escapades in the woods.

One of them.

Many men had wounds bandaged with dirty linen. At the back, carts carried those who could not ride and bodies for loved ones to burn. Despite this, the warriors sang battle-chants as they ducked beneath the overhang of trees along the river.

Greenery had softened the stark brown landscape now, leaves

pushing through a riot of white blossoms on the thorns. Maeve brushed the tiny flowers as she passed, their heady smell drawing her mind from its cocoon.

She slowed her horse, dropping back.

The land had burst into life. Leaf-bud *had* come early. A subtle rush ran through the earth beneath, like an underground stream.

Shading her eyes, Maeve caught sight of the herders who had gathered from the steadings to watch the war-band pass. When younger, she had shared a bowl of pottage many times at the house of Aengus.

Spurring her horse, she sent Meallán along a narrow path that led between the little ridged barley fields. Green shoots were already spearing up from the turned earth, and the boggy meadows along the streams were sprouting new grass.

Maeve sought out Aengus and his family, tugging off her helmet outside their thatched hut. His women broke into awkward curtsies, clutching the hands of their children, all of them gaping at her bloodstained finery.

"Is it true the season has broken early?" she breathed.

Aengus had come in from the fields with his brother, a hoe across his broad shoulders. "Aye, the warmth brought the crop so fast, lady, we are planting more. And the hay sprouts like Davin's head!" Aengus ruffled the flaxen hair of a small boy clinging to his legs. "None remember it like this."

It caught Maeve under the ribs. *Could it be?* Or was she still in that dream?

She pointed at the wicker pens beside the hut, dotted with sheep. "You have your ewes gathered in, though, not out in the pasture."

Aengus squinted, sucking his teeth. "Aye, for they are bearing twins—every one. We have to turn out every night to help some through the birthing."

His plain words rang through her. "And the calves?"

Aengus's brother spread a callused hand, his palm earth-stained. "Twins up and down the valley, lady, and all the herders mad with it."

She wanted to feel bad for them being out all night in rain birthing lambs and calves. She wanted to, but she could not. Thanking them in a husky voice, she turned Meallán back to the procession of warriors.

Garvan had pulled off the track and was waiting for her. "Spitfire, if you can race down a hill into all those swords, you can damn well lead the men through a bit of cheering." He grinned, pushing up his helmet with his sword-hilt.

Maeve nodded, but she wasn't listening. Her mind was soaring ahead, seeking one man above all the hundreds of people now massed around Cruachan.

Garvan insisted she ride all the way along the track through the gold-thatched houses, swept along by a river of overwrought women and children flinging themselves at their men. Maeve knew it should fill her up like a draft of mead, but she could barely focus on their glowing faces, their tears and laughter.

She saw Garvan being pulled off his horse by one of his lovers, and when he was distracted with a kiss, Maeve took her chance. She needed to soak this up alone . . . to know it was real.

Was the power hers, at last—to hold her, to fill her?

She kneed Meallán onto one of the empty paths behind the houses and headed for the stables, sliding from his back in one of the stalls. A shower of windflowers fell from her hair—sticky-fingered children had been throwing them from the earth ramparts. She tossed the reins around a post, patted her stallion, and ignoring the strain in her muscles, vaulted over the rail and bounded out the door.

Outside, Maeve was enveloped in light, the sun catching on all the puddles, wet timber, and soaking thatch. Light . . . lifting her up, as it did at Ruán's side. She loped along the silent pathways away from the king's hall, racing up the green mound of the temple of Lugh.

There were druids before the golden shield. "Where...is...
Tiernan?" she gasped, holding her side.

One pointed. "He is waiting for you, lady, at the gate to the
king's hall."

Maeve limped back down, her face streaked with sweat. Her
legs were protesting, her old scar cramping.

As she reached the crowds flocking about the king's hall, it
took all her willpower to slow to a walk. This was not a triumph
for her on her own—how could she forget? People gradually
hushed and fell back to let her through, as they did when she
trod this path to fight her brother, thinking her life was about to
end.

It was all different now.

Tiernan was standing alone in the gateway between the
wooden towers, his hair a waterfall of gray over his pale robe, sunlight resting on his shaven brow.

Maeve's voice failed when she recognized the veil of the druid
trance that clouded his eyes. So he had also been seeking far for
her.

Breathing hard, she pulled her sword free and knelt before him.
"I triumphed against those who opposed me, and won the loyalty
of lords and warriors. The long dark was mild, and leaf-bud
early. The crops are abundant, the flocks and herds swelling. All is
fertile and unfurls with life."

Tiernan's eyelids closed and opened again. His human self
gradually settled back into him, and he slowly moved his head,
looking down at her.

Maeve raised a fierce face. "*Now* proclaim what you know to be
true!"

Mother of the land. A power that meant safety to her.

Tiernan's gaze sharpened as it roamed over her, and his eyes
filled with wonder. With a nod, he unclasped one veined hand
from his staff and rested the palm on her brow. "It is as I foresaw."

His resonant voice called a great stillness into Maeve's body, and she stopped shaking. Everyone shared that silence with her, that pause.

"Before the gods I give you a new name. Maeve, Queen of Connacht, ruler of the lands of the Western Sea."

The roar of the people came—a wave sweeping her away.

As soon as he was able to get to her through the throng of warriors, Tiernan appeared once more at Maeve's side, a sheepskin cloak thrown over his druid robes. He had come back to himself, though his cheeks bore a trace of high color.

He beckoned Maeve with his staff toward the rampart stairs. Children scampered out of their way, their parents dropping back and whispering.

Up on the gate-tower, Tiernan folded his hands over the globe of white quartz atop his staff. "You wanted this burden, lady, and so it comes. A small party of warriors has raided the northern border."

Maeve's exultant smile faded. "And?"

Tiernan squinted at the sunshine. The rains had washed the sky clean and it was a vivid blue, the new grass on the plain a bright emerald. "They kept close to the rivers, moving fast, barely stopping. Some of our herdsmen took up spears against them and were killed."

Maeve's heart sank. "Did they steal any cattle?"

"No, strangely. They ignored many herds in passing."

Maeve looked down, releasing her breath. "Conor did not take no for an answer." She met Tiernan's eyes. "They are only seeking Finnbennach. If they wanted a fight, they would have killed more people. He wants Finnbennach."

Tiernan frowned. "We have kept the great one well hidden, as you suggested. And...he is certainly not white anymore." He spread his gnarled hand. "I sent riders after the Ulaid warriors, but the best trackers were with you, and mine lost them in the hills."

"Then I will send more, and if Ulaid warriors are still harrying our lands, we will drive them away." It was an effort to brace her shoulders, for they suddenly felt unbearably heavy. "You know this is just the beginning."

He nodded, studying her. "Because of Eochaid's death, Conor may have thought to use your marriage to press some absurd claim of kingship. Now, though, he will discover we have a ruler of our own—and one, I fancy, he was not expecting."

Maeve touched her brow and bowed her head, her heart pounding.

Maeve galloped Meallán along the shore of the lake, and this time she was in control of his reins.

She jumped down, and did not need to seek Ruán with her eyes. She merely let go. As she raced through the marsh, the grasses set up a great murmuring, bending as the wind swept through them. It blew away all memory of gates and ramparts, thatch roofs and smoke, and the bustle of Cruachan beyond the hills. There was only an endless expanse of reeds closing about her ... to lose herself in.

No voices calling for her, arguing, or hammering out demands. *Her fingertips trailed through the stalks, her steps quickening.* No one grasping for her, pulling her in all directions. *She glimpsed water now, the sparks of sunshine beckoning.*

Maeve splashed through puddles with abandon, the wind dragging her hair from its rough braid, and she grew lighter the farther she went from solid land.

Without needing to think, she found Ruán.

He was toiling hard in the sun, cutting bundles of tall reeds for his bed. His long hair was wet, gleaming like an otter pelt, and the sunshine was strong enough now to turn his bare shoulders a faint red.

Maeve leaped up on an old buried log beside him. When Ruán straightened with the stems in one hand, she saw his face and words failed her. "I am Queen." It came out as a whisper, after all.

He said nothing, for some reason lowering his chin, his shoulders sinking. The same heaviness dragged down Maeve's belly, and only then did she realize what thumped so loud in her breast was nothing about being a queen at all.

"You came to me." Maeve unbalanced and fell off the log. Ruán caught her, and her thigh instinctively nestled between his two strong legs, the sweat on his belly penetrating her thin tunic. She looked down at his brown wrist. "*You saved me.*"

He froze, before letting out a soft exhalation. "So it was not a dream."

"You took me from sleep, showed me the men waiting to ambush me. We crossed the hills and attacked them—and we *won.*"

And I lived. Her shallow breaths made them both sway, the soft ground giving way beneath her heels.

His lips parted, it seemed with wonder. Then his forehead creased up. "But how can that be? I did not try to reach you." He glanced into the distance, as if asking someone else.

Confused, a chill again swept Maeve. "Well … be happy at least that you saved the lives of many men." She hesitated, her chin lifting. She had summoned courage in battle, and it still flowed through her.

So she would be raw before him now … risk this even though his brow was heavy.

Maeve freed her wrist and carefully took his face in her hands. She needed to feel *life* rushing through him again, for she had been so near death now—and survived.

At her touch, Ruán's head came up. He was poised in that way he had, as if at any moment he might leap away through the trees or dive down through deep water. Away from her.

Maeve let out a shaky breath and brushed strands of his damp hair over one ear, smoothing the wet nape of his neck and trailing the dark hair back on the other side. His tanned, moist skin was silky beneath her fingers. She swore a shudder went through him.

"So," she whispered, "this means you do not wish me dead, Ruán of the marsh. It means you came for me." She had to swallow a lump, force it out. *"As I would you."*

The tension in him flowed out of his muscles like water, his shoulders lowering. "So it seems, *ceara.*"

Ceara. Fiery red.

Ruán tossed down the reeds in his fist, his palm stained green. The curse that came from under his breath sounded a note of surrender.

He swept an arm about her neck and pulled her in, his mouth crushed fiercely to her brow.

⚏

Out in the dark, the lapping of waves had hushed as the wind dropped. Ruán was curled around Maeve in the nest of hides they had made, both of them facing the campfire. Maeve rolled on her back to look at him, the lush furs brushing her naked skin.

His elbow was propped up, chin in one hand. Under the furs he stroked her arm, but the touch was distracted, as if he beheld the same flames she did and sought for something in them.

She tilted her head up to him. "In the dream, I saw your eyes."

His chin lowered, that invisible regard focusing on her. His loose hair caught on his collarbone, stiffened by the lake-water.

She traced the stubble on his jaw, touching the sweet bow of his lips, roughened by sun and wind. "They were gray because of the moonlight, but bright. They saw into me."

The dips in Ruán's cheeks hollowed, and he shuddered as if a memory blew over him. Maeve nestled the fur around his shoulder and settled her rump into the curve of his belly.

She laid her cheek on his callused hand. His heart thudded into her back.

At last Ruán sighed, leaning his chin on her hair. "They were green."

That secret did not fly out into the dark forest. It stayed between their bodies, along with the scent of their skin.

CHAPTER 18

The day approached where at last it would not be Maeve raising the mead horn to bestow the blessings of the land upon another man as king. Someone would have to gift the cup of plenty to her, the first Queen of Connacht for generations.

"I can't do it." Finn backed up against Nél's stall in the stable. Her tunic was grimed with dirt and there were smears across her soft round cheek. She held the horse-brush before her like a shield. "No."

Maeve frowned as Nél kicked the rail, tossing his head. "You are of Connacht and Laigin, our alliance in flesh and blood ..." She faltered.

The whites of Finn's eyes were showing, her lips drawn in.

Maeve sent her senses along unfamiliar pathways. She had trained herself to read men's hearts, but only for the dark things that threatened her. Women's hearts? Never.

Finn tossed the brush to the straw and turned from Maeve, visibly forcing herself to lower her shoulders as she fingered her horse's mane. "You ride to battle, and I know only that you will most likely die. Then you *do* nearly die, but I only find out you haven't when the servants tell me of your message to Tiernan. Then you take off again—with no word for me—and *now* you want to parade me around, moving when you say, speaking when you say?" Her hands slipped from Nél's neck to the rail, gripping it. "Well, I won't!"

This torrent left Maeve speechless. Since she returned, Finn had never sought her out, and rarely met her eyes when she tried to draw a smile from her. Now Maeve was taken by an impulse to put a hand to her as she would to a foal, for that was all she knew about young things.

Yet as Maeve came closer, Finn spun about and shrank back. So Maeve stopped and searched her face. Finn's braids were shoved beneath a leather cap. From afar she looked like a boy. But the sweaty curls that had escaped at her brow were all Maeve's, and meeting Finn's startling eyes was like looking in a mirror.

That was it. The answer lay in her memories of her own young self. She moistened her lips and cupped her palm along Finn's temple in a touch of equals. The girl would twist away from anything else, like a wild cub.

Finn did tense but did not move, her lip quivering.

Maeve pretended not to notice. "Daughter, any leader would want to take you to battle, for you would make a fine scout. But if you were harmed, I could not forgive myself. The day my blood runs into the ground, it will still flow in your veins. You are daughter of a queen and a king; you have the people of Connacht and Laigin to think about." She moved her hand to Finn's shoulder, just as she gripped Garvan. "And *if* you are going to stay, you must therefore learn what it means to rule a kingdom."

Finn's anger flared into something else. *"Stay?"*

That light in her eye struck Maeve's breast, though for once it was not pain. "Do you want to?" Maeve's voice was hoarse, but, inspired, she drew her sword from its sheath and tilted it to the light from the stable doors. "Can you fight?"

Finn's brows shot up and she trapped an incredulous smile between her teeth. "Father thought such things unbecoming for a woman—and unsuitable for a child."

"The handling of a sword is a fine skill to learn. It keeps you

strong and nimble, and gains you the respect of men." Maeve held
the blade out on her palms, hilt first.

Finn's eyes went round, and with a little, exultant bob on her
toes she clasped the hilt. When Maeve let go, the weight made
Finn's arm dip. Blushing, she hefted it, swishing it through the
dusty air.

Maeve watched the flame of sunlight breathe along the living
blade. "And when you can fight, you don't get left behind anymore."

Her gaze met Finn's. The thrill danced between them, hot and
bright.

The day of Maeve's crowning was the greatest celebration Connacht had seen in years.

Her warriors had chased Conor's raiders away without them
discovering Finnbennach, and she had placed a strong guard
about all approaches from the north. Within that ring of safety,
Connacht's people could indulge in pleasure after the challenges
of the dark and cold.

Games in the leaf-bud sunshine. Races. Prizes. Casks of mead
and spitted pig and beef for the crafters, farmers, and warriors
who came from all over Connacht. Streaming banners. Battle-
horns and drums. A raucous fair, with stalls offering food and
drink, cloth and baskets, leather, beads, and bronze.

The great fire in the king's hall was put out and the ash cleared
away. A new fire would be lit that night by the druids from the
eternal flame that burned at Lugh's temple.

The only thing missing was Maeve herself.

As the sun rose higher, the tension built. Drums beat to
quicken the pulse of the people of Connacht, galloping faster as
the crowds thronged.

At last a glimmer of white and red appeared against the lush
grass along the river.

People shouted and beckoned to each other, scrambling up the gate-towers and lining the ramparts. They clambered onto carts and crawled up thatch roofs to see better.

A hush spread.

Swaying along the riverside path, as if he had taken shape from the Otherworld mists, came Finnbennach, royal bull of Connacht. The chief druid Tiernan led him on a halter, and boys dashed alongside with switches of willow. Finnbennach, however, had been pacified with sweet grass and lush cows. He rolled along now like a great, white swell of the sea, immense and awe-inspiring.

On his back, sheathed in leather and hung with gold, rode Maeve.

Her ruddy hair draped the bull's neck, the Otherworldly hues of red and white mingling together—god-blessed, sacred. She lifted her head at the murmur of the crowd, flashing sun from her helm, and raised her lance. The eagle of Connacht unfurled on a pennant, wings spread in the wind.

A roar of acclaim erupted, echoing far across the plains of Cruachan.

※

The circlet on her brow.

The nectar of the land on her tongue.

The songs of the druids in her ears.

The cheers of the people in her heart.

From the steps of the temple of Lugh, Maeve looked out over a riot of colorful banners and milling crowds, everything gilded by the dusk.

But she saw only light—walked through light—hushed and glowing as silver on the lake.

※

"Ferdia has left Cúchulainn's side." The ragged bard bowed to Maeve, wiping his red nose on his sleeve.

Maeve's hand paused on Miu's head, the cat's golden eyes staring into her own.

Two days after the crowning, the feasts still rolled on, but she had escaped from drunken warriors and red-cheeked chieftains to enjoy a quiet moment by the brazier in her father's old chamber.

Her chamber now.

"Conor's lords hoped he would bury his wrath with the old season, but leaf-bud only sees it stoked higher. No one thought his old trunk could fill with such sap!" The harper cackled and sneezed, huddling into his cloak. "Now his madness has forced Ferdia to seek Naisi and Deirdre in Alba. And Cúchulainn is silent, and no man can look in his face."

Maeve's heart began to race, and she folded her hands in her lap. Ferdia and the great Cúchulainn were more than sword-brothers. They were *one soul*.

Ferdia fought by Cúchulainn's side, drank and ate and, for all she knew, slept at Cúchulainn's side. They were night and day—Ferdia dark and secretive, the Hound fair and fiery. At Emain Macha, Maeve had managed to glean that the mystical bond that forged the strength of the Red Branch was somehow embodied by those two.

She had therefore tried everything to win over Cúchulainn, but he proved one of the few men entirely immune to her, keeping her at arm's length with his cheery bluster. Whenever she tried to speak to him, he breezed on past with a broad grin and glazed eyes, looking over her shoulder for something more interesting.

Bastard.

Maeve reined in her thoughts. Ferdia and Cúchulainn cast a kind of spell over the warriors. Their very bond seemed to conjure exhilaration, the surge of bravery that makes men run at enemy swords. *They* were the war-song that inspired the battle charge of the Ulaid.

And now these two, the heart of the Red Branch, had been parted by Conor's madness. Maeve sprang from her chair like a hound off its leash.

Miu startled and scampered off, and Maeve waved the harper away, too, telling him to warm himself with barley broth. With a bow and another sneeze, the bard tottered down the stairs.

Maeve lifted the royal circlet from her brow and held it in the glow of the brazier. She was queen at last.

Her hands were no longer tied.

By the time the chiefs rode away from the crowning, they had agreed to leave warriors to be battle-trained together on the meadows around Cruachan. It was time, Fraech and Maeve argued, for the bonds of the fighting men of Connacht to be strengthened, and for old rifts to be put aside.

They must be forged into one force, like the Ulaid Red Branch.

Maeve waved away the last cattle-lord and then said farewell to Ailill, who was taking her dowry of hides, mead, and honey to his father—and no doubt reporting back to Ros Ruadh about her crowning.

He rode off swathed in furs and gold. As soon as Maeve lost sight of his spiked mane at the head of the baggage carts, she stripped off her finery, slipped into her buckhides, and sought out Garvan and Fraech.

The two young warriors had climbed the gates of the royal mound to observe their new fighters, for Fraech had set the recruits challenges to unearth who was the strongest and most skilled.

Maeve bounded up the steps to the gate-tower, looking over the earthen rampart to the chaos below.

Men sloshed about in a mire of rain puddles and churned earth, hacking at each other with ash staves. Rows of spearmen were being drilled by the Galeóin fighters. Lances traced glittering arcs, thudding into the grass. Farther out, screeching riders urged their horses around tight loops between stakes in the ground.

When Maeve reached Fraech and Garvan on the platform of the wooden tower, she was surprised to see Finn there, legs dangling through a gap in the rail as she ate a bannock.

Finn straightened. "Fraech has been teaching me to fight," she mumbled through barley crumbs.

Maeve did not take her eyes off the glint of spear-tips. "I said one of the men could train you. The war-leader is too busy."

Fraech shrugged, folding his arms. His back was as straight as one of the staves, his natural bearing now come into its own. "It is no inconvenience to me."

"Lugh's breath and balls...bloody useless!" Garvan jabbed a finger at a clutch of youths who were whacking their comrades and falling over, hooting with laughter. "If those were real swords, their heads would be rolling by now."

In one of the first acts after her crowning, Maeve had named Garvan her champion, the greatest honor for any warrior. He was already enjoying his elevation, strutting about with a new sword and the Champion's torc of gold.

Shouting, two of the youths below now threw their wooden swords away and leaped onto each other, wrestling in the mud.

A rumble sounded in the back of Fraech's throat—the closest he ever came to raising his voice. "They won't think this a joke in battle, with their guts spilled over the ground." He went to swing his long legs over the rail to climb down the outside of the tower.

Maeve stopped him. "I have news of the Ulaid."

All three heads swung toward her: brown, red, and black. Swiftly, Maeve told them of Ferdia and Cúchulainn.

"My father said Conor was the most cunning king Erin had spawned." Fraech leaned on the palisade, his green eyes narrowed in the sun. "He will never lose his grip on the Red Branch."

"He *is* losing it." Maeve realized she had always gnawed on such thoughts alone; she had never had anyone to tell before. "We know he is desperate enough to send raiders after our bull. His lords splinter, and now Cúchulainn and Ferdia are torn apart. What will come next?" She rocked from side to side, unable to be still. "It is time to see with our own eyes if they are weakening, and strike that wedge deeper. Let us return the favor, and mount a raid of our own."

Fraech snorted, shaking the brown tail of hair down his back like a disgruntled stallion. "Cousin, the last thing we *see* will be Cúchulainn bearing down upon us in his battle-frenzy, with the Red Branch not far behind!"

"Perhaps, but if they are truly crumbling, we have a chance our fathers never had—to break Conor's hold forever."

A spark kindled in Fraech's eyes, his calm features drawing tense.

Maeve appealed to him. "Conor is mad enough to want all of Connacht. We have to see if he has the power for more than a raid. *We have to.*"

Coming to a decision, Fraech nodded. "That is shrewd."

"And ..." Maeve heard herself say. "I am going."

Garvan and Finn squawked at the same time.

"Damn blast it, spitfire!"

"Mother!"

Maeve blinked. "I am the queen—"

"Aye, you are." Garvan wiped sweat from his cheek on his shoulder. "Which means you can no longer think only of yourself."

Finn hopped up, her words tumbling out. "You keep telling me that to rule means putting the people first, Mother, especially so soon after our ... our troubles." Finn glanced at Fraech, her face coloring. "You cannot risk your life when they need you here, showing them how strong we are." Finn widened her eyes, her pupils limpid. "That is what you keep saying to me, anyway."

Fraech was regarding Finn with amusement, and Maeve could

swear she saw an answering tremor in Finn's mouth. *Wretched child.*

Fraech sobered. "I will command the raiders, cousin. I am war-leader."

"I am Queen's Champion." Garvan pushed out his chest, gripping his new sword-hilt.

Maeve shook her head. "You are both too young to have fought against the Red Branch."

It was Garvan's turn to snort. "You never fought them either!"

She squared off to Fraech and Garvan. "Have you ever been face-to-face with Cúchulainn? I have. Do you know what you are looking for? I do. Fraech, you must stay here. You were trained in tactics—battle tactics. A raid is a minor risk when set against the future safety of Connacht. That is *your* responsibility."

As she glared at the three of them, Maeve's indignation died. Fraech was pursing his lips, looking at his feet. Finn's eyes were bleak. Garvan was chewing the inside of his cheek as he looked over the meadow, his scowl creasing up his battered face.

Maeve had to clear her throat. "I know what signs of trouble I am looking for. And there is rarely any fighting on a raid. But..." She sighed. "I will stay far to the rear, and if any Red Branch come anywhere near, I promise I will run away."

Garvan also sighed, folding his arms. He scratched at his tangled black hair. "And I am coming to hold you to that."

"Of course." Maeve clapped his arm, then addressed Fraech. "Pick the best riders from these new men. We need speed and horse-skill, though, not brawn."

Fraech had a frank way of appraising someone. Looking in his eyes now, Maeve had the distinct impression she had not disappointed him.

Hesitating only a moment, she slung an arm around Finn, who was still glowering. "Come, daughter, you know I will return." She reached out and gently tucked a strand of hair behind Finn's ear. "Another secret," she whispered, squeezing her shoulder. "I am very hard to kill."

At last she was rewarded with a grudging smile. She left Finn there with instructions to come to her with news of the men Fraech picked for the war-band.

Halfway back down the stairs, Maeve paused, her face turned to the east. The breeze caught the clash of metal and shouts of men and snatched them away. For a heartbeat there was silence in her head.

For once, she shied at any thought of riding to the lake. Ruán had told her to choose a different path. He did not realize she had no choice. She had made herself the bulwark of her people against the Ulaid. They looked to her to keep them safe now—the goddess Macha Mong Ruad.

Who I am here is not who I am there. At the lake, they wandered barefoot and ragged as children. Her heart was light there, and Ruán glowed when she made him laugh. No dark thoughts invaded that place now, and it was a peace she would guard with her life.

But she imagined telling him this, and in her mind saw his face fall. He would not understand what she had to be here, because it was not the Maeve he touched, the one he teased.

She couldn't show him this other Maeve.

It didn't matter, though . . . for one day soon they would all be safe, and she would shed that old self forever and run to him, and there would be no one calling her back.

Maeve shook these strange, tumbling thoughts from her head.

She leaped the last step to flat ground and set her chin north instead. *Conor of the Ulaid.* That summoned a belly-knot she knew much better.

She tugged her breastplate down, twisting her hair back with cold hands.

Ruán's certainty grew that someone was watching him.

As he set snares or gutted fish, he kept catching a shimmer

from the corner of his eye, a disturbance in the silver around him. One of the nearby farmers, or the old druid again?

He began tucking one of Maeve's daggers in his trews, but aside from that did not reveal his suspicions. Whoever it was might also think him sídhe and leave him alone.

One day, Ruán was intent on the tricky task of cooking mussels over the fire without spilling them in the sand. For a few moments he was so absorbed, focusing all his senses into his fingertips, that he became deaf to everything else.

Someone cleared his throat behind him.

Ruán bounded up, the dagger already out.

"By the light of Manannán himself." It was a rich voice, trained to resonate. A druid. "It has been hard to be sure, brother. Your hair is a mess, and you look like a deer."

For a moment Ruán thought he was falling, as when he was first blinded. He missed a step and with burning cheeks planted his feet wide, righting himself. "I gather, Áedán, that since you have been secretly stalking me, you must have come at Lord Mulach's behest. So you have supplanted me at his side, as you always wanted."

"You are bitter, and I do not blame you." Áedán spoke more gently. "I heard about what Mulach and his men did to you, but by the time I returned from the small island you were already lost to us. I didn't ..." He drew a breath. "I did not realize you were like ... this."

Alone with the wild creatures, Ruán was woven into Source. To men, he would always be maimed. He had to prize his cold lips apart. "Has the great lord decided to finish me off after all, then? Is that why you come skulking around, spying on me?"

"I did not want to frighten you—"

"Am I as pitiful as that?" Áedán had looked into his eyes once, known him in his power. His old power. Ruán straightened, planting his soles on the earth. *Remember who you are.* The world was not black; it cradled him in light. He savored the give of the soil now, smelled the mud. A blackbird trilled in the trees.

"Ru, you *are* changed."

Ruán snorted, touching the blindfold. "What did you expect?"

"I don't know." Áedán's tread came closer. "I had to be careful, assure myself it was you."

Ruán squatted, folding a burdock leaf over the mussels. "So do I put my wrists out for the chains, or can I eat my supper first?"

Áedán hesitated. "Can we not sit together, as we used to?"

Ruán pressed his tongue against his teeth, picturing Áedán's grave face shadowed by dark hair. Áedán was awkward as a boy, spindly and owl-eyed. Ruán was ever the bold one, impatient and far-seeking. "Why are you here?"

There was a rustle of wool as Áedán sank on a log at the hearth. "Forgive me, but I have come a long way. Your path was winding, and the memory of you fleeting."

Ruán swapped the knife to his other hand and wiped his palm. "Answer me. I won't be trapped and bound again."

Áedán sighed. "Mere moons after he banished you, Mulach and his warriors came down with pains in the belly and a sweating sickness. They died, Ru, the men who wounded you. Mulach's brother Donn is lord now, but last sun-season brought more trouble upon us. A blight shriveled the root crop, and storms scattered the fish. Leaf-bud has been better, but it is too late for some. Hunger stalks us, taking the babes and old ones. People have begun muttering that we are cursed because Mulach harmed a druid." He paused. "A rumor, I tell you honestly, that I have nurtured."

For Ruán, each word was like a nick of the blade.

"Lord Donn wants to make amends and beg your forgiveness. I've been sent to bring you home."

Silence. A spasm of Ruán's shoulders brought the knife up, and he laughed. "The lords take my sight, and now that they are in danger they *command* my return? I am not to be paraded before the warriors so Donn can look powerful again! No one will pity me, as if I am less than them."

"That is not how it is—"

"It is how it will be!" Ruán slammed the dagger into the sand, causing the nearby wading birds to scatter with splashes. A gust of wind agitated the reeds. "Now go, and forget you ever found me."

Rising to his feet, Áedán turned. "This is not the end," he said. "You mean more to me than that."

Ruán listened to his steps retreating, and when he was sure Áedán had gone, he hastened to the water's edge and sank on his haunches. He could not see the glimmer around him anymore. He touched the lake with trembling fingers and put them to his mouth, placed his palm on the surface so the water clung to him.

Another rustle came from among the trees, this one lighter, more hesitant.

Ruán's head went up. Only then did he realize that all the while he spoke to Áedán, he had sensed someone else was there.

CHAPTER 19

"That is far enough," Garvan said to Maeve. "You will stay behind us now."

Maeve pursed her lips and eyed him, Meallán shifting beneath her. They had crossed the border to the Ulaid and were hiding themselves among the trees on a ridge that led deeper into Conor's territory.

"You promised," Garvan added.

Maeve searched the narrow green valley below. She didn't like it. For days her band of raiders had skirted the lakes and lush swamps that formed the border. Here, farther into the hills, steadings clung to the drier slopes, and there were sparse fields scratched from the drained soil. But those Ulaid houses were deserted.

"Now that I am queen, you boss me around more than you did before."

Garvan patted his restive horse. "Brothers must enjoy some rewards for their troubles."

Maeve grunted. She had promised to drop back with the young warrior Lassar while the rest rode on only because she could not rid her mind of Finn's stark face. Frustration, however, was gaining ground over promises. "It is too quiet."

The plan was for her warriors to head along these valleys to where they spilled into a more open expanse of Ulaid pasturelands, drive off a few cattle, then loop about and head back the same way. It was a test of the Ulaid defenses. If any Ulaid warriors gave chase, her men would abandon the cattle and lose their pursuers in the great swaths of bog and river-marsh that the Connacht fighters knew so well.

A simple plan; Maeve only hoped she could glean something from it.

"If what your harper says is true, and Conor has fallen out with some of his chiefs, the people around here may have retreated inside their lords' forts. It is a good thing, spitfire. They are more afraid of each other than of us."

Maeve relaxed. "You sometimes do speak sense."

Over the next three days, Maeve and Lassar went to ground in the woods. Maeve spent the time on her belly, clinging to the ridgeline above the valley so that she would not be seen from below. Wedged into the roots of a rowan tree, she ignored the rain drumming on her oilskin, her aching back and cold feet.

On the fourth morning she rose before dawn and gazed across the Ulaid, straining her eyes. Where were they?

Dawn revealed a blanket of mist in the hollows. Maeve blinked as she glimpsed a strange backwash of light, a flicker around the hills and the trees outlined against the sky. She thought it was sunrise, but it was in the north, and silver, not gold. The valley before her was a dark tear through those glowing veils, and she thought she saw a shadow stretching along the horizon in the north. She closed her eyes and opened them.

It was gone, but the shadow remained on her heart.

She slid down the hill to where Lassar was breaking his fast with a wedge of stale bread. "Something is wrong." She swiped her scabbard from her pack. "We have to climb that far ridge so we can see more."

Lassar chewed. "The Champion said we must stay out of trouble."

She cocked her head as she belted on her sword. "I am your queen, Lassar. Are you intending to obey me or the Lord Garvan?"

Lassar gulped his bread and hastened to his feet.

Keeping to the line of oak trees on the slope, they led the horses across to the next ridge. The crest was still obscuring their sightline when, on the morning air, they clearly heard the distressed lowing of cattle.

Maeve and Lassar clambered to the top.

The mist had lifted. Some distance down the valley, Maeve could just see a cluster of huts by a shallow river, and the sunlit gleam of red and black hides. Scores of cows were milling about the stockade of brush and hazel saplings. Maeve's mouth went dry. "I know this steading, and those cattle are not quartered here. The lord keeps them on a high hill, inside a rampart."

Lassar looked at her with wide eyes. "Then—"

"They knew we were coming." Maeve's stomach turned. "It is a trap, and our men took the bait." Her mind galloped on. Who would the border lords appeal to if they had broken with Conor? Who could muster men and ride here so swiftly?

She was already jerking Meallán on the rein, scrabbling down the slope. "Hurry!"

⁂

Stripped to the waist, Ruán waded into the shallows. He flexed his bare back, reveling in the strengthening sun, then retied the thong that kept his hair off his face. Finally, he spread his hands over the water, calling the spell up inside him.

He was placing the bream on his hearth-stone, feeling for his scaler, when he paused. He had not heard a step this time, but still he sensed that strange someone. "Who is there?" That glimmer in the air...it was like a deer, shy and delicate. Not Áedán. Ruán tensed and was halfway up when she spoke.

"Ru." Her voice was husky with sadness.

"Orla?"

He heard a rustle of cloth and a tentative tread. "I wasn't sure whether you would speak to me after what you said to Áedán." She caught her breath. "I was never brave like you."

Ruán's fingers unconsciously spread over his blindfold. Orla had last looked upon him when he was whole. He remembered tree-shadows dappling her hair, the amber flecks in her irises. He dropped his hand. "What are you doing here?"

"I came with Áedán to see you."

A trembling had started beneath his skin. It was as if she had walked out of his vision among the stones. He was still raw from those vivid sensations—but that was all she was, a boy's fiery memory. "If you wanted revenge for my cruelty, you have it." He touched his brow. "My eyes."

"I don't want revenge!"

Ruán steadied himself, his new sight coming in snatches. Orla was a small, unflickering light, pale but steady. "Then do you need my apology? For how can you come here after what I did to you?"

"That is nothing to what Lord Mulach did to you."

Ruán groped for his tunic and tugged it over his wet skin. "I brought that on myself. You did no wrong." His arms fell by his sides as he faced her. "Why did you come, Orla? You are grown, with a life of your own."

He heard her picking at the bark on the rowan tree. "We have all suffered for what Lord Mulach did to you. When Lord Donn sent Áedán to find you, I thought...if you would not listen to him, you might..." A shuddering breath. "You might need someone else who knew you *before*."

He sighed. "Then your efforts were in vain. I cannot go back. This is my home."

"This is not a home." She rushed up to him, her little, cold fingers sending a shock through his arm. "Come back to where you belong, to where people can look after you."

"Orla." Ruán took her fingers, curled them up and gently put them from him. He smiled to take the sting away. "I do not need looking after."

"No one is meant to be alone!"

She meant well. Ruán touched the crown of her head, for she only came up to his chest. Her hair smelled of salt and seaweed, so familiar...

"Ru." She bent back her head and her light flared. "I thought you might not trust Áedán because he came from Mulach's kin. But *I* speak for the people, the ones you helped."

Ruán dropped his hand and backed away. He did not *help*. He had killed someone. And he had hurt Orla. He would not hurt anyone again.

His legs chose their own path onto the track he had beaten through the undergrowth. He couldn't think straight and had to resort to halting steps that made his face burn.

Orla chased after him. "They have not forgotten how you sung over their fishing boats. They remember the nights when you braved the mounds of the sídhe to fast and pray for them."

He made an inarticulate sound in the back of his throat. Behind him, she stopped and shouted, "I came because the fishermen begged me to. They thought I knew a boy who was part of the woods and water, who wanted to know *everything* because one day he would be a druid and do good with that knowing."

Ruán halted, his chest tight.

"And all the moons I wept in my bed, I knew that you had something better to do than mind sheep in my father's fields!"

Ruán turned, lifting a hand. "And I've found it here." He gentled his voice. "I want you to have the same peace, for I did you a terrible wrong. Go back to your husband and family, Orla. You always deserved more than a memory."

She was sniffling. "My husband was taken by the sea long ago. My children are years out of breechclouts. And I yearned to see this world you spun for me with your fine words. For once, I wanted more than stone and water."

Ruán touched the blindfold and then his heart. "So now you see that time marches on in every world. The boy you remember is gone."

"*No*. Áedán and I will not give up on you as Lord Mulach did." Her voice receded as she backed away between the trees. "We bide in a steading close by, with the reed-cutters. A druid always gets a bed and broth—you told me that."

"It won't do any good, Orla."

She did not answer, cracking sticks as she raced away through the forest.

As a maiden, Orla had blossomed into a fleeting season of creamy curves. But the Stone Islands did not nurture lush flesh and rosy skin. They wizened people, dried them with salt and wind.

Ruán returned to the fish and ran his thumbs over its scales. He would never know what Orla looked like now, and though she could see him, a heart had a blindness of its own. To her, he would always be the boy whose touch made her bloom.

Ruán gutted the fish, and when it was roasting and he sat by the flames, something unexpected happened. His body gradually settled into the damp grass, an old tightness leaching from him. He rested his head back on the log. The spiral scar flexed as he breathed.

He did not have to fear that any lord was seeking his death anymore.

⁂

Maeve and Lassar slid down a gully on the hill above the river, coaxing their horses behind them. It was hard to make out what was happening among the houses by the ford, the branches and thickets obscuring their view. But their ears soon told them everything.

They caught the clang of iron. Screams and shouts.

They reached flat ground where a bank of oak and hazel trees fringed a green pasture. A stony ford led across the stream to a scatter of thatched huts surrounded by a little stockade. The gate of brushwood was standing open.

Metal flashed in the morning sun. Warriors were fighting all over the steading, churning up the mud paths. Cattle thronged a web of ditches, tossing their horns and kicking out at the stockade as men leaped and ducked among them.

Maeve's eyes darted back and forth as she desperately tried to make sense of chaos. The men were strewn about, scattered knots of them struggling in cow-byres, pigpens, and the paths between the huts. The Ulaid must have been hiding in ambush all over the homestead.

Maeve wiped sweat from her face. The warriors were tussling in the mud, their armor and faces coated in the same filth. Only then did she realize that a few bore shields with streaks of scarlet and gold showing through the dirt, like blooms scattered on dark earth.

Red Branch.

Dropping Meallán's reins, Maeve took off across the riverbank, stretching out her legs and pumping her arms. She splashed over the ford, her hand going to her hilt. Just as she burst through the open gate, Lassar barreled into her from behind, knocking her off her feet.

They tumbled off the track into a ditch, facedown in a trickle of water that ran beneath the stockade. Maeve spat out mud and dung, wrenching herself from beneath Lassar's heavy body. "Get off!"

"I gave an oath to Lord Fraech to protect you," the young warrior panted. "If you die, I die, whether I return home or not."

She threw him off and he crouched beside her, his hand out as if to a spitting cat.

"Lassar!" She wiped her face and eyes on her sleeve.

"I raised my voice for you when you killed your brother," he stammered, white-faced. "You told us you'd protect Connacht, and you can't do that when you are dead."

With a growl, Maeve rolled on her belly. Side by side they crawled to the lip of the wet ditch and peered beneath the stakes of one of the fences.

Screeching warriors were still hurling themselves at each other as the cattle milled around their pens, lowing in panic. Holding their blades high, other men were leaping from the thatch roofs and the palings of the stock pens, stabbing anyone who came close and bellowing war-cries. Their screams of fury and pain pierced Maeve's breast, and she gulped for air as the reek of blood grew more pungent.

She peered around. Connacht men were down, but there were also some scarlet shields thrown into the mud. Of the few Red Branch that were here, two or three had been slain. She recognized those she knew, still fighting.

Ulaid's old king Fergus, a silver bear, was swinging his sword while he bellowed.

Conor's two sons—Cormac the eldest, with his sire's proud face, and Fiacra the youngest, flaxen-haired.

Fergus's son Illan.

Maeve blinked, her sight blurred by sweat and the panicked racing of her heart. Something was amiss...something her instincts could sense. The Red Branch were not fighting in that flowing, deadly dance she had watched in training a hundred times, when they fought as one. Instead, they were in disarray, scattered all over the place.

And then Maeve saw him.

A golden god stood before the doors of the largest house. He was of middling size, graceful rather than hulking, with his fair hair and beardless face coated in blood. Even from afar, however, his eyes blazed out of that gore like beacons of blue flame. He danced, swinging his sword in an intricate pattern of blows and lunges that formed a cage of iron around him, taking down three men at a time.

A revulsion took Maeve at the sight of him, a visceral curdling in her belly. "Cúchulainn." He was the blade in Conor's hand—the blade that would descend upon her people.

"So that is him." A tremor ran through Lassar's voice.

That was him: he had become as great an enemy as Conor himself. By habit, Maeve sought Ferdia by his side, and then remembered Ferdia was gone, driven away by Conor.

Maeve's breathing was so shallow she must have dizzied herself, for the world lurched as if she dipped below its surface once more. The streaked blades and dented shields, puddles of blood and gleam of cattle, were all cloaked in silver ... or was it a trick of the sun?

No, everything glowed from within. She could *see* it.

There was a mystery at the heart of the Red Branch, a bond they kept well-hidden. During those few times she dared risk Conor's wrath, sleeping with Red Branch warriors in secret, they fell silent when she broached it, turning away from her.

Now Maeve was rooted to the spot in wonder—and horror.

Cúchulainn was a towering flame, white-hot. The other Red Branch warriors were fainter spires of radiance. Ruán had showed her the soul-lights in the valley—some drew on a greater power than others. *Cúchulainn.* His flame sent out great flares as if to encompass his Red Branch brothers.

A light that joined them all ... Was that how they moved as one, thought as one?

The soul-lights of Maeve's Connacht-men throbbed in single pulses of desperation and fear, writhing and guttering out alone. The Ulaid appeared as a branch of lightning anchored in their champion, Cúchulainn.

And then it all changed.

The flames of the Red Branch fighters were stabbed by dark rents, the glowing streamers that bound them tearing apart. Soon they were only shreds of brightness, and then they began to die out. As they did, more Red Branch warriors fell to Connacht blades.

The darkness invaded Cúchulainn. The great blaze of him faltered, contracting. Maeve wiped sweat from her face, closing her eyes. When she opened them, Cúchulainn was sending up gouts of red fury.

He threw off the warriors crowding him and raced down the track toward the cattle-pens, spinning his sword over his head.

Garvan was in his way, furiously sparring with another fighter, oblivious to the golden storm approaching.

Maeve's trance shattered. She pushed herself up on her hands and out of the ditch. Lassar lunged for her, but she managed to slide between the fence palings and stagger to her feet. As Lassar scrambled over the rail, Maeve streaked across the churned mud. Something was wrong with the Red Branch! If she could only rally her men, give them courage . . .

The Connacht war-cry was on her tongue, ready to fly free. *The eagle of blood! The eagle of courage!*

A shout sounded behind her. At the same moment, Maeve was blinded by a flash of light that came at her from the side. Fire seared across her flank.

Not flame . . . *pain* . . .

She stumbled and fell.

Cúchulainn did not wash the gore from his face when he stormed into Emain Macha. He wanted the blood of his dead comrades all over him. The guards at the king's hall jumped out of the way as he flung back the doors and passed through the cavernous building like a flaming brand.

Cúchulainn took the stairs to the storehouse behind in one bound. Conor was inside with a druid, tallying the Beltaine gifts. The two men stood in a pool of light from a horn-lamp, which outlined the shapes of barrels and baskets piled against the walls. Chinks of daylight fell through the cracks in the boards.

The king spun around when Cúchulainn appeared. The Champion was trailing his unsheathed sword from one bloodied hand.

"Tell me this was no defeat." The veined whites of Conor's eyes gleamed in the dimness.

"The Connacht warriors fled, though many still live." Cúchulainn's lips were numb, his voice hoarse from shouting.

Conor glanced at the druid, whose pen was poised over the sheet of bleached leather to tally the marks. "Go," the king murmured. "We will continue this later."

A storehouse would not have been Cúchulainn's chosen ground, but the sides of drying beef, the sacks of musty grain, and vats of cheese in the darkness, whispered to him that if his warriors faltered, the fortunes of the people would be next—their safety, their survival.

As soon as the druid was gone, Cúchulainn snapped, "Maine, Brecc, and Curoi are dead, and many others with them."

"Fiacra?"

Cúchulainn shook his head.

One of Conor's cheeks spasmed, an eye flickering. "When warriors fight, they die."

"If you had not abandoned yourself to this folly, uncle, Connacht would not have chosen to raid at the time of the Beltaine feast. They must know of our weakness."

"No," the king rasped, eyes flaring. "It is that the bastards have named the she-wolf their queen." His lip curled as if he tasted something vile. "She was always hungry to humiliate me ... always seeking to bring me down. Eochaid spawned her just to plant a traitor in our midst ..."

Ach. Cúchulainn silenced that madness by striding before Conor, still crackling with the aftermath of battle-fire. Ferdia ... gods, *Ferdia.* His absence had torn a hole in Cúchulainn's heart. Did that weaken him in battle—did the hurt make him fail? Perhaps he did not summon the Source properly, or weave the threads with the other Red Branch strong enough.

Shaking with shame and fury, Cúchulainn brought up his sword.

Conor stepped back, his eyes striped by the sunlight that fell through narrow gaps in the walls. Cúchulainn glimpsed fear in those glazed depths.

The king's gray hair was for once uncombed, and there was an ale stain down his robes. His cheeks, temples, and eyes were hollowed, the flesh being consumed from within.

That skull-like face invoked no pity in Cúchulainn. "I am talking of *us*, not of Maeve. If she was there, I did not see her. What matters is that after our scouts spotted the raiders, we took secret pathways to cut in front of them and set a trap. *We were waiting for them*—so we should have defeated them easily. Instead, our men died because of this rift between us!"

Conor worried a loose tooth with his tongue, his veined eyes hooded. "There would be no rift if the Red Branch turned their backs on that traitorous cub Naisi once and for all. The men should obey their king—"

"Are you so blind?" Cúchulainn's roar made Conor flinch. "This sickness is rotting the very roots of the Red Branch. Connacht will see that we have lost strength, and they will come back again—with an army. Then you'll have no chance to mourn Deirdre at all."

Conor spread a claw over his chest. "The Red Branch will rally. They are the strongest, the bravest of all men. I spent my boyhood listening to that." An expression of distaste bared his teeth.

Conor had never been a warrior, never been idolized that way. Dear gods, is that what it was about? Cúchulainn flipped his sword into both hands. "You still do not understand the mind of the Red Branch."

Conor eyed the blade. "You are not the first to venture that."

"Then listen. It is not only our skills, hard won as they are. In battle, we summon the Source. Our love for our land and each other weaves a net, and in that *we are one*. And this is the unity you now destroy with your lust and pride!"

Conor's throat bobbed in denial...and Cúchulainn's sword wavered closer.

"Unless you do something to right this," the Hound whispered, "the Red Branch trunk will topple, and the way will lie open for the other kingdoms and Alba to fall upon us. People will be slaughtered in their beds, and *there will be no more Ulaid.* No one will remember us, or sing of us, or light fires for us." The torrent burned Cúchulainn's throat. "And if they ever speak of you, great king, it will be with scorn."

Conor blanched, his collarbone straining through his wrinkled skin. "You threaten me, nephew?"

"Not with treason, uncle." Cúchulainn dropped the sword. "My oath was to guard the Ulaid and whichever king sits on the throne. I pledged my sword to you only because *you* took oath as the land's protector." He sheathed his blade and at the door he stopped, reaching out to touch the sacking that contained a wealth of grain. "There is still time," he added, "before you have broken that vow once and for all."

ᘓ

A song trailed from Maeve's cracked lips. Her mouth was muffled in horseflesh. The warm slab of it beneath her cheek tightened, sending a spasm down her side.

Her hand slipped but seemed to be bound in something that kept it from dangling, the other arm tucked beneath her belly. She could not lift her aching head or draw her thoughts into any sense.

The agony came in waves.

Her awareness circled that pain—endlessly, helplessly—bound to this heat that sucked her dry.

She sang, her eyelids pressed closed by a wad of saddle blanket, hoping she did not have to wake again.

CHAPTER 20

SUN-SEASON

E very day for a week Orla had followed Ruán while he gathered food, chattering of old times. She was quick to laugh,
teasing him with a lilt in her voice. She spun memories of the innocent boy he once was—the Ruán who had only come alive again
among the sídhe.

And beneath Maeve's touch.

He could not bear to be cruel to her and so held his tongue,
smiling as she reminisced of climbing the cliffs for gull eggs and
lying in the sun listening to the roar of waves below. It was easier
than facing Áedán and the recollections of Lord Mulach, which
the druid must have known because he stayed away.

Orla never fussed over him or pitied him, and that summoned
a warmth Ruán could not resist. It was strange that just when he
began to sink into the wildness of the woods and lake, the first
person he shared that rush of life with appeared.

At night he asked the sídhe if they toyed with him now.

They never answered.

Maeve had also disappeared, which was confusing. He sent
his senses out, searching for some glimpse of her, but there was
nothing. They had shared such sweetness in the burgeoning of
leaf-bud . . . and this was how she treated him? *Played with him?* And
yet, lately she had seemed truly herself, an intoxicating mix of girl
and woman. Not as if she was lying.

His mood grew darker.

One morning his frustration at the mystery of Maeve threatened to drive him mad. He dived into the lake to wash it away, and
when he surfaced, Orla was waiting on the shore.

With a smile in her voice, she cajoled him to come with her to the steading where she and Áedán slept, to eat a proper meal. On a whim, Ruán gave in—anything to occupy his mind.

By the time they reached the huts in a fold of the hills, a thunderstorm was brewing. The shepherds avoided the lake of the sídhe, and as Ruán walked through the steading, he heard how their chatter fell into silence.

It was then he saw that the hue of fear in others was gray, a cloud that dimmed a person's soul-flame.

Nevertheless, awed by their druid visitors, the villagers sat Ruán in a place of honor at the headman's hearth. Cushioned by furs, cradled by thatch, he sat and listened to wind batter the roof and ate things he'd forgotten: mutton stewed with marsh-herbs and barley, and butter on coarse bread.

Áedán and Orla amused the herdsmen with tales of the islands, Orla sang fishing ditties, and others the tunes they hummed on the marsh, cutting reeds. No one demanded anything of Ruán, leaving him to his silence.

As the music wrapped him in drowsy warmth, he was surprised by a pang of loneliness. He missed singing, the beat of drums and ripple of laughter. There was a childhood pleasure that came from being nestled within strong walls while rain hammered outside.

The storm cleared, and near dusk, Ruán hurried back through the dripping woods, a frown on his brow.

"That was not painful, was it?" Orla trotted alongside. "You didn't choke on the bread, did you?"

"No." His steps quickened. *Through the woods, down the slope, to where the reeds sang in the wind.* He had to summon the sight back into his heart, for it had been broken by human speech. He needed that light or he would be alone when all others had left him . . .

"Bríd's breath!"

Orla's outburst halted him.

"There's a horse by the water, Ru, and it's got bronze rings all over it."

Ruán's belly swooped. "A red bay?"

"What's a bay?"

Ruán broke into a lope, his senses focused. His sight flooded back. The path unwound before him in a spool of glowing white. The trees were pale flames, the lake molten silver. At the shore, Meallán was a flare against the grass—but beside him on the ground was a smear of darkness.

The horse snorted as Ruán reached him, tossing his head. Ruán smoothed Meallán's neck and groped along his flank, dropping to his knees beside Maeve. His hand landed on her forearm. Her skin was burning.

"Maeve." His fingers flew along her limbs, gently probing any flesh not bound by her leather armor. Beneath her breastplate along one flank, her tunic was stuck to her skin. At his touch, she groaned. He cupped her face, moving his thumbs over her quivering eyelids. Her pulse was a panicked moth against his wrist. "Maeve."

A strangled gasp. "The storm. Home...must close the gates. Conor..."

"Hush." He tried to steady her, but her body was seized by a great shudder.

"Put me...d-down." Her teeth chattered. "Let me go. Let me..." Her body curled up and she retched over Ruán's arm. The fumes of vomit stung his nostrils.

"Oh." Orla had come up behind him. "That doesn't look good."

Ruán plunged knee-deep into the lake, ignoring the shock of the icy water.

His clothes reeked of the contents of Maeve's belly and her sour sweat. He pulled off tunic and trews, swirling them in the water and throwing them to the sand, then splashing his face. The drips from his chin and hair counted out a rhythm—a heartbeat running down.

Time sliding from dawn to dusk, dawn to dusk, taking more of Maeve's strength each time. Three days.

"She's not getting better," Orla said from the shore.

"I told you to stay with her."

"The sacred smoke, the broth, the chants you bade me sing—nothing works. Áedán's syrup stops her thrashing, but still she weakens."

Ruán rubbed his face with cold hands. "It is a sword wound. They turn the blood and make people sick." He breathed through the cage of his fingers. "They make warriors sick."

And who was she fighting?

"Ru, who is she? I see she is noble. She must have kin that miss her. Don't you think they should look after her? I mean, she must have healers and servants—"

"She has no one." It fell from his lips. He dropped his hands. "No one who will fight hard enough to save her."

Orla rinsed his tunic in the water again and squeezed it. She was always hovering, her hands moving alongside his in the same rhythm. "But if anything happens, you'll get in trouble. They might hurt you again."

Ruán waded out, shaking water from his bare legs. For Orla, he had taken to wearing a clout at his loins, though what he wanted was to wash the fear from every part of him. For there was one chance, a glimmer of light that was bound by a terrible darkness.

He might fail, as he did before.

"Orla," he croaked. "Go to Áedán and do not come back until the dawn after tomorrow. Do not let Áedán come here. Swear it."

"I swear," Orla stammered. "But—"

"Orla." Now his voice was that of a trained druid. After a moment, Orla threw down his wet tunic and stalked away.

Ruán strained to make sure she had gone. At last he turned from the lake. The woods before him were a wall of black. All the silver of his sight had bled away, because his heart was now tangled and dark.

He knew only a few of the plants that cleansed blood and cooled fevers. He did not know enough.

Ruán wavered. From the forest he caught a faint throb, the ancient heartbeat that beckoned him on another night like this—when Lord Mulach's son died.

He bowed his head. "I am afraid." Through the veils, he sensed a sigh at that last surrender of old pride. He eased the tightness in his throat.

He could almost hear Lord Mulach's voice again, pleading with him as the boy failed. *Send now for the wisewoman*, Mulach had begged him, deep in the night.

A brute warrior he might be, but Mulach's instincts understood that the crone who lived by the spring was more earth than human, her hair woven with leaves, her skin as creased as bark. She was a creature of soil and leaf-mold, mist and rain. She was the essence of earth in a human body.

The Mother.

And yet Ruán did not summon her, because he thought he knew better.

The answer, he was sure, was in the stars. The entrails of a hare. The carvings on the old tombs. He must seek a message from the gods that only he could read.

That night, Ruán left the boy's sickbed, heading for the hilltop to gain a view of the stars. The path to its stony crest ran through the forest.

He had no choice but to plunge into that musty darkness.

He still remembered his feet sinking into the rich loam and how it sucked at him, the twigs and leaves of trees catching in his hair. The smells were overwhelming: rotting stalks, sour mud, and the tang of vegetation. Whispers swirled around him, and he kept glimpsing flashes of light, which he ignored as tricks of the sídhe.

Back then he thought of them as mere sprites. The gods were greater beings, distant and set apart in the Otherworld. Now he knew they were all one, and they were always close ... the Otherworld eternally threaded through Thisworld.

Send for the wisewoman. Even the trees had murmured it to him that night.

Ruán, though, kept his head down as he ran, blotting out the heartbeat of the forest lest it drown him with its wild song. The rush of sap. The rustle of tiny creatures. The creep of roots and stalks. Scared of losing himself in that dark ocean of instinct and feeling, he panicked, wanting only to drag himself free of those cloying branches.

At last he had climbed free of the woods, relieved to reach the stony hilltop, so bare and cold. When he looked up, though, the stars appeared to be spinning, his mind unable to grasp their patterns. Panting, he raced along the ridge to one of the ancestor tombs, and lay in the dark summoning a trance, trying to free his thoughts to find answers.

Nothing came.

He went back to Lord Mulach's fort and sweated his son once more before bathing him in icy water. And yet still the boy's life ebbed, until at last death brought him the silence and stillness Ruán sought in himself.

Now here he was again, and this time it was Maeve's life in his hands.

Ceara.

Ruán touched his blindfold with shaking fingers. His sockets burned, as when Lord Mulach's warriors thrust the poker into his eyes. "I am not that man anymore."

The sídhe's voice floated back to him. *We are the Bridge between Worlds.*

There was no room for fear.

Naked now, Ruán breached the dark trees, and this time let the veils of the forest wreathe about him. In a glade, he lay and breathed in the scent of loam and rich decay. He drank dew from the leaves, dug himself into the soil and let the ferns close over his body.

Gradually, his heart slowed and began to swing to a different rhythm. When his body instinctively fought that cloying air, he only drew it deeper into his lungs, until the forest itself was breathing from his pores.

I am yours now, he said to the Earth Mother. He would strain for answers no more: She would bless him, or kill him. And so Ruán at last let his soul bow down before Her.

He sank, his mind adrift, every muscle surrendering. The spark of his soul spiraled behind his eyes, and he became that flame and nothing else.

Light flooded the glade.

The silver filaments that wove the shape of Ruán's spirit-body unraveled. He was conscious of them taking root, sending bright tendrils into the soil. His fingers appeared to unfold into shoots that spread among the other plants; his hair flowed over the damp ground. He became a riot of growth, the tendrils of his own self weaving through the threads of silver that made up the trees and flowers.

Heal her. That was the only conscious thought he could hold.

Ruán's awareness hovered, watching as here and there on the forest floor a plant kindled into white fire, torches flaring to light the way of his spirit.

He must become sídhe now.

Ruán flung his tiny soul-spark at the nearest bloom of fire, and again, as on the night with the sídhe, he was dancing through the streams of motes within the plant. This time he noticed that his own spark radiated a certain hue and resonated with a particular note, as in a song. As he dived among them, some of the motes in the leaves began to vibrate in harmony with that note. He focused his will, calling them into patterns of his own making. As the plant-sparks swirled around him, they grew brighter.

He was summoning life into the plant. For Maeve.

Ruán woke only slowly from that dream.

His body gradually took shape around him. He was kneeling beside Maeve, and as his human senses returned he became aware of the heat that rose from her skin.

The blooms of fire were still scattered around him. He felt for them with tingling fingers. There were roots smeared with soil, bundles of leaves, and stalks still dripping with juice.

He had gathered what flamed the brightest—the healing plants that sang in harmony with human flesh and blood.

He knew the forest. He was the forest.

Ruán at last looked down at himself with his new sight. The glow of his body was more intense than his memory of the moon: as brilliant as the sídhe were in their dance upon the ridge. So he had not only picked healing leaves. Somehow, he had summoned the Source that ran through the woods, too, gathering it in this vessel of his body so he could bring it to Maeve.

In wonder, Ruán held up his arms, heart pounding. His flesh was radiant, the shape of his hands blurred with light. The ecstasy rushed up his body from his feet, as if he was a tree rooted in the Otherworld itself.

A bridge between worlds.

He laid his hands upon Maeve, and Source flowed from him, borne on an intense wave from his heart.

CHAPTER 21

The fever broke, and sweat washed the poison from Maeve's blood.

Ruán did not take his attention off her, watching how the light of the plants was seeping into her through his healing brews and the poultices he bound over her wound.

For days, though, Maeve continued to slip between sleep and restless dreams in which she muttered as if delirious. At first Ruán wondered if he had missed something, and then realized it was the exhaustion of years, and the wanderings of a strained mind.

Orla returned with some mutton from the little steading, and together they coaxed trickles of broth between Maeve's lips, stroking her throat until she swallowed.

One day Ruán was bathing Maeve, peeling back the covers a little at a time to bare small spans of naked skin to the cool air. It took him a moment to realize Orla was watching.

"I will do it." Her hand fell upon his shoulder.

"You do not have to."

"I have birthed many babes, and buried some," she muttered. "I will do it." She plucked the sponge of moss from his hand.

Just then Maeve arched her back, her arm knocking the bowl of water from Ruán's lap. As he leaned to stop it spilling, Maeve plucked at his tunic, dragging him off balance. "They cannot think me dead," she fretted, delirious. "The queen must rise...or they will all die at Conor's hand! *Die!*"

Orla gasped.

Ruán unhooked Maeve's nails from his tunic and pressed her down into the mat of dried bracken. "Hush, *ceara*." He had been focusing so hard on saving her, he had not even thought of her people. Was it possible they did not know she was alive? Where had she been fighting to make this so? He pushed those thoughts away. "I will get a message to them. Don't be afraid. Sleep now, and get well."

Maeve sighed, and beneath his hand he felt her fingers curl up in the hollow of her throat. A memory jolted him: her chin lifting as he lapped that little dip in her flesh, his hands at the small of her back.

Ruán left the campfire on unsteady legs, seeking the fresh air that blew in over the water. Why did he do this, knitting together flesh torn by an iron blade? They rent bodies, these warriors. He pressed his fingers into the blindfold, over his empty eyes. Maeve kept choosing a path of destruction—and he had now poured his light into her. Why?

His mind tried to answer. Her bravery surely earned her a chance, even if it was not the life he sought for himself. But his heart spoke without words.

I cannot bear this flame to go out. His world would grow cold.

Orla startled him. *"Queen?"*

"Yes." Ruán swung toward her. "Orla, I must get a message to Cruachan." He felt his way to Maeve's saddle-pack, plucking out a finger-ring and an iron pin from her cloak. "Send the herder's boy to the chief druid to report that Queen Maeve is alive and will soon return. The ring is a token of proof for the druids. The child will only have the pin when he has delivered the message."

"Ru...*Queen Maeve?*" Orla squeaked. "You and me, we're humble folk. We have no business with the likes of her."

"Don't be so foolish."

"But it's dangerous! Have you learned nothing?"

Ruán turned back toward the murmuring lake, the little waves being nudged onto the sand. "She brought strength to her kingdom—at least she did that." His own fierceness caught him by surprise. "But to lose that now, her people weakened, prey to their enemies...Letting them down that way would kill her."

"It is not your concern!"

He faced Orla. "If you are my friend, then take these and do as I say."

The air prickled, Orla's flame spiking around the edges. At last she snatched the ring from his hand.

She did not return until the next morning.

The herbs had done their work, and Maeve had now fallen into a true sleep. For an endless time Ruán listened to her deep, even breaths, feeling her brow over and over. At last he felt safe enough to go and check his snares in the marshes.

Orla found him there. She pushed through the reeds and squatted on a dry patch of earth beneath a scrubby alder bush. "It is done."

Ruán gently laid down the pair of dabchicks he had snared, brushing the crests of feathers on their heads. "You do not know the truth of her."

"And what do you know?" Orla's toes cracked twigs as she leaned forward. "The reed-cutters told me everything. *She killed her own brother.* He was helpless on the ground and she stabbed her sword in him until he died!"

The chill from Ruán's wet clothes ran up his neck. That was who she had fought—her own blood?

"She did the same with a lord who challenged her—tied him up and slashed him in the neck in front of his son. *And* she ruts with all the men at Cruachan, hundreds of them," Orla breathed, "to make them do her will."

Ruán's body remembered Maeve's weight bearing him to the sand, her frantic thighs and clawing hands. He wiped a sour taste from his mouth. "Such rumors are borne of jealousy."

"Really? You know none of this?"

Ruán sank to his haunches. Nearby, the lake showed up in his mind as glittering jewels scattered over a dark veil. The sparks did not trace frantic messages of danger. They danced, beckoning... hinting at so much he did not understand.

The intricate threads that wove people's fates together.

Ruán was not ruled by stiff-necked pride anymore; he acknowledged he could not see the greater pattern. All he knew was that raw pull to Maeve—and the push away. So why did he now feel sick? *The scent of blood was still upon her.*

But he did not possess her. If he longed to live as a wild creature, then she also lived free.

She *was* a wild creature.

Ruán had looped his hair back with buckhide. Now Orla touched the sunburned nape of his neck, her sturdy hand still rough with calluses. "Leave the nobles to their swords and blood—that is the world that took your eyes. Now you have a chance to be with your own folk. You will be honored, set at the very heart of our people." Her ardent gaze was the light of a lamp spilling over his face. "I saw how you healed her. Bring that light back to us. *We need you.*"

Ruán barely heard the temptations Orla dangled of food, warmth, and honor. He only remembered what he said to Maeve the night she let out her pain in his arms.

You can only forgive yourself when you make amends.

He leaped up, flinging off his damp tunic. Boots and all, he bounded down the broken bank and into a channel of water, sloshing a few steps to where it opened out into the lake before throwing himself in.

Down he dived, away from air, voices, and colliding thoughts of Maeve.

He sought the sídhe in the depths of the lake since they would not come to him on land. The water closed around him, seeping into his skin. *Tell me what to do!* Bubbles streamed all around him, water rushing into his throat as he cried to the sídhe.

I will not lose you.

His lungs began to burn, and still he sank, until all that was dark turned silver and he dived through clouds of stars. He would drown if he did not get an answer from them.

The sparks behind his eyes whirled faster, and just before he was going to lose consciousness, he heard the sídhe-maid.

Little brother fool, you cannot lose us. We are not bound to the lake. We are everywhere.

⧉

At Emain Macha in the Ulaid, the druid Levarcham lingered in the yard outside the shrine to the Father God, the Dagda. It was set on a mound across a low valley from King Conor's royal fort.

She rarely prayed at this little shrine, for the greatest temple was that to the goddess Macha behind her, with its many circles of oak posts holding up a vast thatch roof. Levarcham wanted to see which stars rose first this night, though, and the Dagda's yard faced east and had a clear view of the sky.

Levarcham bent back her head, hoping to glimpse a pattern that could help Deirdre. The red sunset had cooled into a deep indigo. The air was thick with that after-dark dampness of sun-season. It brought to her nostrils the scent of earth, the fields churned by the feet of the harvest teams. There was grit in it, too: chaff drifting from the threshing sheds. So the year kept turning.

Where are you, my child? What distant grove witnessed the same star-rise, shining in Deirdre's beloved face? Levarcham sent out every sense she could muster, sifting the dark world about her for any clue. Desperation strained her heart.

But an answer came not from the skies.

Instead, the clear air carried a sound to her ears from the nearby hut that was the Dagda's shrine. Someone begging for help.

Levarcham would never disturb someone's prayers, but that hoarse voice was familiar, and the crack in it caught at her druid senses. She limped to the little entrance at the rear of the shrine that the druids used to reach the altar unobserved, and lifted the heavy cowhides across the doorway.

The Dagda's temple was lit by one beeswax candle in a bronze dish. The altar was an unhewn oak trunk, a symbol of the spirit-tree that anchored the worlds.

Kneeling before it was King Conor mac Nessa.

Levarcham fought down revulsion. Since Cúchulainn challenged him over the Connacht raid, Conor had been in hiding. A woman in his household who served Levarcham swore she had heard him sobbing during a drunken argument with his mother, Nessa.

Levarcham hoarded each scrap of insight into the king's mind, in case she could use it to aid Deirdre.

Conor spoke again, and Levarcham made out hissed entreaties to the gods Manannán, Lugh, and the Dagda. "I am beaten. You have seen fit to set the vixen of Connacht as an Erin queen. *A cruel lesson you teach me!*" His anguish flared and he panted and dropped his voice again. "Only you can show me a way out now. Please... *help me.*"

Levarcham's hackles rose. By the feeble glow of the candle, she could just glimpse Conor's gray head buried in his hands.

"At this harvest, there should be a woman at my side, belly swelling with my seed. I can be a true king then—strong enough for any Connacht queen! But I lost Deirdre for the Ulaid. I failed you. Help me right this now. *Help me to be free...*"

Levarcham's blood began racing out of control of her mind.

He had the gall to whine and weep, scrabbling before the gods as if they would forgive him? She wanted to strike him, fling at him all the pain she had suffered since Deirdre was torn from her. Sharpening her tongue, Levarcham prepared to step out of the shadows.

Only she could not move.

The air around the altar had grown even more dense. Levarcham was caught by it, as if she waded suddenly through water. She trembled, heart pounding, until a calmness began to flow through her. It blurred the sensation of her own shape, loosening her awareness of her limbs, muscles, and bones. A humming all around made her light-headed.

Levarcham knew this sensation. The gods were here.

Her body filled with something Greater, a presence not of Thisworld. She surrendered to it as she was trained to do, her own soul shrinking to a tiny spark that hovered on the fringes of her body.

The Other luminescence welled up and took her over.

From the darkness behind the altar, Levarcham looked at the king. Her eyes were now cloaked in a different sight that saw only hues of flame and shadow.

A blackness writhed at Conor's heart.

The candle-flame at last caught the powdered incense in the dish and flared, sending a plume of smoke to obscure Levarcham's body. "You have come for salvation. Ask what you will." They were not her words or her voice. The sonorous murmur echoed off the walls and low roof, colliding and multiplying until it surrounded the king.

Conor clenched his eyes shut, dropping his chin upon his chest. "I have lost my way."

"The gods see all. For your relief, they need utter truth."

Conor gasped, and it tumbled out. "I craved the maiden's sweet flesh in my bed, yes I did, to bury my body in hers. I wanted to possess her—and have men bow to me for commanding such a woman!"

From afar, Levarcham's spirit flickered with disgust. But the greater flame possessing her was lighting up the caverns of Conor's heart. Words flowed forth. "There is more: a man, cloaked in your hate."

Levarcham saw floating before her the fair face of a young warrior. Naisi, Deirdre's lover.

"I am withered," Conor croaked, huddled on his knees. "And..." It all rushed out. "I hated that the women loved him so, with his skin, and his black hair...*yes, I did*."

"That is not all." The breath of the gods was soft. "Let thy burden go."

The king moaned. "And the warriors...*they loved him*."

His impotent fury battered at Levarcham's heart. *All the young ones looked to Naisi...even my sons*, Conor silently railed. *They wanted to be as strong as him. They wanted to* be *him*.

Levarcham watched that thread unspool, winding back into the past and all its hoarded bitterness. Conor had always been a weak child, his mind his only weapon. He *had* to scorn what he could not have, what he hungered for—to win his kingship with a sword. Instead, his mother bought it for him by opening her thighs to Fergus mac Roy. Conor longed for his men's eyes to glow when they looked at *him*—but they only looked that way to Cúchulainn, and Ferdia.

And Naisi.

"Yes," the gods said through Levarcham. "Feel it all."

Conor's body was raging now, the agony making him clutch his belly. At that moment something poured through Levarcham from the godly presence that she did not expect.

Compassion.

"That is truth, our son, at last," the gods sighed.

It was their pity that finally undid Conor. He curled up on the earthen floor, his mouth twisting to hold down pain that never reached his eyes as tears.

Levarcham's spark of spirit was fluttering. Could his heart truly change...? *Set Deirdre free*. It was a fervent prayer, as if Conor could hear her. *Bring her home.* The strength of this human yearning at last sucked her back into her body, and she swayed on the spot as if waking.

The divine presence swiftly faded.

Levarcham staggered back against the wall, her hand out. She became aware then of someone else approaching the main entrance to the shrine behind the king. Levarcham limped through the shadows toward the rear doorway, slipping under the layers of hides.

Conor's final entreaty floated out after her. "If I am led astray by lust and envy, then I must return to what a king should be."

Levarcham stumbled into the night, dragging cold air into her lungs. A dream . . . no, she was awake. She shook her head to clear it of the incense.

At the bottom of the temple mound she stopped amid the birch trees. They lifted pale branches to the stars, as slender as Deirdre's white arms. Yet Levarcham did not need to seek their patterns now.

She trembled with something she thought she had lost.

Hope.

Conor would bring Deirdre home, and Levarcham would hold her child—and this time never let her go.

⁂

Maeve's croak was as faint as a branch rubbing in the wind. "Did you tell them?"

Ruán dropped the spoon into the mutton broth and crouched beside her on the furs at the entrance to his tent. He had tucked her up there to let the sun bathe her sleeping face.

By habit, he felt her brow. "Yes."

Maeve sighed, and when Ruán went to withdraw his hand, she turned her cheek into his palm. "Thank you."

"You should not have ridden here in that state."

"I didn't. I was bleeding, and the men were fighting . . . and

Lassar…." Her voice cracked and a droplet fell upon his wrist. "Lassar must have lifted me onto Meallán and strapped me down before he was attacked again. I think…I saw him…" She could not go on, her breath labored. "But not Garvan. Garvan lives."

Her throat moved against Ruán's wrist, and with shaking hand she touched her heart and brow in a silent prayer. "Meallán wandered, though I was barely aware of it, except for drinking rain when it fell on me. But the lake was closer than Cruachan, and I suppose he…he feels safe here." She paused. "His heart is here."

There was silence from them both.

At last Ruán peeled his fingers from her cheek. "Smart horse."

He fetched water for her and helped her drink, and she groped for his hand again, tucking it beneath her chin. "The shadows still hover close. Stay with me."

She had never pleaded with him.

Though Áedán and Orla had refused to give up and return to the island, at least Orla would not come anywhere near the lake now that Maeve was awake. Ruán had asked Áedán to also stay away; perhaps, Ruán thought, because he did not want to hear the druid speak his own thoughts—that he was mad, and had been since first he kissed Maeve back.

Right now there was nothing but a fire and the two of them, as if they were simple people after all, with simple lives. The pool of warmth and the hushed air pushed all that was real away.

Ruán settled into the deerskins. Maeve put her head on his chest, and all the breath went out of her. She was asleep immediately, nestling into his arms like a child.

CHAPTER 22

SUN-SEASON

R uán was picking raspberries along the edge of a sun-bathed clearing, pleased to find something sweet now that the honey had run out. Early sun-season was unfolding with a rush, the dusks growing long and hazy, the days still.

He recognized Maeve's step behind him. She squatted, the smell of sheep-fat and horse wafting over him from the saddle blanket around her shoulders.

"You should not be walking this far," he said.

Maeve took a raspberry from the birch basket and munched it. "I *should* have gone home days ago."

"Just because you can hobble does not mean you can ride." He eased another berry from its stalk.

"You know very well I'm not hobbling. You hear my every step."

The wound above her hip bone was knitting swiftly. It was not deep; it must have been shock that sent her into a swoon on her horse, the fever then taking hold. "I didn't let you retch all over me just to break your neck halfway home." Ruán turned to the bushes to pluck more berries.

Maeve rose and flicked his hair, leaving a tingling trail on his neck. "Now you've made me feel sick again." She crawled into the hollow, spreading her blanket among the ferns and sprawling on her back. There she let out a sigh from deep inside her. "I cannot see anything but the sky ... there is nothing at all. Nothing." The yearning in her voice bore a darker thread.

Sorrow.

Pulling up the deerskins while she slept, Ruán sometimes brushed her cheeks and still found them wet—tears she did not shed when awake. He suddenly wondered why someone so robust had taken so long to surface from this fever. As if she did not want to come back...

"Come and smell these blooms," Maeve said, "and talk to me."

"I can talk while I gather supper."

She went silent, but the next moment there was a flare beside him, and she caught his legs and dragged him toward her.

"Careful!" Ruán braced himself as he toppled on his back, trying not to fall on top of her.

Maeve propped herself up on one elbow, nudging a berry between Ruán's lips. He pressed them together, but she only squashed the fruit until it burst and dribbled down his chin. Ruán licked it away, tucking an elbow behind his head.

The blaze he saw around him now was not the sun, it was her. *Ceara.*

Ruán's limbs settled into the ferns. *She lives.* Thank the gods. Thank the land. A secret pleasure welled in his heart. *I didn't kill her.*

Maeve traced his lips with a finger, her breath berry-sweet. Ruán became aware of his pulse growing slower, stronger. He knew she must have sensed it, for she bent and kissed the beating vein in his wrist. This pool of sunshine fringed by whispering trees was set adrift, he thought unsteadily. It was a moment of time outside their real lives, their greater desires, as it always was.

She must have thought it, too, for he heard her whisper something into his skin. *Take me away...*

From the weight of sorrow, the darkness in her dreams.

And for that brief time, he could. Then he would wake, and she would be gone, and he would be left in peace again and his mind might clear.

Ruán tilted Maeve's chin up to his mouth, his fingers tangling in her curls as he held her head, parting her lips with his tongue.

This time, wounded in body, she was not frantic or lustful. She melted beneath him, so fluid and abandoned he did not know where she ended and the wild began.

The lake must have seeped into her, too, as she lay here all these days.

Her limbs molded to his with gentle absorption, though he kept his weight from crushing her side. Her face fitted the curve of his neck. Every time he thrust into her, he was diving into silky water.

The salty film over her shoulders and breasts tasted of the lake. When the pleasure broke, Ruán's awareness dissolved and another snatch came of a moment *beyond*.

The rushing wave of light that encompassed the land was *him*—and this time it was all of Erin he cradled. The strength of his arms formed the bounds of her shores, his blood the waters that gave her life.

And then it was gone.

Lying on his back, something dripped onto Ruán's shoulder. He twitched, mumbling and turning his head into the ferns.

"It is *ale*—and still you will not rouse?" Maeve took another sip, planted her lips on his, and as his mouth opened, cold liquid flowed in from hers.

He swallowed and exclaimed.

"There." She sat up, linking her arms about her knees.

Even through the haze of sleep, Ruán perceived the change in her. There was a ragged edge to her flame now. "What is wrong?"

"I walked a long way along the shore while you slept, and..." Her arm tensed. "If I can make it that far now, then I have to get home. I am a fool and have stayed too long."

Ruán knew that taut seam in her voice. While he slept, fear had slunk along the shores of the lake behind her. "You are wounded—"

Her breath exploded. "*Yes, I nearly died!* And imagine if I had been slain...what would happen to them all..." Her voice cracked. "It has all changed now, after what I saw. There isn't any more time to lose. There never was, no matter what I want for myself."

Ruán listened to her rising voice, smelled her sharp sweat. Together, they were a rampart rising between them again. "Maeve, how were you wounded?"

She paused, blowing shreds of fern from her fingers. "I ordered a cattle raid on the Ulaid."

"You attacked the Ulaid at Beltaine?" It was a sacred time, celebrating life.

She went rigid, then groped and flung on her discarded tunic as if she wanted some armor between them. "Conor raided *my* lands to steal our sacred bull."

His pulse was a louder drumbeat now. "And what," he said softly, "were your raiders seeking?"

"Proof of a weakness in the Red Branch."

"Why?"

Her sigh was forceful as she twisted toward him. "So I can bring them and Conor down."

Something was tearing inside Ruán. He sat straight to ease his chest. "If you attack the Ulaid in force, you condemn many to death. Not just warriors, but innocent people."

"My warriors do not kill crafters and farmers!" She clambered to her feet.

"Herders defend their lands and cattle, Maeve, and crafters their homes." He jumped up after her, ferns clinging to his bare thighs. He tried to rein in his rising temper. "Defense is one thing. You had to fight your rivals, or die. But attack the Ulaid in force, unprovoked, and you risk a war breaking out that will draw everyone in, from the poorest cottars to the greatest kings. You risk all of Erin!"

"How dare you question me?" Their harsh voices flushed a blackbird from the branches and it flapped away. Maeve hobbled over the grass, shoving one leg into her trews.

Ruán was struggling with the storm in his head, unable to

think. And then the hurt bloomed, and he finally understood that pain. They had shared a wonder together, opened to each other—and still she would choose to be *this*.

Kin-slayer. Sword-wielder.

An unreachable person who rose again before him, armored and bloody.

He was swamped by betrayal. He had poured all of his light into her, taken what was torn and knitted it back together in one of the greatest moments of his life. *He wove the very sparks that made him* with her own life force. And now, again, she would throw that wondrous form of flesh and spirit before a deadly blade.

Ruán swiped up his tunic and drew it over his head. "Do not speak to me like a servant. Or is that all I am?" He faced her, lips tight. "Am I just another man to fill you, distract you, like the others?"

She gasped, her flame blotted out by a darkness that was terror. "By all the gods—*I will kill Conor now before he kills me!*"

The explosion faded into silence. Ruán's blood was pumping. Could it all come down to that?

Maeve plucked up the saddle-blanket and tossed it back down, cursing. "I was *wed* to Conor. He wants to be high king of Erin. His pride is savage, only few see it because of his cunning." Her words tumbled out, senseless. "*Don't you see?* The flight of Deirdre has dealt him the final blow. He is seeking a way to prove his strength to his men again, to show his power."

"You don't know this—"

"I *do*! He has always been Connacht's greatest threat, and I won't risk *my land* based on scruples you wish I had!" They regarded each other, breathless. "It's not the same for you," she hissed. "You are safe here."

He gestured at his blindfold. "Was I safe from nobles like you, who never care about the havoc you wreak?"

She stifled an exclamation. "*I care.*"

"Do you?" He was dragging on his trews, fumbling with the laces. "Because from the moment you took that sword from your father, you have been seeking out danger and bloodshed. Anyone would think you crave it, thrive on it."

"I do not crave it." Bitterness seeped through her voice. "I never chose rape at the hands of men who saw me first as a prize and then as a threat they should destroy."

Ruán laughed, grinding his palms into his temples. "Listen to yourself! What are you going to do, kill every man in Erin so no one can hurt you again?"

Her obstinance beat upon his senses. He growled, sweeping in to grasp her face between his hands, caging her cheeks. Their legs entangled, hot breath mingling. "Open your eyes, Maeve! Use that strength of yours to *build*, not tear down." He caught his breath as her tears ran into his fingers. "I feel such fire in you—use it to make something no one has thought of before. Conor has ringed his territories with ramparts; you can do the same. Find a way to forge the strength of the other kingdoms into something greater than one tribe alone. *That* is what will make you unassailable."

Maeve's back went rigid. Her flame, now a turmoil of black and red, sent up a desperate flare. "*Gods, you are right.* The kingdoms must band together to attack Conor. It is the only way."

With a curse, Ruán thrust her away. He took a step and turned. "What are you doing here with me, Maeve? I am not a warrior. I am not a lord. I cannot give you anything to make you safe from men like Conor of the Ulaid. You choose that life ..." He sketched a hand at his eyes. "But I left that world long ago." He dropped his hands by his sides. "So tell me what I am to you. What we are."

And if she answered ... he would know for certain himself.

That pause was full of struggle. "It does not matter." Her voice was ragged, despairing. "Whatever I try to hold for myself ... it will be torn away from me by Conor and men like him. So no one ... no one can be anything to me."

Ruán's chest deflated, and he nodded, his chin down.

"There is not only *my life* to consider ..." She faltered. "I have people to protect—"

"People you put in danger every day by setting them on the battle-path. Can't you see it? Your fear of Conor takes your sense."

"I do not fight for me, I do it for *them*."

"If that is what you tell yourself at night."

Maeve choked back a cry and struck him in the chest, her fist on his breastbone.

That blow forced all the hurt out of Ruán, and in the shocked silence that ensued, a calmness poured over him. His mind cleared into a dawn of understanding.

He had saved Maeve's life three times: the sacred number of the gods. Connacht needed a strong ruler, and she had stopped the kingdom from disintegrating—that was undeniable. She was born to be a shield, a sword. That was what her druid dreamed, only Ruán had not fully believed it. He couldn't fight his way through that ... but as she said, it did not matter.

He would make it not matter.

And now he knew what to grasp for—his fate was only ever to help the Queen of Connacht to her throne.

Ruán went light-headed, his ears ringing. Maeve had brought the life and vigor back into his body. He helped her to power. It was a bargain, as she had always said.

A bargain fulfilled.

The glimmer of the sídhe washed through Ruán. He heard their singing, faint as wind in the reeds. "I miss the one who opened to me, and wept in my arms."

"If I weep, I break—and people die." But in Maeve's voice was the force of will she was marshaling to speak this way. She wrapped herself in the saddle-blanket. "Perhaps the Shining Ones did help me to my hall, but kings who fail to protect their flock are sacrificed to the gods."

"If you were blessed by the sídhe, it is because of the surrender that has happened in your heart, not the blade in your hand. For someone so brave, it's the one truth you will not face."

Maeve was backing up. "The Red Branch wield a weapon we

do not understand. The only way to be safe is to attack Conor when he is weakened."

Pity throbbed in Ruán, and his reply emerged with tenderness. "And all you do is stoke his wrath higher."

"No! You do not understand."

"Ceara—"

"No." The despair in her whisper pierced him, the hopelessness of a wild thing ensnared. "I know what I have to do." With a catch in her throat, Maeve spun about and hastened away.

Ruán heard the faltering of her step, the wound paining her. There was nothing to do but let her go.

He sat down cross-legged, his face lifted to the sky as he tried to slow his breath. He could muster no sight, could only cling to the lifeline of the sunshine soaking through him.

At his heart, though, there was only ice.

At the stables of Cruachan, Maeve was easing Meallán's saddle off when Finn burst through the open doors. The girl's face was bone-white, her eyes glittering. She went to fling herself at Maeve and stopped a hand-span away, rocking on her toes as if she did not know which way to fall.

Maeve drew breath, her eyes lifting to her daughter like someone in darkness seeking the glow of a fire. She had passed the funeral pyres of the men who died in the raid on her way across the plain, the ashes still smoldering. The reek clung to her hair, to her dead heart.

But more deaths would come if they did not stay strong.

"I..." Finn's voice cracked. Her face was all twisted up, a cub in pain.

It stirred Maeve's instincts, piercing the fog around her. She curved her palm behind Finn's head, then stepped close to crush her child into her chest. "I told you I was hard to kill."

Finn's breath leaked out of her, her brow upon Maeve's breast. "But you did not run away from the warriors, as you promised."

"No." Maeve stared over Finn's shoulder into the dusty shadows of the stable. Her eyes were glassy. "I could not live with myself if I ran away. It is my duty to stay." Her embrace tightened around the one in her arms, so vulnerable as she huddled against her. She was meant to shelter them all...she made an oath. "I brought the wrath of the wolf upon you, so it is I who must fight. I have to be more ruthless than he is, lunge first, or he will defeat us. I have to be ..."

"Mother...?" Finn raised her head.

Maeve's lips parted and she looked into Finn's puzzled eyes. Blinking, she brushed a strand of Finn's copper hair from her brow. "Go tell Fraech I am back and that I will see him tomorrow, when I have rested." She turned and left, her head pounding so hard she could barely see.

As sheets of rain blew in, Maeve sought out Garvan to assure herself he was alive, watching him from afar training on the waterlogged meadows with the men. She slipped away before he saw her, and managed to evade Tiernan and everyone else as well, pleading that she needed her sleep.

Her throat aching, she eased herself into her bed in her bedchamber, ignoring her soaked hair and chilled body.

She could not face anyone. No one must touch her raw skin or drag her back with their questions, not yet. She conjured again every touch in the sunshine, the way he murmured to her, the taste of his lips. *She could hoard that...*

She was staring into the sputtering lamp when Ailill came lumbering up the stairs.

"Lugh's ball's, but what were you thinking?" Ailill unhooked his dripping cloak and threw it over a chair. "What madness possessed you?"

She squinted at him, her eyes gritty with unshed tears.

"As soon as I heard of this fool raid, I rode back from Laigin. I only wished I'd caught you before you left...*damn and blast it, Maeve!*" He grabbed the jug of watered wine on her dresser and drank from the spout. The rain and mist had turned his spiked brown mane into a limp tangle.

"Ailill—"

He slammed the jug down, wiping his beard. "*And then* we feared you dead, until some scraggly brat ran in with a mysterious message for Tiernan, and scampered off before anyone could find out where he came from!"

Ruán of the marsh. Maeve pressed her temples, closing her eyes. If she clenched her belly, it curdled her sorrow into anger at Conor instead. Make the deaths of Lassar and her men count for something. *Use* what they won against the Ulaid.

If she did not, she betrayed them all.

She eased herself to her feet, her legs weak. "There is something wrong with the Red Branch. They ambushed us and should have beaten us easily, but most of us escaped." She bit her lip, eyes on the lamp-flame. "Most."

"They nearly killed *you*, you rash idiot!"

Maeve's head went up. Good gods...he did not care like that?

A flush crept over Ailill's heavy cheeks, veiling the web of ale-veins. His glance was defiant. "If you die, I lose all that you promised me."

Ah. She nodded, scraping her wet hair back with one hand. "I have seen the Red Branch train at Emain Macha. This time they were broken, and Cúchulainn could not hold them. I saw it with my own eyes—that is what the deaths of our warriors bought us. This unrest among them has dealt a fatal blow to their strength."

Ailill's glare faded.

Maeve balled her fists over her chest. "*Now* is the time to throw everything we have at Conor and bring him down! Go back to your father, and this time ask him for men. We need more than a war-band. We need an army."

Ailill folded his burly arms, planting his feet. "My father is still too afraid of the Red Branch to risk an outright defeat, you know that."

Lassar's face loomed before Maeve. More of Connacht's young ones would die. "You must do this." Sweat broke out over her lip. "It is our only chance."

"Must?" Ailill advanced on her, reeking of horse and ale. "I don't know why you think I'll do your bidding when you hardly ever share your thoughts with me—let alone your body!"

She blinked, her sight coming back into focus. Ailill looked peevish, his eyes small and hard beneath bushy brows. "I am a queen," she said, "not a hearth-wife. That is what your women are for—you certainly brought enough of them with you."

"You used to be true to your promises." Ailill clamped her arms, his tone darker. "I will play the part you charged me with when you play yours."

Maeve's nostrils flared as she bent her head up at him. Everything she had buried at the lake now came rushing up her body.

She pushed him away and, turning, ripped off her damp tunic and trews, breast-band and clout. Her wound was a branding iron pressed to her side. Balling the clothes, she flung them at the wall with a gasp of frustration. All her promises had been given away, one by one, to forge the shield for her people.

And so now she did not own a moment of peace for herself.

She had spoken vows to her husband, too. *An ally.* She made herself remember that, though it felt empty to her now. She faced Ailill, crooking her hands on her naked hips, her chest heaving. His eyes went wide as he saw the bandage. Then his gaze dropped lower.

Maeve's curves had been pared away by illness, riding, and weapons: the muscles at her waist built up, the flesh of her hips worked off. It was not a lush body to excite a man. Perhaps the vulnerability of her injury affected Ailill, though, or the trembling she could not hide.

Desire began to warm his eyes, and he smiled.

It took a week for Maeve to bring her wrath to heel and return to the lake. Ruán had saved her more than once. She owed him every apology she could muster, and even more gratitude. She had to show him what really lay inside her, so he would again call her *ceara* with that catch in his voice.

I was yours long ago. Be with me through this, and soon it will change.

As she rode, Maeve comforted herself—a little—that at least Ruán already *knew* her pride was abominable. Perhaps he could forgive her.

He had to forgive her.

At the fringes of the reeds, Meallán came to a halt, his ears twitching back and forth. He had already sensed what was only dawning over Maeve. The silence of the lake had deepened. For the first time, the emptiness felt threatening, the wind tearing at her cloak.

It was a wild place now, and nothing more.

Maeve slid to the ground, the hammering in her chest drowning out the subtle shifts in her surroundings. She crossed the shore. The dew coated the grass, unbroken by footsteps. She reached the place where they put up his tent in the hailstorm. The shelter was still there, though the flap had come undone and the furs inside were wet. Everything she had brought was laid upon the bed—pots and platters, the fire-dog to spit meat over the hearth, deerskins and blankets.

They were already musty with damp.

Her thoughts flew around, crazy as moths. Perhaps she had furnished this place in a swoon of madness, and there had never been a Ruán. Perhaps she had been led astray by the glimmers of the lake, the murmuring reeds.

So why had the emptiness crept inside her now?

Maeve forced herself to move, squatting by the hearth. He might be off fishing after smooring the fire to save the coals. She reached out a quavering hand and let her palm hover over the ashes.

Cold. Long dead.

Her chin sank to her breast.

At dusk Maeve rode into Cruachan.

She did not pay any mind to the blur of people who flowed out of her way. At the stables, she uncramped her fingers to wave aside the boys who came running to catch Meallán's bridle. She forced a stiff leg over to dismount.

She came back to herself with a jolt, ankle-deep in straw in the darkest stall away from the doors. She was standing with her palms on Meallán's sweaty flank. Her horse had splashed through the lake, and still smelled of sour mud and weedy water. If she let go of him, that smell would be gone, too. She would have to face the harsh light of day, the bustle of the dun.

Meallán's hide trembled, as if something poured into him from her touch. Maeve jerked her hands away.

"Mother."

This time she longed to turn from that voice, lurking in cold shadow until she went numb.

"Mother?"

The voice was insistent, tugging on her. A touch came on her shoulder, her arm. Maeve lifted her aching head and flinched as the pale light from the doors caught her face.

Finn searched the tracks on Maeve's cheeks. "Are you sick again?"

A familiar denial surfaced. But she was only talking to herself, wasn't she? No one would know her weakness if she whispered it to herself in the mirror. "The pain...it burns. I can't...I can't breathe."

A pause. "Then let the servants fill a bath for you, Mother, in the women's lodge. That will soothe you, and I will wash your hair."

As Maeve walked across the grass, everything was a haze of

color: snapping red banners on gold thatch roofs, white clouds scudding across a bright sky, the green plains beyond high, dark ramparts. She longed to burrow away from it all.

Only when she huddled in steaming water, a sponge spilling heat down her back, did her shivers slow. Her knees were against her chest. Water poured over her hair. Fingers massaged her head.

Dimly, Maeve became aware of footsteps approaching the screen of woven willow around the bath. Finn dropped the bone scoop to the flagstones of the bath-chamber and dashed out. "My lord?"

"I have news for the queen." It was Garvan.

"Can it not wait ...?"

"No, it cannot, little Red. I'm ready to leave for Mumu, to see King Niall."

"But ... she's not dressed!"

A snort. "It is nothing I haven't seen before."

Garvan was standing by the bath. Maeve looked up at a thatch of black glossy hair, a glint of bright eyes. "I thought you should know Ailill has gone to see his father, spitfire. He was all primped, his guards and horses scrubbed. He listened to you, after all."

The words fell through Maeve. She stared down at the water, red in the light of the brazier. She put her hand on the surface so the skin of it clung to her.

The shining lake reflecting the sunset ... Ruán singing as he built the fire behind her. Gazing out, she had not been able to turn away from the burning sky and glowing water, even though she was in ankle-deep and growing cold. She had longed for that peace to flow into her, to fill her forever.

"Maeve." Garvan's step dislodged a sponge from the tub and it fell in the water, shattering the surface.

Maeve forced her chin up.

"Did you hear what I said? Ailill has gone to Laigin. I am for Mumu."

She gazed at him wide-eyed. *It had begun.* There was no stopping it now ... the warriors were gathering their strength, champing at the bit.

Her hands fell on the sides of the bath, gripping the rim to push herself up. Naked she was, but she must be clad now in the heavy robes of a queen.

That was what her people needed. She had made that vow to them on the steps of the temple of Lugh, the day the sacred mead bound her to the land.

CHAPTER 23

Cúchulainn sat at his own fire for once. He had retreated to his fort Dun Dalgan, near the eastern shore of the Ulaid close to the border with Laigin.

His was not a formal household, and everyone from the boys who led the cattle to the cooks and weavers clustered into his hall at night. At the still of dusk, though, when the stock was being penned and servants were roasting meat and stirring broth, everyone left Cúchulainn and his wife alone beside the flames.

Emer and Cúchulainn nestled close, her head on his shoulder as they shared one cup of mead. The glow on Emer's soft cheek and the gleam of her dark hair let Cúchulainn pretend, for a moment, they were simple herders at their hearth, the cattle safely in for the night.

Emer's heart beat against his arm where she pressed her breast to him. Cúchulainn sighed.

"My father was here today." Emer's husky voice was comforting. "The other chieftains are growing angrier with Conor, but Fa doesn't think anyone will act against him. They are too afraid."

For a mad moment it occurred to Cúchulainn that if one of

the lords usurped the king, their problems would be solved. *I could*. But his oath was to protect the Ulaid, and if anyone seized power without the acclaim of all the chiefs, battle would ensue. Conor had bought many of them with land and other riches, and for some, that would hold more power than loyalty to the people.

This could still be mended...if Ferdia found the sons of Usnech.

Poor Ferdia. He had not been back long from Skatha's— empty-handed—when Levarcham sought them out. The silver-haired druid, her face now so haunted, told Cúchulainn and Ferdia that she had nearly killed herself with the druid herbs, but had at last glimpsed in her visions something of Deirdre's where-abouts.

She was certain that the girl and the sons of Usnech were hiding in the west of Alba.

Ferdia immediately took off again, desperate to get to them before Conor did. This time Cúchulainn had pressed hard to go, but Ferdia talked him down once more. "You must stay, Cú, and hold the Red Branch together. That Connacht raid was too close." Ferdia's smile was tight as he hefted his pack into the boat's hull. "And I am expendable."

"Not to me," was Cúchulainn's sharp reply.

Ferdia's face was still hovering before him in the flames as Cúchulainn rested his chin upon Emer's brow. She reached a hand up and ran it through the hair at his temple.

Suddenly, the Hound went alert.

Cúchulainn heard the challenge from one of his guards then, and the scrape of the gates and thud of hooves. A panicked horse—it had been ridden fast.

Emer sat up. "What?" Dark curls drooped over her face as she rubbed her nose.

"Ferdia." Cúchulainn spoke his longing aloud. But...no. His guards would never challenge Ferdia.

The rider ducked into the hall, mist dampening his hair and muddy cloak. It was a warrior Cúchulainn had planted in the king's hall at Emain Macha long ago. With a taut face, Cúchulainn shoved a cup of ale in the rider's hand. He gulped and spoke between swallows. "Conor has at last discovered the sons of Usnech."

Emer gasped, a hand flying to her mouth.

"The king heard rumors of three Erin men at Dunadd, the western stronghold of the Epidii tribe. The king has sent someone to identify them before he does anything else."

Does what? Cúchulainn wondered, sick to the belly. Pay the Epidii king for prisoners in chains? Dispatch someone to kill them? Or send someone dear to Naisi, who would bring them home safely, with their honor intact?

Ferdia did not get to them first.

Chilled despite the flames, Cúchulainn asked his servants to feed the man and find him a bed. Then he swung back to Emer.

"Conor knows that the eyes of his people are upon him," Emer said swiftly.

"Aye." Cúchulainn swallowed, determination hardening. "He cannot harm them if everyone knows this news. I must ensure it is spread among the Red Branch—and shouted from the walls of Emain Macha." He beckoned to the men on the wall-benches sharpening their spears. "Bring my weapons!" he cried. To Emer, he muttered, "I'll need jewels and clothes. Are my best robes clean, my boots? The horse-tack and chariot need polishing..."

"Husband." Emer gripped his arms. "We will ready it all. The king and his men know there is only one Hound of Cullen, and they will hearken to that glorious sun when it rises in their midst."

He filled his lungs, focusing on her again.

"But...you go tonight?" Emer's voice dropped as she searched his eyes.

Cúchulainn gathered himself, brushing a curl from her cheek. "At dawn. So come with me now, wife, and we will make a flame of our own to drive back the dark. I will take it with me when I go to challenge the king."

In the blessed darkness of the storehouse, Conor, King of the Ulaid, sprawled among his riches. His head swayed, so heavy on his neck. The room spun and he threw an arm around the bulge of a grain sack, piled up as the harvest was gathered in.

He had crept there to escape it, but the blaze that was Cúchulainn still hurt his eyes, as if Conor had looked into the sun.

Just after dusk the Hound had come, slamming open the doors of Conor's hall. The firelight reflected off his gold and bronze as he paced around the hearth, and every flash speared Conor, pinning him to his chair. So he knew that he had at last found Deirdre and Naisi.

"Bring them home with honor!" Cúchulainn had bellowed, prowling before the Red Branch heroes—shaming his king before his warriors. "Bring them and feast them, and mend what has been riven, and make us one again."

Conor wanted to. Since he felt the touch of the gods in the temple, he longed to. He had already sent someone Naisi loved to Alba to fetch the exiles home—Fergus mac Roy and his sons Illan and Buinne.

Conor's gaze darted about the storehouse. Even here, moonlight found its way between the timbers, picking out all the wealth he possessed.

His breaths were muffled by jars and barrels, sacks, baskets and pots piled up against the walls. On a shelf, a gleam of wood bound by iron bands. Crawling over, Conor reached up and clawed out the bung of the little keg, opening his mouth beneath. He gulped, greedy for oblivion, mead spilling down his chin. When he thought he might be sick, he shoved the bung back in, collapsing against the wall. His throat burned.

He swallowed the sweet juices of Deirdre's mouth.

No. His nails dented the timbers beneath him. They were not his thoughts. He summoned the ecstatic vision from the temple instead. That was real, and sacred. The voice of the gods.

Deirdre.

Even now she might be flying to him over the waves. She

would shine a light over his kingdom, her beauty binding his fractured people back together. Conor crawled back to the sacks, the floor bucking beneath him. He scrabbled with the flax tie until he tore one open. *See…grain.*

Deirdre would stand beside him at the temple and bestow upon him her gifts of plenty. Conor grabbed a handful of barley seeds, crushing them to his nose.

Wife, came a dark whisper. *Queen.*

Conor gasped, scattering grain over the floor. She was Naisi's. They were both so young and beautiful…If his people saw them together, and *then* he wrenched her from Naisi, they would all cry out against him. There must be some way his possession of Deirdre could become a sacred duty.

The walls shivered away, and Conor saw himself at the shrine of Macha, holding Deirdre's hand and being cheered by his people. And there, on her other side…there must stand Naisi in some position of honor, to show all was forgiven.

The Red Branch would revere him for that.

Clutching another handful of seed, Conor pushed himself up and stood wavering from side to side. Slowly, he poured the grain over his head until it streamed through his gray locks and caught on his eyes and wrinkled cheeks.

Turning his hair gold again—making his skin gleam once more.

He longed to be the Good God, the father of the land who made everything fertile, who brought safety and plenty to his people. That was why he must elevate Deirdre into a goddess—an idol—whom all would worship. For if they worshipped *her,* she would bestow that sacredness on him.

Conor staggered, the seeds of plenty spilling from his shoulders onto the wet floor.

Maeve's illness appeared to return to her.

Her body became exhausted—a weariness she could only

overcome with an effort of will. Her mind, though, was fevered, and her heart would not be still. She would not allow it, even for a moment.

There was no way to exist but to push on.

Aching in every bone, she rode the rounds of the harvest feasts, waiting until the dancing was frenzied and the mead flowing before she begged the lords for more men to build her warbands. She sorted tithes and cattle-portions; heard complaints and dealt with trade ships; settled marriages and chieftain disputes.

She paced the ramparts, studying the sparring warriors with burning eyes. If she had only sacred duty to drive her on, then that is what they must summon, too.

Then Ailill returned from Laigin with the news that Ros Ruadh would not support any plan for a full-scale attack on Conor. Despite Conor's demands for the bull, and the raid on Connacht, Ros Ruadh thought the Ulaid were still too strong to defy. They still possessed the Red Branch.

He is old, Maeve stormed to Ailill. *His fear makes him weak.*

Without Laigin, the secret appeal to Mumu also came to nothing.

And then came worse—much worse.

"Conor has found his fugitives in Alba," Garvan reported to Maeve. "He's forgiven Naisi and his brothers, and Fergus is bringing them and Deirdre home so he can set them back in a place of honor."

So they were too late. The Ulaid would bind themselves back together, closer than ever, and be too strong to ever face again.

And so Conor would come in force for Connacht. For her.

Too late, Maeve fretted, as she dragged herself up the stairs to the gate-towers, slipped on and off her horse, and raised her hollow voice in laughter among the fighting men. She gulped mead with the chiefs until they fell over and she was left staring into the bonfires and seeing nothing but destruction.

"You never stay still," Ailill complained one day from the hearth-bench in the king's hall, as Maeve pulled her mantle on and squatted to lace her boots. "You never come to bed, and you won't sit and eat."

"I am a queen," she muttered, head down. A wave of dizziness hit her, and she sat on the rushes, blinking to clear her eyes. "If you want a kingdom to rule, then this is what I must be."

I can only be this.

Memories of *him* kept creeping in, each drawing a blade that hacked away at her roots. But if she let them fell her, she would huddle and weep and her strength would bleed away. Instead, she crushed that pain into a ceaseless ache that merely walked beside her.

She would not even think his name.

Maeve returned in the dark that night when Ailill had already drunk himself into a stupor. Aching all over, she removed her armor beside the low bed. She flinched when she brushed the welts her breastplate had worn under her arms. The sword's weight had rubbed blisters beneath her belt, and battered bruises down her thigh.

She accidentally touched the thin scar on her flank. *Tenderly knitted back together.* Her fingers leaped away as if scalded.

Shivering, she crawled in beside a snoring Ailill and sat with her back against the mud wall. In the dark beneath the thatched eaves she could clench her knees to her chest and no one would know.

That day, Erna told her of something Tiernan had cried out during a vision in the grove. The druids who witnessed it were whispering among themselves in dismay, the rumor spreading among all the priests like a blight.

All riven, all burning!

Blood shines in the fire, amid the flames.

And after, there is only ash blowing through empty halls.

Sorrow becomes a fog over the land, light perishes.

Cruachan. It must be.

There was little Maeve could do without the support of the other kingdoms, or at least an agreement from her own chieftains to send their men into battle. She could throw herself into Connacht's defenses, however.

The Gates of Macha were part of a network of ditches, banks, and ramparts that Conor had delved and raised over many years along the border of the Ulaid. There wasn't time for earthen defenses for Connacht, though—only wood.

Day in and day out Maeve rode the borders as teams of crafters and warriors threw up stockades at river crossings and on the ridges that crossed the marshes. They would not stop a large warband, but they would halt a horse charge and give shelter to Connacht spearmen.

The days were long and Maeve was able to stay out late, suffering only brief nights of dreams she could not control.

Someone hovering over her, his breath warm on her lips.

Her face cradled in the nook of his shoulder, as she breathed in wolf-scent.

She woke from such dreams curled up, holding her belly against an ache she barely remembered.

One blustery day, she and Garvan watched a row of stakes being hammered into a boggy spur between two lakes. The sun was beginning to sink into the reed-fringed water when a rider came streaking along a track from the east.

It was his reckless speed that caught Maeve's eye as he wheeled his horse out over the rough ground, weaving between ruddy marsh pools and jumping streams. She stopped listening to the carpenter beside her, who was complaining he needed more oak.

Garvan was already vaulting onto his pony, shouting at the rider to slow as he drew his sword. Maeve recognized the young spearman, though, and that his face was contorted with excitement, not aggression. She ran forward, waving Garvan back.

The youth hauled his horse up before her. "My lady," he panted. The sunset turned his face scarlet, and it was sheened with sweat. "More than two hundred warriors have crossed from Ulaid lands on foot. They skirted the Great Lake and came upon the Fort of the Birches."

Maeve's tender belly turned over. "An attack?"

"No! They have women and children with them, and they sheathed their weapons. They say they come in peace."

Maeve's eyes narrowed as she tried to think past another wave of sickness, a prickling of heat across her neck. A trick?

"They want to be brought before you. They said you alone would know them."

When she dwelled among the Ulaid, Maeve had been mostly confined to the royal halls and their surrounds on Emain Macha's heights. The only warriors she knew by sight were . . .

She clutched the boy's bridle, making his horse shy. "Do they bear red shields with a gold tree? Armbands of braided bronze, the fastening a spearhead?"

The boy gulped at her fierce tone. "Armbands, yes."

"This is some act of treachery," Garvan growled.

"No, my lord." The muddy scout shook his head. "They had druids with them, and all swore on every god we know that they spoke true."

It could not be. "Is there a slight man among them," Maeve demanded, "someone easy to overlook, lean but muscled, fair hair, no beard, and blue eyes that do not flinch?"

"Maeve . . ." Garvan put in doubtfully.

"Not that I saw." The youth's face cleared. "But their leader is an enormous old man with lots of silver hair."

Maeve dropped the harness, her lips falling open. She glanced at her filthy clothes. She had been in the saddle for days, sleeping on the ground at night. Her hand went to her stomach as it stirred again.

She was so overwrought she'd hardly been eating, and her insides had begun to rebel. She would meet no fighters of the Ulaid in this state.

"Hold them at the Fort of the Birches," she squeezed out, "and bring them to my hall at high-sun in four days. Hurry." She gave the pony a smack on its rump and stood with her cloak flapping around her as the boy galloped away.

"I'll be back," Maeve muttered to Garvan, and dashed into a nearby cluster of birches that feathered the darkening marsh. Clutching one of the trunks, her belly rippled and brought up a few scant mouthfuls of porridge.

She stared at her feet, panting.

CHAPTER 24

LEAF-FALL

The King's Hall of Cruachan was packed with Connacht fighters draped in their finery.

Maeve gazed at her warriors. Their wives had pinned swaths of imported scarlet and blue cloth on them, with brooches studded in coral and amber. Their heads formed a sea of jagged crests, hair limed into spikes. Swords hung prominently on leather scabbards embroidered with gold beads, shell, and bone.

They looked a match for the Ulaid.

Two whole boars sizzled over the hearth-fire. Every lamp blazed, shining on Connacht's wealth of furs and embroidered hangings, the tables and chairs of oiled wood, the bronze and horn platters and cups.

Maeve's buttocks were barely touching the seat and her brow was clammy. *You will stay down*, she ordered her stomach, and broke a piece off the bannock on the arm of her chair, swallowing it as she nodded to her steward to bring the Ulaid leaders in.

She had ordered her women to sew raven feathers all over a

scarlet cloak, and she wore it with her leather breastplate, tunic, and kilt, her battle helmet on flowing red hair. Her sword lay along her bare thigh, where it would catch the light. She would only appear to the Ulaid-men in armor, so they would remember their warrior-queen Macha. Beside her, Ailill was attired in costly wool and furs—the power of Laigin and Connacht together.

The first man had to collapse his great bulk to get under the lintel, straightening and filling the room. A craggy face, scarred nose, and hair a great silver sweep from wrinkled brow to hulking shoulders. Fergus mac Roy. So it was true.

As the Ulaid filed in, the Connacht warriors all bristled, crowding them with a forest of spears. Maeve had been the payment for a peace treaty that did not last, and old enmities had asserted themselves once more.

She flicked a finger at one of her ale-maids, who tripped forward with a two-handled cup of bronze. "My mistress and master welcome you to Cruachan Aí," the girl said to Fergus. "Accept a sip of their finest mead, and wash the road from your throat."

Fergus glanced at Maeve from under his brows. By accepting her mead he could not harm her at her own hearth.

He stretched out massive, scarred hands to the cup, straining the mead through his long moustache then handing it to men ranged to either side. Maeve could not see any of them clearly in the firelight and shadow.

She hauled her weary body up, the raven feathers fluttering, and touched her brow. "Fergus mac Roy. It is an unexpected pleasure to welcome a former king of the Ulaid, a warrior of the Red Branch, and kinsman of Conor mac Nessa."

Fergus's face spasmed. "I do not lay claim to those titles anymore," he rumbled. His sagging cheeks grew red, his mouth twisting as if something was trying to force its way out. "We have foresworn our allegiance to Conor. We come to offer our swords to you."

The exclamations of the Connacht warriors drowned out all

else—a tumult that rose to the roof-beams. Maeve's heart bounded with it. Breathless, her eye fell on the blond man beside Fergus. "Cormac mac Conor."

Amid the din, Conor's eldest son saw her lips move with his name.

Pride had always been stamped on his thin, bony face as it was on his sire's, his sharp nose tilted above icy blue eyes. Now he was stubbled and red-eyed. He stepped forward, and when Maeve lifted her hand, her baying men fell silent.

Cormac's voice cracked. "I no longer bear his name."

Guests were supposed to be feasted before speaking their business, but Maeve threw aside all manners, gripping her hilt with white knuckles. *"What has happened?"*

Fergus's great shoulders slumped, sorrow dragging down his mouth. He beckoned to someone behind him. The other man stirred wearily, the colored stripes of a *fili* barely showing through the mud on his cloak.

"Not a bard." Maeve pointed at Fergus. "Once, over a fidchell game, you told me you spoke only the language of the warrior, sharp and clean as a blade. I want that." She swirled her raven feathers about and sat down, gazing at Fergus.

The old warrior sighed and, waving his bard away, stepped ponderously into the glow of the fires. He looked around the throng, the emptiness in his eyes making people draw back. Only then did he begin to speak.

Fergus's deep voice told a tale that was indeed too raw for poetry. Maeve forgot she was clutching her chair...forgot everything.

He and his sons, Buinne and Illan, had been sent over the sea to bring Deirdre and the three sons of Usnech home. Once back on Erin's shores, they were making their way to Emain Macha when a messenger on the road drew Fergus away on unexpected business. Buinne and Illan agreed to go on with the fugitives to Conor's stronghold, for Naisi's pride bade him seek Conor's pardon with all haste. Conor, meanwhile, had sent all the Red Branch heroes and Naisi's allies on errands away from the fort.

Once the fugitives were inside Emain Macha, he betrayed them, trapping them in the empty Red Branch hall.

"No one was there to aid them but my sons." Fergus's eyes were glassy, fixed on the wool hanging above Maeve's head. "Buinne abandoned Naisi in exchange for Conor's promise of riches. But Illan..." He stopped, wiped his mouth as if he could not bear the words. "Illan stayed in the Red Branch hall to defend the sons of Usnech."

Unbeknownst to anyone, Conor had summoned to him a chieftain from a far-flung province who was not Red Branch and had no loyalties to the brothers. This chief and his men surrounded the Red Branch hall. Conor stood outside the doors and demanded that Naisi surrender Deirdre, even though he had vowed they would all be safe in his hands. When Naisi refused, Conor's wolves set fire to the hall. The sons of Usnech sought to escape at the back, while Illan held the great doors at the front alone.

At this point in his story Fergus began to shake.

Naisi and his brothers could not escape and had to break out through the flames. By then, Red Branch warriors had heard the news of the brothers' return and were hurrying back to Emain Macha. Conor's own youngest son, Fiacra, raced to the hall. There was terrible confusion, misunderstandings—and Fiacra and Illan, twin souls, ended up fighting each other amid shadow and flame.

"And then..." Fergus faltered, and forced it out in an icy stream. "Our Red Branch brother Conall arrived. Unable to see clearly in the smoke, he charged up to defend the king's son, Fiacra. And...he mistakenly stabbed my Illan from behind. To the death."

The silence throbbed. A single tear ran down Fergus's whiskered chin, but he did not move. Mac Roy had loved his younger son Illan to distraction, Maeve knew.

Cormac stirred and took up the story. "I also rushed to the burning hall. There, I saw Illan bleeding, and what I thought was an enemy warrior bending over him with a sword. So I...killed him." His breath wheezed out, eyes sank closed. "I killed my brother Fiacra, my little brother."

Gods. Maeve crushed her hand over her mouth as mutters of horror ran around the room.

With Illan and Fiacra dead, the three sons of Usnech and the girl Deirdre were surrounded. Conor offered Naisi one last chance to give her up—a chance he did not take. In the face of all those swords, Deirdre also spurned the king.

Then the last Red Branch hero arrived—Cúchulainn.

At the mention of that hallowed name, someone behind Cormac stirred. Maeve ignored the disturbance, enthralled.

Cúchulainn thought Emain Macha was being attacked by enemies, and charged in to defend the three sons of Usnech. Even with his strength and skill, the four of them were no match for the sheer numbers of renegade warriors. Cúchulainn saved the girl, but Naisi, Ardan, and Ainnle were slain.

People gasped, swept along by the story as if they watched it play out in the writhing flames of the hearth-fire.

Fergus lifted his grizzled head and resumed the tale. He left Emain Macha to bury Illan at his own fort, while Cormac and many of the other Red Branch heroes lay wounded. Still Conor would not leave Deirdre alone, even though she was bedridden in her grief for Naisi. He tried to force himself upon her, but when she cursed him, he punished her by vowing to give her to the treacherous chieftain, Naisi's killer, for his bed.

Maeve's mouth twisted as she was overtaken by a memory of Conor's bony limbs jabbing her, his cold lips capturing hers. When he took a woman, she knew, his eyes were lit with the zeal of conquering something.

On the day she was to be given away as a slave, Deirdre came out of the lodge entirely naked but for her long golden hair. Vulnerable and proud, she approached Conor and all the warriors with her head high.

Now Fergus bent his shaggy head into his hand. "I watched her walk to us like a queen, a goddess. And I—still clad in the ashes of my son's body—I knew if that girl could defy Conor, then I had to. I could never again breathe the same air as the murderer of *my son*. I could not call myself Red Branch when he had ruined that brotherhood by turning us on each other. I could not stay in a kingdom that was tainted with such foulness."

Tiernan's prophecy shuddered through Maeve. *All riven. All burning. And after, there is only ash to blow through empty halls.* He was speaking of the Ulaid all along.

"I broke my oath of allegiance to Conor," Fergus finished. "And I led from Emain Macha all those Red Branch who felt the same as me, and other warriors and their families. Now, as exiles, we seek shelter in your kingdom."

Maeve was barely clinging to the chair. The tale had summoned Conor for her in all his dark glory, the memory making her heart hammer. But this...

This was her chance to rid herself of that fear forever. *The Red Branch was now in her hands.*

Cormac spoke. "My father is a murderer of innocents. His blood-taint made me a kin-slayer." He choked on that word, mangling it. "I left Emain Macha forever, lest my shame rot me through bone, flesh, and all the blood in my body."

Maeve stared at him, but her thoughts darted back to something Fergus had just said. *All who felt the same as me.* Tensing, she searched the other Ulaid men obscured by the shadows near the door. Her gaze came to rest on a hooded figure at the back. Who would shield his features in shame but Cúchulainn, the most honor-bound man in Erin?

Maeve shot from her chair in a flurry of feathers, pointing. "You...show yourself!"

The warrior hesitated, but Fergus growled under his breath

and the man slowly emerged into light. Battle-scarred hands reached up to his hood and eased it back. Dark hair. Lean, secretive face.

Ferdia.

Disappointment washed over Maeve, and immediately receded. Ferdia would never leave Cúchulainn, which meant that the Hound must be on his way to join him.

Still, she was shocked by his appearance. Ferdia had always been handsome, if too sinewy and self-contained for her. Now, though, his skin was waxen, black hair hanging in tendrils that shadowed his bruised gray eyes.

She remembered a different Ferdia at Emain Macha, so smug, so insolent. Every time Cúchulainn breezed past, ignoring her, Ferdia stopped to glance over his shoulder at her, slyly amused. It had occurred to Maeve then that perhaps he saw through her desperate ploys because he was *like* her. He was clever, for all he tried to appear pure, his heart full of unexpressed hungers.

Cúchulainn's name was on the tip of Maeve's tongue when the entreaty in Ferdia's eyes stopped her. She halted, puzzled, then realized she would get nowhere by shaming him in public. "Welcome, Daman's son," was all she said. "We are honored to feast such heroes in our hall tonight."

Ferdia nodded. He wore his famous armor—a set of overlapping cow-horn plates bound with sinew that encased his torso like scales. They rattled as he dropped his chin, shuffling back among his men.

Maeve gazed at Fergus instead. She still needed to know. "What of Cúchulainn?"

Fergus's face set in hard lines. "The Hound is still Conor's champion. He would not renounce his oaths."

Maeve's glance flew back to Ferdia, but his hood was over his cheeks.

Courtesy could no longer be delayed. "Come and eat," she said to them all. "You must be tired." She gestured Fergus and his men to cushioned benches at the hearth-fire, and waved the servers in with oak platters of pig and beef from the spits, and jugs of drink. Warily, Fergus led his men through the muttering Connacht warriors, but once they sat, they ravenously fell upon the food.

"What do you think?" Maeve muttered to Ailill from their chairs, trying to absorb the implications but still stunned. *Conor could be beaten.* She wiped a trace of sweat from her lip.

Ailill flicked a slice of roast boar off a passing platter and folded it into his mouth. "My father always said Fergus is a man without cunning." He smirked as he chewed. "That is what lost him his throne to Conor."

"He wasn't lying about his son, or Cormac about his brother."

"Aye. But this could still be a ploy to trick us, so they can attack us."

"It could. But Fergus is as straight as a spear-shaft; I never met a man more honor-bound."

Ailill's small eyes darted back to her, a frown on his brow.

Maeve urged kegs of ale and mead on the Ulaid warriors and sat back to watch the result. They barely spoke, gulping as if they were hoping for oblivion. The shock was Ferdia. He was famous for refusing any drinks that blurred the mind, for he always guarded Cúchulainn's back, keeping a clear head when all about him lost theirs.

Now he was pouring ale down his throat.

Ailill got up to join his Laigin men, but Maeve's eyes never left Ferdia. When he staggered up and made for the doors, she rose in his wake. Outside, farther around the curving stone wall of the great hall, Maeve came up behind the Connacht guards who had scrambled after the Ulaid warrior. She waited while Ferdia passed his water down the slope of the mound and into a shallow ditch at the bottom.

She waved the Connacht warriors back into the shadows. All of the Ulaid men had been disarmed. "Unless he is actually strangling me, stay here." Drawing herself up, she strode to the lip of the mound that lifted the king's hall above the plain. The grass and mud below were a dark river that lapped at the inside of the high stockade surrounding it.

Clouds streaked the stars, a moon the hue of old bone gleaming through the rents. Ferdia was lacing his trews, his beaker gripped in his teeth.

"Ferdia mac Daman."

He grabbed the cup from his mouth and peered at her, the yellow light falling upon his hollowed face.

She touched her brow in greeting. "I heard Fergus's heart speaking beneath his words. I believe it when he says his pain absolves him of all loyalty to Conor mac Nessa. But that is him." Maeve tilted her head. "What secrets are you willing to give me in exchange for *your* life?"

Ferdia gulped another slug of ale, making the plates of horn armor scrape together. "Don't think you will use me against him," he slurred. *"I will not harm him."*

Maeve's blood quickened, and she took a stab at the truth. "But Cúchulainn abandoned you. He rejected the bonds you share by clinging to Conor, even after Conor killed so many men you loved." She swayed closer. "A man who is the sword-arm of a king acts in his name. By staying with Conor, Cúchulainn forgives him those deaths—"

"No!"

The guards bristled.

Behind Ferdia's back, Maeve held up her hand. She bore her sword at her waist, and if a man managed to wrestle that off her, a blade was strapped along her thigh under her cloak, and another down her boot at all times. Her body had not forgotten the brutal touch of her brother's men.

Ferdia lurched about, to face the dark plain beyond the rampart, speckled by campfires. "We thought...differently...about what was right." His hand shook as he drained his beaker, the night wind lifting his hair.

"Which is why you are the greatest prize in all Erin. You alone are Cúchulainn's equal." She sidled nearer. "I am happy to offer you every honor and luxury. You will be safe with us."

His head swung around. "I know what you do," he mumbled. "You take men to your bed to make them yield things." He tossed the cup into the ditch and threw an arm about her waist, dragging her against him. "So take me, then! I will stoop even to that if it will blight my mind. But I *will not* give you *him*."

Maeve wriggled a hand up and gripped his jaw. The ridges of horn dug into her belly, and the fumes of his breath stung her eyes. Ferdia's chin sprouted an untidy beard, though he'd always been clean-shaven like Cúchulainn. His face was thinner, his glazed eyes those of a trapped beast. She gave him a little shove.

He stumbled, chuckling and scraping his hair back with an unsteady hand.

"Why are you here?" Maeve demanded. "If you have not come for revenge, and you won't give up your secrets, then why trail behind Fergus like a whipped cur? Why not wander Erin alone, or take service with other lords? Unless..." Her mind pounced. "Because here you can cling to the Red Branch, and you cannot bear to sever that last bond to him." She smiled and pressed a hand over Ferdia's heart. "Because you know that my army will carry you to him again."

Ferdia struck her hand away. "You are a banshee, Maeve of Connacht."

A banshee flew across the battlefields, screaming in victory over the dead. A chill invaded Maeve, and she flung her feathered hem about her neck. "I only know that Conor mac Nessa is the most dangerous man in Erin. And so we share something, you and I, for we hate him just the same."

"But you must destroy Cúchulainn to get to him, and that I will never do."

"Then why would I give you good food, a fire, and a bed?"

A stagger nearly toppled Ferdia, before he hiccupped and bared his teeth. "I don't care if you throw me out in the cold."

"Yes, you do." Ferdia wanted to see Cúchulainn again, even if it was across a blade. Maeve caught her hair as it blew over her face, twisting it into a hank and holding it at her neck. "I will shelter you, Ferdia," she murmured, "and you may find there is more to me than the she-wolf you and the Hound named me."

That night, in a blazing trail of torches, Maeve took all two hundred of the Ulaid warriors to the temple of Lugh. There, in faltering voices, they swore on the altar of the god they shared—and again to Macha, their goddess—that their loyalties were now given to Connacht.

Ferdia was the last to swear, so drunk he could barely walk and had to be propped up by Fergus. As soon as Ferdia mumbled the words, he staggered out the door and retched them back up again on the grass.

It was done. Maeve had Red Branch in her hands.

A great sword to lift to Conor, to turn his own blades from her people.

Her blood thrumming, she halted beside Ferdia as she went to leave. He was now sprawled on the temple steps. Her torch-bearer paused with her, and the ruddy light of the flame fell upon the Ulaid warrior's face.

Ferdia looked up. The glaze of ale fell away, and Maeve saw a moment of clarity in his eyes, at last.

Filled with utter despair.

Somehow it invaded her, and as she made her way to the women's lodge in near-darkness, she stumbled, stopping in the shadows and gazing up at the stars.

There was no point in dwelling on the struggle inside her: how every morning she longed to curl away from the voices and clank of metal, the weight of words on her lips that sent smiths to the forges and warriors to the sparring green. She wanted to sink back into dreams where she was light and fluid, swimming through bright water.

There was no point.

For now, the gods themselves had truly spoken.

Red Branch.

The will of the divine ones swept them all up, as the stars themselves swung and wheeled, reshaping the world.

CHAPTER 25

D*eirdre is dead.*
The night whispered it to Levarcham, creeping around her in the Ulaid forest. It trailed its cloak of dark and cold about her until she could not breathe or think or see.

No.

Through the rocks beneath her and the mound of fresh-turned earth, she could surely hear a heartbeat. Deirdre must be alive under there, in Naisi's arms. *She was alive.*

Levarcham's ragged nails broke on the stones as she once more scrabbled to shift them, blood sticky between her fingers. They would not move. At last she collapsed over them, gasping. Cúchulainn had built the grave mound so high she could not crawl in to join Deirdre.

Wild-eyed, Levarcham turned her cheek to the stone, straining to hear. She did not recall stumbling all the way from Emain Macha, but her bruised soles now stung, and her shoes were torn.

Through a haze, she did remember reaching this shadowed, dripping glade near the seashore. The Hound had snarled at her like a wolf, and all she could do as the day lengthened was watch him pour his shame out in tears and sweat as he labored over the mound, his rage let loose in growls.

Only afterward did Cúchulainn tell her everything, his pictures so vivid she could not rid herself of them even though she ground her palms into her eyes.

Deirdre trapped in a chariot between Conor and Naisi's killer.

Their cart flying along the low sea-cliffs on the Ulaid coast.

Deirdre, lifting her arms into wings...

...leaping onto the rocks below.

No. No...no.

Levarcham twisted onto her back. Cúchulainn was gone now. The dark sky was billowing with low clouds underlit by a crescent moon, and the wind burrowed through her threadbare robe. The plangent call of an owl dragged her spirit back into her body.

Cúchulainn said that after he lifted Deirdre's body from the sea, three swans glided in, a fourth rising from the shore to join them. Did Deirdre remember her teaching, Levarcham wondered, sending her spirit into a swan as her body fell? As if Deirdre were there, Levarcham reached up to brush her face now, remembering it glowing with excitement the night the girl's spirit-self first flew with an eagle over the forest.

Levarcham's hand closed on air.

She curled on her side, gullet spasming—all that was left of her screams. *I failed her.* She must weep blood to release the guilt, and then slip into the cold and dark beneath the ground, yes.

A restless stirring in her belly would not subside, however, something forcing its way up. At last Levarcham crouched on all fours. "What do you want with me?" she hissed to the sídhe, staring into the forest. *Let me go to her.*

Then her back went rigid, her eyes unfocused. If she died, too, Conor's triumph would be complete. He would extinguish all memory of Deirdre's radiance.

Levarcham gasped.

She had to live beyond him, so that light at last would eclipse his darkness. *For Deirdre.*

At dawn Levarcham dragged herself up on unsteady legs and

staggered back through the woods toward the distant ramparts of Emain Macha. They drove her, the sídhe ... the gods.

She had to obey.

※

Conor mac Nessa struggled within another tortured dream. He was surrounded by flame and screams, and the glint of swords. There ... something white and blurred rolled to his feet. Fiacra's head, his fair skin bloodied, his neck split by his own brother's sword.

His eyes were open, looking at his father.

Conor cried out and shocked himself awake, a dagger clasped to his breast.

An acrid smell assaulted his nose, and for a moment he was disoriented. He was sleeping in different places each night, afraid to be caught in his own hall by burning cinders or cold blades. There were many empty houses now—the homes of dead men, or warriors who had left him.

He lay beneath a bundle of blankets in a grain hut, he remembered. It was on stilts, a trapdoor set in the floor to let out the threshed grain. A way to escape, should someone stalk him and overpower his guards. Fergus. Cormac.

Cúchulainn.

The room was being tossed on a river of ale. Gripping the sides of his cot to keep it from bucking, Conor strained to hear the warriors warding the door outside. The old guard of Emain Macha had been overturned. Fergus and his Red Branch traitors had left him, but the lower-ranked warriors who remained were afraid and confused, and did not question his orders. They looked to him to take control, and he would. He bared his teeth, blinking. He was still Conor the wily—most powerful king in Erin.

The last drops of seal-oil flickered on the wick of the stone lamp. He could not abide darkness. The pool of light drew in from the edges of the hut.

He was being watched.

Conor opened his mouth to call his guards.

No sound came out, though, as a wraith stepped from the shadows toward him. The King of the Ulaid was paralyzed.

Her hair was twisted into long hanks with blood and earth, and the stink of burning wafted from her filthy gray rags. All he could see were white eyes gleaming from an inhuman face caked in ash.

Conor's drunken mind gibbered. *She* had come for him—the three-faced goddess of battle and death—cloaked in funeral ash and wreathed in the smoke of the temple in which he'd promised to honor Deirdre. This was not the glow he felt that day in the Dagda's shrine, the sense of compassion, the love.

This was Her darkness. The Goddess of Three.

Nemain, of the frenzied death. The Morrígan, foreteller of a man's demise. And Badb, battle-crow, whose wings brushed a man's cheeks as the blade entered his heart.

Conor whimpered, desperate to brace his dagger but unable to move.

The apparition glowed, it seemed to him, with a baleful light, the figure towering to the roof. She pointed fingers of bone at his breast, blood-tipped. "You have betrayed the Goddess, for your greed slew her fairest daughter." It was a voice torn by battle-screams, harsh as a raven caw. "You used your strength not to honor womankind, but to destroy Her. For this, She will have revenge. You will not die in battle, honored and bard-sung, or in a soft bed." She thrust her chin forward, teeth glinting. "You are cursed, Conor mac Nessa, to die by the hand of Woman... shamed and reviled for all time!"

Conor gurgled his horror, and with a great effort twisted his back until he managed to throw himself onto the floor. His blade clattered to the boards as he scrabbled to roll over, blinded by his hair and the lurching of his ale-sodden senses.

A moment of silence outside was followed by exclamations,

and the guards scraped back the door and rushed in, their feet slipping on scattered grain. Conor wiped his mouth, peering through his stringy hair. The wraith was gone.

The pool of lamplight flared in the draft, banishing shadow. His gaze raked the dusty walls. They closed in, collapsing on him...

"Back to my hall," he stammered. He didn't care about anything but cowering in his own bed now. At least there were servants there.

The next day, sick to the belly, Conor hobbled feverishly between the huts of the crafters, the lodges of the warriors, the stables, dairy, and weaving sheds. His voice was shrill, the orders clear. All women were hereby banished from the king's fort. The female servants, and the wives of the nobles and fighting men, the jewelers, smiths, iron and leather workers, bone- and wood-carvers— all had to leave, with their brats.

You will die by the hand of Woman.

If any men balked at this decree, Conor growled that the old ways were gone. There were absent places beside him now, waiting to be filled by those who were loyal.

The king stormed to his mother's house. "You will also be gone, woman, and never come back."

Nessa remained striking even at sixty-five, but the past weeks had leached the remaining beauty from her. Her back was bowed, her painted face ravaged. "My son—"

Conor struck her across the cheek. "I will not let you twist me again, trick me again, rule me again. I will triumph now as myself alone—without you!"

His spearmen bundled Nessa and her servants out of her lodge, throwing her glossy furs, Roman glass jugs, silver platters, and jewelry into the mud. Blood trickled down Nessa's face where Conor's ring had cut her. Without a word, she gestured to her women to gather up her belongings, and they hastened toward the stables where the chariots were kept.

Finally, Conor staggered to the temple of Macha.

His chief druid, Cathbad, had died the night of the battle at the Red Branch hall, and the druids were all in disarray. The only one who ever defied Conor was Levarcham, and he was told she had already fled. If she showed her face, this time he would kill her with his bare hands.

Conor singled out a thin, clever druid who had been angling for Cathbad's position for some time. "Fergus and his men have turned on me. Such dangers need to be met with extraordinary measures, and the warriors must hoard their strength. All women are therefore now banished, including your druids." The priests clamored in dismay, all arguing at once. Conor struck the roof-post of the temple with his sword, making the timbers shiver. "This is my will!" he bellowed. The terror kept choking him; he needed to vomit it up. "The priest who obeys me now will be my new adviser, set above all others."

A crafty excitement passed over the face of Conor's candidate—someone was always hungry for power. With shaking hands and a sour mouth, Conor crawled back into his den.

Emain Macha would henceforth be a fort of men, all of them united against the Red Branch traitors and any who sheltered them.

A stronghold of war.

Days later, King Conor fumbled with the strap of his sword-belt, trying to still the abominable tremor in his hands. At last he settled the sheath over his thigh and drew the seal-pelt around his neck. Bracing his shoulders, he stabbed the pins in, one on each side, and smoothed his gray hair.

There were no women here to dress him, and that was how it would be.

He straightened his linen tunic, and head erect, descended the stairs to his hall. The firelight lanced his eyes, but he drove through the pain. The Red Branch tree was hewn, the branches splintered. He must now resurrect it. *He* would be the power behind a new Red Branch.

The assembled messengers watched him glide to his great chair. They had helmets tucked under their arms, riding boots laced up their legs. They had young, bright faces, eager to jostle for favor now that so much had changed.

Conor crooked a finger at them one by one. At first his voice faltered as the drink left him, but soon it was swelling with his old power. His orders flowed out on a tide of fervor.

Every man across the Ulaid who could fight was commanded to Emain Macha.

The warriors would have the chance to prove themselves in a feast of games and sparring, where the prizes would be more than bronze rings and carved spears. The reward for the most skilled, the bravest, would be... elevation to a new Red Branch.

All those warriors who had previously been defeated by its near-impossible initiation feats and mystical challenges would now enjoy the glory that had once belonged to Naisi, Fergus, and Ferdia.

Riches and women, a place beside the gods when they died— and the honor of being reborn into an even more wonderful life.

Conor knew warriors. Such a rare opportunity would draw fighters away from their own lords, these chiefs who nursed their grievances against him. And then once he had them, the oath this new Red Branch took would be to him alone. From now on it would be more binding than the oath to their clans, and more sacred than the vow of Red Branch brotherhood that had wrought this disaster.

They would be avowed to the king and no one else.

In twos and threes the riders bowed to him and swished out of the hall, heading for all points of the Ulaid.

Conor beckoned stewards forward, and his new chief druid. The coffers and storehouses of the chiefs still loyal to him must yield an extra tithe, the tribute from every cattle-lord and crafter must be increased. He would assemble the greatest treasure the Ulaid had ever known—by order of the priests, for the safety of the people.

Next, Conor waved toward him a clutch of weathered men, sailors of trade ships and fisher-boats. To warriors and disaffected clansmen in Alba and the British lands, he threw out a challenge.

"The Ulaid of Erin have an army to build, and riches to pay it with."

The boatmen trooped out, muttering in wonder.

The hall was nearly empty. With labored breath, Conor drank from a beaker at his side, flexing his other hand and watching the rings upon it. *Damn you, nephew.*

Cúchulainn had avoided Emain Macha since he witnessed Deirdre throw herself into the sea, and though Conor was glad to be spared the memory in the Hound's eyes, the young warriors loved Cúchulainn with a passion. They would clamor to join the Red Branch just to be close to him, to be taught by him. He *must* come back and sit at the feasts and games and show that Conor remained strong.

"You." Conor called the last rider to him. "Go to the Hound of Cullen and tell him I demand he attend me here. Tell him ..." He gnawed his lip. "Tell him we need him to bind what has been riven. Tell him warriors are gathering and *they* need him to lead them, to make our people safe." Pricking the Hound's conscience usually worked.

The youth gulped and bowed, hurrying out with shining eyes.

A wind slammed into the hall and the timbers creaked. Conor's eyes darted to the shadows. In dreams, the red-haired vixen of Connacht crept through the woods toward him, a lance over her shoulder. Her triumphant smile always woke him, panting and sweating.

He remembered her watching him thus from the shadows—just before she betrayed him and fled. She must have been planning it from the start, masking her ambition with that cool self-possession. Other royal daughters would have been proud to wed Erin's most glorious king, but her face always radiated a subtle defiance he could never quite extinguish.

He tried, striking her sometimes to glimpse that fire for which she was renowned; taunting her to make her eyes flash. It was just enough to harden his shaft so he might get a child on her to bind him to Connacht.

To give him Connacht.

Now he knew that smoldering gaze had been hiding a devious plot to seize her own kingdom, in order to defy him. She had only been waiting for a chance to usurp her kin so she could then strike at him.

Die by the hand of Woman.

Conor quelled a tremor. Where else would Fergus run but to that vengeful bitch? She came. *They all came for him.*

Conor was on his feet, the hall fading away. Yes, they came, weaving among the roof-pillars...the trees...their swords glinting. Ferdia, Fergus, Cormac, *my son*...dead to him now. Ailill.

Maeve.

With a growl, Conor threw his bronze cup at those ghostly faces, and it fell and shredded the smoke, and they were gone. The cup bounced into the fire and sent up a fan of sparks.

Conor kept his hollow eyes on those flames. Fire could cleanse, as well as ruin—cleanse this land of his enemies. He would strike them before they could him. And one by one all their kingdoms would fall, until there was one left, for him alone.

CHAPTER 26

Maeve poured a stream of wine into the gilded horn clutched in Fergus's massive, scarred fingers. He needed to see what luxuries he would gain by keeping his oaths to her. She didn't trust him—yet.

"I am surprised you would be alone with me." The former Ulaid king strained the wine through his silver moustache, glancing around the house where Maeve had lodged him, Cormac, and Ferdia.

This day, Fraech had taken the latter two and all the other Red Branch hunting boar in the hills.

Fergus and Maeve sat alone on cushioned chairs by a crackling fire, feet on soft furs. Wool hangings woven with the Connacht eagle warded drafts from the door. The last of the cheese glistened on a platter next to a basket of honey-cakes. That morning Maeve had even lent Fergus her bathtub, hauled by servants and then filled with hot water by her prettiest maids.

Maeve smiled, proffering a cake. "You are famous for your sense of honor, Fergus. You, of all men, would not break a guest-law."

Fergus could not hide his pleasure. His blue eyes were small but shrewd in his battered face, and gray hair sprouted from his bulbous nose and ears.

Maeve poured for herself. "Nor do you lie—unlike Conor."

Fergus swallowed. "Do not name me in the same breath as that bastard."

She watched the coiling of those enormous slabs of muscle, the hands that could crunch bone, and suppressed a shudder. She leaned her elbows on her knees, cradling her cup. "This could still be an elaborate plan of yours to betray us."

Fergus spread a hand on his thigh, looking down. His gray mane still dripped from the bath, spattering his clean trews. "All my heart was poured into Illan. He was pure and brave, like Lugh come to earth. And *I* sired him—lumpy, broken old me." His knuckles turned white. "Now I do not care what oaths I once made. There is no more for me to lose. If you think I trick you, you are wrong."

Maeve was enthralled by the passion in his gruff voice. "But why come to me?"

"Because one day you will face Conor in battle—and I want to be the one to take his life."

Maeve spilled wine from her mouth, the back of her hand covering it up. She rested the beaker on a log by the fire and lifted a little table between them. A carver had gouged and burned a grid of lines and black squares into its top. On that was a buckskin pouch of bone and jet counters.

Life sparked in Fergus's eyes when he saw the fidchell game, his ragged brows arching.

"I know." Maeve spread the counters out. "I played you at Emain Macha and lost, but the skill of a player changes when the stakes are raised. Some are spurred to greater heights." She glanced at him. "Some snap under the pressure."

Fergus grimaced, swilling his wine. "Old oaks have withstood so much, they do not snap."

The game commenced, Maeve refilling his horn over and over, sticking to pleasantries until the drink had taken its toll. When she judged he was bleary-eyed enough she changed tack, her eyes on the board. "If you want me to defeat Conor, of course, then you need to give me better weapons." She did not mean iron.

Fergus's jet piece clattered to the table. "I will not allow the slaughter of my people," he slurred, frowning. "Or the ruin of my kingdom."

Maeve moved her bone piece on top of his. "I don't want to ruin it. The Ulaid needs farmers and herders, smiths and weavers. Your people are as sacred as the land itself. They will not be harmed." *And nor will mine.* It was a tremor in her very bones. "I want to keep the Ulaid prosperous and happy."

"It *was* that." Fergus slid his piece awry, leaving an opening for Maeve to win. "No more."

She ignored the opportunity, her gaze sweeping up to fix on him. "As it could be again—with you as king." He gaped at her, and she smiled, lifting a finger. "Only if you acknowledge me and Ailill as your overlords."

Fergus slammed his wicker chair back and it slid on the scattered floor rushes. He passed a hand over his eyes, his mouth trembling behind his wrist.

"What did you expect?" she asked softly.

He dropped his fist to his lap, his face haggard. "An alliance of equals."

"The Ulaid have a habit of forgetting alliances. I cannot afford you becoming a danger again."

"We will not, with my honor staked on it."

She sprang from her seat and came around the table. "To risk so much, I need more than honor. And if you do not swear this, you will not be able to rid your land of Conor's stain." She dropped her voice, touching the white hair on the back of his wrist, turned ruddy by the firelight. "You will not get close enough to put *these* about his throat as you dream of doing."

Fergus stared down at his meaty hands and flexed them. The scent of death hung about every great warrior.

Her belly sinking, Maeve raised her voice. "Come! I heard you were bored with the business of ruling, anyway. This way, you can content yourself with hunting boar and deer, bedding women and making your hall glorious." With a flourish she leaned over to move her last piece.

It was a deliberate suicidal position.

Fergus smacked his counter on top of hers to claim his triumph, then swept all her warriors off the board, toppling the table and spilling his wine. He lowered his head to his chest, breathing hard.

The hairs had lifted on Maeve's neck. "I see you agree." She threw her sheepskin cloak about her and rubbed her arms beneath the soft fleece.

At the door, she cast an eye over his slumped shoulders. "If you will be Ulaid king, Fergus, it would be prudent for us to do all we can to gild your reputation. Your men are grief-sick and afraid. They have to believe *you* can knit them back together."

He bristled. "They know that."

"They will be doubting all they know right now."

He raised his head to her, frowning.

"You must be expecting I will offer myself to you, Fergus. Everyone does."

His eyes flared, his mouth falling open.

She summoned a dry smile. "I do not want to lie with you, however, and I see you share my lack of desire." She waved a hand at the scattered pieces. "We will continue to play fidchell together, and everyone will assume we are embroiled in...other games. It will raise your standing among my men and yours if they think you alone can tame the vixen of Connacht."

Outside, Maeve for once let her shoulders fall. For a moment her mind slipped into an unguarded daze. In that stillness came a throb of pain, stirring as if it saw its chance.

Hastily, she spun around. Something must have to be done... someone always needed her. Rubbing the ache from her breastbone, she ran into a bulwark of flesh before she could stop herself.

Ailill was blocking the narrow track between two houses, their thatch roofs nearly sweeping the ground. Dusk had already gathered here, cold and damp.

Maeve stifled a curse as she stepped on his toes, and would have pulled back but he grabbed her wrist. "Just why," he ground out, "were you alone with Fergus mac Roy?"

Distracted, she tried to step around him. "You know I must win him over, more than all the others."

Ailill followed. "Why? He is our *prisoner*, Maeve."

Her laugh was brittle. She desperately needed to get away and think. "He is not very useful as a prisoner, Ailill. He is an exile, and brought his kin with him. No one will pay a ransom for him. But he *is* useful as an ally."

"An ally? You are going to set him loose to join Conor again?"

She sighed. "Were you too drunk to listen to him the night he arrived? He hates Conor with every drop of blood in his veins. And...." She stopped and turned to the Laigin prince. "I believe he will keep his oaths to us. I told you I never met anyone so bound to his word as Fergus mac Roy."

Ailill's glower deepened, the purple twilight casting shadows over his heavy brow.

Maeve moved her hand to his arm. She realized she had been too busy with the exiles to discuss this with him. "I said we would restore him as Ulaid king—"

"*What?*"

"*If* he swore allegiance to you and me."

Ailill opened his mouth, then snapped it shut and drew back. He flung his bear-fur cloak over his shoulder. "You are mad, Maeve. He will gain his freedom and turn on us."

Maeve chewed inside her lip, breathing through her nostrils. She did not pick Ailill as husband for his cunning. "Treating him well now means we will never have to fear the Ulaid again." To be rid of that tension inside, her nerves pulled tight—she could hardly imagine what it would feel like. *Soon…it comes soon…*

Ailill only grunted in the back of his throat and knocked her arm aside, before stalking away.

Maeve rubbed her wrist. Then she ground her heel into the mud to spin her around, choosing a different path. Ailill would come to his senses when the riches of Emain Macha fell into his hands and he was wreathed in Ulaid gold.

But as she walked, her heart thought only of silver, iridescent and flowing, a radiance sweeping her on a tide beyond hurt.

And nothing brutal grasping for her, ever again.

A squall pounded the warriors who were hard at training on the meadows of Cruachan.

Ferdia smeared the rain over his face, wiping sweat away. Turning his back on the sparring swordsmen, he squelched over to a little stream that was becoming swollen, breaking into rapids over the rocks. He could not squat easily in his horn armor, so he braced himself full-length on the ground and drank, then dabbed away blood from a cut on his brow.

Standing, he tested his nose. Not quite broken. He probed his teeth. Still firmly rooted.

He had been fighting all morning—blindly, fiercely. Though the men were only using wooden staves, he had thrown himself into the Red Branch trance, diving into the silver light in the hope it would drown him. He vaguely remembered howling as he cracked wrists and ribs, bruised skulls, shattered oak, and drew blood.

Baying, the Connacht warriors had started leaping onto him, throwing punches. Ferdia was even more thrilled with that, flinging away his staff to let loose a flurry of fists. In the end the Connacht champion, Garvan, had dragged him off, threatening to toss him in the dung pit and damn what the queen said.

But Ferdia knew Maeve needed him.

The rain had ceased at last, the clouds lighter as the wind shredded them. By the stream, he lifted his oak stave, testing its weight. He had stabbed his iron sword into the ground at Conor's feet before walking away from the Ulaid. Now he tried to summon that joy again—the tingling fingertips, the satisfying swing and clang. The Source flowed from a weapon into its master's flesh, and from the master into the sword, so they were one.

Did his body remember?

Rain gleamed on the soaked wood in his hands, and in it Ferdia glimpsed a mischievous grin and mop of blond hair. *Spar with me, brother, and we'll work that fat off your belly!*

He flinched, the stave thudding to the ground.

A shadow rolled over him. Ferdia blinked to clear his eyes. It was Fergus.

Ferdia nodded to him. "I wonder when they'll trust us enough to give us real blades."

Fergus scooped water with his hand and straightened, silver beard dripping. "Soon. They want us to fight in their war-bands."

Ferdia's smile died. Fergus knew that Maeve was interested in only one battle. His temper was too strained to leash. "That she-wolf only wants us to fight the *Ulaid*—you know this! And Cúchulainn will be foremost in any battle line. How can you consider fighting him, your own sword-brother?"

Fergus clutched the hilt of his stave, his dripping face a granite crag. "I love Cúchulainn."

"He is your Red Branch brother!"

"I am no longer Red Branch." Fergus stared down into the foaming water. "The Hound protects Conor, and I have to remove the poison I inflicted on the Ulaid years ago." He drew a shaking breath. "I have to cleanse our land of a sickening king, a mad king, so that we can make our people safe again. If I have to go through Cúchulainn to do that, I will."

Ferdia flung his weapon into the wet ferns with all his force, shredding them. He wanted to sink a fist into Fergus's stony face instead, make it crumble. But he couldn't.

"Cúchulainn is a man," Fergus snapped. "He had a choice, and he chose Conor."

"*He had no choice!* He felt responsible for our people. He's the only one to keep them safe after *we* abandoned them." That is exactly what Cúchulainn had yelled at him that last terrible day. Cú had taken oaths to the people as their champion he would not break. Now Ferdia gulped. So why could *he* not bend his heart to stay?

Deep down he knew why. He could not rid himself of the memory of Naisi's dead face, or the ruin of Naisi's loins, mutilated by Conor for bedding Deirdre. He could not forget the three brothers in their grave, piled like pups in a den. "I cannot shed the Hound's blood, or he mine."

The coldness in Fergus's eyes seeped into Ferdia. "My son *was* my blood. Though I love him, still I will smite Cúchulainn to get to Nessa's cur."

"As will I." Cormac appeared behind them. His wet hair looked like the pale reeds dragged in the current of the stream, the bruises under his eyes stark against cold skin. "If Cúchulainn stands in my way to justice, he is my enemy, too."

Ferdia spun about. "You say this only to escape the truth that *your* blade cut your own brother's veins!"

Cormac gasped and swung up his fist.

"Enough!" Fergus came to life, shouldering between them. "Such fiery words will finish us!" He gripped Ferdia's arms, looming over him. The rain trailed from his moustache, his brows. "Once we kill Conor, and the Hound knows we come not to ruin the Ulaid but rescue it, he will be freed of his oaths." He shook Ferdia. "Think on this, brother."

Letting out his breath, Cormac placed a hand on Ferdia's heaving shoulder. "And we can have our land back the way it was."

A distant, high-pitched shout from the eastern roadway cut over the din of the Connacht fighters. All three Ulaid heads lifted, as wolves that know the howl of their own pack. They dropped their weapons. Ferdia and Cormac bounded away through the last veil of raindrops, with Fergus lumbering after.

In the middle of the track by the outer ramparts, a group of warriors were arguing beside a horse. Ferdia slowed. Connacht spearmen were struggling to restrain someone. "We said we would take you to the queen."

Ferdia recognized a pack of Red Branch exiles crowding them. "No, take him to Fergus!" they were baying. "Fergus needs to see him."

Ferdia glimpsed a streak of scarlet and his heart went into his throat. He broke into a run, splashing through puddles. *Cú . . .*

The man at the center of the fuss was trying to free himself. "Get your hands off me, pup," he growled, "or I will break both your arms and stick that spear up your arse!"

Ferdia came to a halt.

Cormac shot past him. "Conall!" Cormac yelled. Shouldering his way through the men, he clasped Conall Cearnach, the red-haired Ulaid warrior, to his chest.

"Watch the wound, boy," Conall croaked. He was one of the older Red Branch, tall and rangy, with a shock of red hair. Ferdia saw the scarlet shield tied to his saddle, but his weapons had been stripped from him at the borders, as had theirs. Conall was wounded in the battle at the Red Branch hall and left abed when the exiles departed—the only great hero besides Cúchulainn still remaining with Conor.

Ferdia's insides sank again.

Conall was clasping his flank as he turned to him, his soaking tunic bulked out by bandages beneath. Another strip of linen snaked up his forearm. "Mac Daman."

His thin face grew wary as the mountain that was Fergus approached. It was Conall who had mistakenly killed Illan, Fergus's son.

But the red-haired warrior was a jester, and now he broke into a pained smile—the only way to cut to the quick. "You left me behind." He pushed his dripping hair back with his good hand. Facing Illan's sire, though, he could not hide his shame. "I would have come with you if I had been well."

Fergus folded his arms. "Why are you here, then?"

Conall's face fell. He pulled himself straight, bracing his shoulders even though he winced at the pain. "As soon as I could ride, I came to join you."

Cormac was looking between them, trying to smile. He clapped Conall on the back. "You were always one of the best of our trackers!"

"It was not hard to guess where you would go."

Aching, Ferdia half turned away. Cúchulainn would also know, but he had not come.

"I don't just bring my sword," Conall added, speaking to Fergus as if they were the only two there. "I bring news—and all of it grave."

"I said you must come to the queen," one of the young Connacht warriors protested, brandishing his spear as if he might poke Conall in the rump with it.

Fergus growled and struck the lance away. "We have taken Connacht oaths," he said to Conall, glaring at the terrified spearman. "There must be trust between us. Speak your news." The hollowness in his voice said there was nothing Conall could say that would be worse than what Fergus already suffered.

"The maiden Deirdre is dead. She threw herself from Conor's chariot the day you left, over a sea-cliff." Conall's eyes slid toward Ferdia. "The Hound retrieved her from the sea, buried her with Naisi and the sons of Usnech. Then he took himself to his dun and barred the gates to everyone, even me."

Cormac cursed, and Fergus dropped his grizzled head as if its weight pained him. Ferdia stared at Conall with burning eyes.

"The king went into a frenzy. He banished all women from Emain Macha, and put a new chief druid in power. But there is more." The lump in Conall's skinny throat bobbed, his hand on his wound. "With few Red Branch left, he has sent a call across the Ulaid. All fighting men can come to show their skill in the games, and he will choose the best and turn them into a new Red Branch."

The men around them gasped. Red Branch training took many years, the required prowess difficult to master—but that was what made them exceptional. Fergus spoke slowly, brow lowered. "Without the sword-feats? The shield and spear-feats?"

Conall glanced at the Connacht warriors. "Without the Source," he muttered, before swallowing the rest.

Ferdia wiped more rain from his face with a shaking hand. Some Red Branch were better able to summon the Source when they fought than others. But all conjured it to some degree or they could not be Red Branch. It is what joined them, bound them, so they fought as one.

Conall raised his chin. "Conor is building a war-band that has no loyalty to clan or chief, only to him. And he sent out messengers to summon more warriors. To *pay* for more warriors—from Alba and Britain."

The gasps became cries of disbelief.

Fergus's face was not cold anymore. Dark red, it was, wisps of pale moustache blowing out with every gust of breath. "Come," he said to Conall, waving the spearmen away.

Maeve was pacing by the hearth-fire of the hall, throwing orders at scouts who dashed for the doors with every wave of her hand. Servants scurried about, furnishing the riders with food, handing over rings and other tokens to sweeten Maeve's appeals to her chieftains.

Ailill had roused himself with an aching head and bleary eyes, determined, it seemed, to dog her every step.

Maeve came to a stop when Fergus appeared. Ailill dragged himself from his chair.

Fergus stomped up to the roaring fire, his face like thunder. A tall man was trailing behind him. Maeve squinted. She knew that weathered face, that red hair. Conall Cearnach.

As Fergus swept toward her, Ailill surprised them both by stepping between them, facing Fergus as if protecting Maeve. He braced his shoulders, his scarred hands hooked in his belt. "What do you mean by storming in here like this, mac Roy?"

Fergus's furious gaze barely touched upon Ailill's face. Instead, he locked eyes with Maeve, raising his bearded chin.

"Here is the weapon I promised you." He gestured Conall forward, slicing the air with his hand. "Tell her."

That night, Maeve called all her kin and commanders together, and this time there were no arguments. Conor was gathering a war-host.

At dawn Maeve lurked in the mist outside the little shrine of the goddess Bríd until she heard that Erna had finished chanting. Then she slipped inside the hut, buried in her shaggy fleece cloak—a futile shield against what lay within her.

Sheep-fat lamps burned around the curved walls, illuminating a lump of sandstone carved with the suggestion of head and breasts, cleft and legs. Its belly was a swelling curve. Indents of eyes suggested a tranquil expression, compassionate. Bríd was the protector of women in childbirth. The ewes and lambs were sacred to her.

The Mother.

Maeve suppressed a shiver as Erna got up off her knees. "I am sorry to disturb you here," Maeve said, "but I had to be sure you were alone."

Erna looked as if she'd been gazing upon something wonderful, her dark eyes glowing. As before, Maeve felt a strange pang at seeing her face like that.

Erna lifted her chin, assembling her usual grave expression. "How may I serve you, lady?" Her breath turned to vapor in the cold shrine.

The days had long since turned from the warmth of sun-season.

Maeve's gaze slid to the altar. Bríd was looking at her now, the shadows casting her face into...admonition? *Sorrow.* Maeve's eyes stung, and for a moment she could not speak. "You said you could uproot a seedling already sprouted." She could not look away from the statue of the Mother.

Images flitted past, burned behind her eyes. The cold tombs by the sea. The little goddess carvings with empty faces. She made herself breathe. Finn was *here now*, sleeping nearby.

But...the other, the boy. *Dark cave walls seeping water, furred with moss.* Maeve caught herself with a tiny gasp.

"I can make a potion for you, lady." Erna was frowning, rubbing her chilled hands. "But it is not as simple a matter as the tea. I...assume...you stopped taking that?"

Maeve's hand went over her belly as if to a wound, and she turned her chin to look out the doorway at the muted sky and the houses blurred by fog. "When I was taken ill after the raid. I confess your herbs were not on my mind at the time."

"The cleansing of the womb is more complicated," Erna murmured, glancing over her shoulder to the goddess statue. "The potion is strong, taken over many days, and the sickness very severe."

Maeve dragged her attention back.

"There is retching and fever, weakness...the bowels are loosed." Erna was biting her lip. "I would suggest a woman who takes this treatment lie abed for at least two seven-nights if not longer, and will be weak for a long time after."

The cramp that came was faint: Maeve thought it was her belly and realized it was her heart.

A brief sickness, then...better than becoming powerless, which is what would happen if she let the child grow. Her body would slow, her mind soften. The warriors, cattle-lords, and kings would no longer hearken to her, but smile upon her as a milk-cow and nothing more. A difficult birth, and she might even die.

Not now, with Conor gathering a battle-host.

Maeve swallowed, her sight glazing over. *I have made vows.* She had looked in the eyes of people already alive who needed her now more than ever: the crafters, the children, Aengus and his flax-haired son. The sacred oath to protect them came above all others. She said to Finn she could not turn away from them.

I could not live with myself.

And now the gods had put the greatest weapon of all into *her* hands—Red Branch—and she would have her army, and they must fight the Ulaid before they themselves were attacked.

"Prepare it for me." Maeve managed a cracked whisper. "I will...I will consider when is best."

A few nights later she left yet another feast—the Red Branch warriors must be showered with favor—and crawled into her bed alone. The belly sickness was constant now, and her mirror revealed sunken cheeks and a waxy pallor. Curled on her side, Maeve picked up Erna's little jar, fingering the stopper. *Open it, drink it. Have it done.*

She spread a hand beneath her ribs as she gazed down. Flashes came of blood between her thighs, and a tiny, pale body, his fists grasping for life. Another torn from her when she tried so hard to keep him close.

She squeezed those memories away, tears caught between her

lashes. *I am sorry,* she said to the nub of life now within her. *So many need me.*

She had no choice. It flickered in her then that she was as trapped as she had ever been by her father.

No. In lurid detail she summoned the faces of children, thousands of them, looking up at her as they were riven by Ulaid blades. How could she beg their forgiveness if she failed them now? When Conor was defeated, it would all change. Perhaps there might be other babes, when she was safe.

Maeve raised her face to the blackness beneath the eaves. *I am sorry.* She wiped her cheeks, but the cramp in her heart would not ease.

Wait. Her pulse jumped.

She wasn't thinking straight. Conor had shown his hand, and she had Red Branch. The Mumu and Laigin kings *had* to support an immediate attack on Conor now. And if so, she could not be stuck in bed bleeding, vomiting, and burning with fever.

Perhaps there was no time for Erna's draft, either.

Maeve dropped the jar on the table, her cheeks hot. *Of course there wasn't.* The answer was that the attack must happen very soon, while she could still ride and fight. It must happen before she swelled into something all the men would pity. She would conquer Conor while the warriors still saw her as great Macha the Raven.

And after...

She would think about *after* when it came.

Now that Conor's plans had been revealed, Maeve told Ailill that he must lose no time in turning around and riding straight back to his father. As his Laigin men were preparing his weapons and horses, Ailill sought her out in the forge. She was consulting with the smith about the supplies of swords and spears.

"Word just came there has been a raid on the Laigin border," Ailill said, tightening the strap of his sword across his broad back.

"One of my father's chieftains has lost a herd of cattle—ten warriors died, and the herders were also killed."

Their eyes met. Maeve's lips parted, mind racing.

"Aye." Ailill's blunt face was furious in the lurid glow of the furnace. He clapped his helmet on his head, stocky in his layers of leather and mail. "Conor has sent his new wolves out on their first hunt."

Conor has attacked. Maeve's blood quickened, and she could not tell the difference between fear and relief.

Fraech, meanwhile, was ordered to fly south to the Mumu king Niall—her former husband Diarmait's brother. Diarmait had died in a raid a few years ago, but at least his brother held no rancor for her. He had refused Garvan's first entreaty, but for political, not personal, reasons.

Now, with the cream of the Red Branch on their side, Fraech was going to demand that Niall join forces with them, at last.

Maeve hurried into the stables as Fraech was preparing to leave. His head was bent close to Finn's as they tied the saddle on Fraech's horse and strapped on his packs. They drew apart at Maeve's appearance, Finn swiftly retreating to the stallion's muzzle and patting it.

Maeve cradled the back of Finn's head in passing.

"So…" Maeve looked Fraech up and down. The cheek- and brow-guards on his helmet sliced his face into hard lines, making him look older. Despite the weight of a mail-shirt, two swords, and jerkin of toughened leather, his lithe body moved more easily than before. "This time, cousin Fraech, I see you will not advise us to be prudent."

Fraech's teeth gleamed as he drew to his full height. "Everything has changed. Conor has shown his hand at last."

Maeve was arrested by the fierceness that ran beneath his skin. She searched his eyes, vivid with a fire he could not hide. "You *want* this," she said. "As a matter of honor."

Fraech glanced at Finn, who kept her gaze on the horse, murmuring to it. He gripped his sword-hilt, nodding to Maeve. "I have not slept through a night since my father ... died. I will not have it said I cower from a fight."

"You did not cower from the first one."

"And yet I have not had a chance to restore my family name—until now."

Maeve nodded, shoulders lowering. So she could never be a warrior or a lord, after all. It was not a name she wanted to win, or honor. It was simply *family*—the lives of the crafters who had sheltered her at their hearths.

She thumped Fraech's shoulder. "Get to it, then. Tell Niall of Mumu that though he might feel safe behind his mountains, if Conor's host takes Connacht and Laigin, it will be battering down his ramparts soon after. Tell him Conor has given in to madness and will try to take all of Erin's kingdoms for himself, as ard-rí."

Fraech nodded, face aglow.

As Maeve hastened out, she called to Finn. "Daughter, ensure our war leader and his men have decent food in their saddle-packs. And I leave you to pick gifts for the Mumu king, to sweeten the vinegar I send him."

Maeve strode up the track to the king's hall. The morning's rain had stopped, and Cruachan was hung about with glints and gleams of light, the sun catching on dripping thatch and timber, and spangling the grass. She dodged the puddles, squinting at their bright assault on her eyes.

Spying her, Erna came hurrying down the steps of the gate-tower, the hem of her dark robe stained with mud. "Lady, someone has come from afar, requesting an audience with you."

Somebody else demanding her attention? Maeve's head was pounding, too much squeezed into it. She was going to refuse when she was halted by Erna rocking from foot to foot. Color stained the girl's cheeks, her deep, brown eyes snapping with excitement.

"Who?" Maeve demanded.

"She was the druid of Conor mac Nessa—and tutor to his lost betrothed."

CHAPTER 27

Unlike the grand welcome for the warriors, Maeve received her visitor by the fire in the women's lodge. The voices of the servants sewing around the glow of lamps were hushed and singsong. Fragrant steam wafted from a cauldron of barley pottage on the coals.

The druid Levarcham was a shard of ice amid that warmth.

Like a crone playing Badb at the festivals, she had ground ashes into her skin and frosted hair. Her eyes were a twilight hue that was potent when they were full of life, Maeve remembered from Emain Macha. Now, they were frozen.

"What I do not understand is why you would come to me," Maeve continued. Miu, dabbing her nose at the druid's robes, leaped into Maeve's lap and settled there.

Levarcham's jaw creaked open. "I need a fire, a bed."

"You are a druid. You could find that in any cottage in Erin." Maeve sounded harsh, but she could not help it. Horror was creeping from this dead thing beside her into her own warm flesh. She rubbed Miu's head so hard the cat chirruped, batting her fingers.

Maeve forced herself to sit back, lowering her shoulders. "I am surprised you would let Conor out of your sight after what he did to your charge."

"My child." It was a ghost of a whisper, those empty eyes on the wavering lamp beside Maeve. "Though I did not bear her."

"Then I would have expected you to kill him yourself."

A cold gust of a sigh. "He was asleep in front of me, but he clasped a knife. He would have roused his guards, and I would have lost my chance forever."

"You had him helpless before you, and did not act?"

"I tried to...but then it was not me standing before him. It was *Her*."

When druids spoke like that, they meant a goddess. So the reek of Badb death-bringer did cling to this woman.

"And I could not move..." Levarcham confessed, her eyes dropping. "I could not use my own knife on him."

Maeve pulled at the embroidered neck of her tunic, a prickling breaking out over her chest. Miu shot her a dark look and hopped down, shrugging off Maeve's tension as she scampered away.

Deirdre was dead.

A girl Maeve had never met, but with whom she shared a unique kinship. Pity tried to stir in her, but tenderness of any kind was under strong guard in Maeve. A sigh escaped instead.

By taking Conor's attention, Deirdre had rescued her. By running away—and now dying—Deirdre had put her and her people in even greater danger. Maeve wet her lips. "If you suffer so, then why not take your life and join this child of yours?" She kept her eyes blank, as if she had never toyed with holding that same knife at her own veins.

Levarcham's smile was bitter. "I thought to. But Deirdre was so hungry for life. She drank it in—next to her I was an empty husk. And when I pressed the blade to my wrist...I saw her face in the rain on the leaves at my feet. A glimmer...silver. And I could not do it."

Silver. Maeve turned her chin from the fire, her fingers across her throat. *His* face still came to her that way.

"I could not take from myself what Deirdre had lost."

"Except that *she* did."

Levarcham's brows rose like two brandished swords.

"She leaped from the chariot, and killed herself."

The druid's gray eyes flashed. "She chose a different life in the Otherworld." Her nostrils flared, her lashes lowered. "But I know I must still serve. Atone for...my failings." She brushed flakes of ash from her colorless lips.

Levarcham did not sound as if she truly believed Deirdre lived on. The pain was too deep for belief, no matter how long this druid had trained. For her, Deirdre was gone.

Maeve knew.

She tented her trembling fingers under her chin. "So you balked at killing Conor, and would not take your own life. Yet you came to me instead of disappearing into the woods. This tells me, Lady Levarcham, that you do want revenge."

Levarcham started. "Perhaps you are right, mistress." Her back lifted with its old haughtiness. "As you know, I was Conor's talking-woman. I understand him better than anyone. However, I will not be responsible for the deaths of my people."

Fergus's words. Maeve exhaled through her nose. Everyone thought her soulless, indeed. "I have no intention of slaughtering your people."

Maeve tapped her fingers together. Levarcham had treated her with cold disregard the entire time she was Queen of the Ulaid. And yet...they were now the two women who most hated Conor mac Nessa. Who knew where that might lead? The druid needed to abandon some of that pride, though. "Your counsel might be in question, lady, if you bade Deirdre flee with her lover, and so bring about his death."

Levarcham turned from Maeve, gazing into the reaches of the lodge beyond the fire, where the indistinct shapes of looms, piled baskets, and blankets disappeared into darkness. The air seemed to ripple around her, and her mouth curved. "Before the end, Deirdre told me she had lived a lifetime with Naisi in two years; that she would give her pulse a thousand times over for such love—give up kin, warmth, safety, and Erin's very air to stay with him."

Maeve's eyes flickered at that, her hand pressing below her ribs. She managed to get to her feet.

Gazing down, she glimpsed the pitiful woman beneath the film of ash, her thin face haggard. "Then I offer you a place here, give you time to mourn and bind yourself back together." Her voice was strained. "You cannot serve me otherwise—and you *will* render a service to me, Lady Levarcham."

The druid nodded. "So be it," she whispered, as if it was a spell.

Outside the lodge, Maeve turned her steps from the king's hall and climbed the ramparts around the mound. She strode well away from the guards and the watch-towers, curling her fingers about the stakes of the palisade until they cut her palms.

Smoke billowed from the campfires of the gathering warriors below on the river meadow. A waft caught her throat, blotting out the washed blue sky and wet grass.

For a moment she thought she was falling into mist, with no solid place to land. Her belly heaved, and she retched into the hollow where the posts were dug into the earth. Wiping her mouth, she sank down with her back against the stockade.

Only then did she realize what burned in her the entire time she sat with Levarcham.

Envy.

The druid had torn open her own heart, taken that agony and smeared it all over her body as ash and ground it into her hair. Thereby did she cry to the world, *I have lost! I am broken!*

Maeve put her hands over her face, craving that stink of burning and soil; hungering to mark herself so someone would understand. But she was a queen, and must give strength, not show weakness.

And there was no grave for her to delve, only a cold hearth by a lake, spattered with rain.

Maeve made Levarcham accompany her all over the dun, consulting with her on endless matters—how many days away was Samhain, and what could they do then to gain the favor of the gods on their endeavors? What was a good blessing for the calves as they were weaned? Did she know better herbs to keep

ewe-cheese from turning rancid? How many boars should they
salt over the long dark? How many did Conor serve his warriors?

Levarcham's mind had all but seized up, rusted by tears. But
she still knew when she was being played—Maeve could get any
druid to help her with this. And yet, shock had melted and Levarcham was no longer numb. Maeve's powerful presence had become a lifeline, stopping her from drowning in the flood.

This windy day, as she limped beside Maeve, Levarcham's
more vital conversation carried on inside her. If the gods had
beckoned her to death, she would not have survived thus far. Instead of dying of cold in the forest, or rotting into the soil, she
was still here, like a weathered old stick. *Is it revenge you want,
Deirdre-chick? You lost your voice, but if Conor dies in your name then all of
Erin will remember you. Is that what you need?*

Deirdre, as usual, did not answer.

Maeve had stopped beside one of the storehouses, talking to a
red-cheeked woman curing bacons and hams in salt. Food was
being gathered, as leaf-fall came upon them again.

You will die by the hand of Woman.

Levarcham's glance slid sidelong to Maeve. The queen's cloak
blew out in a green flurry, her hair blood-red.

Macha. Battle raven.

For the first time in weeks Levarcham's heart quickened.
When Maeve turned and asked her about hams and sausages,
the druid's hoarse voice strengthened. "There was a way we made
blood pudding in the Ulaid, with herbs and a scalding of the
blood that keeps it for longer. I will show you." Levarcham forced
her bowed shoulders back, rolling her sleeves and gesturing
briskly to the servant.

I will show you, fledgling.

That night, for once Levarcham did not flail awake, searching
for Deirdre in her nightmares. She surfaced slowly, almost

peacefully, with the sense that she was beckoned upward by a soft glow.

She opened her eyes. Maeve had bade the servants clear a little storage alcove at the back of the women's lodge for her, screening it with hurdles of hazel and willow. The tatty furs at her chin smelled comfortingly of wood-smoke and the bog myrtle scattered among the bracken of the bed.

The glow was the last light from the hearth-coals.

Levarcham's fingers were around something at her neck. She strained to remember. It was the little pouch in which she kept her rowan carving of the Mother Goddess. But that was from *before*. On Deirdre's grave, she had flung that amulet away, crying that she did not know her goddess anymore. *Forgive me*, she said again.

The pouch was still lumpy in Levarcham's fingers.

She fumbled it open. The dim glow picked out the sheen of a tiny antler figurine. Someone had shaped the eyes and graceful head of an enchanted deer-maiden. The curve of the neck captured the hind pausing, torn between the man who beckoned to her and the song of the wild. Would she spring away...or turn and be his forever?

Naisi had made it for Deirdre before they left Alba, his love capturing her spirit. Deirdre had worn it bound to the pulse in her wrist.

She only took it off once—to press it into Levarcham's hands the last night they were alone before Deirdre was sent away with Naisi's killer. The night before...

Trapping a moan, Levarcham caressed the little deer. When Deirdre gave it to her, its surface was still warm from her skin. *The night before her blood stopped flowing, and her flesh grew cold.*

Levarcham scrabbled from the bed, wild-eyed. A shudder took her. She had to banish that terrible cold. She could look into the dark no more.

She stumbled to the hearth, on the opposite side from the snoring servants on their pallets. Prodding back the banked turves, she fed the coals with tinder and a few pieces of kindling. As the little flame spat into life, Levarcham rested her chin on her bony knees.

The shivers wracked her, but as the heat grew they slowed. Staring into that flame, a different memory now flowered in Levarcham, one her grief had crushed. It had been too agonizing to relive Deirdre's pain for Naisi that last night together.

Deirdre's grief for Naisi...

Levarcham straightened. Through a crack in her soul, Deirdre's words drifted once more. *I know he is not gone, Mother, he is just on the Other side. And...I found something in Alba, a way to reach him, to do many things. Look, I can show you in the fire.*

With a gasp, Levarcham was on her knees, palms on the hearthstone as she leaned close to the little flame. *What did Deirdre tell her?*

What seemed solid and hard was not at all. Everything was made of tiny specks of glowing dust that streamed together in patterns. The patterns wove the physical shapes of people, trees, rocks, and water. The light that made them glow, that drew them together and filled them with life, was Source.

Quivering, Levarcham gazed hungrily into the fire. *She* had taught Deirdre how to shrink her spirit into a tiny star and send it into the body of a bird. It was a sacred druid skill, though no one knew how it worked.

A gift from the gods.

Deirdre had trained herself to see more than a druid, however. More than her teacher. She had spun herself into one of those tiny, bright motes, and then dived into the whole dance of sparks and stardust around her.

Mother, I can melt into water, and earth. Sink into trees and flowers. Fly with the birds.

Levarcham blinked, and a tear dropped onto her hand.

A charge like invisible lightning bound all the motes together, even those far from each other. In a stream, Deirdre had been able to shape the water droplets with her hands to glimpse Naisi fighting many leagues away, and thereby know he was alive.

And there was time, too.

Somehow, moments were captured in the webs of Source like droplets of dew. Past moments, as well as things that were to come. Time was made of many threads of these droplets all woven together; what humans knew as *before, now,* and *after* all drifting close to each other, all *alive at the same time.* At a spring, Deirdre had discovered an echo of the past captured in the air and water. She felt the presence of priestesses who worshipped at the sacred place long ago, and their memories helped her to save Naisi's life.

Deirdre said she also glimpsed things in fire.

Levarcham leaned closer to the hearth now, her hand out, fingers shaking. The craving in her heart reached for the fire, willing it to dissolve into tiny sparks so she could fly among them. *Deirdre.* Her mother-longing was the strongest force in all the worlds.

The little flame wavered, and bent toward her.

Maeve waited for Ailill and Fraech to return with the support of the other kings, for the sword to fall one way or another. The flesh melted from her, but she could not be still.

At night she cradled the little swelling between her hip bones, more prominent now that she was thinner. In her mind, it all became tangled. This babe was *all* the children—and the women with their weaving songs, and the men who tilled the earth in the rain.

In the dark, an instinct whispered that she must use her power to cradle this vulnerable womb-place. Not *her* womb, but the young ones who were Connacht's future, the pastures that gave them life.

Mother of the land. It called to her, but did not feel like the cold of iron now, or the fierce flame. Instead she sometimes sensed a vast pool within her, a slow upwelling of brightness. She did not understand it.

It was the slowness of pregnancy trying to drag her down, that must be it.

Afraid she was faltering, Maeve flung her doors open each day to search for answers. There must be a key to beating Conor, more than just numbers of men. He was gathering more men.

There must be a way she could triumph in battle.

"You will teach my warriors the Ulaid war-feats," she ordered Fergus, over one of their fidchell games. She gripped his arm, her fingers small and pale around his thick wrist. As the reality of war grew closer and his grief disintegrated, something was also weighing more heavily upon Fergus—fear of facing his own people in battle.

Maeve pinned him with her gaze. "And ... you will also give my men at least some glimpse of the mystery, the secret, at the heart of the Red Branch."

Fergus balked. Maeve got up, dashing the game-board to the floor. "We will not defeat Conor without that—and you will never rule the Ulaid again by cowering by this fire!"

Fergus glared at her, fists braced on his thighs. He said nothing, though, and the next day appeared fully armed on the meadow once more, sweeping through the fighters like a silver-crested wave.

Ferdia had also retreated since Conall's arrival, hiding away to drink, and refusing to train at all.

"How dare you defy me?" Maeve demanded, holding up a lamp over his bed in the musty guest lodge.

Sprawled on the deerskin covers, Ferdia blinked at her, his narrow face flushed. "Kill me anytime you want." He groped for the mead-jug, gulping from the spout. "Though you seem to need me alive for something."

"Ask yourself why you want to *be* alive—for you will only reach it through me."

He merely laughed, and Maeve slammed the lamp on a nearby table and stormed out. Someone must hold some secret about how to defeat Conor. His face stalked her dreams, a sheet of flame playing over it. She did not know whether she glimpsed future or past—only that his mind bent toward hers.

She came to a halt on the muddy path. *The druid.*

Levarcham had not appeared for many days. The servants said she was mired in sorrow, huddling in her bed and muttering, and they were too afraid to go near her. Busy with the men, Maeve had left her alone to grieve.

Now her steps turned for the women's hall.

She strode to Levarcham's chamber, shuttered by a willow screen. Peering through a crack, she saw the druid crouched on her bed cradling a stone lamp bowl, her gray hair hanging over her face. Maeve cleared her throat. "Lady."

Levarcham's ghostly face lifted. Her eyes showed only a reflection of fire, and Maeve could have sworn the little lamp-flame swayed toward her outstretched fingers. As Maeve stared, the unearthly light in the druid's pupils turned from red to silver.

It drew her in.

Maeve saw a great expanse of water under a twilit sky.

She flew across the lake on swan wings, endlessly calling to the emptiness below...He was gone.

Maeve's shins hit something, and she came back to herself to find she was standing beside Levarcham's box-bed.

"I have not seen my child," the druid whispered. Her hand turned over, uncurling toward Maeve's belly. "But I have seen *yours.*"

Maeve drew a sharp breath. Levarcham lunged for her wrist, pulling her onto the bed, enmeshing her in that spell and the glow of the lamp. "This child is made of light. This child was *sired* in light." The druid's torn nails curved over Maeve's belly.

A gentle touch. Maeve's mouth crumpled.

"Shh," Levarcham crooned. "The Shining Ones themselves sang the babe through the veils. Close they hovered, weaving Source into a cradle and beckoning the child to take root."

Maeve groped for the mattress beneath her. "But...all children come from the Source."

Levarcham's eyes were dreamy, radiant. "No, this babe was sired *between* the veils. It is an Otherworld child. The sídhe gathered so close at its seeding the babe is theirs, too."

Cold washed over her as Maeve scrambled up. She did not part the veils—but he did.

He lied to me. The glow of twilight in her drained away.

Levarcham's smile faded as she sensed what now roared up in Maeve. *"Ah, so black..."* the druid hissed, covering her heart and bending her face away. "The pain rots, it gnaws, held in check for too long. You must lance it, or it will fell you, queen of ravens."

The shadows closed in, spinning. Maeve's hand flew to her lips. The druid groped for a bowl beside her and shoved it at Maeve, a film of water glinting in the bottom. Maeve retched, fouling the water of seeing. Shaking, she wiped her mouth.

"Rid yourself of the darkness," Levarcham whispered, rocking on the bed, "or you will fall."

She and he had been walking among the Shining Ones all along. Loving amid that light.

Maeve hobbled out of the lodge like an old woman. A squall had blown up, sending everyone scurrying inside and emptying the paths. The drops hammered her bare head.

She had sent a tracker to find him, of course, sniffing along a trail of rumors and whispers. A young druid and a woman had come to the shining lake. He had left with them and headed west. The Stone Islands.

Maeve knew where he was, but pride had caged her. He didn't want her, so he left her.

Hidden behind the dairy-shed, she let her legs buckle. She groped for the slope of thatch roof and bent her brow upon it. Stifled sounds were caught in her throat, choking her. She turned her cheek so the rain needled her face and filled her open mouth.

Ruán. Ruán. She let his name storm through her heart at last, let it be washed from her lips.

Eventually, Maeve pushed herself back up on unsteady legs and wiped her face and nose.

When the men of Mumu, Laigin, and Connacht mustered, she must be here to lead them. She had vowed she would be Macha to them, and call down upon them the blessings of the gods. She must become a strong blade, proudly raised.

So she had a little time left to take these shattered pieces of herself and hammer them back into something that was whole. To lance the poison in her heart.

The swiftest horse in Erin could reach the western shore in days.

He lied.

CHAPTER 28

꙰꙰꙰꙰꙰꙰꙰꙰꙰꙰꙰꙰꙰꙰

Maeve hobbled along the stormy shore of the Western Sea. The coast opposite the Stone Islands was a bleak landscape of exposed rock, lichen, and dark pools. Her back cramped and she halted.

She did not want anyone knowing of this madness, and so had kept it from Garvan, taking three young warriors from her guard with her and swearing them to secrecy. They had endured four hard days of riding over mud, gravel, and the wooden trackways her people built across bogs.

Few women could hold a child in the womb through that. She should be bleeding, but still it held on. Maeve moved her hand to her stomach and drew in her lips, too exhausted to make sense of the stirring in her heart.

In the dawn, the fishermen's huts looked like sea-wrack cast up by storms, turf roofs rattling with strips of dried seaweed and crusted nets. The clink of bronze in her palm soon had the fishermen scurrying to launch a curragh, and the women stabling their horses in the byre.

They set off—Maeve, her men, and ten rowers in a long blade of a boat.

The ocean was calm in the dawn. As the sun broke, the Stone Islands reared in three humps on the horizon, gray-scarred whales breaching from a dark sea. Maeve's face was set to the cold wind. "What do you know of the druid Ruán?" Her tongue twisted on his name.

One of the fishermen spoke, his breath broken by the strain of the oars. "The gods returned the red druid, the islanders say, lady. The blight on their crops passes and they no longer cry from hunger."

Maeve flinched as she was spattered with seawater. He had been *her* secret. No one else must speak of him. He could not walk in daylight, amid the noise and bustle. He was always twilight, soft and silent.

Waiting for her.

The Big Island was shaped like a wedge, the low coast facing east, the thick edge a wall of cliffs that plunged into the Western Sea. There, the fishermen told her, Lord Donn lived in a fort on the edge of a great drop.

In the sheltered turquoise bay where they disembarked, women were unloading creels of fish from long curraghs. Men knotted ropes, others gutting the catch.

The village was a shoal of tiny huts roofed with seaweed. There was a single ox to haul rocks from the sparse fields. Maeve unclasped another arm-ring, and she and her men were soon swaying in the back of the cart while a squint-eyed farmer drove the ox westward along sandy tracks.

The island was mostly treeless, grooved rocks breaking through the thin covering of sheep pasture. Lord Donn's dun reared on the skyline, an enormous stone fort buttressed against the wind. It was guarded by immense walls, cold and forbidding. Ruán would wither here, Maeve thought, dazed. A barefoot girl was driving geese along the track. Maeve moistened her lips and beckoned to her. "I need to send a message to the druid Ruán."

"The Red Man?" The girl pointed. "He doesn't bide in the dun, lady. His house is by the spring."

Looking around, Maeve saw that some of the breaks in the ridges were filled with green leaves, copses of hazels, oak, and rowan speckled with brown and gold. *Of course.*

Maeve left the men and cart on the track and made her way down a slope through a small patch of woodland. Despite the sun, she pulled up her hood with unsteady hands. There was a glade with a stone hut at its heart. Its door stood open. She approached, then saw no one was inside.

On the grass before the door stood a lathe, a bench with pedal and flax rope to turn a piece of wood against a chisel. Maeve approached carefully, touching the array of tools and the little curls of shaved wood. Slowly, she picked up a carving of smoothed oak. Although crude, already she could see life emerging, a suggestion of curves and rounded head narrowing at one end. A seal.

Maeve cradled the creature, her head bent over it.

A sound drew her back. Voices. The spring.

She crept along the path, willing herself to disappear into the dappled shadows and rustling leaves. A smaller clearing opened up through the trees. Springwater ran off the ridge and seeped down a rock face. It was gathered in a pool at its foot by a little well built of stones.

Maeve pressed herself against a hazel tree, hiding among its fluted leaves.

Ruán sat on the lip of the spring. His ruddy hair was longer, the tangled hanks held back by two thin braids tied at his nape. The sun hit his cheekbones, picking out the dips that ran to the bow of his mouth. He was lightly browned, the glow about him copper and golden now.

Silver no more.

The man and woman beside him were barefoot and thin, dressed in threadbare tunics. The man stood back, clutching a scrap of fishing net as a sack. The woman crouched, holding a babe on her lap and trying to make it drink from a wooden cup while an older boy clung to her skirts.

The babe squirmed, pushing the cup away. Even from where she stood, Maeve could see he was flushed with fever, his hair damp. All of them were hollow-cheeked, the parents weathered by salt and wind.

Ruán spoke to the woman and held his arms out for the babe. Maeve froze as Ruán nestled him in his lap, pointing into the pool and murmuring. The child stopped crying, gazing down at the water.

Absently, Ruán began stroking him from his crown down his back. Maeve could not take her eyes off his hands. As he whispered, Ruán paused to cradle the babe's head, then the nape of his neck, and finally he spread his palm on the child's back. The sunlight rippled, glowing brighter to Maeve's eyes. A trick of the light, she told herself.

Except she had felt that warmth flow from Ruán's hands when she was ill. She had felt it *in* her. She had to stop her body from being drawn to it now, holding to the tree trunk, her knuckles white.

Ruán groped for the cup and sprinkled something in it from a bowl beside him. He tried again to make the babe drink. This time the boy gulped, distracted by Ruán's murmurs. The older child ran over, leaning on Ruán's knee to gaze into the water. Ruán held the cup out, bestowing the same touch on his golden hair.

He placed the younger babe in his mother's arms, and with a gentle smile proffered a package of leaves wrapped in twine to the father. The fisherman bowed, stowing it in his sack. Stammering their thanks, the couple swung their children up and plodded away down the track to the village.

Ruán bent his head, touching his fingers to his lips and then to the surface of the spring. He sat for a moment, face lifted to the sun, his shoulders sinking.

Maeve's attention was caught by his blindfold. The stained deerskin had been replaced by one of brown-flecked wool. The edges were embroidered with blue sea-waves, and in the middle there was a spiral to echo the one on his chest.

Maeve was shaken by an urge to tear it from him, for in those stitches she saw another woman's touch.

Ruán looked up when he heard her step, his face still soft. *He thought her someone else.* Maeve tasted bitterness, squeezed up from the black inside. "You lied to me."

Ruán's dreamy smile faded.

She stumbled closer. "I know the sídhe were there all along— *you* were with them all along." She wanted him to deny it. She longed for it.

Ruán got up, uncurling with grace to his full height. His tunic was rough-spun, his trews scattered with shavings of wood. He wasn't draped with jewelry and furs, but he stood as if he was. She wanted to see in him what she felt.

"My journey to the sídhe was not about you, but about me." Ruán's voice was deep and even. Distant.

Maeve's throat burned. "You knew I sought them."

"You didn't need them. You won your hall, you gathered an army. News comes even to us here on the edge of the world." That wry smile was so familiar. He lifted a shoulder in a shrug ... as if he had never craved her at all.

"That is not the point." Her words were strangled. "You lied to me, after all we shared." *What we share.* She fought the instinct to hide her belly with her hand. He would know the truth if she even thought it, and she would not reveal that hold he had over her. Still, her weakness broke through. "I ... trusted you."

I only trusted you. If he had not guessed, if he had not seen it— when he saw everything—then he must not want it. Pride kept that turmoil silent.

But something was tapping on her mind. His tense face and curled hands formed a shield—but against what? Was he not calm after all? Her pulse skipped.

Ruán felt for the bowls beside the spring, his hair falling over his cheek. Tiny shells were threaded through the copper braids at the sides. Someone else wove those in, too. Maeve dragged her eyes back to his face, and swore his jaw betrayed a tremor.

"I did not break your trust, Maeve. I told you that every person's journey to the sídhe is theirs alone."

"You could have helped me! You could have shown me!"

"*I showed you enough!*" The roar stunned them both.

Stifling a curse, Ruán charged past Maeve to reach the path back up through the trees. She spun about and followed.

Ruán's lope kept his feet low to the ground, feeling for the clear trail he had beaten in the sand. At his house, he hit the wall of mud and wattle, then felt along it before ducking through the door. Maeve came to a halt inside.

The hut was starkly furnished, with a fire-pit, an oak bench, a chair made of driftwood, and a bracken bed against the wall. Bunches of herbs scented the air, however, and amulets of stone, shell, and wood hung in the breeze by the door. Maeve caught a pearl shell in her hand, carved into a glimmering fish. There were otters, deer, and gulls shaped from memory, from yearning.

Ruán gripped the back of his chair, using it as a barrier. "This is my home. You cannot charge in here without my leave."

Maeve did not trust herself to answer, her eyes stinging.

He sighed, lowering his shoulders. "Because of me, you gained the anam of the otter and defeated your brother. I walked the dream with you and saw the ambush. I drew the fever from your body. What more could you want from me, Maeve?"

"The truth." Her voice cracked. "For once, for someone to not hold anything back."

His laugh was bitter. "And you did not hide yourself?" He moved to the shelves pegged to his wall, fingering a row of little stone carvings, his hands restless. "This fire in you overrides everything, and so I could not expose the sídhe to you. I could not let you drive them away."

Maeve lifted a hand and dropped it. "But … that is not all I am." Did he not remember the warmth of the furs, the whispers in the darkness?

"It doesn't matter." He drew a breath, drawing straight. "I know now they are beyond your power and mine, and did not need my protection. And I *did* tell you truth—you have to bare your heart to the sídhe. I cannot deliver them to anyone."

The meaning in his words slipped from Maeve, drowned by desperation. She saw herself with a sword raised against an Ulaid warrior, his blade smashing hers. She imagined strength surging through her, because behind her at the lake Ruán waited. There, amid the peace and beauty was … *love*. Something for herself, alone, that gave her a reason to survive.

She was eclipsed by a terrible bleakness. It was only a dream. There *was* nothing for herself, now, on the war-path to the Ulaid.

Her ragged breaths echoed off the roof, and Ruán frowned. "You told me I would do a service to you, Maeve, and you saw true. My fate was to help you to power." He wet his lips and swallowed. "And so it has been fulfilled."

His face was closing in again—he sought to shut her out. Maeve flung herself on the chair and grabbed his hand. "*I don't believe you*. The people here offered you something you missed, shelter, belonging … I don't know. But I will give you all of that."

And you will stay long enough to come to love me, too.

There was a white line around Ruán's mouth, his forearm like iron. "What could I ever be in your world: the blind, scarred bedmate of a queen? It would taint you, weaken your power with the warriors. Would you give up all you've won, Maeve, for me?"

Yes. It went to fly from her heart, gloriously free.

But at once it was caught in the cage of her ribs. The lords would cry against her bringing what they saw as infirmity into the king's hall, and demand a leader who was pure. The warriors and crafters would think their goddess Macha lost to them. The Ulaid would crow that they were weakened. The derbfine would splinter, turn their swords on each other and forget Conor creeping up behind them.

She must hold them all, somehow.

Maeve hesitated only a moment, but Ruán smiled.

She knelt up on the chair. "You could join the druids at Cruachan." Her voice shook.

"I am needed here, by good people. I can make a difference, as I wanted to long ago." He lifted his head, as if drawn by the power of the spring.

The longing in his face, the tenderness, pierced her. "We could live by the lake. I would protect you with my life."

"I do not need your protection."

"Then stay there alone! I'll give you land, build a house. No one will ever come there but me."

Without warning Ruán's hands gripped her cheeks, dragging her toward him. "You saw me as part of the Otherworld, but they tell me I must be a man in *Thisworld* now. And I am starting to discover what I can do for my people." He shook her. "*Maeve*, let me be!"

The back of the chair pushed the air from Maeve's lungs. She drank in every pore on his face, every speck of stubble. He smelled of thyme, and there was sand in his hair.

Nothing else of them touched but their swift breaths...and yet still, his lips parted at her nearness.

A footstep outside made Ruán spring away from her. By the time a slight, fair-headed woman tripped inside, Maeve was backed against the wall near the door, Ruán by his hearth-bench.

"My lady!" The woman bobbed her head.

The braids about her crown had once been golden but were faded now, like barley cut from the stalk. Her hazel eyes were still shrewd, but for the rest, she was salt-dried like all the people here, her face shrunken, the harsh sunlight off the sea carving deep lines around her eyes.

The woman's wind-scoured cheeks grew even redder. "I heard

you had blessed us with a visit, my lady, but we have no comforts here for a great queen, and—"

"Orla." Ruán was composed, sinking to the oak bench. "The queen only came to thank us for our care during her sickness. She knows we were not expecting her."

Maeve was glaring at him when she realized this other woman *could* see her. She folded her trembling hands in her sleeves. "Yes, please do not distress yourself. This is a sudden visit."

Orla clucked, shaking her head and spooning porridge from a fire-pot nestled in the coals at the edge of the hearth. Despite her frazzled manner, she cast sharp glances at Maeve. She bobbed and held out the steaming bowl. "Please, mistress, sit and eat."

As if she had the right to invite someone to this home. "Thank you, but I am not well after the journey." Maeve could not keep her furious gaze from flying to Ruán.

Orla approached him. "You have it, then," she murmured. "You've been with the fisherfolk all morning." She nestled the bowl in Ruán's lap with chapped hands, pressing a spoon to his fingers and muttering about drafts.

Ruán smiled at her as he set it aside. "I'll have it in a moment."

Maeve thought she might be sick again, and wished she would not. She scrutinized the room. There were no spindles or loom, no quern-stone for grinding grain, no needles or cloth. One wooden cup, one bowl. This Orla was not his woman. Yet.

Orla set herself behind Ruán. "I am sorry we do not have better food," she mumbled, eyes cast down. "We are humble folk here, but Lord Donn enjoys all the comforts you are used to. Shall I send a girl to tell him you're coming?" Her little red hand crept onto Ruán's shoulder.

Maeve could not take her eyes off it. "No," she managed. "I will go myself." Only then did she realize she could not say anything that would make any difference. Queen Maeve *could* only be here to thank Ruán for rendering her a service. And he didn't seem to want anything more.

She dipped her head to Ruán. "I hope you find what you need

here. I do, truly, only wish that for you." She glanced at Orla, and caught a hint of triumph about the woman's cracked lips. Defeat settled over Maeve. "Good-bye."

She had just crossed the threshold when Ruán caught her outside, staying her by the wrist. The sun poured over them, blotting everything else out. Maeve looked at the glinting hairs on the back of his hand.

"To win your victory, *ceara*, be brave enough to face yourself. Something whispers to me that you must know your own heart to understand that of others—and that will win you freedom." Ruán's nostrils flared. "I fear you are in grave danger if you don't heed me."

Her scalp rippled. He called her *ceara*.

And he bade her go.

Crushing her pride, she let herself touch his cheek. There was a rime of salt on it; this island was claiming him. She wanted to rub it away, draw his mouth to hers so there were no words. "As you said, I won my army. That is all I can rely upon now. But I do...thank you...with all I have in me."

His lips thinning, he nodded. She thought he was paler now, that something else hovered that he might say.

If he begged her now, could she turn from her duty to her people, as Deirdre did? *Break faith with those who trusted her...watch them die...be rotted by shame and pain, forever?*

But Ruán did not ask. He released her wrist so slowly she did not sense the moment their flesh parted, until the cold breeze blew across her bare skin.

At the lip of the dell she paused and without thinking lifted a hand to him. Ruán remained at the door, unmoving.

Maeve turned, and her hand curled into a fist at her side. "We will return home now," she said to her men. She could not stay a night in this place of jagged rocks and harsh sea-wind.

There was only one path left to her now, and it ran north.

The Ulaid.

By the time Maeve and her men clambered out of the curragh,

dark had nearly fallen. The low black clouds pressed on her breast so that she could hardly breathe.

They led their horses behind the fisher huts and into a rolling expanse of bare rock, bog, and black pools. Maeve suddenly halted, thrusting Meallán's reins into the hands of her nearest guard. "Go, all of you, over that rise, and wait for me."

Exhausted, they did not argue, casting fearful glances at her before hastening away with the horses.

Standing on the brink of a dark lake, Maeve watched them go, trembling from feet to head. There was no place to hide in this blasted landscape, only pockmarked rocks and a black sky that began to weep rain on her head.

Alone, she collapsed on the peaty ground, her elbows braced above the opaque water, her head hanging. The single cry that came from her was swallowed by the cloying mass of moss and sedge beneath her knees.

Dark disgorged to dark.

Maeve drove Meallán and her men home through curtains of rain that followed them from the sea. She let it run in rivulets down her face and did not wipe it away. The stone of the islands had seeped into her body.

Her head drooped and she stared at her fingers in Meallán's dripping mane, for she did not want to see life going on around her. She had the impression of dark banks closing in on either side as they passed between the outer defenses; gates dragged shut behind her; watch-towers looming beneath a clouded sky.

She closed her eyes. This time she had built her own trap. Her vows—sacred vows—had taken the one treasure that had ever been hers alone.

As she grew closer to Cruachan, the rain began to clear. One of her guards whistled. "Lugh's balls." His exclamation dragged Maeve from her stupor.

She looked up, blinking sore eyes.

The green turf of Cruachan had been transformed into a great war-camp. What she had thought in her daze was the sun catching on raindrops was instead a vast sea of metal. A forest of spears was staked between scattered tents. Helmets were hooked over poles, shields piled up, studded with iron bosses.

The meadows had been churned into mud, swarming with ranks of men sparring with each other, practicing the battle-feats or wrestling and cheering each other on. The glint of their swords and spears was like lightning among dark clouds.

Maeve and her men passed from the western fringes of the plains toward the royal halls. One flank of tents were of sheepskin, the rain clumping the oily fleece together. At the heart of that encampment, yellow banners sagged from tall spears. *Mumu*. The Mumu mountains nurtured great flocks of sheep. There must be a thousand warriors here at least.

Another field held more familiar cowhide tents. The spears of the Galeóin were in rows of holders, tracing spirals of sharp iron on the ground. They bore green banners—Laigin. And closer to Cruachan were gathered Connacht-men from many far-flung clans.

In the camps, warriors huddled about smoky fires, their clothes steaming as they stirred pots over the flames and cleaned their weapons. They fell silent as Maeve passed, lifting their faces to her. She saw dripping moustaches, hair drawn into crests or greased with ocher, fur mantles hanging limp and wet.

The men began to get up to watch her ride by. She heard the mutters being passed along. *Rígan...Macha Mong Ruad*. They called her Queen or Macha of the Red Mane—it did not matter. Perhaps they were one and the same now.

Maeve drew breath as if surfacing from black water. She put back her hood, shaking out her wet hair.

More men left off what they were doing and lined the track. The sparring ones halted, shading their eyes and raising their swords. Scarred hands gripped spear-shafts, thudding them

across broad chests in a mark of respect. Mumu, Laigin, and Connacht. More than three thousand warriors.

Maeve tried to draw her weary back straight, to brace her
shoulders.

She was the land.

She had once inhaled its mist at the lake, cried out pleasure
that was sun-bright. Her body had unfurled beneath Ruán's hands
like the green shoots themselves. But that was over now; he had
told her so.

If she did not have that, then she only had the cold stone of the
land, the hewn wood, the iron to fill her. *If you see me only as a
warrior-queen*, she said to Ruán, *then that is all I will be.*

Wolves and bears had claws, but the people had only their
warriors to protect them. And the warriors had her—*the Maeve,*
battle-queen of Erin.

The new Red Branch warriors filled Conor's hall at Emain Macha
to the rafters, piling up the stairs to sit with legs dangling from the
gallery. As the feast wore on, those crushed around the hearth-
fires below were showered with mead and ale, eliciting gales of
laughter.

Most of the young revelers were beyond caring. Two hundred
British and Alban warriors, lordless and landless, had answered
Conor's call, drawn by the promise of battle-spoils.

In their honor, Conor had brought in barrels of the finest
heather ale that he had captured from an Alban ship. The Alban
kegs had been set up around the room, and as the men got
drunker, they turned to draining whole pitchers in a single gulp.

Conor himself only took one small sip from a ceremonial cup,
then signaled his slaves to bring him water. He could not assert
authority over these cubs if he heaved his supper over his feet.
That was over now; he was strong now. Clear.

Buinne, Fergus's elder son, sprawled near Conor, barely upright. He slammed his cup on the table, shoving a hand into a mound of salmon cooked in milk and smearing it onto his tongue and red beard. "Where is the Hound?"

Conor eyed Buinne with distaste. "Cúchulainn will come. I ordered him to." He picked up a duck bone and held it to his new pet perched on a stool beside him. The creature had come off a ship from the Middle Sea. It was a furry little man-shape with long arms, no tail, and bulbous eyes. The ruff of fur above its eyes made it look doleful, which amused Conor greatly. He had tied its gold collar to his chair with a chain.

"This is my new adviser," he announced to the drunken men around him. "It will serve me better than any druid I've endured, for it cannot answer back!"

The warriors roared, and the ape rocked on its haunches. It took the bone in delicate fingers, sniffed it, and wrinkled its nose before tossing it away. The men laughed even harder. Conor's attention only lifted from his pet when all the heads of the warriors began turning, like barley with a wind through it. The din subsided.

Cúchulainn had come.

Conor waved his cup. "I summoned you days ago." He squinted at the Hound, clearing the smoke from his eyes. Cúchulainn stood there unmoving. "Come!" Conor cried. "See these fine new Red Branch I have here."

The last time Cúchulainn came to this hall was to force Conor to bring Naisi home. Then, he had blazed with finery, and the druids all murmured in awe that it must be true that Cúchulainn's sire was the god Lugh, the bright one.

Now Cúchulainn was diminished, a shadow in a dark leather cloak and lank hair. Only his vivid eyes still burned.

Slowly, the torch of his gaze alighted on the ale barrels, and dropped to the men passed out on the floor, the straw stained around them. It rose to the carcasses of cow and pig flung about in gleeful waste, and drink spilled over platters of half-eaten food.

It roamed over the youths still staggering up the stairs and retching in corners.

Finally, it fixed upon Conor. "The initiation feats of the Red Branch are trying, but their purpose is to uncover the most skilled fighters, the bravest, the most dedicated." Cúchulainn's voice carried through the hall. "You must not abandon them."

Conor scowled. "Do not cross me, Hound. We will talk of this in my chamber, or not at all."

Cúchulainn did not blink. Rain had plastered his blond hair down his cheeks. "The weaving of the sacred bonds requires careful teaching and practice, fasting and prayer. The light we draw upon arises from a communion with the forests and seas." His lip curled. "*This* is sacrilege."

Those warriors still in their right minds could not face the Hound, looking down and shuffling their feet. Conor frowned and gestured to an ale-lad behind his chair. "Get the Hound a measure, and see if we cannot sweeten his temper."

The boy scrabbled on the tables for a mead-horn or bronze cup, but most were strewn on the floor. He surfaced at last with a clay beaker. As he proffered it to Cúchulainn, the king smiled. "I should have welcomed you properly, Champion of the Ulaid. It has been long since you graced my royal hall."

"I would not come when I could still smell the reek of my brothers' burned flesh."

Another hush fell. Conor had indulged the Hound's lack of respect before because he needed the Red Branch for protection against his border lords and Connacht. The worst had now happened, though—the Red Branch was broken, and here he was, still standing.

The new Red Branch might need the Hound's prowess, but never again would he let Cúchulainn claim the loyalty of warriors that should be his. "You are honor-bound to sit by me as Champion of the Ulaid," Conor ground out, "and accept the homage of these men."

Cúchulainn's face went white. He put his hands out and accepted the cup of ale, and the servant let go and fled behind Conor's chair. Cúchulainn looked down into the pale liquid, head bowed.

Conor hauled himself up in his chair. *He knows he's beaten.* Cúchulainn might hate his uncle, but his responsibility to the people of the Ulaid still shackled the Hound to his will.

"I no longer drink ale." Cúchulainn spoke so softly, everyone strained to hear him. "To honor my brother Ferdia, who always kept his mind clear to cover my back."

Conor slammed the arm of his chair. "You will take the sacred drink that binds us as one!"

Cúchulainn lifted his head, and only then did the king understand that his stillness was not an admission of defeat. Even Conor could recognize the force in those vivid eyes, the pause before a killing blow. The king's muscles instinctively braced. *He can't kill me at my hearth!*

He didn't.

Cúchulainn spun on his heel and hurled the cup with such force it shattered into a hundred pieces against a roof-pillar of oak. It showered the young men with shards and ale, and, panicking, they scurried away from the flame of the Hound's eyes.

Without a glance at Conor, Cúchulainn threw a fold of his dark cloak about his head. The men gaped, crushed against the walls, as the Hound swept from the hall like a cloud on the crest of a storm.

CHAPTER 29

For the first time in a generation, the king's hall at Cruachan hosted a council of war, the fragile alliances that bound the four kingdoms now fractured.

Hidden around the back of the great building, Maeve crouched on her haunches in the sun, her eyes closed. Young warriors had always raided cattle, burning off the fire in their blood. But a great battle? There had been none for many years.

She had brought this thing into being.

The leaders sent with the Mumu and Laigin forces were gathered on benches around the hearth-fires inside, along with the foremost Red Branch exiles. The kings of Laigin and Mumu had offered a thousand warriors each. Ros Ruadh had also sent a crusty old warrior to command his forces alongside Ailill—a sign he was still cautious.

And here she was, belly-sick, her back against a mud wall.

"Maeve." It was Garvan. His shadow fell across her, blotting out the sun. "They grow restive. The Laigin war-leader is saying we should think twice about something from which we cannot turn back." He grunted. "Coward."

It was her legs that might not bear her up. But they had to. Stiffly, she pulled herself straight, lifting her head.

Garvan searched her face, worry in his eyes. As she forced her thighs to move, he rested a hand on her back. "Soon enough, spitfire, you'll be riding, spearing, and screaming to your heart's content." He grinned. "*That* will wipe the frown from your pretty face."

"Lugh's balls," Maeve replied. But she could not summon a smile.

Caught in the shadows inside the doors, she wavered. *She*

could turn and slip from this place before they saw her, and then the momentum might be lost—and the killing never happen. Then Garvan swept past her, his stride nudging her out into the firelight. A score of heads turned to her: grizzled hair, battle-scarred faces, huge shoulders draped in furs of wolf and fox, seal and stoat.

Wetting her lips, Maeve walked out before them. "There has never been a chance like this to rid ourselves of Conor—and there never will be again." She glanced down, taking a breath. Yes, remember this...it used to fill her with such fire. She gestured toward Fergus, whose bulk was spilling over her father's old chair. "We have the true strength of the Ulaid on *our* side now."

"Conor mac Nessa can still field thousands of warriors," the Mumu battle-leader growled.

Maeve glanced at Fergus.

The former Ulaid king lumbered to his feet, heavy rings of bronze and gold gleaming at his arms and throat. "Conor has lost most of his best fighters. The Ulaid lords near the border are strong, but they also resent him, and for the past year have stayed away from Emain Macha. He is having to *buy* foreign fighters, and cobble together a force from boys who have barely held a sword. *The Ulaid are no longer bound by strong ties.*" Fergus's lashes flickered, and he caught up a cup and drank, spilling ale down his silver beard. "So." He shaped their path with scarred hands. "We cross the border in the west of the Ulaid, where the lords are sundered from each other and from Conor, and overcome any resistance there. The road to Emain Macha lies open after that."

Maeve put her hand on Fergus's broad shoulder, facing the others. The leaping flames of the great fire made her cheeks flush and her skin prickle. "We do not want to lay waste to the Ulaid, only unseat Conor. Then Fergus will regain his kingship, and all four kingdoms will swear to one alliance, to make Erin stronger."

Ailill was staring at Maeve's fingers where they gripped Fergus, his eyes narrowed and cold. "Why," he asked, "should we struggle across the marshes in the west when we could head east to the coast, then turn north? If Conor's guard is weakened, we should target the easier path to Emain Macha." He glared at Fergus. "Or is the great Fergus mac Roy playing with us?"

"Ailill," Maeve said softly.

Fergus's brows lowered, his heavy cheeks going red. Before he could answer, a voice floated from the outskirts of the circle.

"They won't go east." Ferdia was seated against the wall, legs crossed on a table, bronze cup balanced on his chest. His dark hair hung over reddened eyes. "They won't go east because there lies the famed dun of Cúchulainn—great Hound of the Ulaid." He lifted his cup, his smile savage.

The other warriors muttered. Fergus glowered at Ferdia, and then at Ailill. "It is true. We must avoid the Hound's lands. That is why the west is better."

"We will die either way," someone grumbled.

At that moment the doors opened. Maeve wheeled around to greet the one they were waiting for. Tiernan leaned on his staff as he broke out into the flickering pool of firelight.

"Tell them what you told me, chief druid." Maeve touched her brow. "The druids know this is the time."

Tiernan also appeared to be carrying a weight on his bowed shoulders. Nevertheless he nodded, fixing his gaze upon the battered shields and swords of old kings that hung from the walls and rafters. Maeve had never asked him to speak anything but truth.

"I saw that Emain Macha would burn, and that Fergus mac Roy and his men would come." His aged voice still resonated with power. "Since then I have seen other things. A woman whose red hair flows over the land, her power a mantle that covers the hills, her breath the winds." He faltered, his awareness turned inward. "She gathers the Source from the Otherworld in a great vessel, her power making it purer, brighter. A silver lake, she makes, before she pours it through Thisworld and fills it with light."

He had never used those words before.

Maeve rubbed a shiver from her neck, and as the men all

stared at the druid, she had to clear her throat. "It is Macha—the chief druid sees Macha's red hair because she blesses our endeavors."

"Or it's the blood of the Ulaid flowing over the ground." Drunken Ferdia took another swig of ale.

"There is more," Tiernan said, closing his eyes. "I saw the people gathered on a hilltop, and Maeve, daughter of Eochaid, circling the mound with a sword. As she rode, she struck the four great shields that protected that throng, screeching a war-cry that echoed over the land."

Maeve could not look at Tiernan; many nights ago he had told her this dream. She had thought it would fill her with her old flame, but as she walked from the sacred grove, she reflected only on how lonely it was: she on a deserted plain, bracing a sword and shield.

The gods had chosen this, though. She it was who had drawn Conor's wrath. Her duty in return was clear, and for that she must be grateful. Fewer paths meant fewer thoughts.

Instead of Tiernan, Maeve gazed around at the battle-leaders, as well as Ailill, Fraech, Garvan, Fergus, and Cormac. As one, their eyes rose to her. The flame of the Great Raid upon Conor mac Nessa had been lit, for she saw it in their faces.

A hand crept around Conor's throat, thumbs pressing his windpipe.

He flailed awake, grabbing his dagger and slashing out. The knife swished through empty air. The walls and roof were tilting, collapsing in on him...

"My lord."

Conor tried to focus, but the flame of the lamp kept swelling and shrinking.

"My lord! Pray the sickness does not have you, too."

An icy clarity gripped Conor and he shook his head. Pain shot through him that was not the dregs of ale; he hadn't drunk enough for that. The glint of steel was only a terrified boy holding a spear. No one had touched his throat. "What?" he croaked.

"All the warriors have been taken deathly ill," the boy stammered. "I was told to wake you. You've been asleep for a night and a day."

Conor recalled a burning in his dreams. There was a pitcher and cup of water by his bed. Bracing himself, he pushed back the bed covers, which made the room reel again. The linen sheets were crumpled with sweat, the furs damp.

A wave of screams and shouts echoed up the stairs. Conor's aching head rolled toward it. "What is that?"

"R-Red Branch. All the men at the feast, struck down by an illness the druids have never seen before. Hurry!"

Conor got up and teetered as he drew on his cloak, the boy kneeling to lace his boots. The youth helped him down the stairs. At the bottom, Conor's belly lurched and he emptied it into the stinking straw. He wiped his mouth. "Where are all the servants?"

"The druids have spent themselves trying to heal the warriors, and with no one to order them, the servants all fled, afraid of the sickness."

Conor staggered into the firelight and stopped. For a terrible moment he thought he was looking into a wound full of squirming maggots.

Naked men sprawled on filthy cushions or hangings wrenched from the walls. Some writhed as druids bathed their brows, clasping their bellies like women in the grip of birthing. Others retched, the fumes of vomit and loosed bowels making Conor gag and shove an arm across his nose.

A nearby priest was holding one of the warriors down. The sick man was arching his back and swatting the air, filled with horror at something only he could see. His cries were those of a frenzied animal.

"Where is the chief druid?" Conor barked.

The priest wiped his face on his shoulder as he pinned the man's arms. "In the temple, praying this scourge be taken from us!"

A wave of dizziness took Conor. "How many are sick?"

"Hundreds, my lord. All the noble houses in Emain Macha and the guest lodges boast men as ill. The warriors from Alba and the east are also stricken, screaming and shaking their hands and feet. But we have run out of herbs, and water does not stop the burning." His thin face was bloodless. "We do not know what to do!"

Conor collapsed on the stair, his thoughts slipping as he tried to grasp them.

The border lords...I need more men.

No! When they hear of this they will attack and unseat me.

No one must know...

A scream split the fetid air. One of the sick men shoved the druids aside and stumbled across the hall, gibbering. Conor could barely make out his words as he fell, trying to burrow into the wall. "She comes...great wings...save me...*Nemain, Nemain!*"

Conor snapped straight, his head spinning. Nemain was one of the battle frenzies, the crow goddesses. Red-haired Macha was her sister.

Fear wiped away his dizziness. He groped for the young guard, who was rooted to the spot with his spear braced, terrified. "Take me to Macha's temple," Conor rasped. "We must sacrifice everything we can to beg her favor. Hurry!"

Maeve left Cruachan at the head of a glittering column of warriors. That day, the cold wind clawed at them, the sky the hue of beaten iron. In defiance, as it flowed over the plains, the great warband was afire, blazing with scarlet cloth and painted shields, polished metal, red horses and flaming hair.

The sickness in Maeve's belly had gone. She was swept along now as part of this great beast, with its teeth of iron and its scales of bronze.

The north of Connacht was a realm of lakes and bogs threaded with streams. There were few places for a heavy force of horses, chariots, and baggage carts to cross the great river, and few passages between the mud and high ground. They picked the only good trail, a wide funnel of drier land flanked by ridges.

Four days later the Great Raid had come to a halt.

Maeve sat her horse on a low ridge with her battle-leaders around her. Down below, the pass was blocked by a ditch, the soil heaped into a rampart behind it, topped by oak stakes. A track through the rampart was guarded by barred gates, and the bank ran for a league over the hills to either side.

Garvan's whistle was snatched by the wind. "The Gates of Macha."

Maeve realized she was grinding her teeth. She glanced at Fergus. "The stockade is new."

Fergus shifted in his saddle, his stocky horse bearing him with a stoic expression. "With the Ulaid forces weakened, I did not think the gates would be heavily guarded."

As the scouts had already reported, they were guarded. Ranks of Ulaid men darkened the top of the earth and wood ramparts, their spear-tips clipped by the dull leaf-fall daylight. Their glinting lances waved in agitation as more of Maeve's forces drew up along the valley.

"You cannot hide a war-band this big," Cormac put in. "The border chiefs must be better prepared than we had hoped." His lip curled, his eyes reflecting the bleak gray of the sky. "Perhaps their hatred of *him* has brought them together after all."

Maeve nudged Meallán to the edge of the ridge. She had galloped over these hills the day she fled Conor, with their coarse marsh grass and wind-bent trees. She'd been friendless then, everyone and everything arrayed against her.

That had changed, and yet still she sat here and her legs felt the same...the jelly of marrow in bone. She dragged a hand through her fringe to pull sense into her head.

Fraech spoke up, his horse prancing. "If we do not challenge them, we give the lords time to send to Conor for more warriors, or to gather more themselves. It has to be now."

Yes. She could not bear to flee through these hills again, with fear riding her.

Fraech caught Maeve's glance. He was arrayed for once in the riches of his kin: a green cloak caught with a gold brooch, a shirt of mail polished to silver, and bronze bands around his upper arms. Feathered iron wings spread up each side of his helmet, and the brow-guard was incised with the suggestion of a beak: the eagle of his mountain home. Maeve's heart lifted. Her men would follow him, and they would win.

Fergus and Cormac agreed they should attack. With Fraech and the other battle-leaders, they all hastened down the hill to summon their men. At the last minute, and to everyone's surprise, Ferdia had joined the war-band. Maeve, though, knew he would not fight; not now.

She understood what he really wanted.

As the others left, she dismounted and plucked at the bindings that held her raven helmet and sword to her saddle.

Ailill spurred his horse up. "*You* are not fighting, firebrand. You have my kingdom's hopes as well as others in your hands now." She glared at him, and his fingers closed upon hers on the strap. "You nearly died last time. See sense for once, woman!"

Beltaine. Soft hands lifting furs about her naked shoulders as she burned with fever. The rush of life back into her limbs, a sunlit glade. Sired in light.

Maeve gasped and tried to yank her hand away, but Ailill's grip was too crushing.

"Brother." Finn spoke behind them. "I heard the Galeóin leader calling for you."

Maeve turned. Finn teased or cajoled Ailill, but never had Maeve heard her sound sharp with her brother. All that time the girl had spent with her as she went about the business of queenship these past moons must have seeped into her, after all.

"Then *you* speak sense to her," Ailill muttered, turning his horse down the slope.

When he was gone, Maeve ripped her scabbard from the

saddle and stomped to the lip of the slope where it dropped to the valley. Her warriors were arming themselves, sheltering in copses of trees that were red-brown and yellow, the leaves already scattering on the cold wind. "Do not bother," she threw over her shoulder to Finn.

Ailill was right. She just needed to feel a sword in her grip, in the hope she would feel nothing else. It didn't work. She ached to her core; a wound, it was dawning over her, that would not heal.

"Just remember," she added, "you begged me to let *you* come, and I did—against my better judgment."

Finn reached her side, tentatively resting a small hand on Maeve's shoulder. "He *is* right, Mother, but not just because you can't afford to be hurt." She braced herself, the wind blowing her copper hair over her face. "You seem ... different. Something has happened to make you falter, and ... it makes me afraid, like Ailill."

Maeve had to dip her head to the sodden ground beneath. Her breastplate was tightly bound to hide the slight fullness in her belly, and she could hardly breathe. Her hand covered Finn's warm fingers. "Little Red, Garvan calls you." She glanced sidelong at her daughter. "How foolish for a mother to pass her stubborn will to a child. I should have known better."

Finn smiled.

Squeezing her hand, Maeve turned. "I was not well for a time, but I am not faltering." *I have borne much; I will bear this.* She looped the sword-belt around her waist, settling the scabbard behind her thigh. "I will watch from up here, but *you* will listen to sense and go back to Levarcham at the wagons."

Finn's face fell. "But ... No! I need to see—"

"I order you not as a mother, but as your queen! What is the point of you training at weapons if you will not obey me?"

Finn chewed her lip, a rueful glint in her eye. "Fraech is the war-leader, and I know he will let me."

"Except that I rule you both. Now go, before I get angry." Maeve kissed Finn's brow, turned her by the shoulders, and gently smacked her on the rump.

Creeping close with a small guard of warriors, Maeve took up position at the end of the ridge near the Ulaid ramparts, sheltering in a clump of trees. As she scrambled into position, war trumpets blew, rebounding off the hills.

The Connacht war-band began a charge on foot up the valley, and were greeted with a hail of Ulaid spears in return. The attackers dodged the falling lances, hurling themselves at the ramparts like a wave upon rocks.

Breathlessly, Maeve watched Fergus driving through his milling Red Branch warriors. Fraech was also tall enough to outshine the men around him, his helmet throwing off flashes of silver and bronze. His fighters eddied about him as he calmly shouted orders and encouraged them on. Ailill was bellowing at his Galeóin to throw their own lances back, driving the Ulaid down behind their stockade.

Spears sliced the air in all directions now, glittering like rain.

A wave of Connacht warriors swarmed in under the cover of the Galeóin lances to catch at the ramparts and swing themselves up in acrobatic flips. They grappled on the stockade, the Ulaid defenders desperately trying to hack them down as well as strike falling spears away with their shields. Maeve's gaze darted back and forth. *Fergus taught them that.* Such feats bore the stamp of the Red Branch.

More of Maeve's forces poured in. The great tide of Connacht spread up the sides of the hills that flanked the gates. The Ulaid defenders screamed "Macha! Macha!" stabbing down with their blades. Connacht-men fell into the ditch, tangling in knots of limbs stained with blood.

Something flashed in the sky, and one of Maeve's guards bellowed.

She instinctively crouched. A spear clattered against a nearby birch tree, another embedding itself in the trunk. Showered with splinters, Maeve touched her cheek, her fingers coming away bloodied.

"Hurry!" her guards shouted, flinging up their shields as they

scrambled back. More spears struck the shields and bounced off.
Then one came in low, skewering a young warrior's calf, and he
howled and fell.

Maeve swept up his shield and shoved two warriors toward
the wounded man. "Lift him, quickly!"

She looped her forearm through the strap and hauled the
heavy shield over her head, pushing it against the others to form
a roof of wood. As they shuffled away, Maeve's foot caught and she
stumbled, landing on her front. Her hand went to her belly, but
then another of her men cried a warning and she had to wrench
her shield up with both hands.

An impact shivered through her wrists.

Maeve stared, gulping for air. A spear had nearly come
through the shield, its shaft lodged in the wood. Its glinting tip
was frozen in flight toward her heart. Someone had scratched a
mark into it—the horned moon of Macha.

She could hear the roar of blood in her ears.

She limped away with her men, her thigh strained, the embedded spear and shield dragging down her arm. At last the rain
of death ceased and she tossed the broken shield away. As the
others tended to the wounded, Maeve threw her back against an
ash tree, breathing hard. She looked again to the fighting.

Ulaid reinforcements.

The border chiefs had kept the bulk of their men hidden in
the hills behind the ramparts, their spearmen creeping out to a
distance either side. Now all the Ulaid came pouring out from
their hiding places, and the valley rang with their savage cries.

The momentum of Maeve's warriors slowed as they clashed
with the new fighters, the rivers of men seeping like thick blood
now, and not water.

Standing on each other's shoulders, some brave Connacht-
men had forced their way over the gates; Maeve thought she saw
the eagle on Fraech's helmet among them. The next moment the
gates began to creak open, and the fighters from inside and outside all swirled together.

Maeve blinked cold sweat from her eyes.

A bearlike figure was striding up the hill toward her, hauling a scrawny fighter. Maeve pushed herself from the tree and limped toward Fergus. His silver hair was splashed with blood, which streaked his wrinkled cheeks like war-paint. His sword was dark with gore.

Fergus threw down his captive and pinned him with a foot. His chest rose and fell, his face fey with bloodlust. "The cattle-lords have put aside their differences after all, it seems." He shook sweat from his hair. "We cannot force our way through easily. We'll be mired in these ditches."

"We can if we persevere—"

"No!" Fergus roared, eyes battle-glazed. "We will spend ourselves before we ever reach Emain Macha!"

And Conor.

Maeve looked at the squirming man trapped beneath Fergus's foot. "What do you bring me?"

He sneered. "The ones who run are scared enough to bargain." He leaned on the whimpering Ulaid fighter, who was eyeing Fergus's sword. "Tell the queen what you told me, and I will spare you."

The man turned his face into the churned turf. "M-My lord is Aed son of Cumhall. These are our men and those of the lords Finbar and Cainnech."

"Not the king's men?" Maeve demanded.

The man shook his head, gathering a mouthful of mud. "No riders have come from Emain Macha for many days."

Fergus bared his teeth at Maeve. "There are no scarlet shields on this battlefield, no gold tree." He pressed again to squeeze the last words from the prisoner. "Tell her why."

"W-We hear strange things. The Red Branch has been struck down by a sickness, pangs in the belly. They are abed and cannot move!"

As the stink of blood swirled around them, the eyes of Maeve and Fergus met, fierce and bright.

CHAPTER 30

At dusk Maeve drifted through her war-camp like the pall of smoke on the air.

The fighting had come to a stalemate by dark, the ramparts and hills giving the defenders an advantage over her forces, even though they were superior in numbers and skill.

Neither could break through and deliver a crushing defeat.

As honor demanded, both war-bands retreated at sundown to nurse their wounded and farewell their dead. The Ulaid hauled trees to fill the gap in the rampart, and bonfires now glowed on both flanks of the valley, the stink of the pyres sickly sweet on the air.

Maeve would not mindlessly send men to die in that darkness, however close those fires. It was supposed to have been an easy entry into the Ulaid.

She paused, listening to the moans of pain around her. Piles of scavenged weapons glinted beneath a bronze moon.

She had vowed that if she sent men to battle, she would not veil her nose from the stink of blood or fevers, or her eyes from the spasms of the wounded. So tonight, as dusk fell, she had knelt beside them with the druids, held their hands and bent to hear their last words.

This night she was Bríd to them, Eriu, and Danu—the soft, loving Mother calling them home. But her heart stirred, and twisted, and her own gentle words tasted bitter in the face of their pain.

Now, at the fringes of camp, Maeve knelt at a stream to wash the ash from her throat. Here in the dark, tears could run down her face and drip onto her empty hands, and she did not have to move or speak or mask anything.

Levarcham found her there.

The druid had climbed the hills for a view of the Ulaid, she told Maeve, hoping for a vision. A glimpse had come to her in the mist, in water, of the sickness among the Ulaid Red Branch.

So the words of the captured warrior were true.

When the druid fell silent, Maeve faced the gathering darkness. The mother goddess Eriu must fade away now. She had to call Macha the battle-queen back from Her shadowy realm.

Maeve and Levarcham made for the great command tent, strung together from cowhides and rope. Inside, Maeve's swollen eyes adjusted to the glow of horn lamps hanging from the roof-poles and a brazier filled with coals. Flaming wicks in bowls of oil splashed a brighter light on a folding table set with food.

Unpinning her cloak, she instinctively sought for three faces: Finn, Garvan, Fraech. They were safe.

Ailill, Fergus, and Cormac were also sprawled on cushions, drinking ale. Hangings of wool and fur kept out the cold night air.

Fraech was slumped in a chair, filthy from his boots to his bloodstained tunic. His face was black from the ash of the pyres. Finn crouched next to him, darting glances at the scratches up his forearms. The eagle helmet glinted at his feet.

Maeve went straight to Fraech and bowed her head, touching it with her fist. "You were in the heart of the breach at the gates. Your bravery was the glory of this day."

The mask of soot made Fraech's green eyes more vivid, and despite his weariness, there was a glow of pride in his smile. "I thank you, cousin."

Turning, Maeve offered her wrist to Fergus in the clasp of warriors. He snorted as she struggled to get her fingers around his great forearm, until she gave in and slapped his shoulder. He had proven his loyalty, if not to her then to their cause. Cormac had also fought well, and she murmured to him and touched his arm.

There was a rakish cut above Garvan's eye, and a scrap of linen about his wrist seeped blood. Maeve could hardly look at it. He had been one of the first to fling himself over the Ulaid rampart. "Get that wound seen to," she said in his ear as she hugged him.

"It is nothing." His smile was wry. "When I agreed to follow you, spitfire, I had no idea where it would take me."

"Surely this is better than endless boar-hunts and dice games?"

"Hmm—a toasty fire, a vat of ale, a girl on my lap...tempting right now."

Her smile was weary as she turned, nodding at Ailill, who lifted his cup to her, his mouth grim. He bore no wounds or dirt, having stayed back with his spearmen.

Gods, her tongue was dry as sawdust. "Here, Mother." Finn hopped up and poured ale for her.

Maeve drank, placing the cup on the table. "Levarcham—Conor's druid and a great seer—has received a vision of the place she once called home."

Everyone turned as Levarcham limped across the rug. Fraech hauled himself up and gestured to his chair, and with a nod Levarcham sat down.

"What your captives told you was true," she said to Fergus, her voice as dry as wind in reeds. "The Red Branch has been struck by a terrible illness." She gripped the chair, her eyes far away. "Conor has banished all women from Emain Macha. He has dishonored the Goddess herself, slain Her innocent daughters." She licked her lips. "This is Her punishment."

Fergus's brows knitted as he stared at Levarcham. He appeared conflicted, still.

Maeve strode before the men. "Macha has cursed the Ulaid because of Conor's greed. She longs for someone to rid the land of him and protect the people again. This news has changed everything." She stopped before Fergus. *Show what you are, mac Roy.*

Fergus had taken from his tunic a little deer amulet, a carving of antler that young warriors wore hunting. Now he smoothed it, tucked it back in his clothes, and heaved himself to his feet. "There are more defenders here than we foresaw, and because of the marshes, there are few good tracks for a war-band as large as ours to cross the Ulaid. We risk getting mired in these ditches, but if we retreat, they will pour after us, and our strength will be spent defeating them in these bogs rather than at Emain Macha."

Maeve broke in. "The Ulaid have the advantage of the ramparts and the high ground: we cannot break through without great loss of life. But our men could *hold* the Ulaid war-band here, keeping them busy while a smaller force finds a drier road around the marshlands. After all, we only want Conor."

Fergus cocked his head at Ailill. "You are right about the coast trail. If the Red Branch are struck down, they cannot defend Emain Macha. We take a smaller war-band east, then come upon Emain Macha from the south."

A curse flew from Cormac. "An eastern road will pass through the Hound's lands! And Cúchulainn—"

"Is also sick," Maeve finished.

"The Ulaid prisoners at my fire say they heard Cúchulainn is at Emain Macha burning with fever like the others." Fergus smacked a fist into his palm, hunger kindling in his face again. "*This* way we can surround Nessa's bastard and catch him in his den."

Fraech spoke up. "My heart says the gods themselves have shown us this path. It will deliver Emain Macha to us without a ruinous battle and many deaths."

"We cannot become mired in these bogs," Ailill agreed with Fergus, though his glance at the former Ulaid king was sullen. He got up and stretched his back, rolling his broad shoulders. "If we do, Niall of Mumu and my father will call their warriors home."

Garvan strode to Maeve, hand on his hilt. "Then as Connacht Champion, *I* would be honored to command the war-band that holds the West, if you will it."

"I do." Maeve gripped his shoulder. He had the least pride of any man here. Ailill, Fraech, Cormac, and Fergus could never miss the taking of Emain Macha. "We leave at dawn," she said to the others. "Pick your best warriors to accompany us east." Levarcham and the men left, Finn hopping up and trotting out with Fraech.

Maeve held Fergus back. "Let me tell Ferdia."

"Be my guest. That pup will snap off my hand when he hears this."

Exhausted, she smoothed her smoky hair back. "Perhaps not."

"Maeve." Fergus swilled the ale in his cup, glancing at the tent flap before cocking a beady eye at her. "You have played your part too well. Ailill believes what he sees of us. Beware that bite of *his*."

"Ach, it is only ever a bark." Maeve grabbed her cloak. "I chose him as husband precisely because he's never jealous. He has a hundred women to satisfy his desires."

"You are not like other women." Fergus belched, picking clods of mud from his gray hair.

She arched a brow. "*Now* you woo me?"

He closed his eyes and shook his shaggy head. "Woman, I couldn't hump a maid to save my life. I need a wash ... and bed."

"Then enjoy both. Our greatest challenge is still before us."

Outside, Maeve drew up her hood and plunged back into the camp. After a moment she stopped. The hushed grief of twilight had given way to wildness.

Women had flooded in from the baggage carts, gathering with the warriors around great bonfires and draining skins of mead and ale. Wild tunes were picked out on bone pipes, drummers beating a frenzied pulse. Skirts pulled up, the women danced with bloodied men around the flames, as the warriors put back their heads and howled in savage relief for surviving another day.

In the shadows, Maeve stood rooted. The air throbbed all around her, and gradually she was taken over by the beat of their drums, the rush of blood.

She understood.

Her shield-arm ached from the thud of the lance. The glint of its tip still burned behind her eyes. When it missed her, for a moment the wind had smelled sweeter again, as it used to, the sun blazing through her once more.

This is what warriors craved, this fire. Death and life, close together.

Her face burning, Maeve prowled through the camp. All around, couples rutted beneath scraps of deerskin or shelters of branches. Their cries of abandon quickened her breathing, a sweat prickling her breasts. If a man grasped her now, she would kiss him back. For the next spear might take her life. Her hands still reeked of smoke and death. She could still see the twisted faces of the dead men behind her eyes. And suddenly Maeve knew she could not after all leave Thisworld so cold, so empty.

She reached the edge of camp and sought out Ferdia.

Ignoring the din, he huddled under a dome of branches, wrapped in deerskins. In the glow of the fires he looked like a moth in a cocoon. With no warning, she dropped to her knees and crawled inside—knowing, with Ferdia's training, what would happen.

The moth unfurled and pressed a blade across her throat. Its touch made Maeve's pulse hammer, shooting heat into her groin. *She was alive.*

"I see you are low on ale," she squeezed out. She lifted a goatskin under her arm.

In the firelight Ferdia's pupils were empty, his soul flown far away. Maeve's eyes watered at the fumes on his breath. He lowered the knife. Despite the discomfort, Ferdia slept every night now in his armor. The plates rasped together as he went to pull away.

Maeve caught his tunic. "I have news of Cúchulainn." As she told him, Ferdia's body drew tight. "Do not think to leave us," she warned. "The Hound is sick and will raise no weapon against us. And *if* you can make peace with him, I will spare him."

Death already sat heavy upon her, its ash in her throat. She could think of no more tonight.

Nor, she realized, could she remain so numb if she was to hold her ground among all these hot-blooded warriors. She *must* find the flame again, the fire of spirit and body that had poured forth with . . . Her breath caught. She could not help it.

Ferdia's head swung around.

By firelight Maeve looked at that broken man before her. She saw a wound, deeply cut. The agony of unbearable loss in every line and hollow of his face.

Herself.

All sense snapped and she gripped his chin. "For the sake of all the gods, Ferdia, if you find him, go to him, and feel *this* no more." She struck him in the breast, to shatter this pain for them both. "*Go to him and end this*—for you, at least!"

The muscles beneath Maeve's fingers tensed.

Ferdia uncoiled, grabbing her hair and crushing her into his shoulder, bearing her into the deerskins with his weight. A faint sound escaped Maeve as his hands fumbled with her trews.

Ferdia's face brushed hers, and he tasted the salt tears from her eyes. He paused. "So you do feel, raven queen," he hissed.

She turned her head, her hand over her mouth. *Not that. Feel only the fire.* His body pressed upon her, belly to loins. *Feel the flame,* she cried to herself. She must catch alight again.

But suddenly Ferdia's bulk was squeezing the breath from her, the life from her. *No.* Maeve gasped it aloud, striking him in the chest, trying to throw him off. "*No.*"

At the first blow, Ferdia recoiled. At the second, he let out a growl of inarticulate disgust and rolled away, sitting up with hands over his face. Maeve huddled into her arms. With his back turned, Ferdia groped for her aleskin and drained it, then tossed it aside. "Leave me." He burrowed back into his furs.

The wildness of the night still beat in Maeve's wrist and neck, but as she looked up at the stars, a chill crept over her. Ruán had smiled when she tried to rut like that, slowing her with a touch. Her hand crept to her neck. He had breathed secrets into her skin ... here. Sacred things.

Maeve sat up, yanking down her tunic and curling her arms beneath her legs, shivering. *Forgive me. Forgive me.* The first time she had spoken to him in weeks.

She was his, whether he wanted her or not. It was not going to end. For the first time, that understanding sank through all the layers of her soul. Being sundered from someone did not mean the heart was unbound.

There was nothing tangible to slash, no bindings or ropes. No flesh to cut or bone to break, no vein to sever. It could not be undone. It could only be borne.

This truth ran from Maeve in tears that welled with no sound, and dripped from her chin until her tunic was wet.

When Ferdia let out a snore, she got up on shaky legs and stumbled back through the camp.

Most of the revelers had collapsed where they stood or crawled into their sleeping hides. The drumbeats from the fires were chaotic now, the screeches no longer human. Near her own tent, Maeve caught her foot on a rope and began to fall. Someone grabbed her, dragging her into the shadows. Twisting, she brought her knee up into the man's groin.

He chuckled, blocking it with his thigh. "Y'don't think I'd fall for that," he slurred. "I've had lots'f practice with *you*."

"Ailill!" She struck him in the chest. "You scared me."

"If you can creep about at night, so can I." He hiccupped. "Where've y'been?"

She was still gathering her wits when Ailill dragged her close, snuffling her neck like a rooting pig. "Who've you wrapped those thighs around now?"

"Don't be ridiculous." Her voice sounded hollow, her nose swollen from tears. "My body is my own. That was the bargain."

"The 'bargain' was I bed you 'ny time I want."

"It was to enjoy privileges, power—"

"Power?" Ailill hissed, staggering back. The starlight caught his bared teeth. "You keep *that* for those you hump, your black-haired bastard and stuck-up cousin—"

"Stop it." Wrapping her arms about herself, Maeve turned away.

Ailill's meaty hand grasped her throat, squeezing. "And who rode you t'night? Fergus? Everyone knows that. D'you think I'm *blind*? Slaver over'm instead of giving *me* what you promised!"

His eyes were senseless. Struggling to breathe, Maeve refrained from provoking him further. "*Fergus?* We play fidchell and I make him talk about the Ulaid. He's old enough to be my father!"

"No..." Ailill's grip slackened as he swayed. "It's always power y'want. All you've ever wanted."

She wanted to laugh, but the bleakness took her remaining breath. No one knew her at all.

Maeve knocked his arm and sprang away. "You are unbelievably stupid," she muttered, backing over the shields behind her. "I won't listen to the rantings of a coward—and a pickled one at that."

Ailill lunged at her, but the rope sent him sprawling. Maeve hurried away before he could get up.

⊠

The wind sheared across the bare hillside on the Stone Islands.

It dragged at Ruán's cloak and tore his hair from its braids. He welcomed its chill, pausing to drink in that taste of sea, rock, and thyme. Now he let no savoring of his bodily senses pass him by.

Focusing once more, he resumed his path between the humps of turned earth. Under his guidance, the fisherman had hauled seaweed and sand to build up soil on the rocky hillside so they could plant barley. Now he called the Source into that barren ground, just as he called life into the fishing nets each day.

Ruán's senses flowered inside him. Instead of brown earth and blue sky, the world appeared to him in flares of silver and gray shadow. He saw it clearly at last, and strode along the plowed rows like a sighted man, arms out as he beckoned the Source to flow through the soil.

Slowly the ecstasy filled him. Glowing like a beacon, he wreathed it around the grains of earth beneath his feet.

The ground fell into hollows, but he did not falter, weaving around piles of rocks the farmers had dug from the fields. He turned, ready to sweep down the slope once more...

...and saw another crop littering bare earth...fallen bodies with twisted limbs, blood sinking into the soil instead of Source...

Ruán stumbled, eclipsed by blackness. He lost his sense of the ground and fell on his hands and knees. Sitting up, he brushed the soil from his palms before getting to his feet. He shook his head to clear it. *Go away.*

He breathed in again and endeavored to melt back into the light through the veils. Glimmers of radiance returned, and he began to walk.

Across his path was a river...broken bodies among the rocks. A woman was on her knees, blood flowing from her loins into the ground...

Ruán's heart threw itself in a great bound, quicker than his mind could rein it back. *Maeve.* His body also reached for her, forgetting itself; his hand out, a cry on his lips.

Immediately, he staggered into a pile of stones and barked his shin, the world lurching as the blackness closed in again. Sprawled on the rocks, he strained but could kindle no flame behind his eyes.

Gods. He could not bless the fields like this.

Using only touch and hearing, Ruán managed to make his way over the hill above the fields. He took his frustration out on the land, dragging himself up the rocks, sweat beading his brow. He needed to seek a wild place, where the Source was not disturbed by houses, fields, or tracks.

The sea-cliffs in the West.

By the time Ruán reached the edge of the cliffs, he could sense dusk falling. As the air cooled, the scent of damp grass grew stronger. The cold of the wind on his cheek was now unleavened by sunshine. Below him, waves thundered on the rocks, sending spray to drift over his face and wet his hair.

He felt her take shape behind him, the presence of sídhe lifting the hairs on his neck.

You would have been better born a gull.

Ruán's palms were turned up on his knees, his legs dangling

over the drop. "I did once yearn to fly from these cliffs," he said aloud. Not now. Now he was resolved to be happy with what he had. A simple life. Alone.

She indulged in a very human snort, and before he could answer, her radiance brought to him an inner dawn. Close to her resonance, his sight opened upon Thisworld once more. He gazed hungrily at the swells of the waves, gilded by the red, sinking sun. The grass was dark bronze between his fingers.

Next to him, her black hair streamed in the wind, her dark eyes glinting.

So you can see farther now than before—as far as the Ulaid.

His cheeks grew hot.

But this is no failure. She curled up, oblivious to the terrifying drop below. *You are able to use this sight now for your people, to summon Source and heal them and their island.*

"Then why do these visions take me *from* them?" He struck out, sweeping stones off the edge into the roiling spume below.

The silence throbbed.

Breathing out, Ruán lowered his shoulders. "I helped Maeve to become queen, and now her war-band marches on the Ulaid. This fate of ours is fulfilled."

She looked sidelong at him. *Is it?*

When he did not answer, she dug a handful of sand and flung it in the air. It glittered as it fell, as if with a life of its own.

When you dance with the sparks of Source, you can bend time and place. So why, though you anchor your mind here, do you see her far away? Her eyes betrayed a glimmer of sympathy. *Few humans part the veils as you do. Could your fate be greater than you imagined?*

"All you do is taunt me with questions."

Then I give you this answer. Your heart has greater power over Source than your mind. That is why it seeks far even when your thoughts are rooted here. Also know that you do not find peace in a place. She rested her hand on his chest. *You carry it here. Go to her.*

Her words and touch were an arc of lightning through Ruán's

body, setting it alight in a way he barely remembered. As the heat swept him, he made himself laugh. "I am blind, and you think I can travel the breadth of Erin to find her?"

You see more than you would with eyes. Go alone, though. With others, you will lose your thread to the Source.

"I prefer your questions." When he wiped spray from his mouth, however, Ruán found his hand was shaking.

She smiled. *You came here to be forgiven, and find the power you always longed for. But it is not to be wielded for your people alone, or to save the raven queen. It is to save the lives of many.*

Ruán's heart was already soaring out of his control. "Why did you not tell me this at the lake?"

That brought a swift laugh, her black hair gleaming. *Would we bestow all the riches of knowing upon an ignorant child? How can you understand a path without seeking it yourself? We did not take your blindness away. You had to open your own eyes.*

His choice; so they always said. "You say the paths we pick are of no consequence to you." For the first time in moons, he curled a finger about her arm. The Source rushed in from her flesh, which felt like molten silver. "Except that I do not believe you."

Her eyes glinted and it was Ruán's turn to laugh, strangely light-headed. "You saved my life and took me into your dance. *You* share some purpose with us, or you would have left me to die in the lake!" When she did not answer, he sat back. "So if I come to harm, you do not care?"

I will see you in spirit either way, brother.

That brutal truth left him speechless.

The sídhe smiled. *You and she both have more courage to find before this fate is won. If you do not find it, do not conquer, that future can no longer be yours anyway, and will become someone else's, perhaps.*

"Conquer what?"

She hopped up, weaving her feet along the cliff edge like a child on a branch. *Only you can discover how powerful you are, and what you can be.* Precariously balanced on one foot, her teeth flashed as white as the gulls that plunged into the sea. *Go to her.*

And she let herself fall.

Caught up in instinct, Ruán cried out and his fingers reached to snatch her back, but the sídhe disappeared into the veils of spray.

CHAPTER 31

The army of Connacht split. The greater part of their forces would hold the Ulaid warriors in the West, including Ros Ruadh's old commander and the Mumu battle leader. A smaller band headed east, swifter and more nimble.

Maeve said farewell to Garvan in a little brown-leafed grove on the ridge. His men were nearby with their horses, murmuring together.

Conscious of them, she drew Garvan into a king's embrace and thumped him on the back. "Be as crazy as you like," she muttered, "but *do not* get yourself killed."

"Spitfire, the crazy one of us is you. Still, you have tried hard to kill yourself and not managed it yet." He searched her face, his smile fading. "Keep it up."

The sun had browned him, the cut on his brow hardening his eyes. His dark hair was tangled with leaf-litter. Maeve picked out some stray pieces and dropped them. "I will if you will." Suddenly careless of who watched them, she held his face and kissed his lips.

The teasing glint in Garvan's eye stayed with her as she rode away.

Traveling fast without carts and women, two days later Maeve's smaller war-band came down upon the Plain of Muirthemne near the eastern sea.

Since her disastrous night with Ferdia, he had withdrawn even further, barely leaving his tent when they camped, and riding at the rear of the war-band. Even if he hated her, though, she knew he must be brought into the fold. He was a threat otherwise, unpredictable. Gifts did not sway him. Her very presence obviously now repelled him.

Maeve called Finn to her tent, and observed her as the girl swept inside. She had bound her amber hair into tight braids, which revealed how these past moons had melted away the roundness of her face. Her features stood out more cleanly now. The sea-wind had stained Finn's cheeks, and her eyes snapped with life. She looked young and vivid, dressed in trews and tunic and a leather cap.

Ferdia would dismiss anything too soft or lush. He revered courage; the nobility of a sharp blade, the simplicity of a skilled feat. Bravery. Purity. They ached in his voice when he spoke of Naisi and in his rare mentions of Cúchulainn.

Did he worship those traits because he feared he lacked them?

"Ferdia should be attending our councils," Maeve told Finn, "and readying himself to fight for Emain Macha. We need him."

Finn's bright expression dimmed. "I doubt he will fight," she murmured, brushing dew from her brow where she'd ducked beneath a tree. "He seems broken, as if he can find no place for himself."

"Then we must give him a place." Maeve paced along her trestle table, picking at blackberries. They tasted like pebbles, sitting heavy in her gut. "Ferdia is an unusual man, daughter. His father was a smith from a poor village in the far west of the Ulaid. The other Red Branch warriors came from kin-lines of great fighters, and gained their swords from the Red Branch hall. Ferdia did not learn such skills at his father's knee, so he had to train much harder to win his way into the Red Branch as a grown man. This set him apart. In all my time at Emain Macha, he rarely dallied with women for longer than a night. He had no wife, children, hearth, or kin. All he had was Cúchulainn."

Finn's eyes widened. "Poor man!"

"Yes."

"You don't sound sad," Finn ventured, cocking her head in the shaft of sunlight that fell through the tent flap.

Maeve chewed and forced the berries down her tight throat. She rubbed her stomach as if it might ease away this constant dread, but nothing would help. "The lives of many thousands of people are at risk—the very safety of Connacht. Set against *that*, my sympathy for Ferdia has its limits." Her smile was rueful as she spread her hands. "He is lonely—if he is going to stay with us, then we need to make him feel he belongs, even a little. Just take him some mead. He won't listen to me anymore."

At last Finn returned an unhappy nod.

Maeve put her hands on her daughter's shoulders. "Unlike *me*, you are sweet-tempered…" She gently rocked Finn on her heels. "…and good-natured…"

That drew a grudging smile from Finn.

"And you have a better chance of making Ferdia feel at home with us." Maeve grew sober, holding Finn's eyes. "I know some things about warriors, daughter. The pain you see is his shame. If he fights, he can hold his head high again, gain his soul back. It is for his good he should fight, not ours alone. Comfort yourself with that."

⚯

That night, Finn reluctantly sought out Ferdia.

It was the coldest night so far, and the wind swept across the grassy lowlands north of Laigin. For once Ferdia had sought warmth, if not company. He was wrapped in his cloak on a knoll at the fringes of one of the Mumu campfires, his head resting on his fists. Sparks streamed into the starry sky on freezing gusts as the Mumu fighters sheltered the flames with their saddle-rolls.

With a heavy heart, Finn lugged a jug of mead toward Ferdia, her cheeks burning as all the warriors stopped talking to gape at her. "The queen sent me to bestow this gift upon you."

Ferdia lifted his head. His eyes were bloodshot in the firelight, his dark hair knotted in clumps over his brow. "So she still thinks she can buy me." His laugh was a croak. "I can hardly keep it down. She may as well pour it on the ground herself."

"It is the best mead in Erin," Finn stammered. "The bees are grazed on heather, which gives a taste—"

"Grazed?"

Finn was arrested by a spark of dark humor in Ferdia's eyes.

"Like cows? So she commands bees now, too?"

The Mumu warriors laughed as they rubbed their swords with pig-fat. Finn's face flamed brighter.

"Go back to your warm bed, princess," Ferdia muttered.

"I can't." Finn bit her lip to stare him down. "Let me pass some time, or I will only have to come back."

The others, all shaggy, wild-eyed mountain men, sniggered and leered at her. At last Ferdia took pity upon Finn, shrugging and shifting along to make room. While she lowered herself to the windblown grass, Ferdia gazed hard at the Mumu warriors until they dropped their heads back to their weapons.

Finn flipped open the stopper of the jug, poured mead into a cup, and handed it to him.

Ferdia held the beaker before the flames, the curve of transparent horn glowing. His armor was made of the same plates, speckled cream and brown. "I thought my life would come to more than drowning in mead."

Finn could not bear to see this noble, gray-eyed man brought so low. "It *is* worth more," she blurted. She touched his knee without thinking, drawn to wounded things as she'd always been, with her hounds and horses. "You could leave all this behind, my lord."

It was an odd conversation, but the war-camp was untethered

from the old world she knew. The familiar scents of her father's hall had been replaced by the metallic tang of blood, the jingle of iron, and always, all around, harsh voices. There were no warm hearths or lowing of cattle or children crying. Finn had long since fallen into a kind of daze, unsure what was real and what a dream. Now she blinked, the firelight wavering. "You should find yourself a woman and fill your hearth with babies and your fields with cows."

Her fierceness surprised them both, for Ferdia laughed. "Should I, now?" He sobered. "How old are you?"

"Nearly seventeen."

"I am twenty-six. And *you* are giving me advice?" His sagging face was despairing, though, not angry.

Finn's pity pained her, and she recklessly grabbed the cup and drank the mead. "You think I am young and therefore ignorant. But people forget that the quietest person sees the most, watching from the fringes."

His weary eyes flickered to life. "I know that."

The wind blew hair across her face, and she peeled back the strands. "I am the daughter of a king and queen, sister of princes. What I have seen is that people do things because someone said it is their duty, or because they want something—power, alliances. Few people do what they *truly* want, when their hearts cry out and they *cannot* ignore it ..." Finn trailed off, for Ferdia was staring at her. She shoved the empty cup back at him.

"Well, little watcher ..." He laughed again, bitterly. "You may be right. It is true I must find a way to breathe again."

By the yearning in his face, Finn guessed where his thoughts had flown. She got up. The one thing this poor man never had was peace. She could give him that, at least, and blast what her mother thought. "I will go, then."

Ferdia cocked his head at her. "On a dark night, princess, you made me remember there can be a dawn."

Finn nodded, confused. At least his face was softer now. He might sleep better.

She wove back through the tents, and for some reason her heart seemed too full for her chest beneath that swollen moon. Her limbs tingled with the tension of the war-camp around her. She approached a familiar tent with a limp banner hanging from its peak, wriggled into the shadows behind the flap and waited.

Men thumped by, swords swinging on their belts, their voices low. At last Finn recognized a certain set of shoulders, a proud carriage of head. Her heart banged out of rhythm, unbalancing her, and she cracked a stick beneath her feet.

Fraech's chin swung about, and he stepped over the rope and gripped her arms. She yelped, and immediately his fingers softened, rubbing her sleeves. "You're freezing. Why are you skulking out here?"

Finn's breath came in plumes of mist. "Waiting for you."

"This camp is full of men with battle in their veins—and loins. You must be careful."

His possessive growl sent a shiver up her neck. "If a man did that to me against my will, Mother would roast him on the spit and serve him for supper." Shyly, she linked her hands about his waist, and then more daring, pressed her breasts against his chest. They had kissed many times, but there had been no more than that. Now, the fire of the camp was running through her limbs. She might die...they might all die. She needed to know the mysteries of him—his smell, the warmth of his skin—before she left this life.

Fraech's thumb brushed her cheek. "She will probably do that to me anyway."

"She won't. She needs you." Finn went up on tiptoe to reach his face. "And anyway...I don't care..." And after such reckless words with Ferdia, she didn't.

Their lips met, and Fraech took a sharp breath at the new force in Finn's kiss. Then his hand was cradling the back of her head, holding it so he could drink more deeply of her mouth.

"Be alone with me," Finn gasped against his cheek, as his lips trailed down to her throat. "In the woods, where no one will find us."

In the bloody darkness of a war-camp, Finn blazed for a moment, and all considerations of duty fell away.

At Cúchulainn's hall at Dun Dalgan, the shadows had voices only he could hear.

Emain Macha.

Red Branch.

Men are dying.

Where is your duty?

Cúchulainn glanced up as those hisses skittered over the thatch roof. It was daybreak and the hall was empty but for Emer, for he could bear no man's company except Ferdia's.

Again he reached for the jug to dull the wound, and again he stopped.

For many years, Ferdia's control had enabled Cúchulainn to sometimes shrug off the weight of duty, the pressures of being King's Champion. It let him revel in being a warrior like any other, drinking ale until his mind blurred, laughing at foolish things.

Now, only Emer watched over him, her eyes clouded. No sword gleamed in Ferdia's hand as he burnished it by the fire... only Emer's needle glinting in the cloth.

Cúchulainn knew he must keep a clear head for himself now. He had not drunk in weeks.

The Hound took up his adze instead, peeling the bark off a new spear. The porridge sat in his gut like glue as the whispers began again. Emain Macha. The men were sick, people muttering of a curse. Macha's curse. Did the fact he tried so hard to hold to his honor save him? He didn't know. And why had he received no word from the lords in the West?

At last he could take no more. The spear clattered onto the

hearth-stone as Cúchulainn swept out, through the gate in the high timber stockade. In the dawn, he threw himself into the icy river below the fort, seeking to numb himself.

When the sun was up, Emer found him on the riverbank. Cúchulainn's home was set on the crest of a hill, guarding a southern pass into the Ulaid. Higher mountains rose on the eastern horizon, bleak and cloaked with purple.

He sat naked on the meadow, combing out his hair. His weapons were arrayed about him. He had washed them in the sacred spring, and the fittings of bronze and horn were sheened with gold in that low sun, the iron spear-tips and sword-blades embodying a colder light.

Emer halted. Grieving, Cúchulainn had not bothered with his appearance since returning from that terrible Red Branch feast. Her fists curled up. "You are not going back to Emain Macha now. You said you would not, in case you catch the fever."

"I have to. The voices will not let me rest."

"That is only guilt talking, husband. Your honor is pricked. That does not make it right."

"Of course it's right!" As Cúchulainn leaped up he knocked over a pot of wool-fat. He kicked at it. "What does a man have to guide him if not honor?"

Emer reached out to her husband's chilled skin. Her dark brows were drawn in, wiping away the droop of her eyes he loved so well. "Look what happened the last time you wielded your honor in the service of Conor mac Nessa."

Cúchulainn let out a strangled grunt and stalked to the riverbank.

"All those you loved were lost!" Emer was undaunted, striding behind him, holding her dark curls back with her hands. "Naisi, Ardan, Ainnle, Fiacra, Illan, Fergus—Ferdia! Your *duty* is to men of good faith. Conor mac Nessa is cursed."

"My duty is to the Ulaid!" he roared. "What shield will they have if I, too, abandon them? The king needs me to hold the Red Branch strong."

"There is no Red Branch." Emer turned before him. "If you go to Emain Macha you will also be struck by their sickness, and if you die, you will abandon *all of us.*" Her hand cut the air. "You *will* not go!"

Cúchulainn's bellow was inarticulate. His hands itched for release, and he caught up a spear at his ankle and flung it into the dappled brown woods with a howl.

The tip sank into an oak tree, the shaft breaking and catching in the branches. Birds scattered from the trees. Afterward, the only sounds were Cúchulainn panting and the clatter of the broken shaft as it fell among a shower of gold-edged leaves.

He glimpsed something over the river then, a streak of fawn hide—a deer. Without thought, he threw himself into an old warfeat he'd learned with Ferdia.

To expend his rage. To imagine Ferdia laughing.

Cúchulainn ran toward another lance on the grass and vaulted over on one wrist, plucking up the spear with his free hand. On landing, he sent the force of the somersault down his arm, driving the lance through the undergrowth.

Just as he let go, something barreled into him. Emer. "It's a boy!" she yelled, both of them falling in a tangle of limbs. The spear yawed and missed, bringing down a scatter of broken twigs.

Cúchulainn found himself staring into Emer's blue eyes, his hands crushing her arms. The battle-fury had been suppressed for too long now, rekindled by Ferdia's memory this morn. It flared brightly, blotting out all his sense. The plume of Source began to rise through him ...

Emer knew only one thing to bring him back. She planted her lips on his, kissing him desperately while cradling his cheeks. The warmth and silkiness of woman-flesh began to penetrate his fading awareness, dragging him back from that font of flame. With effort, Cúchulainn quenched it. He reminded himself who he was.

A man.

He took an unsteady breath, and only then did Emer hop off. "Hurry!" she cried. "The poor thing will flee."

Emer splashed across the shallow river and ran up to the ragged boy. He was rooted there, staring at the spear embedded in a tree beside him. Both shaft and boy still quivered.

"Are you hurt?" Emer dropped her voice.

The boy's face was as pale as the goatskin around his shoulders. He opened his mouth, but when the naked Cúchulainn came loping up, he could only gargle something incoherent.

Emer put an arm about his shoulders. "This is Dun Dalgan, and this is the Lord Cúchulainn," she murmured. "You are safe here."

Dazed, the barefoot boy pointed back the way he had come. "M-Mamaí...Fa...my sisters...behind me."

Cúchulainn glanced at Emer and, reading her face, softened his voice. "Take a breath, lad."

From within Emer's arms, the child peeped at the myriad scars that knitted Cúchulainn's body. "We come from Muirthemne." Gulping, the boy drew free of Emer's embrace and clapped his hands along his flanks, standing straight. "Fa said to find warriors and tell them many men have crossed the plain from the South. We fled before them...left everything."

"They killed your people?" Cúchulainn demanded.

The boy shook his head. "They move fast toward the Calleach's Hill."

Emer now looked more frightened than the boy. The Calleach's Hill was in the East, looming over one of the passes into the Ulaid.

By dusk more fugitives arrived, families of herders from the South. Emer bedded them down on bracken in their hall. From the older men, Cúchulainn gained an idea of the numbers of warriors, armor and weapons, their clothing and spear-standards.

"It is Connacht," he said to Emer when they at last retired to bed. "Maeve is queen now." He sighed. "Her marriage to Conor was never happy from the start, but by the end I saw how she hated him. And now she is wed to Ailill of Laigin. Laigin, and Connacht."

"But...Mumu as well?" Emer whispered.

Cúchulainn's eyes were on the wavering lamp-flame by the bed. "They must know we are weakened." He could not speak what lanced his heart. Where were the Red Branch exiles? Ferdia? He cleared his aching throat. "Maeve must have gathered them together. To wipe us out." He leaned and blew out the lamp, plunging them into darkness.

The next day Emer was so busy feeding the new arrivals she did not look for Cúchulainn until the sun was high above the far hills.

The Hound saw her from the stable, skirts flying as she ran across the yard, her hair falling from its braids. She stopped at Cúchulainn's chariot.

He and his servants had greased the wheels, rubbed the wicker with sheep-fat and polished the mountings. The horse-boys had brushed his stallions, the Gray of Macha and the Black of Sainglu, until their coats gleamed.

Bracing himself, Cúchulainn hoisted down the last shield from the loft and came out to face his wife.

Emer put a hand across her eyes as the sun flashed off Cúchulainn's body. He stood resplendent in ceremonial armor, draped with every weapon he possessed. His helmet was crested with a boar, its bristles standing up—it was his battle-helm.

Her mouth twisted behind her hand. Only then did her gaze fall upon his chariot. He had brought out the gae bolga for the first time in years.

It was a vicious spear that Skatha had given him when he and Ferdia left her battle school in Alba. A druid smith had forged it from sky-metal, and Skatha said since the sun-god Lugh was rumored to be Cúchulainn's true sire, it must be his.

The smith had set hinged spurs in a spiral pattern down its shaft. The spurs were threaded with sinew. In flight they lay flat, but the end of the sinew remained tied about the spearman's wrist. When he thrust the gae bolga into his enemy and yanked his hand back, the spurs sprang out like fish-fins and tore his opponent's innards to shreds.

Emer eyed the fearsome weapon. "Now I know you are mad." Her voice shook.

Cúchulainn's body had filled with a calm glow now, as of a welling tide at dusk. It had drowned all doubt. "I want you to gather our people and lead them to safety on the other side of the eastern mountains. They need your strength, Emer. I will track Maeve's war-band and find a narrow place where I can hold them."

"Hold them alone?" Emer's features contorted. "Your sense of duty takes your wits." Such bitterness had never darkened their door before.

"The Red Branch is struck down. Emain Macha is in disarray. There is no one else."

"You have your men here." She huddled into crossed arms. "*You* trained them."

He smiled. "Aye, wife. And they have to guard you, and the women and children, and keep them safe in the mountains." He paused. "This is my fate, I feel it: a great destiny that for some reason I must face alone." He held out his sword in its sheath of wood and horn. He wanted her to belt it upon him and give him her blessing.

Tears were rolling down Emer's face, but her nostrils flared and she shook her head.

Cúchulainn lowered the sword. His blood was beginning to drum. The Source was drawing in from the silver light of the world-behind-the-world; he saw it glimmering around the edges of sight. It beckoned him to let go, to be flame, storm, and thunder. To be Cúchulainn the man no more.

"Emer," he whispered. "You knew I was the Hound of Cullen when you let me court you." He gestured to the iron and bronze that armored him. "If this is wrong, then our nights together— when you say I make you blaze like the sun—those moments are also nothing. For the man who burns with you then is the man you see now. The glory between us comes from the surrender into Source, and now it asks me to defend my land." He clasped her hand to his breast so she could feel that beat. "This is the only way. The gods will it."

Emer wept, shuddering. All at once she dragged her hand from his. "I know this, husband, and you dishonor me by saying so." She wiped her face. "Don't you dare think I am less than Emer, heart-wife of Cúchulainn, and that your faith in *me* is a lie. Don't you dare let your eyes darken when you look at me!"

He laughed, pulling her close and smoothing her wild dark hair as her fists smacked his ribs. "Emer." He murmured in her ear as he did in the bed-furs. "The crow goddess has shown me the place of my death in dreams. She waits for me beside a gray stone beneath a dark cloud: that will be my end. On the night I ran to defend Naisi at Emain Macha, she crooned, 'It is not time yet,' and so I lived." He rubbed Emer's cheeks with his thumbs, the sun catching her tears. "She is silent now, hovering far away over Maeve of Connacht. I will come back to you." He kissed her, gathering her resisting body against him.

Emer swallowed, husky. "Will you take no one with you?"

"I will not risk another's blood." Cúchulainn cocked his head at her and smiled. "You rail at my sense of honor, and yet it is this that will save my life. My heart is sure of it."

Emer wiped her face on her sleeve, taking deep breaths. Smoothing back her hair, she held her hands out for his sword-belt.

If Ruán had asked, Lord Donn would have given him a horse. Baffled, Áedán tried to urge one upon him, while Orla wept and wrung her hands and would not take any comfort he could offer.

It would have been easier to be mounted, but Ruán knew he needed to feel the ground with his own feet. He must be anchored to the land in order to draw upon the Source and make Erin burst into light around him.

He was as strong as he had ever been, young and straight-limbed. The urgency in his breast to reach Maeve only grew greater day by day, and that gave his feet wings.

At first Ruán followed the great track built across Connacht by Cruachan's kings. Buoyed by the last touch of the sídhe, it unspooled as a glowing thread before him. It was so bright he was able to break into a lope, losing himself in the sense of Source. He let go, trusting he would feel the hollows, the ruts and stones, before he reached them.

The smile of the sídhe girl still glimmered in his mind, and he did not stumble.

The song of the land enveloped Ruán, and he lost track of time. The earth softened beneath, becoming a gentle wave that lifted and swept him onward. The trees were beacons marking out the rises and gullies in the ground, their light shimmering as if they resonated with his pulse and the gust of his breath.

Luminous streams traced the undulations of the lowlands and marshes, weaving patterns he could follow. He was drawn by the glowing heart of the great river, Sinand, and after a time turned along to follow it north.

That brought him close to his old home.

The strange flashes of farsight returned, catching him unawares and snapping his immersion in the song of the land.

He glimpsed warriors in dark leather and fur, so blinded by fear and fury they could see nothing but those others who ran at them with swords, seeking their deaths. Men struggled on the slopes of a rampart topped by stakes. Fighters dueled by a stream, screaming as blood poured from pierced flesh. And always, the morass of scarlet, black, and dull brown was shot through by the glint of iron blades.

Their hopelessness stabbed him, and their pain began to gnaw at his heart.

Sometimes, as he ran, the glowing veils were now marred by dark rents. At night, around his fire, he searched for glimpses of Maeve. Men were dying around her, but though he tried to see her flame—that familiar fire—his sight was obscured by her armor and an iron helmet that cut her face into lines he did not recognize.

Where, days before, the light-song of Erin had swelled in his heart, now a darkness was growing. What was the point of seeking them when death was all he saw? How could one man change this? He could not throw himself before every sword.

Ruán was following the banks of the River Sinand, but as these doubts grew and took root, his steps slowed and the webs of light behind his eyes began to falter. Every now and then the flames wavered as if in a wind, before flickering back into life and allowing him to press on.

As the whispers grew in his mind—*nothing will halt this madness…I cannot stop them dying*—so the river of molten silver and the torches of the trees began to gutter out. At those times he walked in blindness once more, feeling his way through the undergrowth, straining to hear the rushing of the water to guide his way.

You can do this. Remember who you are.

His limbs ached, weariness assailing his body as the land no longer flowed beneath him. He passed close to his marshland home, and it was then that memories began to invade Ruán, as if still imprinted on the veils of Source about the lake.

He saw himself stumbling to the water and throwing his body in, wanting to die. He heard his terrible cries among the stones, lived again the shame that had been burned from him.

Stop, he told himself. Memories *were* left behind as an echo in the Source, but he did not need to claim them again. He was different now. He summoned all his strength to call back the light, trying to melt into it once more.

Still, the doubt crept over him like a dark ocean drowning a bright land.

The whispers began again. How could he let himself believe he had some great fate to fulfill? That was his mistake before. Pride had brought about his fall—pride had taken his eyes.

One day the old pain of his blinding began to burn his sockets, and it made him stagger. The wash of light flickered out once more. Ruán halted, panting.

He smelled mud and water and rotting plants. The air was

growing cold as night fell. A gust of wind brought a snatch of cattle lowing. So ordinary. His blood raced, making his heart beat faster.

This was the world he was bound to. The other must have been a dream born of desperation, because he longed too much for something greater than himself. This yearning must have conjured up a grand fate that belonged to someone else.

Nor could he sense the sídhe. The veils opened on their Otherworld, but it was surely folly to think he possessed the power to part them himself. When he ran with the song of the land across Connacht, it must have been the trace of the sídhe-maiden's spirit that lit his way.

And now it had faded.

It was even more dangerous to believe he could carry the light to others. Such a desire had once led him down terrible paths, and if he ventured along them once more, what if he failed again?

You can save many people, the sídhe said.

Or he could kill not one person, but many.

That pain eclipsed his heart with despair, and drowning in its blackness, Ruán lost all sense of the ground beneath him.

A moment was all it took.

He stumbled, and one foot landed heavily along the edge of the raised riverbank. The bank collapsed. The earth gave way in a landslide of pebbles and river-mud.

Ruán tumbled down the slope and landed with a splash in a scoop of reeds and water.

He heard the crack of his leg before the pain hit.

CHAPTER 32

Maeve dreamed, floating in the peace of the lake.
It was twilight, the sharp outlines of day blurred into silver. Dusk made the water gleam and laced the reeds with jeweled droplets. The sky and lake melted into each other.

He padded up behind her and laid his lips on the curve of her neck. Silence...nothing need be said. She reached a tender hand back to cradle his head, his ruddy hair streaming through her fingers—

"Mother." Finn was shaking Maeve awake. "You have to come now. *Mother!*"

Maeve opened her eyes and squinted. All the silver bled away, replaced by battle-hues of black and red.

A lamp swung in Finn's hands, its feeble light swelling and shrinking on the slope of leather above Maeve's camp bed. Finn's mouth was crumpled. "Fergus and Ailill...drunk," she stammered. "They are fighting. You have to come!"

The fear in her voice dragged Maeve to her feet. She rubbed her face, groping for the cloak she had thrown on her bed-furs. "They are always drunk." Her tongue stuck to the roof of her mouth.

"With blades!" The lamp-flame leaped as Finn's hand shook.

Maeve blinked as she laced on boots and belted her sword on. She struggled to focus as she and Finn hastened through the camp, the night mist clinging to their skin.

"Ailill asked Fergus to drink with him and his men in his tent," Finn explained. "They have been guzzling since sunset."

Maeve glanced up to see that the weary moon was already sinking through streamers of cloud.

"And then Ailill taunted Fergus and they started fighting and..." Finn trailed off.

Maeve thought of her lost dream with a pang. A moment with him...she still felt his kiss. "But why are you awake, daughter? Why did the men not send for me?"

Finn opened her mouth to answer. At that moment a terrible bellow echoed over the camp, screams and shouts erupting behind it. Maeve and Finn broke into a run, dodging the dark humps of brushwood shelters.

They reached Ailill's tent, an unwieldy collection of cowhides that took twenty men to move each day. Maeve flipped her dagger from her belt and with it swept the flap aside, flinging herself in.

Warriors were milling about: Ailill's swordmates from Laigin, Ulaid fighters, and Fraech with his Connacht-men.

Maeve saw Cormac first. The face of Conor's son was a mask of horror, his eyes flaring as he screeched incoherently and tried to claw his way through the throng, a naked sword in his hand. Connacht warriors were holding him back.

"Out of the way!" Maeve's shrill voice cut the din, and the men parted.

Like a felled tree, Fergus was sprawled between an overturned table, scattered fidchell pieces, and spilled cups of wine. The mound of his belly was scarlet, blood spreading in a gory tide from a great wound. Fergus was gurgling, scrabbling at the rent in his tunic and flesh beneath.

Ailill stood beside him, gaping at the dripping sword in his hand and then at Fergus.

Maeve felt the thrust of that blade through her own vitals. Her mouth spasmed, her hand over her lips. *Fergus.* The horror froze her. *Oh, Fergus.*

The warriors were howling like wolves.

Fraech was gripping Cormac's hilt, bending his arm until at last his blade dropped. With a blow of his fist, Fraech knocked Conor's son to the ground, and some of the Connacht-men sat on him as he thrashed. Other Ulaid fighters were cursing and trying to reach Ailill, his Laigin swordmates shoving them back.

Maeve dropped to her knees by the wounded man. "Fergus..."

His eyes rolled back and he tried to speak again. Maeve bent down, groping for his hand. Nothing came out of his throat but a burble, and then a great spasm overcame him. His back arched and blood welled through his fingers. Maeve glimpsed the purple gleam of innards and her own belly turned over.

When Fergus collapsed, his limbs spread out, his head flopping to the side, mouth open. His eyes saw no more.

The cry that went up then hammered Maeve's ears.

The Ulaid warriors were calling on the gods for revenge, Laigin and Connacht-men struggling to stop them from attacking Ailill. With trembling fingers Maeve closed Fergus's eyes and mouth. A king of Erin should not die like this. Her hair over her face, she looked up at Ailill.

His skin was yellow, his features set into a rictus of disbelief. Only when his gaze met hers did he flinch, and squeeze out a gasp.

Maeve got up. "Traitor," she hissed, the first thing that came. Fergus was a great man. He had bound himself to them with oaths. And Ailill had put them all in terrible danger, too, for what if the Ulaid warriors turned on them now?

Ailill swayed, his cheeks now reddened above his beard. "*Me* a traitor? I know why you wanted him. You threw your enchantments over him as you did me, so you could rule Erin between you! You found a better bull, didn't you, Maeve? A king in his own right...*Red Branch!*" He spat that out. "You think I'd let you toss me aside like dog bones because of *him?*" His chin wobbled and he stabbed the air with his sword. "I am Ailill mac Ros Ruadh, and I will be usurped by no man!"

Drawing up, Maeve stepped in and struck Ailill across the face. He bellowed in senseless rage and would have brought his blade down on her if Finn had not yelled Fraech's name.

Fraech whirled, shoving his shoulder into Ailill's side and pushing the Laigin prince to his knees. The blade fell to the rug and lay there, bloody as a hewn limb.

Ailill threw back his head and howled. His Laigin warriors swarmed about him, and dragging him up, helped him stagger through the throng to the tent flap. The Connacht fighters were still holding back the Ulaid men, who cried and reached for him.

Maeve scrabbled for sense. She looked up at Fraech. "Get your men after him and protect him from any further stupidity. If he dies, too, we will have a war with Laigin on our hands."

Fraech gestured at some Connacht guards. "Surround the prince and keep him safe—hurry!"

Bleakly, Maeve looked at Finn huddled by the door, her fingers over her mouth. As Fraech tried to calm the Ulaid warriors, Maeve sank to her knees beside Fergus again and buried her face in her hands.

She had ignored Ailill's growing anger, treating him like a bull content to chew his cud. She was used to being underestimated by men, and now she had made the same mistake.

Death. Somehow, though her heart had reached for life, and freedom, longed for safety and peace ... she had beckoned death to her. She meant to wield it for justice, but had unleashed it instead.

Now it followed her, a dark wolf at her heels.

Dawn brought creeping fog and haunted silence.

Men whispered as they stirred up the coals of their fires. In the encampment of Ulaid warriors, the sounds of revelry had been replaced by keening. The women who accompanied the exiles smeared their faces with ash and wailed. Fergus's men beat their swords on their shields, the horrid thuds like a ghostly battle in the mist.

Maeve donned her jewelry and best seal-fur cloak. Ignoring

the glares of Fergus's kin, she made her way to where they had laid his body out on a grassy knoll, beside an old cairn of the ancestors. The chill vapor clung to her, and she shivered as she draped an embroidered blanket over Fergus's stained cloak and added a dagger to the pile on his breast.

She bowed her head and let the keening wash over her.

As the sun broke over the hills, changing gray to gold, the jingling of sword-belts drew up Maeve's head. Cormac trailed up the hill, his fair hair wet, as if he'd dunked it in a stream. His cheek and jaw were bruised, eyes red-rimmed.

Behind him Ferdia wove an unsteady path over the wet grass, looking at Maeve as if she had stabbed Fergus herself.

Maeve faced them. "What happened to Fergus was an abomination. We of Connacht grieve with you, rage with you. But it was a mistake wrought by jealousy and ale, not treachery. We should leave such things to Conor."

Cormac gritted his teeth. "You do not have the right to speak mac Roy's name."

Sorrow bore Maeve down, and she did not mask her raw expression. If they splintered now, worse evils would come. They would turn on each other, and those left alive would be easy pickings for Conor, even in his weakened state.

"If you leave now, then Conor has already won," she croaked. "Do not let that happen because of a terrible mistake. Fergus fought hard for this. He wanted to be avenged. He wanted to save his own people from Conor—your people."

Cormac cradled the elbow Fraech had bent in the skirmish in the tent. "That murderer Ailill has to pay for what he took from us."

"He will accept his punishment, but only after we are victorious. We must stay strong, together, until then. If you go now, we lose everything."

Cormac jutted out his jaw, his lips thinning as he gazed at Fergus's draped body.

Maeve had no choice but to wield a greater weapon. And she hated it, for she was deathly weary of such things now. "Only my forces have the strength to take Emain Macha. So stay with me and rule your own lands, or leave us now and become our enemies forever." She drew what fire remained into her eyes. They had to understand what was at stake, for all of them.

Framed by his tangled hair and dark stubble, Ferdia's gaze was hot with accusation.

Maeve turned to him. "And if you do walk away, Ferdia, soon Cúchulainn will either be dead or avowed to me in surrender. His honor will not let him break an oath to follow you all over Erin, will it? *It didn't before.*" The broken shard in her heart pricked her. *But it is necessary.* There were enemies behind and in front of them: she had to hold them as one or die.

Ferdia's lashes lowered. He staggered as he turned away, barely staying upright. Cormac threw the hem of his cloak around his neck against the cold mist. "Ailill will pay," he hissed, crossing to the other side of the pyre with Ferdia.

Maeve left them to mourn their leader.

For the rest of the day and night, Fraech and Maeve fought to knit the war-band back together. Summoning all their skills of persuasion, they cajoled and coaxed, calming Laigin men who bristled at the insults thrown at Ailill, smoothing the hackles of Connacht warriors who had been struck by Ulaid and Laigin fists.

And yet still the murmurs rustled across the camp like a foul wind. *They were cursed by the gods.* Around every campfire warriors hunched, casting fearful glances over their shoulders to the sky, the looming hills, and the fading woods along the stream-banks.

Lugh, Manannán, and the Dagda had withdrawn their favor because of the murder of the great king Fergus mac Roy.

Despair invaded Maeve with every breath of that dank, heavy air. She sought out Ailill. If *he* left, he would take his Laigin fighters and the Galeóin, and the superstitious Mumu would probably follow after.

Ailill lay hidden in one of the crude tents his warriors slept in, guarded on all sides. His men did not let her in at first, but Maeve stared them down. "Your king, Ros Ruadh, blessed this raid. He is allied with *me* as Queen of Connacht." At last they dropped their heads and let her through.

Maeve crept into the tent and sat beside Ailill in the shadows. She smelled reedy water on his hair, as if he had dunked it, but his breath still reeked of sour ale and vomit. She bent her knees up. "I never rutted with Fergus, and I was never going to set you aside. I do not—" She cut herself off, by habit shielding her heart.

What Ailill said was wrong: she had never wanted to rule Erin. Huddled in that cold forest, the howls of grief rising around her, Maeve now realized a more bitter truth.

She did not want to rule Connacht, either.

Not now that she knew death and pain were the cost of power, and it was her people who bore it. She had only ever wanted to rule *herself*, and if she could, protect her people. How did that become this?

Strong they might be, but they all paid the price. Idath and Felim's men. Lassar and his swordmates on the raid. Their women, their children.

Fergus.

Now it was too late to go back. She could only bind together what was left, and bring Conor down before he did them.

Maeve cleared her throat. "You saw a chance to grasp at power by marrying me, Ailill, and now you have set all that at risk." She laid a hand on his wrist. "If you return to your father so dishonored, he will refuse to name you his heir and your lords will never follow you again. You will lose everything you ever wanted."

Ailill's hand curled into a fist in the dark.

Maeve's breath stirred his hair. "Or...redeem yourself. Fight alongside the Red Branch exiles to win their kingdom. Only battle glories can outshine this dark deed."

There was a rustle of bracken as Ailill turned his back to her. "Go away, Maeve."

She dragged herself up. Outside, dread still hung over the camp like the stink of something rotting. In the darkness, she looked down, realizing that her hand had come to rest beneath her breastplate.

All the children of Connacht. She could not bear to think of that swell in her belly as anything else. With a sharp breath, Maeve bound her other hand over the first, clutching herself.

Macha. Hold them safe.

✠

The fragile ties that bound the war-band held.

They left the Plain of Muirthemne and passed north, close to Dun Dalgan. Cúchulainn's fort and all the lands about were deserted, the scouts reported. The cottages were dark and empty, the cattle driven away.

The only things that stirred were the dying leaves on the trees, the grasses, bleached by cold and wind, and the red bracken. Clouds of white fleece scudded in the sky, but there were no sheep-flocks dotting the slopes beneath.

"There is the way to Emain Macha." Cormac pointed at the range of hills that ringed the great whale-back of Cullen's Mount.

A pass led inside this circle of lower peaks, and from there a good cart track skirted the sacred mountain and headed north and then west. The trail of gravel, packed-down mud, and timbers dug in across boggy ground made for swifter riding, and speed was of the essence.

This path through the hills also provided cover for them, Cormac said. Nor were the defenses of Macha as strong here: the ditches shallow, with no timber rampart.

Cúchulainn's presence had reassured Conor that no war-party could ever come this way.

They continued north along the trail until it was squeezed between the slopes of Cullen's Mount and a long, dark lake. "It is a narrow way," Maeve observed at dusk, from the far end of the valley.

"It is the swiftest." Cormac rubbed his stubbled jaw. His eyes were still veined from the smoke of Fergus's pyre.

Maeve glanced at the tremor in his hands where they grasped his reins. She needed a swift victory before all the Ulaid-men lost heart, and she lost them. "If this is the quickest way," she murmured, "then tomorrow we will take it."

After a night huddled beneath barren, wind-scoured slopes, they came into the valley of Cullen's Mount at sunrise.

When the scouts came galloping back with their reports, their faces were ashen. "Lady," one stammered, "you must come and see what the dawn has revealed, or you will not believe us." The mingling of wonder and fear in his eyes brought Maeve upright in her saddle.

Maeve, Cormac, and Fraech rode their horses with the scouts and a few guards, approaching the narrow throat between the lakeshore and the slope of the great mount. The woods clinging to the hollows at the base of the mount breathed early mist, the browning leaves dripping dew onto their faces.

The rising sun warmed their cheeks as at last it flooded the landscape.

"I would not go closer," the scout muttered. He pointed with his spear, his horse stamping in a cloud of warm breath on the cold air.

Maeve squinted, then blinked to clear her gritty eyes.

The sun spilled from behind their right shoulders in the east, but a brighter flame flared *before* them—on the western shore, beyond the sheet of bronzed water.

A second sun dawned this day in the Ulaid.

A stream cut the path, spilling down the hill and flowing into the lake. On the other side, someone had erected ranks of felled saplings, a procession of spears with no bearers. Each sapling was topped with a polished shield, and the branches were hung with bronze armbands, horse harness, necklets, and buckles—anything that would reflect the rising sun. Rows of real lances flanked the trees, the light playing over the mass of iron spear-tips just as it rippled across the lake.

A movement caught Maeve's eye. She shaded the glare with her hand. Two horses galloped out of the trees, one gray and one black. The whites of their eyes flashed, their mouths speckling their harnesses with foam. They pulled a chariot encrusted in gleaming shields and every sort of weapon. Red banners streamed from spears that stuck out of the wicker sides.

The figure in the chariot shouted and flicked the reins, and the horses streaked along the processional way formed by the bronze-hung saplings. At the last minute before hitting the stream, the warrior slid the chariot into a broadside, the fittings of metal and oiled wood setting off another sunburst in Maeve's eyes.

As the chariot yawed, the man leaped up and, dropping the reins, expertly ran along the yoke. He paused between the shoulders of his streaking horses, balanced despite the lurching wheels, and brandishing his sword, let out a mighty bellow.

The valley sides gathered that challenge and crashed it back on itself, over and over. The shrieking waves hit the rocks, building up an assault of sound. Meallán reared and shook his head as Maeve scrambled to grab his reins. The other men were also dragging back their horses, their faces pale.

Cormac swore.

Using the jolt of the ground, the warrior launched into a somersault, soaring back into his chariot. He caught the reins and hauled his horses about a heartbeat before they collided with the slope. The sun lit upon his fair hair, crowning him in gold.

The Connacht scouts stared with mouths agape. "The Hound," Cormac whispered.

Maeve snapped her mouth shut, choking on the name.

Cúchulainn.

CHAPTER 33

"That is the sign of the oak." Cormac sounded dazed as he watched Cúchulainn stake a branch into the ground on his side of the stream. "He wants to speak."

Maeve dragged a hand over her lips to wipe away a tremor. Cúchulainn was a golden god to everyone else, but to her, he was so much else.

A vicious sword that Conor wielded. A wolf set free of Conor's leash, to tear her world to pieces.

Her response to him was primitive. Heat swept her and the hairs stood up over her arms and neck. Unconsciously, she bared her teeth, her shoulders rigid.

He was her death. Or she was his.

"I will go to him." Fraech's eyes were fixed on the Hound with great intensity.

Cormac came to life. "I, too."

"Take druids with you," Maeve said. No warrior would harm a priest under a branch of sacred oak.

Two of the Connacht druids hacked a branch off a tree, murmuring to its spirit, and holding it up, walked before Fraech and Cormac's horses as they rode down to the stream, which was a golden ribbon in the dawn light.

Like wildfire, Cormac's utterance of the Hound's name had spread to the Connacht camp behind them, borne on the tongues of the scouts. While Maeve waited on Fraech, the men of her warband began gathering, spilling along the path by the lake and spreading up the slopes to crouch in the bracken, even though it was soaked with dew.

Maeve glanced at them, alarm stirring.

They jostled to see Cúchulainn, craning their necks, even

climbing trees and clambering up the mossy boulders that had tumbled down from the crest of the mount above them. The dark mutters of the past few days were replaced by bright chatter.

Every boy in Erin had heard of Cúchulainn—one of his greatest exploits took place on the other side of this very hill. Many years before, Conor and his Red Branch were gathered at the fort of the smith Cullen for a feast. The plucky boy known then as Sétanta was running late, and coming to the gates after dark was attacked by Cullen's great hound. Sétanta slew the hound in self-defense—a feat that amazed Conor's warriors even as it grieved Cullen. To compensate him, Sétanta vowed to protect the smith's fort himself for a year, sleeping at his gates like a dog.

This legend earned Sétanta his adult name: Cúchulainn, Hound of Cullen.

At the Samhain feast soon after, the Ulaid druid Cathbad foretold that any boy who took his first weapons from the Red Branch hall that day would enjoy the greatest renown of any warrior, but in return a short life. Cúchulainn was the only youth waiting at the doors of the hall before the sun cleared the hills.

A short life, Maeve repeated to herself now, rubbing gooseflesh from her arms. *That means he can be killed.*

Fraech and Cormac returned. Fraech dismounted, hesitating before Maeve.

Cormac cut in instead, breathing as if he'd just run up the slope. "Cúchulainn says he is the Hound who guards the territory of the Goddess Macha. He defends this path into the Ulaid by the grace of the divine ones."

Maeve could not decipher Cormac's expression. Dismay, fear...relief?

Cormac's color was high. "Cúchulainn therefore sends out a sacred challenge to every man here. He will fight the warriors one by one, in single combat, and only if he is beaten will this army pass, for then all will know it is the will of the gods."

Maeve looked to one of the druids, who bowed his head. "It is as he says."

The voices of the warriors rose behind Maeve, leaping into life like the splashing of the sunlit stream. Maeve caught their sentiment. Cúchulainn bore the most blessed name in Erin. Any man who defeated him would *become him*.

Her stomach plunged, understanding what had happened before her mind caught up.

Around her, warriors were crowing that *they* would be the first to triumph over the great Hound of Cullen. Their swordmates chorused that the gods must have taken their wits. Speculation flew about Cúchulainn's wondrous weapons and all the gold that would become the winner's spoils.

Fools. They truly thought they would be the first to defeat Cúchulainn? Maeve gazed around at their glassy eyes, heard their delirious laughter. To make himself run toward the sharp glint of swords, the stab and slice of flesh, a warrior *had* to think he was invincible.

"We are a war-band," Maeve declared over the noise. "We cannot be distracted by some prancing horseman while the rest of Conor's warriors circle around us!"

They must reach Emain Macha swiftly, break Conor's power with the fewest deaths, in the briefest time.

"The Hound has bound us with his oath." Cormac's voice was flat, unassailable. "There is no war-band behind him. There will be no treachery."

More warriors were streaming in from the camp behind them. Dark Galeóin spearmen now mingled with Mumu fighters. Men of Laigin and Connacht crushed together in a throng, faces lit by the same zeal. Their enmities had been forgotten.

The irony of this pushed Maeve off her horse. As she slid to the ground, an intense pain speared her, and she halted, biting her lip as beads of sweat broke over her brow.

The cramp eased, and forcing herself to straighten, Maeve limped before her men. "The Red Branch are struck down by a curse. Lord Garvan is holding the West. We are nearly at Emain Macha, where we can defeat Conor and rid our land of him forever. And here stands the most famed warrior of the Ulaid—our greatest threat—*alone*." She swung back. "If we charge now, the path to Emain Macha will lie open before us. Now go and arm yourselves. This triumph will be ours before the sun is high."

No one moved, men looking at their feet or up at the red hills. Most merely stared at the gilded Cúchulainn. One bold soul spoke up. "The gods curse us for the death of Fergus mac Roy. A grievous taint has fallen upon our names, our kin."

There were mutters of "Aye."

Someone else turned to yell at his sword-brothers. "The gods have shown us how to claim our honor again, so that our names are bard-sung once more. If we take up the Hound's challenge, they will bless us forever, even in death!"

The roar of approval drowned out Maeve's protests.

Maeve turned to Fraech. "Order them to attack," she gasped.

But Fraech shook his head. He had found an eagle's wing-feather on the trail and stuck it through the braid at his neck. A call for courage from the gods, he had named it. Now Maeve could not look away from the taunting flash of it among his brown locks.

"Each man must stand alone before the gods in the Other-world, proud of name and deeds. Only then can we be reborn in honor." Even Fraech's eyes betrayed a smoldering desire. "No warrior can turn from this chance to fight Cúchulainn, and reclaim his pride after the death of mac Roy."

"You mean be killed by Cúchulainn," Maeve retorted. She noticed Cormac, watching the shouting men with a slight smile. "Anyone would think *you* do not want to defeat your father and set the Ulaid to rights."

Cormac's expression soured. "The death of Fergus has angered the gods." The warriors close to him grew hushed. "Though I want to regain my hall, I will not pile treachery upon treachery. I have been suffering for too long—but now the Hound himself shows me the way from pain to glory."

His words were met with an enormous roar of approval.

Cormac joined Conall and his Ulaid sword-brothers once more, and exclaiming among themselves, they turned back to camp. Other warriors from Laigin, Mumu, and Connacht began streaming after them, preparing to bathe and arm themselves.

"You are supposed to obey me," Maeve growled to Fraech.

Fraech sighed, taking off his helmet and propping it on his saddle. He rotated one shoulder, flexing his sword-hand. "A king—or queen—rules a man's body, but his spirit answers to the gods alone." He shot her a look of grim humor. "There are other unstoppable forces in this world besides you."

"And I suppose you have a notion to redeem yourself by smearing your guts all over the Hound's sword?"

For some reason, Fraech's eyes flew toward the camp. He dragged his attention back, running his fingers through his forelock. "Without your champion here, I should fight first."

"You have a duty to all of these men as war-leader."

Fraech paused. "I know."

"Good." Maeve's side throbbed again, and she leaned on Meallán's flank to ease it. "For I remind you of your vows to me, given in return for your life. You will stay out of this. It would not be *honorable* to abandon your leadership when our men need you."

"But you are honorable, too, cousin—and five hundred men piling upon one is not glorious, it is slaughter." Fraech cocked his head, the rising sun hitting his green eyes. "That is not what *Maeve* would do. It is not why the men followed you."

She winced, turning her chin. The Maeve who stood at the temple of Lugh as the crowds cheered had burned with the passion to be a just leader, to rule nobly.

With honor.

"Go back to Cúchulainn..." Maeve could hardly get the words past her instinctive revulsion. Swallowing it, she looked across the shining river at the golden god who held death in his smile. "...and say we accept his challenge."

Fraech put a hand on her shoulder. "Do not despair," he said. "He must weaken in the end. He is only a man, after all."

Cúchulainn rubbed down his horses and set them to graze beneath the trees on his side of the river, and then unpacked his chariot, arranging a great number of weapons and shields on the grass.

Excited murmurs went up from the Connacht-men whenever some particularly fine sword or spear-tip flashed in the sunlight. With a dark fascination, Maeve sat on Meallán's back and watched the Hound wash his head in the tumbling stream and bind back his hair before donning a helmet with a bronze crest. Some of his weapons he also blessed in the water and presented to the sun, his lips moving.

His manner was flowing and graceful, head high, back straight. His hands seemed to move of their own accord, as if he was in a trance. He rested braces of spears on rocks, and stuck shields and unsheathed swords into the soft ground where he could get at them easily.

More armed warriors poured from Maeve's camp. They had polished their swords and spears and bathed themselves clean, tied back their wet hair with fur or scraps of their women's skirts. Arm-rings were bound over sleeves, brooches stuck through tunics.

Anything that shone, to catch the eye of the gods.

Druids from Connacht, Laigin, and Mumu had sacrificed three hares to the gods and were now marking out the boundaries of the river meadow with blood, chanting. Their spells conjured a sacred doorway through which the spirits of warriors could pass in glory to the Otherworld.

Maeve's Champion should fight first, but Garvan was in the West. Numbed, she looked down at Fraech. "How will we decide...?"

Fraech shaded his eyes, looking up at her. He was about to answer when the mutterings of the warriors at the rear of the throng turned to exclamations, rushing to the front like a wave.

A thick-set man parted the crowd, his brown hair spiked with lime. His tread was heavy and faltering. Ailill.

She had not expected him to appear at all, and if he did, that he would arrive on his chariot flanked by spearmen, pennants streaming, horses prancing—a defiant prince for all to see.

This Ailill bore nothing but a sword, shield, and mail-shirt. His trews and tunic were unadorned and he wore no armbands. His broad shoulders were slumped, and though the glitter of his mail was cold and hard, his eyes were blank.

No one made a move to stop him.

Maeve watched Ailill, her lips quivering. Only then did she notice he had even put aside his royal torc. She slid to the ground and dashed between the warriors toward him, as light as the girl who once raced through the Laigin woods. She stepped in front of her husband.

Ailill halted, swaying.

The crowd grew hushed. Maeve searched his eyes. *You do not have to do this*, she wanted to say. But in his battered face, heavy with pain, she saw that he did.

She placed her fist on her breast and bent over it—an honor a king or queen rarely bestowed upon another. She touched her brow as she straightened, and holding Ailill's arms, kissed his cheeks. "Go, husband, with the affection of your wife in your heart, and the honor of your queen on your brow. The bards will sing of your courage from this day forward."

Ailill's eyes were red-veined, but as he gazed down at her, they softened. "Well, firebrand, this is a better end than moldering away at my father's fire." Wonder lifted his drawn face and he laughed. "Lugh's balls, but you were right after all."

She gripped his arms. "*This will not be your end.*"

Ailill's only answer was a dazed smile, and he dragged himself free of her to plow on. Maeve's arms fell by her sides as she watched him go.

Limping, Ailill made his way down to the stream at the base of the great hill. The silence around Maeve was broken by a great clang, and then another. The Laigin warriors lifted their arms above their heads and beat their shields with their swords, drumming out the battle-song for their prince.

More men joined them, the Connacht warriors and even, at last, the Ulaid men. The din echoed off the steep, fern-clad slopes above, hammering on Maeve's ears as she returned to her horse.

Ailill reached the stream-bank.

Cúchulainn was ignoring the noise, tightening his buckles and picking up a sword and long dagger. He turned to face his first challenger, but as he came out of the shade and the sun hit him again, Cúchulainn stopped.

He closed his eyes, tilting his head back, nostrils flaring. In the midst of that wave of drumming and cheering, Cúchulainn crossed both blades over his chest and drew in great breaths all the way from his feet to his head.

Was he filling himself with something? For though she was almost blinded by the flash of iron, as he extended his back and broadened his shoulders Maeve wondered if she imagined he looked bigger than before.

The Hound's eyes snapped open. The sunlight played over his helmet, chain mail, and blades, sheathing him in a glow that seemed to breathe as he breathed.

Cúchulainn was alight.

In a blaze, he crossed the grass to the stream-bank. A druid stood by the water beside Ailill, arms raised to summon blessings for both warriors. The moment the priest stepped back, war-cries burst from every Laigin throat. They were joined by the rest of the war-band, shouting, yelping, and bellowing. The battle-songs of the four kingdoms pierced the hammering of shields.

Silent and still, Maeve could not take her eyes off the armored figures below.

Cúchulainn stared at the prince for a long moment, recognizing him. He said something in anger and Ailill replied, both of them tense. Cúchulainn lifted his chin, and even from afar his eyes held power, framed by the steel of his helmet.

Maeve could tell by his stance that he was taunting Ailill, as warriors did in single combat. Next, they would charge back and forth, working themselves into a frenzy until one of them struck a blow.

Ailill, however, did not puff out his chest and toss insults back. He simply shrugged a shoulder, lowering his shield and sword to his sides and bowing to Cúchulainn. The Hound returned the bow. Ailill lifted his shield and braced his blade in the combat pose.

The warriors around Maeve screamed even louder, trying to force their frenzy into the Laigin prince and set his blood on fire. Mounted again, Maeve squinted, gripping Meallán's mane.

Cúchulainn's shoulders were heaving; he snorted like a pawing bull, gathering his fury. Ailill, in contrast, was heavy and still, his feet dug into the muddy ground, his muscles rigid.

Blaze, Ailill! Maeve found herself praying. *Find the fire in you.* But Ailill had never been fiery.

The Hound of the Ulaid became a streak of light.

He bounded over the mossy stones in the stream and came at Ailill with a whirling sword. Startled at his speed, Ailill threw up his shield and Cúchulainn's sword bit deep into the leather and wood.

Cúchulainn pulled it out and spun, raining down another blow from behind as Ailill was still trying to turn around. Desperate, Ailill flung out his arm and caught the Hound's blade with his shield boss. The rivets in the center of the shield struck sparks off the sword, but Ailill had left his flank exposed.

Now Maeve saw why Cúchulainn bore no shield himself. With both hands ending in blades, he could whirl them into a web of silver around his head. Blinding ... distracting. Dazzled by that display, Ailill swayed back on his heels. While he was immobilized, Cúchulainn threw himself into a little bound, vaulting over on the spot, both blades spinning. One of them slashed Ailill's hip.

Ailill cried out and staggered to the side, and the men around Maeve bayed louder. Ailill limped a few steps, blood pouring down his thigh from a wound on his flank.

Maeve dropped her chin, staring at her fingers knotted in Meallán's mane.

One brawny fighter who could only strike out with brute force; one lithe opponent who could duck and spin, and draw in the light behind the world. Maeve remembered that other fight a year ago with two such combatants ... and its outcome.

She forced herself to straighten, but her breast was hollow.

Cúchulainn leaped and raced around the prince of Laigin, spinning that net of metal into a web to trap him. Ailill was forced to keep turning, and from his stance, Maeve knew he was growing dizzy. Only Red Branch warriors fought like that. It took many years of practice ... and an awareness that was not entirely human.

Ailill kept lunging, crouching close to the ground with his shield to his nose then swinging in with all his force. Every time, Cúchulainn danced out of the way, landing a cut on an arm or leg and making Ailill bellow like a bull.

Running with sweat, Ailill at last lost his temper and threw everything into one wild sword-swipe. He stretched too far over his knee, though, and his shield dropped back.

The Hound snapped up the chance.

Tossing aside the prancing and leaping, Cúchulainn gathered his flame into one focused point. He struck Ailill's sword-arm down at the elbow, and in a blur, immediately flicked his wrist to reverse that blow.

Even as Ailill was stumbling, Cúchulainn drew his blade across the prince of Laigin's neck.

Ailill toppled and sprawled on the grass.

The swiftness of it stunned everyone to silence. Maeve shut her eyes, and the next moment a great cry of grief and anger rose from all the watching warriors and crashed over her like a wave.

By the time Maeve opened her eyes, wild-eyed Laigin men were throwing down their shields, shouting and waving fists, and rending their tunics with their daggers. The ground around Ailill's head was bright scarlet, his face in the grass.

White-robed druids swooped upon Ailill's body, and his

Laigin swordmates tore down the slope after them. Cúchulainn, meanwhile, bowed to Ailill and, before anyone could reach him, leaped back over the stream to his own side.

He was still sheathed in light, blurring the streaks of gore that ran down his armor and the skin on his arms. Cúchulainn turned to salute the men on the slopes with his stained sword, and visibly breathed out, his shoulders lowering.

The body of Ailill of Laigin was gathered on a bier of shields and carried past the waiting throng. Maeve stared at the bloody ring around his neck, a cruel imitation of his torc, and it was then that she cracked. "A great woe has been done this day!"

She saw Ailill again as a boy, the first time he held her in the moonlight. Pretending to be bold, she had tilted her chin to kiss him, but her trembling gave her away. Young as he was, Ailill had merely smiled, gathering her against his beating heart, his skin smelling of river-water. *So you're not as brave as all that, little firebrand.*

Her throat burned at the memory. "The prince of Laigin has died needlessly. Storm Cúchulainn now, all of you, and no more will share his fate!" She flung her hand toward Cúchulainn, who'd taken himself to a rock and now sat carefully upright, the sun bathing him.

Surely the Laigin warriors would want revenge.

Ailill's swordsmen were indeed weeping by his body, which they had now rested on a patch of ferns by the lakeshore. They knelt with helmets in their hands, heads bowed. "We honor you," they cried, dabbing blood from his wounds and smearing it on their blades.

Then, one by one they got up, the tears scouring tracks down their filthy faces. "I am next in rank," one said, his sword across his breast. "I will fight Cúchulainn, and be the first to walk with my prince through the veils."

"No," another argued. "My father is the king's elder cousin by a moon."

"We must draw lots," a third put in.

Maeve's arm slowly dropped. Soon the Laigin fighters would

be taken, and then the Galeóin, for Cúchulainn would make short work of those spearmen, however skilled. She turned from all the men and the fervor in their faces.

Right at her feet was Ailill's shield. She got down and heaved it up in both hands. It had been battered by great blows, the outline of the painted bull flaked away by the Hound's sword.

Tears pricked Maeve's eyes. She saw herself galloping through Tiernan's vision, circling the mound of her people and striking great shields just like this. Each blow cried out to the world that she had vowed to shelter them as their mother: not the strutting warriors, but the vulnerable ones they had forgotten.

For if these men died, one by one, Cúchulainn would stride up that hill to batter her at the end, pulverizing bone, shredding flesh. And then there would be no one to guard the mound and its glowing souls.

A faint sound escaped Maeve. *Help me help them.* She didn't know who she spoke to anymore. And then the desperation seized her. It had to stop, now, while there were fighting men alive for Laigin, Mumu, and Connacht. She must pull them away, turn them all back . . . *surrender*, if that was the only way.

For once, that word did not terrify her.

Maeve opened her mouth and cried it out. "There will be no more deaths! I order you to fall back, all of you!"

She realized no one was listening to her anymore. Her voice was drowned out by the cacophony of arguing men and the clang of swords on shields. They had their backs to her, everything in them bent upon Cúchulainn and the field of death below.

As strong as it was, her spirit could not triumph over warriors after all.

Gray eyes floated into her mind. Dark hair, dark face. *Ferdia.* Gods, she had forgotten Ferdia.

Maeve stumbled through the camp, fear leaching the sense from her mind. It took her some time to discover where Ferdia had gone. As she ran, she had to block out the roars of dismay, turning her wet face from the wounded men and bodies already being carried past her to the druid tents.

At last she found out that Ferdia had retreated into the forest behind the ridge.

He was sitting on a mossy log in a sunny clearing, his face in his hands. His flask, sword, and pack were propped on the stumps around him. Maeve was arrested by the impression of an unseen presence sitting with Ferdia, as if by a campfire.

Ferdia's pain had summoned a shadow of Cúchulainn.

"So the Hound is not sick, or at Emain Macha." Maeve loomed over him. "Instead, he picks our men off one by one. The stream runs red with blood, and Ailill is slain!" She grabbed Ferdia's arm, making him collapse, his limbs unraveling across the log. His pupils were empty pits that saw nothing, the shadows of the branches slicing his face into broken pieces.

Maeve shook him. "*You* are the only one who can beat Cúchulainn and save us all!"

Ferdia wheezed like an old man, blinking bleary eyes. "You do not know what you ask."

Reining in her fear, Maeve grabbed Ferdia's face. Gods, he was drunk. "You and I have listened to the bard songs about Cúchulainn on many firelit nights. But fight now, Ferdia, and *you* will be champion! It will be your name carried in sacred songs to the gods. The women will yearn for *your* eyes, *your* shoulders, *your* loins. You have always been alone. Now you can have it all. You came from nothing, but fight him and you will be remembered forever!" She did not miss the flare that cut through the ale-fog. Did *jealousy* lie buried in the great Ferdia?

He wrenched himself free, nearly falling off the log. "For that to happen, he must die."

"Cúchulainn knew the fate he chose by taking up arms on that Samhain day. A glorious life . . . a swift death."

"And you think this fate will be sealed by me." Ferdia stared into the imaginary flames at the heart of the grove.

"How do you know what the gods have in store for you, Daman's son?"

Ferdia twisted up to see Maeve. The darkness in his eyes had overflowed, delving bruises below his lashes and hollows in his cheeks. "You are asking me to kill the dearest soul to my soul, the dearest heart to my heart. Is there someone, queen of ice, who means that much to you?"

At the unguarded expression that crossed her face, Ferdia's eyes widened.

"For the safety of my people, I would do anything." Her fist shielded her breast. She had already killed herself, for duty had become a living death. And there was no love left for her anymore.

"I do not believe you." Ferdia smiled with the daze of a man who has just relinquished a fight. "You wept for someone that night in my tent; I felt your fire for him. *You* would rail at fate, bend it to your will." His chin dropped to his chest. "Bend it..."

"Ferdia."

When Maeve reached for him, he slapped her away, an action that sent him sprawling into the wet ferns. Gods. If she shoved him before Cúchulainn like this, he would be killed before drawing his sword.

With a curse, Maeve kicked the log. Bits of rotten wood scattered, grazing her cheek, though Ferdia barely flinched from his stupor. The kick drove another pain through her, and she wrapped her arms over it. A wild fear was rising in her, threatening to shatter the last of her sense.

Everybody was going to die. The gates of Cruachan would fall. *The people's blood...*

Maeve flew back through the woods to her tent and called for Finn, who had been sitting with her brother's body at the lakeside. Once they were alone, Maeve dragged her gaze from the blood on Finn's tunic and the smear on her cheek. *She must have embraced Ailill...*

Instead, Maeve looked at her bed, trying to breathe. The mattress was lumpy from her restless sleep, the sheets tied in knots she did not recall making.

"Ferdia must fight Cúchulainn," she forced out, "or more good men like Ailill will die. Only he knows every war-feat that Cúchulainn does, every stroke. He is not moved by promises of cattle, jewels, or a dun of his own—not even pride and honor." Maeve began pacing, her nerves on fire. "There is only this: every time Cúchulainn returned to his wife, Ferdia was left alone."

Finn was shockingly pale. But as she absorbed Maeve's words, the daze in her eyes faded and her cheeks flushed.

Maeve tensed every muscle, bracing herself as she never had before. *For all the children of Erin.* "And so all I have left to turn him, Finn—all any of us have—is you."

Finn's mouth dropped open.

"Promise to become his woman," Maeve ran on in desperation. "You will be the reward for Ferdia defeating Cúchulainn. He is a good man, young and handsome. He will make you happy, I know it."

"No." Finn's voice was unrecognizable, her brow lowered. "I will not be given in marriage to someone I do not love. Not ... not now."

Maeve felt for the camp table, one hand beneath her ribs. "What did I say of love? This is an alliance, more urgent than any other—"

"I do not care. I will not be given away." The ice in Finn's voice was deceptive, for her eyes kindled with a terrible passion.

The throbs of pain were making it hard for Maeve to think. "People's lives are at stake."

"*My* life is at stake!" Finn clenched her fists, throwing up her head. "And when my brother dies, it only makes me want to hold to mine more dearly. Others might suffer for duty, but I do not care for anything but love—and you cannot force me to!"

Maeve groped for the meaning behind this outpouring, but terror was gripping her, sickening. "This is what happens to women!"

"It is what happened to *you*. But I am not you!" Finn struck her breast, her eyes blazing in her stark face. "*You* never loved anyone, so you don't understand I want this more than anything you can promise me."

Maeve could not see anything but Ailill before her. A boy's face, beardless and shy. A dead thing, with florid cheeks and blood-flecked lips. "Men are dying."

"I did not bring them here," Finn shot back. "And I will not be their sacrifice."

Maeve managed to straighten, limping toward her daughter. It was slipping away, after all she had endured. The loss of Ruán tore at her... it was all for nothing. "You will defy *me?*"

Finn was a savage fox-cub now, teeth bared. "Yes."

With this, the specter of Conor rolled over Maeve, darkening her heart like a cloud over sun. It pushed terrible words out of her—Eochaid's words to her as a girl. "Refuse this and you will be banished, stripped of name and rank, a kinless exile with nothing but the clothes on your back."

Finn's laugh made the air shiver.

Only then did Maeve realize what she had said. It tasted vile, as of something old retched up. In horror, she thought, *What have I done to her?*

"You wouldn't defy your father because you were afraid to lose him. Well, Mother..." Tears spilled from Finn's eyes and her hand slashed between them. "I never had you when I needed you, and so I am not afraid to lose you now!"

The blow thrust Maeve back. She watched Finn spin on her heel. She was leaving. Another one... never to be seen again. "No." Maeve groped for her daughter. "No, I was wrong..."

But Finn was no more than a shadow at the flap of the tent.

Maeve's cry broke out. *"I will never force you!"* She thought she saw Finn hesitate before the darkness claimed her.

Maeve sank onto her bed, gripping the covers. The doors to the Otherworld must be open tonight, for the ghosts of the past came crowding in. Eochaid hovered before her—not his face, just his eyes. Gray flint, they were, strong and unyielding. And so he died bitter and alone, hated by his children.

Maeve stared at him so hard her own eyes burned. "I am not afraid to lose you, Father," she whispered. "So now I banish *you*— to be me, myself, alone."

Chin up, she defied that thickening of the air until it dissipated. At last her chest released and she slumped on the covers, a hand pressed to wet eyes.

CHAPTER 34

The early dusk of leaf-fall was creeping over the shore.

The hillcrest on the eastern flank of the lake caught the last sun. The slopes on the west, where the war-band camped, were steeped in purple and blue shadows beneath Cullen's Mount. All color was leached from the red bracken, the russet leaves, and the bright banners and furs of the warriors.

All that remained was the gleam of iron, cold as the shadow.

Fraech was with the guards on a knoll above the stream. Leaving the vigil over Ailill's body, Maeve picked her war-leader out in the growing darkness by the particular way he always poised on the balls of his feet. He was very still, with erect head and back, and at the same time radiated a readiness to strike, to break into flowing motion.

Maeve stood beside him. The rushing of the stream echoed off the rocks, a night-mist beginning to curl across its broken surface. On the opposite bank, a glow picked out Cúchulainn's campfire. The Hound trusted this honor of warriors so much he would mark where he slept.

A chill crept beneath Maeve's cloak. She rubbed her arms. "I was an idiot," she whispered, "and argued with Finn. You often know her whereabouts…" Her voice caught and she buried her chin in the fur ruff, inhaling woodsmoke. "Please don't let her leave. I don't want her to go back to Laigin."

Fraech gazed at her, his face indistinct in the dark. He turned back to Cúchulainn's fire. "She will not leave."

His confidence…that odd note of…possession? Heat rushed over Maeve. "I see," she said, more evenly than she felt. "It is you."

Fraech shrugged one shoulder.

Maeve's laugh was bleak. "Lugh's balls. I am not only heartless, but blind and foolish as well."

"Not foolish. I remember how you fared when your brother sought your death. Cunning runs through your blood." The lake glowed with the last of the twilight, and the silver caught his eyes. "You were blind to Finn and me because we do not threaten you, and that is all you see. And because this thing is not about you; it is ours alone." He let that fierceness fall into silence, folding his arms and setting his face toward the Hound like a wolf scenting the air. "If she wants to leave, I will go with her afterward. But I will not abandon you like so many others, for you have always been honorable to me."

Maeve had to look away, focusing on a crow that crossed the pink sky, black wings flapping. Of all the things to unravel her… She cleared her throat and gave his arm a slap, leaving her hand there. "Then you'd damn well better not get yourself killed."

⚜

At dawn Finn emerged from the damp woods in which she had been hiding, and eventually found Ferdia huddled in his deerskins in a small glade.

She emptied his ale and refilled the flask with water from a stream. Then she squatted beside him. Dew spangled his black hair and lashes, sparkling on his cloak. His features were fine and drawn, beautiful even.

Finn flicked droplets from the flask over Ferdia's face, making him flinch in sleep. It wasn't until the sun spread slowly over his face that he began to stir. He finally blinked awake and rolled on his back.

She held the flask out and let him drink. "You should leave here," she whispered, as if the twittering birds could hear. "You are a good man. You should leave and forget about all this—the greed, the blood."

His eyes were dark and deep now, his gaze slipping into wildness—as if he was finally shedding his human self and melting into the woods. The same trance took hold of Finn, that sense of a blurring of the worlds.

Time out of time; a place of magic.

That must be why she, a mere girl, gripped the shoulder of one of the greatest warriors in Erin as if they were equals. "Follow your heart's desire," she whispered. "Love is all that matters as we stand before the gods."

Ferdia's awareness groped up toward her, as if he was drowning and she was air. At last he surfaced; she felt their souls brush. His mouth formed a word, and Finn did not know what it was.

Or perhaps it was just love, after all.

The wind whipped up the little lake below the temple mound of Emain Macha. It battered Conor's head, blowing away the reek of the sick men that still clung to him.

His new chief druid and the older priests had also fallen ill now. The healers had run out of poppy-syrup, and the warriors were being dosed with more Alban ale to keep them from leaping up to fight with the fire-shadows.

The little flock of gangly novices beside Conor were all the priests he had left.

"Hurry," he croaked. The pain in his gut made it hard to straighten, and he was plagued with dizziness. He wanted to stay in bed, but he had to drag himself out for another sacrifice. At least it gave him some respite from the screams in his hall.

The young druids on the shore shivered, four of them holding long, curling trumpets. Others waved smoldering branches of rowan, sending up blue smoke. The bronze horns had hung in Conor's hall for years uncounted, and were blown at the crownings of kings. He was running out of offerings for the gods. "I said hurry," he spat, narrow-eyed.

The chanting quickened, until the priests were stammering over their pleas for the divine ones to heal the Ulaid warriors. Conor had instructed them to address the Dagda, Lugh, and the sea god Manannán, but not Macha. Father gods might be more inclined to heal warriors.

The last blessings tumbled out, and the horns were given to the lake. The early sun traced their graceful curves with flame, which went out as they sank.

One of the novices looked around, his hearing keen. Conor turned. A man on horseback was streaking down the track from the temple. Conor clutched his sodden robes and waded back through the reeds to dry land.

The rider was a boy, sweating and coated in mud, his teeth and eyes the only pale streaks in that filth. He stammered it out. A war-band had attacked the Gates of Macha in the West. The western lords were barely holding them at bay—the enemy kept swarming over the ramparts before being beaten back.

The ground fell away beneath Conor, and he lurched to one side, the dizziness returning.

The boy murmured, "My lord?" and nudged his horse closer.

Conor grabbed for the pony's mane. He stared at its gray coat between his swollen fingers. It was as mottled as burned bone. As gray as the ashen face of the goddess. *You will die by the hand of Woman.*

Conor pulled his cracked lips apart. "Who leads this war-band? *A woman?*"

The boy shrank from his bulging eyes, his clawed hand. "I do not know."

"Useless! Off with you!" Conor slapped the horse in frustration, sending it flying back up the track.

The Ulaid king wove a broken path toward the sacred temple of Macha. The spire of smoke from the sacrifices was torn into rags by the wind. Bleats floated to him—the last goats being killed, to plead for mercy with the divine ones. He had few animals from his own flocks left.

Conor glared at the great thatch building. *Macha.* He had ruled the Ulaid justly, and in return been scorned by faithless maidens, strutting bucks, and jealous lords. He barely stopped himself from cursing.

Macha of the Red Hair, ruling over his fate. How often had he knelt before her statue in the temple and raged at the empty hollows of her eyes? He only heard that deep, gentle voice, felt that godly light that one time, in the Dagda's shrine.

The Father God.

Buried in his fox-fur cloak, Conor turned his back on the goddess and clambered into his chariot to return to his hall. Inside the cavernous building, his sick Red Branch warriors no longer screamed. The air was filled with an endless moaning, like wind through a rent in the thatch.

He crawled back in his bed and snuffed out the lamp. In the dark he did not know who hovered about him: Levarcham with hatred in her eyes, Maeve with a sneer of contempt, or Deirdre arch and fey, always dancing out of reach.

"I *will not* let you win," he muttered, his fury filling him with strength. He would conquer Woman still.

***

Maeve took to watching the fights from a cart drawn up beneath an ash tree. Its leaves were already falling in gold about its feet. As if god-blessed, the days remained clear and sunlit. Connacht eagle banners were tied to the bare branches above her, drooping around her head. Her warriors spread up the hill, wedging themselves in trees and crouching on rocks.

One by one her warriors strutted down the slope, armor greased and hair spiked, as if that would make them fight better.

They did not all die.

Cúchulainn deemed some unworthy of even bloodying his sword. If they gouged furrows in the turf with foolish blows, or tripped when trying to run, or preened too long before the crowd of warriors, he attacked them only with the flat of his blade, delivering a beating as to a child. He could shear clumps of hair without drawing blood, sending them away bruised inside and out. "Begone!" he cried to them, lip curling, "for I have drawn ridicule upon you." That was the worst defeat of all for a warrior.

As time marched on, though, Cúchulainn began to spear those witless ones before they even reached the stream. Then, Maeve detected a frustration in the Hound's throws, a desperate weariness of spirit.

When braver men barreled into Cúchulainn with swords held high, the fights were bloody and snarling from the start. Cúchulainn let *them* be carried from the field in honor, limbs hacked, bellies rent.

Finally there were the warriors, well-trained in their kingdoms, who put on shows of war-feats.

They launched themselves into tumbles and springs, horse and chariot feats, fights with slings, lances, daggers, clubs, and finally swords. These games got the audience excited again, as they could pretend they were on the sparring green, pitting their skills against each other for the glory of the gods.

At those times, the cloud lifted from the throng, and they forgot death for a while.

With such opponents, Cúchulainn also changed. He shrugged off his stoic manner, this grim dispatching of doomed targets.

The sun breathed along the crest of his boar helmet again, and flickered around the Hound's head.

He and his opponents would hurl insults, the poetry of warriors—lewd chants about their ability to please their wives and their prowess. The men watching would roar with a release of laughter, and as Cúchulainn matched feat for feat, his movements quickened and he grew in stature until Maeve could barely see his face for that glow.

Soon after dawn on the second day of fighting, the crowd grew hushed as Cúchulainn's latest opponent was borne past Maeve.

Maeve stared down from her cart. One of the dead man's arms flopped out and swung from the bier. The other was missing, the stump obscured by his blood-soaked cloak. His head was back, neck ringed by a gaping rent.

Since the fights began, she had felt every wound as a stab in her own body. Now she tried to ignore that pain, touching her forehead with a shaking hand. *May the gods bear you swiftly, with honor on your brow.*

The men had stopped cheering now. They watched in silence, a spell fallen over them, making time stand still. Expectation and awe trembled in the air.

Maeve looked at Cúchulainn on the other side of the river.

Since delivering the last death-blow he had been still, barely breathing. His head was uncovered, the helm on the ground. The sun no longer shone from his hair because it was lank and bloodied, his armor and weapons streaked with gore. Coming back to himself, the Hound gave a bow toward the dead man then plunged into the stream, scouring all the filth from his face and hair and gulping water.

The sun kept climbing. More men breathed their last.

Defeat bore down on Maeve, and she crouched in the cart with arms under her knees. She turned her cheek toward the lake to take a breath that was not sour with death. Tiernan must be wrong, she decided. The savage fire in her must be wrong, too.

She wasn't going to use the power in her for any good at all ... not for the helpless ones of Connacht.

She had not tried to turn the warriors' minds again—fate had them all in its jaws now.

Her eye fell upon Fraech on his horse. Despite the deaths, he was as straight in his saddle as the ash tree beside her, and did not look away from the slaughter. He was determined to bear witness to the fate of every warrior under his command, as a matter of honor.

Maeve realized a man like that would keep Finn safe, always.

She had not seen her daughter face-to-face since they argued, and would not hurt her further by seeking her out now. She could at least give Finn some peace amid all this death. She was only grateful the girl had not left with those taking Ailill's body back to his father.

Maeve closed her eyes on her knee.

At first she did not stir when the silence was broken by the progress of yet another warrior through the crowd. But then the whispers of the men grew into disbelieving murmurs. Maeve's eyes flew open.

The first thing she saw was a small white hand clutching at Fraech's leg, and a glimpse of tumbled red hair. *Finn.*

Maeve lifted her head a moment before Finn's cry brought her to her feet. Upright, Maeve spun about to follow Finn's gaze, looking out over the crowd of men.

Ferdia.

The Ulaid hero wove a careful path through the milling warriors, who took one glance at his face and peeled back. Each step of Ferdia's was deliberate, as if he focused hard on it. He had dug up clean tunic and trews, and his horn armor encased him from breast to groin, the cream and brown plates polished to a shine. He wore Fergus's helmet, the brow-guard casting his face into shadow.

The only glimpse of the man Maeve knew were his brown hands—one about his sword-hilt, one his shield grip—and his dark curls stirring in the wind. The Red Branch band was prominent about his arm, a braid of bronze that met in two spear-points.

Behind him a Laigin man drove Ailill's chariot, which bristled with Galeóin spears and the banners of Mumu and Connacht.

Maeve parted her cracked lips. What could *anyone* have said to move him now?

At that moment Finn took a few steps from Fraech's horse, her fingers uncurling toward Ferdia as he passed. He did not acknowledge her, plunging down the slope.

Finn's pinched face was drained of color as horror dawned in her eyes.

The sky spun above Cúchulainn where he lay on the damp grass. Stream-water dripped down his cheeks, cooling in the breeze. Across the water, the Connacht war-band sounded like a swarm of bees.

He knew he must get up.

But he had been fighting for nearly two days, and was afraid if the Source possessed him for too long it might consume him altogether. He did not know what would happen if he let the silver flame roar through when neither Ferdia nor Emer were there to bring him back. He supposed his spirit would keep expanding, rushing outward to join the Source all around him. That would mean his death, though, and he would not be here to defend the Ulaid from Maeve's army.

No earthly vessel could hold the blaze of Source continuously, which is why he quenched it after every fight. As a great wave peaks in majesty and then crashes, so he must let the Source lift him, surge through him, and then be cast adrift as it sank away.

In the aftermath, the weariness bore him down.

Cúchulainn put an arm across his eyes, pretending the sun glinted on dew and not spear-tips and swords. His array of cuts and bruises stung to varying degrees depending on their depth.

There were slices from swords and grazes from lucky spear-throws. A few sling-stones had cracked his jaw and shin. One giant had caught him across the shoulder with an oak club. Someone had even heated his sword before charging. The weal of that throbbed on the Hound's forearm. His ribs ached where someone had landed a kick during one of the war-feats.

The swarming of the Connacht bees grew louder.

Footsteps crunched on the other stream-bank. There was the creak of wheels and whinnies of horses. His throbbing pains pinned him down. He must get up. *A moment,* his body whispered. *One moment to sink into the earth, to rest.*

No. His mind was unyielding. That moment of nothing must be enough. For once there was no one to keep watch over him.

Taking a breath, Cúchulainn sat up, blinded by the flash of the spears, shields, and bronze rings that hung on the stakes all around. Though the tendons behind his knees screamed, he did not stumble, turning his back on his enemy. He would have to look into his face soon enough.

Cúchulainn reached for weapons without looking: an array of daggers shoved through the loops on his belt, like wolf teeth; short spears tossed into his back-carrier; a helmet pressed onto his itching scalp. Patting his scabbard, he tugged on his mail-shirt, easing the jerkin beneath. The glint of his Red Branch armband caught his eye, and Cúchulainn touched it.

Red Branch. Red Branch.

He had yelled that war-cry many times, but that had been with Ferdia at his side, and Naisi, Illan, and Fiacra. Then they had howled it out. Now, he did not have the heart to even whisper it.

Cúchulainn spun and strode across the grass. *Come,* he beckoned the Source. He could be weary no longer. *Fill me. Come.* He closed his eyes, summoning a silver flood. By the time he reached the stream-bank, his shoulders had expanded once more and his body hummed, taking the pain away.

His challenger had not charged over the river or thrown anything. He stood with a long shield raised up to his eyes, obscuring his face. A chariot sat behind him: so he would indulge in the war-feats.

An ache of loneliness rose from nowhere, surprising the Hound. He craved someone worthy, someone to join with him in that blaze of Source for an ecstatic moment before one of them died.

Cúchulainn stared and squinted, mind adrift on the Source. That helmet...did it bear wings along the side? A man too small for Fergus...someone had taken Fergus's helm.

The warrior planted his legs wide, and Cúchulainn swore he saw the gleam of horn. He blinked, going blank. *His armor...someone had donned Ferdia's armor.*

"Give me your name." Cúchulainn knew his voice was not as strong as it should be.

The challenger did not answer. Instead, he nudged up his helmet and stepped forward, lowering the shield. The sunlight at last fell upon his exposed face.

The Source drained from Cúchulainn in a rush, and he staggered at the force of an invisible blow.

CHAPTER 35

Ferdia dropped his shield and strode up to the stream, the bank churned into mud, the torn grass slick with blood.

There, separated by the shallow rill, he and Cúchulainn studied each other as Skatha had drilled into them long ago in Alba. Cúchulainn heard her hoarse voice. *See if the muscles of your enemies tremble from strain, if they are uneven, revealing old injuries and weaknesses. Look for them favoring certain limbs. Mark slumped shoulders, slackness, weariness, or defeat.*

Ah, Ferdia.

Cúchulainn marked his friend's sickly pallor. Ferdia had no injuries or weak muscles, but his fire and grace were dimmed, his shoulders drooping. It was when he met Ferdia's eyes, however, that Cúchulainn discovered the depths of that emptiness, for there was no end to it. "You do not look good," he blurted. If he did not know better, he would say Ferdia was rotted by ale.

Ferdia's smile was bleak. He tugged a flask from his belt and poured it out. "Water," he croaked. "Now, anyway."

Cúchulainn's throat ached. "You were the last man I expected to see at Connacht's heel." It came out wrathful.

Ferdia flinched. "Fergus knew Maeve would not kill us, that she sought revenge on Conor." He swayed on the spot. "They want to unseat the king, not harm the Ulaid."

"Is that what you tell yourself at night?"

Ferdia's eyes flashed and he drew himself up. "My honor makes me stand with those who oppose Conor." He swallowed, staring Cúchulainn down. "And I would not lose the only brothers I have left."

First blows had been exchanged.

Cúchulainn took in Ferdia's hollowed face and haunted eyes, and something rushed up and he uncurled his hand. "*My brother*, you do not belong with the she-wolf of Connacht, or whoever else she has bought. You belong on this side with me and the Ulaid. Lay down your weapons and cross the water."

Ferdia gasped and turned his jaw, gripping the hilt of a dagger in his belt. "I will not defend that murdering traitor again. The people of the Ulaid will not be harmed—"

"You cannot believe that! Maeve will want to rule us all!"

Something darker crossed Ferdia's face. "I once served a king I thought just—a man I bled for—and he took everything I loved. No ruler could be worse than that."

Cúchulainn's frustration boiled over. "You were once a man of sense."

"I was *bound* by sense." Ferdia plucked his dagger from its scabbard as he flung out his hand. "Always quiet, watching, waiting.

Always second to you. So why can't I be the unyielding one now, the pure one?"

"You were not second," Cúchulainn said quietly. "You watched, and guarded, only to lessen my burden. We lead the Red Branch together, for the Ulaid. I could not do it without you: we are as strong as each other."

"Strong?" Ferdia stalked along the river, his face a taut mask. He whipped out his sword, so he bore a blade in each hand. Cúchulainn knew then he was not in his right mind. "If I was *strong*, Hound of Cullen, I would have walked away from everyone with head high—Maeve, Cormac, Fergus..." He faltered. "I would not have rotted myself with drink and lain with women in a stupor—"

"Ferdia..."

"I know what they all think!" Ferdia's eyes were wild, the borrowed helmet trapping greasy tendrils of dark hair around his face. "It is what everyone has always thought—I can only ever be your shadow."

"*No!* You are the brother of my soul. You fight by my side. We are twins in all but blood."

Ferdia bared his teeth. "But I am the only failure, for here I am ruined and useless, and there you are, defending a kingdom."

Cúchulainn's breast burned. "I could do with your help."

"And be known as an oath-breaker forever?"

"For the sake of all the gods!" Cúchulainn stormed, pacing a furrow in the soft mud. He saw the ripple of his outburst pass over the men up the slope. "Put down your weapons, and join me."

"It will be said I come to your heel, and have no mind of my own. That I am a coward."

"Hang what anyone *thinks*, Ferdia!"

Ferdia's toes were almost in the rushing water, for he had been unconsciously edging ever closer to Cúchulainn. All of a sudden, though, he spread his arms in an embrace, both hands ending in blades. "If we are equal, Cú, then lay *your* weapons down and come to *me*. If you love me, as you say."

Cúchulainn's muscles tensed from feet to head. "If I do that, these warriors will march past me and lay waste to the Ulaid." He withdrew his own sword and slashed at the ferns as he swung past. His gaze darted over the grassed slope above the lake and he thought he glimpsed a banner of red hair. His hackles rose and he growled and swung back. "Many eyes are trained upon me. If I show any uncertainty, the warriors will rush me and the way will be open for Connacht to destroy our people."

Ferdia stabbed his sword into the mud, the hilt wavering. "Prove that you will humble yourself, put your love for me first for once. I asked you to do it the day we left Conor, but you would not be foresworn, not the great Champion of the Ulaid. So you can cling to your honor but I am not allowed mine?"

Cúchulainn's heart twisted. "Do not let the lies of others part us."

"Surrender, then."

Cúchulainn came to a halt, his breath gusting. "We can surrender to each other."

"So we will stand aside from this fight, and you will no longer defend this pass or that traitor who calls himself King?"

Cúchulainn hesitated.

"Ha!" Ferdia's grin was savage. He kicked someone's discarded helmet into the bracken. "After all you've won, Cú, you cannot have the last thing sung of you that you *failed* to beat Connacht, that you gave up and let enemy warriors trample Ulaid soil."

"Why do you do this?"

"Because this is what you ask of me—that my name be scorned as the weak one, the oath-breaker, the traitor." Ferdia's mouth crumpled, his cheeks haggard. "That I be the dark so you can be light!"

It was a gush of bile, and Cúchulainn's hand instinctively shielded his heart.

Ferdia realized what he'd said and staggered back. Then he laughed. "See? I am not noble like you. But I will remain strong until my last breath, at least." He brought his heels together, sword over his heart. "I will fight you, brother of my soul."

"No!" Cúchulainn cried, and threw his blade with such rage it carved a gulley in the turf. "*I will not.*"

"Then I will cross this river and jab this blade at your guts until you do." Ferdia tilted his helmet with his sword-hilt. "So...the war-feats. Chariots first, I thought."

Cúchulainn's relief poured over him. If they started with distance battle-feats, he might be able to disarm or disable Ferdia. He bowed a heavy head. "As you will it."

His friend saluted and made his way back to the chariot. Cúchulainn watched that long, lean lope, the familiar tense line of Ferdia's shoulders. Always guarded.

"Go with love," Cúchulainn whispered, but only the stream heard it.

※

The Connacht war-band watched Cúchulainn and Ferdia pull off their boots to go barefoot, then approach their chariots. The warriors realized the spectacle that would ensue and rushed closer, fighting for better vantage points.

At a signal from Ferdia, the Connacht battle drums began to beat, soon joined by the blare of bronze trumpets. The noise whipped up the audience and they broke into cheers. Leaping into Ailill's chariot, Ferdia urged his horses along the grassy slope, walking them in time with the sway of hundreds of fists, and bare knuckles striking hide.

Cúchulainn watched Ferdia lean his head back, breathing deeply as he braced himself with the reins. The Hound had no drummers and pipers. Instead, he began to strike his sword-hilt on one of the shields tied to the posts. Each blow resonated through his body, drawing the Source up until it surged in time with the swing of his arm.

Cúchulainn heard the jingle of Ferdia's horse-bits and his eyes flew open. Ferdia's stallions had broken into a trot, shaking their manes. The music took on a wilder edge.

Cúchulainn ran for his own horses, and a moment later he was driving his chariot around. Mirroring each other, he and Ferdia raced the teams, scything matching ruts in the turf on either side of the stream.

The rawhide platform beneath Cúchulainn's feet was suspended on a net of ropes from its arched sides, keeping him level. The pole of polished wood caught the sun, the rein-rings gleaming with coral, enamel, and bronze. The crowd of men screeched as one.

Cúchulainn's blood coursed with them, and Ferdia also loosed a great shout of release. For a moment they could forget they fought at all.

The chariot-feats were a song, with verses they both knew. First the turns grew tighter, wheels spraying up mud. Then they set the horses toward the slopes, at the last moment skewing the chariots around on one wheel-rim.

Cúchulainn crouched low, feet wedged against the wicker arches, coaxing his horses with a delicate touch despite the juddering of the chariot. The thrill of the near-miss made him laugh. He glanced at Ferdia, seeing the same glee on his friend's face.

They picked up speed toward the lake, flinging the chariots into another loop. Ferdia reached for the spears in their carriers. *Now it came.* Cúchulainn also plucked a spear, and as the chariots streamed back over flatter ground, they both dropped their reins and ran a herringbone with bare feet, up the poles between the racing horses.

The watching warriors screamed with delight.

The chariots yawed from side to side, bumping over stones. The horses reached out their necks, manes streaming. The drums and horns reached a climax along with the cheering of the crazed spectators. Cúchulainn and Ferdia leaped onto the yokes of the galloping horses, feet splayed, and with twin shouts went to fling their spears.

Aflame with Source, Cúchulainn sensed the unusual angle of Ferdia's throw before his friend even loosed the lance. Ferdia had tilted it to fly high—it was not aimed at his body.

Cúchulainn adjusted his own lance to the same arc, releasing it. As they dashed back along the pole, leaping into the driver's seat, the spears smacked into each other over the stream and fell in the water. Once more they hauled the horses about just before being dashed to pieces against the hill.

The audience all came to their feet, roaring and waving their arms.

When they slowed the panting horses, Ferdia's eyes were blazing once more, his chest heaving. He saluted to Cúchulainn with a shorter lance, and Cúchulainn grinned.

The chariot-feats went on until they were both pouring with sweat, the horses foam-flecked. Spears littered the riverbanks. Some throws would have seemed near-misses to the warriors, soaring close to Cúchulainn's head or Ferdia's shoulder.

Cúchulainn, however, knew that neither he nor Ferdia were aiming for each other's flesh. *It buys us time*, was his fervent thought. Time for Ferdia to collapse, for Maeve to surrender, for the Red Branch to shake off their illness and join him.

The sun sank lower. Cúchulainn's clothes were dark with sweat and his hair dripped.

At last they ran out of chariot-feats. He and Ferdia dismounted from the battered carts, the sides scratched, the ropes frayed. The audience grew hushed.

The two approached the opposite banks of the stream and squatted where it pooled in a hollow. They drank, spat out sweat, and drank again. The fighting must have drawn the Source into Ferdia, washing away some of the ale-rot. For Ferdia never took his eyes from Cúchulainn, and the silver blaze there pierced the Hound's heart.

Ferdia stood with a slight wince. "The thunder-feat," he croaked. "On horseback."

Cúchulainn nodded. Horse-feats. Good.

Ferdia got a fresh mount from Maeve's camp. Cúchulainn only had the Gray of Macha or the Black of Sainglu. He unharnessed them, pulling off the yoke-pads of fleece and rubbing down their sweaty backs. He gave them a long drink, smoothing the gray's neck. "A little rest, brother, is all I can give." He rode the gray into battle the night Naisi and his brothers died. He was the steadiest with Cúchulainn on his back.

The gray raised his dripping muzzle and leaned his forehead on Cúchulainn's chest.

Ferdia shouted at Maeve's warriors, and men scrambled to stake rows of spears and tie shields to them, making targets like those of Cúchulainn's. The Hound spent his time moving his own stakes on his side of the stream so they formed not an avenue, but a wall.

Astride their horses, they took turns galloping along the stream-banks, whirling leather slings of stones over their heads. The whirring slings gave off the sound of distant thunder, and each released stone hit their opponent's shield with a crack like lightning.

Rocks fell in a deadly hail. The exchange of missiles grew frantic as they sought to hit more shields, and faster.

Soon, Cúchulainn found he could not be skillful while keeping the Source at bay. He was helpless to stop the flood of silver overflowing, spreading out to the sky and spilling over the ground. Its power coursed down his arm, and at last he let go into that brilliant tide.

Instinctively, he flung a stone along the most direct path, forgetting to avoid Ferdia. The rock just missed Ferdia and shattered on the shield. The shards sprayed Ferdia's face and his horse shied, nearly throwing him off. The shouts of the other warriors faded away.

Ferdia put a hand to his cheek and then stared at his red fingers. *First blood.*

Cúchulainn gulped, forcing the light back down, soothing his stallion with one hand. Ferdia gazed at him, drops of scarlet speckling his cheeks and brow.

Cúchulainn had to look away.

The feats went from stones to spears—spears blocked by spinning shields, thrown with feet, flung in threes and fours. At last the overbreath feat was all they had left—the most difficult horse-feat of all. Cúchulainn called it in a heavy voice. A shadow crossed Ferdia's face, but he nodded.

They must stick a spear into the ground, then gallop past it while standing on the mount's bare back. At the precise moment, they had to somersault backward off the horse, and as they landed, pluck the spear out and fling it at their enemy.

There was no way to deliberately miss now.

Ferdia and Cúchulainn had drilled this feat into their reflexes, their nerves and muscles, over many years of training. To land in the right place, catch up the spear and move the body into the throw took perfect focus. If a man tried to disrupt the spear-flight, his vault would be off and he could fall and break a limb—or his neck.

Ferdia went first. He flipped off the horse, his lance spinning straight at Cúchulainn. Seeing that ripple in the Source, the Hound was already ducking, knocking it out of the air with his shield.

Ferdia leaped around and flung both arms up. His bellow of relief echoed off the hill, disappearing among the whistles and cheers of the men. This feat was always his greatest weakness; for some reason he often misjudged it.

"I see you stopped being so stubborn," Cúchulainn called, "and put your feet where I said to."

Ferdia wiped more trickles of blood from his brow. "Aye, in my own time." His smile, though, was bitter.

It was Cúchulainn's turn on the Gray of Macha. He focused the Source in two places: his legs, to balance him on the gray's back as the stallion galloped in; and the spear in the ground, which became a spire of light. The Source told him when to jump, sweeping him up as if in a wave. He spun, weightless, already picturing his throw so that the moment he landed his arm became a blur, sending the lance at Ferdia.

Ferdia struck it away with his shield rim. Only when Cúchulainn came back to himself did he see how Ferdia panted, as if forced to lunge far aside. Glowering, Ferdia went back to his horse for another run at the feat, and so it went in turns.

Soon the spears were flying back and forth with deadly force, the hooves of the horses thundering. Cúchulainn's arm ached from knocking them aside. Points splintered the wooden shields, and he kept throwing them away and grabbing another from the pile by his chariot. His back grew sore from the endless jarring as he landed on the ground.

He had always beaten Ferdia at this. Perhaps this was why Ferdia seemed unable to stop, bracing himself for each somersault with a feral snarl.

Shield arms faltered; tired limbs slowed.

Bone-weary, Cúchulainn misjudged one of Ferdia's throws and it soared under his shield-rim, catching his hip below his mail-shirt. It burned and he cried out, clapping a hand over the wound. Blood trickled from the rent in his tunic.

The cuts had dried on Ferdia's face, the red mask distorting his expression. For a savage moment Cúchulainn fancied he saw a smirk of satisfaction. *Blood for blood.*

Anger bloomed in Cúchulainn, as potent as the thrill had once been.

His next spear carved the air with a life of its own, striking Ferdia on the helmet and knocking him down. Enraged, Ferdia leaped up, and as the men on the ridge all screamed, he tossed his shield aside, ducked, and flung one of the discarded lances straight at Cúchulainn.

The Source flared.

Cúchulainn dodged the spear, tumbling over on the ground. By the time he bounced to his feet, another shaft was on its way back to Ferdia.

Spears hissed back and forth. Soon Cúchulainn and Ferdia were bruised on jaws and collarbones, thighs and backs, from the blows of the ashwood shafts. Such was their skill at acrobatics, that though their arms and legs were sliced by glancing points, neither sustained a serious wound. Blinded by wrath, Cúchulainn did not know if in some kernel of their souls they still held back, or if they were so well-matched they saved each other.

The first shadows engulfed them. The sun was lost. The far hill slopes were turning red.

Panting, they both stopped, peering at each other. The gloom darkened the blood on Ferdia's face. He saluted with his spear again, but there was strain in his arm now, and a sway in his body.

Cúchulainn clasped his lance across his chest. *My heart honors you.* He staggered to the Gray of Macha and caught his reins, limping toward his campfire. All the way, the Hound blocked out the wave of jubilation that greeted Ferdia's return to the war-band, the triumphant blare of horns.

Cúchulainn settled his horses with stiff, aching hands and a deliberately blank mind. Stretching his back, he poked up the coals in his fire so there was a glow of something alive beside him.

Then he gathered the folds of his cloak about him and sank down. He knew he should bathe his wounds and bind them with Emer's beeswax salve. *In a moment...* The silver wave of Source receded, leaving him limp on the sands of Thisworld. *One moment of rest and I will do it...*

One—

⁂

The war-camp among the hills plunged into dusk.

Ferdia was carried to Ailill's great tent, tossing in delirium, and laid upon soft furs. Maeve leaned over him while the druids untied his horn armor, a lamp swinging over his head in a draft of evening wind.

Ferdia muttered under his breath, his lashes dark smears across pale cheeks. Grazes webbed his hollowed face, larger spearcuts slicing his arms and legs. His tunic and trews were so torn they almost fell off him. As the druids bathed him with sponges, Levarcham mashed knit-bone leaves in a mortar nearby.

Her eyes were sad as she sat at Ferdia's side and began to smear the green paste over his wounds.

Maeve gently wiped the dirt and blood from Ferdia's brow, then stood at his head and held his temples in her palms. "You fight like the Tuatha dé Danann themselves," she whispered to him. "You are a god, Daman's son, and your father looks upon you this night with pride."

Ferdia's eyes flickered open.

"You are fighting for us all," Maeve added. "Protecting so many people."

Ferdia's laugh startled her. His eyes rolled, the pupils glassy in the pool of lamplight, as if he watched something on the roof of the tent. "Did you see how high I jumped?" he slurred.

Maeve leaned down, her heart thudding. Why would he speak like that to her?

"My vault was higher than yours." Ferdia's smile was delirious. He cocked his head, listening to something she could not hear. "Balls! Skatha said higher was better than faster. Remember how you kept rolling when you landed?" A hoarse laugh. "Yes, you did, you bastard. Come, let's do it again before supper. I'll show you. Come..." His fingers uncurled to empty air.

Levarcham was watching him, her hands leaf-stained. The western sky sent a shaft of rose through the tent flap, illuminating a yearning in her grave face that threaded Ferdia's voice. A flicker of the past, when much was whole that now was in ruin.

Maeve backed away.

"We can give him syrup to make him sleep," one of the druids said.

Maeve touched Ferdia's shoulder as she passed. "No. Leave him with Cúchulainn."

She turned to go and the pain in her belly came out of nowhere, a spear thrust deep. Maeve's breath escaped in a hiss, and with smarting eyes she hobbled out of the tent, away from all those druid eyes.

"Heal them!" Conor strode around the temple mound at Emain Macha, stabbing a finger at the druids. "Do it, or die!"

Dark had fallen, and the world was wreathed in flame as it had been the night of the burning of the Red Branch hall. Great bonfires roared all over the expanse of grass around the temple, the wood breaking with loud cracks like thunder, the streaming flames charring the turf.

All the sick Red Branch and Alban warriors were piled between the pyres now, writhing, retching, as their naked bodies poured with sweat.

Dancing druids whirled among them to drive out the sickness, beseeching the goddess Macha to lift her curse. They were mostly the young ones, the novices, for their elders had been at the feast when the sickness spread.

Prowling, Conor watched a druid collapse in the dance, exhausted. Conor hauled him up by his robe. "Break this curse now, or I will kill you myself!" He needed these fighters alive, strong enough to send to the border lords who were now under attack.

Strong enough to defend Emain Macha.

The druid's head fell back, eyes glazed in trance. Conor cursed and let him fall. The shrieks of the warriors clawed at Conor's ears, and he spun away and hastened to the temple steps, where novices were sacrificing any animal Conor could get his hands on. A river of blood spilled down the slope, the carcasses of sheep, goats, and bulls thrown in the ditch.

"More," Conor growled. *"More!"* So Macha wanted to punish him, did she? She cursed him, drew this attack upon him from the west. Well, she was a goddess of the battlefield. She must desire blood—he would give her blood! He would offer her anything to destroy this war-band that tried to invade the hallowed land of the Ulaid.

He would damn well *buy* her favor. No king could abase themselves as he did, give as much as he did, and that *must* make even a goddess relent.

The young priests looked at their king in terror, their faces blood-spattered.

Conor staggered to the makeshift pens where sheep milled, kicking at the palings. His heart sank as his eye fell on the sheen of horsehide and a tossing mane. He hardened it, gritting his teeth, grabbed the halter of one of his chariot mounts, Lúath, and hauled the horse to the temple steps.

Maddened by the smell of gore, Lúath tried to tear himself away, but he'd been hobbled. Conor threw back his head, howling his despair to the dark sky. *Macha!* Then he struck out, slicing the vein in the horse's neck with his dagger. Blood sprayed across his face. Panting, Conor let the beast crumple to the stained earth at his feet.

A chittering interrupted Conor's rage. The ape was tied to a post by its chain, writhing and trying to break free.

"Is it my pride you want, then?" Conor cried to Macha. He had shredded his once-fine tunics, that silk from the East, and burned his furs. He had poured out his wine, sacrificed all the riches he had boasted from the trade ships of the Middle Sea. Now he grasped the monkey around its neck and held it in the doorway to the great temple. The creature squirmed, clawing at him. *"What else can I give?"* Conor screamed to the faceless altar, and stuck the monkey with the knife before tossing its limp body down.

Outside the temple, he stood swaying.

The fires lit the underbellies of the sickly clouds. The druids capered like madmen, black against the flames while the sick lifted their hands, begging for water. No water, Conor had ordered. Only flame and sweat would purge them.

Someone spoke, and Conor spun around. A youth stood below the temple, his eyes rolling toward the dying men. "M-My lord."

Conor squinted, cobbling his scattered thoughts together as the boy stammered.

"...so Ronan and I heard rumors from the herders... and we went to see for ourselves."

Conor blinked.

"A war-band is approaching from the south. And..." The youth gulped. "Cúchulainn is there—holding the ford by himself!"

Conor stumbled down the steps, groping for the boy. He shrank away, but Conor caught him by both arms, crushing him. "A woman," he rasped. "Is she there... armored in fury... flame-eyed, red hair? Did you see her with your own sight?"

The scout swallowed. "Aye, I saw that woman, yelling at her men to fight."

At last.

She was here. All the churning and pain inside Conor came together in one flare that went up his spine to his crown. He snapped upright, thrusting the boy from him and hurrying down the path away from the temple. It led through meadows and houses up to his fort on the next hill.

Halfway there he pulled up. The crafter-men and the Ulaid guards from the ramparts were gathered across the track. Some of the new warriors had joined them, those youths who'd come from the western hills and northeastern farms, barely knowing one end of a sword from another, but able to clutch a spear. They had not been as ill as the Red Branch fighters, and many had now recovered.

Conor flung out a hand. "The Hound holds a ford on his own against the hordes of Connacht. You must defend our land, drive back the she-wolf and her pack." The men looked slack-jawed from him to the flaming hilltop, the whirling druids. "Do your duty to the Ulaid or we will all die!" Conor yelled.

At first no one moved. Then Conor realized the crafters and gate-guards were backing away, leaving the young warriors wavering. And so it burst upon Conor.

He had to lead them. He would not cower here, waiting for *her* to come. He would be a war-leader at last, with glory on his brow and fire in his veins, his sword held high. Men would cheer for him, die for him as they did Cúchulainn...as they once did Fergus mac Roy.

Conor mac Nessa would be the god who stood against Maeve—the bards would sing *that* song and no other once he had triumphed.

Nothing of Deirdre. Nothing of anyone but him and his brave heart.

"I order you to follow your king! Raid the walls of my hall and take up the shields and swords of all the heroes who came before you—*you are Red Branch now.* When you triumph, the arms will be yours, along with the riches of Connacht. Defend us now!"

The eyes of the youths lit up, for they would never otherwise have the chance to bear such noble weapons, let alone win them. But older, battle-scarred men murmured and shook their heads, disappearing into the darkness.

Conor growled, dragging out his sword and thrusting it into the sky. "All who are worthy, go now and arm yourselves. We will ride out to glory as the dawn lights our way. To the fire of Lugh!"

They cheered, these wild-eyed boys, and streamed back to the fort.

Giddy, Conor turned, his smile dying. At the temple the flames lit up splayed bodies and groaning men. The goddess Macha had not stopped the Connacht bitch from coming for him. She was not going to protect the Ulaid.

Macha had turned her back on him. It was over.

Conor staggered and broke into a run, throwing himself back

up the bloody steps to the temple. There, he howled and flung his dagger. It arced, catching the light of the flames, and thudded into the ground before the doorway. He wove his way to the young druids who were still drumming with empty eyes. "Burn the temple," he ordered. "If She will not champion us, then we will not worship Her."

The drumming tailed away, the dancers collapsing on the ground among the sick men. One priest spoke, his face coated with soot. "It is...sacrilege," he rasped.

Conor swayed. "We cleansed this place of living women, now we must do the same for dead maidens and heartless goddesses! I will be cleansed of Her, and then I will kill Her she-wolf with my own hands."

The panting novices crowded together, murmuring that they must rouse the chief druid and their elders, that the king was mad. Growling, Conor lunged at the nearest one with his sword. They cried out and broke ranks, pulling their brothers away from the writhing warriors on the ground and fleeing into the dark.

Head back, Conor bellowed to the sky. Fire would heed his call.

He plucked up scattered pieces of wood by the bonfires, sticking the torches into the flames until they were alight. Smiling, he stalked around the temple, every few steps touching them to the thatch. By the time he reached the door again, the roof was flaming. Dodging the cinders, Conor staggered inside and threw the torches at the wooden idol of Macha. "I now defeat you. *Burn!*"

He hurried back outside and stood on the grass, wheezing.

The flames ate up the thatch and wood until the great temple of Macha bore a crown of fire that streamed into the sky, making the clouds glow a lurid red. At last the roof caved in with a whoosh of sparks, and Conor laughed, tasting the ash on his lips, his face scorched. The conflagration would be seen far across the hills, and everyone would know there was a new power at Emain Macha, the power of man and god.

The power of the king.

CHAPTER 36

A scout was waiting for Maeve when she left Ferdia in the healing tent.

In the shadows of the camp she could not see him clearly. Holding her side, she dimly recognized the splotches of mud up his legs and spatters on his cheeks. He had ridden far, through bog and swamplands.

Dread halted her, her hand falling loose.

Tucking his leather helmet under his arm, the scout went down on one knee before her. "The battle still rages at the Gates of Macha." He bowed his head. "But I have been sent to tell you that Lord Garvan has been speared in the attack." He wet his lips. "He is slain."

Maeve's body instinctively turned from that truth, one hand clutching air as if it might hold her up.

What are you getting me into, spitfire?

In the dark under the trees, Garvan's pale face hovered—she could almost touch his cheek. A shudder began at Maeve's feet and ran up her back. Garvan, heart-brother. It was not the taste of his lips that came to her, but the quirk of his smile. *Damn you, Maeve.*

Pain ripped through her belly, and then again. The patchwork of red sky, glowing fires, and dark shadows began to spin. When Maeve's knees sagged, Levarcham's arms came around her, their fingers knotted together.

"Come and sit," the druid murmured.

Bending over, Maeve groaned. The scout was standing back now, his face a pale blotch in the gloom. Other passing warriors had also stopped to stare at her. Hard eyes, scorning her ... always scorning her.

"Get me away from here," she forced through her teeth. "I cannot sicken before them."

Levarcham did not argue, holding Maeve around the waist and helping her stumble along into the trees at the edge of camp. When they were out of earshot, the druid said, "If you do not lie down and let me help you, the babe is certainly lost."

Lost. All lost. *Garvan*. No tears came, just the pain that doubled her up, though not all of it was her belly.

"How long has it been hurting?" Levarcham asked.

Maeve blinked. She had not been able to separate this agony from all the others, her heart swamped by the death around her. "A day...two."

Levarcham hissed under her breath, shaking her head.

"Not here," Maeve gasped, her eyes watering. "Away from iron...and their voices. The woods. Quiet. And...water. Let me be by water."

Levarcham peered at her face and nodded. "Let me get my bag and some furs, then."

By the time she returned, the pains had subsided enough to allow Maeve to walk.

Every step labored, they left the camp on a track that wound out of the trees and skirted the bare slopes of the hill. Here, at last a bronze moon soared free of the horizon, and by its light they could just follow a path sheep had cut through the heather. Levarcham limped along, a bundle strapped to her back, her arms about Maeve.

"It is far enough," Levarcham urged.

Maeve shook her head. "Farther." She wanted to be by water that flowed into Connacht.

Around the shoulder of the slope, she knew the streams must drain west. Some water might seep away from these eastern hills, flowing through bog and lake and the broken rills that meandered over her kingdom's green plains. Eventually, some drops might empty into the River Sinand...Connacht's river. West, Sinand flowed, out into the sea, and there some trace of her might be carried by the waves to the Stone Islands. It was all that made sense to her at this moment.

Time slipped away, and every now and then a pain went through her.

They were the sword thrusts that her men had suffered.

The spear that broke Garvan's back.

※

At first Ruán had been able to crawl to the water, then drag himself back to the little copse of trees to cover his body with fallen leaves at night.

The snapped bone had broken the skin of his thigh, though, and when his hands felt the wound, it was now growing hot. The pain began to gnaw, and he was no longer able to move that far. An arm of the river had caught in a bend, scattering itself into weedy puddles. He could only lie there among them in the mud, scooping water into his mouth and resting in between.

It was always dark now, an endless night.

Why will you not come to me? he called to the blackness, thick as pitch. The sídhe had saved him before—the Source connected them to everything. *Help me.* That plea was hard for his pride, even now.

The sun rose again and Ruán stretched his chin to the warmth. *You walk your own path,* they told him, many times. And he had stumbled, and fallen, and so they would not come. Perhaps they did not hear him any longer ... or care.

He lifted his face to the sun, grasping at a spark of old humor to keep himself alert. *Well, this is not your finest moment. I cannot say I blame them.*

Then a wave of loneliness swept over him, and his bleak smile died. It was not a good end. He wanted to remember the moonglow shining from the eyes of the sídhe, because it was the most beautiful thing he had ever seen. But he could not summon even that.

Ruán slipped into troubled dreams.

Maeve knelt behind him and curled her belly about his back. The great flame in her warmed his cold skin. She wrapped him in heat, her hands across his heart.

Farewell, *she breathed in his ear.*

He turned his chin to her, stifling a shiver. Why farewell?

She pressed her lips upon his, smoothed his brows with a finger. I do not know.

Ruán jerked awake. His hair was wet, his cheek pressed into cold mud. He rolled on his back, gripping his leg. The pain had become fire and ice at the same time.

At that moment he felt the throb from far away. It drove all the pain aside. His head lifted as he strained toward it. The pang came again, from *outside of him.*

This time his spirit-self registered an even blacker agony than the one consuming his body.

Maeve . . . she was in danger.

Ruán's head fell back in the reeds. In a burst of frustration, he struck the ground, and water splashed over his face. The stab of pain cleared his mind. It was in Maeve's power to save the lives of many, the sídhe said.

It was in his power to reach her.

Damn it, Ruán. He had seen for himself how fear dimmed people's soul-lights. He had let it conquer him so far . . . but he would not let it defeat him now. Maeve's life was at stake. And those of others.

Ruán breathed deeply, filling his lungs. *Either I perish here like a useless fool, or I gather what strength I have left and find a way to send it to her.*

That was a better way to die.

He nodded, and carefully skewed his body with his arms, dragging his wounded leg behind him. He bit his lip until he tasted blood, focusing on hauling himself through the mire to the main channel of the river. The sídhe maiden said he would be on his own, that he would have to find courage.

She said he had the power.

He did. He knew he did. How could he forget it? His body might be trapped beside this river, but the spark of his soul was not.

Another creature had come into his mind, one that danced through water as freely as he danced through the bright motes of Source. And Erin was threaded with streams and soaked by rain, so the water-drops themselves must also be joined into one vast web. His will could surely shape the silver motes of Source, spinning a pattern of his own making—a vessel for his soul.

Maeve.

At last he allowed his heart free to reach for her. *I want only you. I want to claim you for my own. I want to give you me.*

He let his breast fill with the memory of her face in the sídhe vision, the sound of the smile in her voice, her hands upon him, gentle and absorbed. He let his loins burn again with the fire of their joining.

And so Ruán's blindness at last lifted, as his spirit-sight flooded back. Looking down, he saw that the most intense flame around him was spilling from his own self.

He must expend all of it now, for her.

Dragging on his belly, Ruán forgot all his pain as he plunged his hands into the fast-flowing water in the shallows. There, he began to call to the Source, singing to it under his breath. Perhaps he only summoned one small flare in the great swirl that was Erin's life, but it was enough.

Gradually, the Otherworldly light around him and the water droplets of Thisworld began winding together, both of them streams of silver glimmers. Between Ruán's hands, woven by Ruán's thoughts, the creature took shape that would hold the spark of his soul.

Long and sleek, its body curling along its spine. Snub head diving, tail rippling.

An otter, bright as moonlight.

Maeve collapsed on the banks of a slow-moving stream that formed pools glowing under the moon.

It reminded her of twilight on a lake.

A copse of hazels drooped over the water, their dying leaves rustling in a cold breeze. Levarcham built a tiny fire, helped Maeve take off armor and trews and wrapped her in furs. Then she felt Maeve's belly over with a gentle touch, bending to place her ear on it and finally sitting with hands spread.

Maeve watched Levarcham's eyes moving behind her eyelids. "Is it ... gone ...?"

The druid lifted her hands, pulling down Maeve's tunic. "No. There is only a little blood yet." She drew the furs about Maeve's bare legs.

Maeve curled on her side, shivering. She stared at the stream ripples breaking up the moon's reflection. "What can you do?"

Levarcham sat back on her heels and sighed. "With a draft of herbs, it depends. Once the pains have been going that long, there is little to be done to calm the womb."

Maeve's lips parted. "I do not mean to hold the child in. I mean ... make me well." *Well enough to fight to the end.* That was all that remained: to raise a shield for those who were still left to her.

Levarcham hesitated. "I told you what I saw of the child—"

"And it is going to die anyway!" Another pain ripped through Maeve, and she cried out. "They are all dying. We are *all lost.*" A second stab drove her awareness from her body. Everything reeled about her: trees, moonlight, broken water. "H-He is lost. *Lost.*" Garvan.

And Ruán ... her heart.

As the waves of agony broke over Maeve, so the stars kept wheeling above. They swung past her, turning time, even though she soon lost their rhythm as the night wore on.

Her skin ran with sweat, but at her core she was ice and her teeth chattered. Levarcham brewed something from her pouch of herbs and forced it down her. Maeve was barely aware of the bitterness on her tongue, the druid's callused hand on her brow.

And Levarcham singing ... not Ruán's watery streams of sound. These were druid chants, low and earthy, calling the Mother to hold her.

Maeve's smile cracked. The Mother saw no kinship in her, nothing to love.

The agony tore her in two—a punishment she deserved. She had not crooned to the babe as she longed to, stroking the sweet bud of it. *Forgive me, I beg you.*

The child was wrapped in her pain over Ruán. If she had given in to that love, held it close, gazed at her belly with soft eyes... then sorrow for Ruán would have risen up and weakened her beyond all repair. She would have failed·everyone.

She *had* failed everyone.

On her side, Maeve curled her knees to her chest. Her arm fell out as if to touch the stream-water. The moonlight blurred on the surface and grew brighter. So beautiful. She wanted to sink into it and never surface. Be filled with sídhe light, blessed by it ...

Not after all I have done.

Maeve whimpered. She tried to turn from that glory but found she could not move, captured by the silver on the water. The Great Mother was the vessel for the Source, Her face this moon that beckoned the tides of seeds, sap, blood, and oceans. Her eyes beheld all creatures of Thisworld with compassion, offering shelter and belonging.

Ruán had told Maeve this.

Adrift on pain, her mind kept spinning. No, she could not be drawn into the Mother's arms. *I abandoned them.* The cramps in her belly spread to her breast. *Finn and—* She cut off that thought. *I abandoned them.*

As if answering her, the moonlight suddenly ignited into a brilliance that was blinding, penetrating Maeve's half-closed eyelids. She gasped, shielding her face. But nevertheless the radiance overflowed, reaching for her.

She dropped her hand.

And so at last she saw in it the glints of Ruán's eyes, the warmth of his smile. *Ceara*, he breathed. *Come to me.*

Maeve choked back an exclamation, as something stirred for the first time in her womb. A flutter. She dug her hands into the mud, forcing herself onto hands and knees and crawling to the banks of the stream. The furs fell from her and she was bare-limbed, her damp shift clinging to her thighs.

Behind her, Levarcham's singing faltered, then resumed with greater force.

Maeve sprawled on the pebbles and thrust her hands into the stream, yearning for Ruán to bear her away into that light she had always sought. She lost the ache in her legs and the hurt in her body. Looking down, she saw ripples now in the brightness of the water, swirls and shining eddies, as if the droplets were being drawn to form a shape.

A creature of light.

Sleek and sinuous, he glided up to her, curling his long body in a spiral. *Ruán.*

The stones beneath Maeve disappeared, along with the murmurs of the trees, the icy water, and the cold wind. Only the flame of Ruán's anam enveloped her. And then she felt she was somehow floating, the otter weaving about her. Where Ruán paused, curling around her belly, heat pooled there. She sensed his wonder, and a flicker of a different light deep inside.

Surrender the poison, ceara, and cradle what fills you now.

He said it to her the night she first lay with him in love—when she wept at an old black memory. The denial was swift. *No! Too much.* More memory would take her to even darker places.

Cold stone. Mossy walls. A cave from long ago.

When you hold this trapped in you, you cannot be anything else. Swim with me.

Sleek and bright, the otter looped circles about Maeve's wrists and shoulders, pulling her farther into the stream. *Come, ceara.* With a tail-flick he swam downward, his glow disappearing fast.

Do not leave me! Without hesitating, Maeve slipped from the last vestiges of her body, abandoning it to dive after him. *Love... my love.* As a tiny spark of awareness, she plunged deep into the water.

Down there, the light began to fade. Maeve hesitated.

Turning, Ruán streaked back up to her, coiling about her once more, making the water swirl until she could see nothing. *I said come with me.* With one undulation he plunged again.

Leaving her behind.

Wait! Maeve cried. She grasped for Ruán, but he was nothing but a diminishing flame in the great darkness below. Spinning wildly, she sank, and the impenetrable black claimed her, and it was too late to flee the past now.

She was seventeen.

Her moan of pain echoed off the rock walls, the final one after so many agonized hours.

The narrow cave pressed in on the girl-Maeve, the weight of stone almost crushing her. Her throat ached from holding back the laboring screams. No one must hear.

Her old servant Brenna huddled between her legs, bony arms sticking out of ragged clothes. Tears ran from her eyes as she eased the child onto the blanket of fleece. Panting, Maeve hauled herself up on her elbows. "Light," she croaked.

Brenna reached for the lamp with trembling hands, pulling it nearer. "A boy," the old woman whispered. She rubbed him all over to make him breathe, wrapping him in an old tunic and resting him on Maeve's belly. The rough handling made the little wet thing at last stir, though his cry was no more than a mew. Maeve drew him close, peeling back the bloody linen.

The cave was a hidden hole beneath a hillside near Cruachan. It was sacred to the sídhe, a doorway to the Otherworld, so she knew no one would come here. She had given birth among people's offerings of dried flowers, rings and pins, and bones from sacrifices.

The power of the sídhe was supposed to help them.

"It was too soon." Maeve turned her face to the rock. Moisture glinted on the thick moss. The cave wept. "It was the ride, so far ... too fast."

Brenna's back was a hump of sorrow. She groped for Maeve's hand. In the dim lamplight she looked like the gnarled hawthorns on the surface above, her faded hair tangled with leaf litter. Seventeen years before, she had brought Maeve into the world like this, on the night Maeve's mother died.

Brenna was old now, though, her mind shrinking along with her wizened body. She knew nothing of kings, or why Maeve would be scared enough to gallop a horse across Erin with a belly so ripe.

Maeve looked down at the child. He stretched one hand and it touched her nose, then curled up. She clutched him to her. *They can't take you from me now.* She gave herself those moments while she waited for the birth-cradle to be expelled, her cheek on the child's wet head, her eyes closed. His breaths were tiny flutters, three to every one of hers, both of them still woven together.

Shuffling, Brenna massaged Maeve's belly, singing under her breath. Maeve bit her lip as she felt the second rush, and clambered to her knees, holding the baby with one hand. When the bloody cradle came, Brenna cut the cord and wrapped it in cloth. Normally it would be buried, but Maeve was already within the earth.

She bid Brenna curl up with the lamp, Maeve's son nestled in her lap. And willing herself past the pain, Maeve crept deeper into the cave and left it as an offering to the goddesses. Reaching for a flask of water, she then cleaned herself up, binding two breech-clouts on, one over the other. Wincing, she awkwardly drew on trews and tunic.

Brenna's eyes were frightened. "You cannot go so soon."

"I have to." Maeve stuck a brooch through her cloak with shaking fingers. "They will come looking for me. Father's trackers are the best in Erin." She crawled to her pack. "Here are skins of goat-milk. And food for you. I brought as many furs as I could, and tallow—enough for a few nights." During the day, light crept into the cleft from above. Maeve gripped the thin bones at Brenna's shoulder. "I know I ask much of you, but it is the only way."

Brenna's smile was tremulous, her voice cracked with age. "You are my own child. My heart."

Maeve cradled Brenna's cheek, kissed the baby's head, and trying to see through tears, hauled herself back up the cave and into the tangle of thorns that covered the entrance. She caught the reins of her pony and gritted her teeth as she lowered her raw loins onto the saddle and turned the horse into a walk toward Cruachan.

Giving herself up now was the only way to keep her father's wolves from sniffing along the trail that led to her baby son.

When Maeve at last reached the king's hall, she saw that her new husband, the Mumu prince Diarmait, had already arrived from his southern mountains. Diarmait's banner flew from the gatepost along with the eagle standards of her father. She gingerly dismounted as the guards ran forward.

She was dragged before father and husband, biting the inside of her lip to drive away the cramps still gripping her. Eochaid leaped from his great chair and charged toward her.

Maeve swallowed, raising her chin.

"Where have you been?" Eochaid stormed, his battered warrior's face as red as his hair. "What dishonor do you do our kinsman, stealing away from him in the night?"

Would he whip a woman in her state? Maeve did not know. She must chance it, because she would not answer his first question.

Diarmait's gaze went to her slack belly, his eyes sharp beneath a furrowed brow. "Where is my child?" He was a burly man whose great muscles were beginning to run to fat, which had stretched his skin smooth. A thatch of yellow hair topped a florid face.

Maeve's lip curled. "It is dead. The ride killed it."

Eochaid growled. Diarmait's expression did not change, which was worse. He merely stared at her with burning eyes.

"Willful, faithless cub!" Her father's massive hand caught her a stinging blow. "*You* killed it by fleeing your lawful husband. What madwoman rides a horse for days with such a belly?" Looming over her, he shook her by the arms.

Maeve squinted through the pain, her ears ringing. She would get beaten anyway, so she may as well speak truth. "If it had lived," she hissed under her breath, "it would have been *his*. And you would barter me to someone else, and I would lose it anyway!"

As I did her. I lost her.

Eochaid's eyes flared, flickering toward the Mumu prince to see if he'd heard. Another cramp came, and a trickle of blood between Maeve's thighs. She ground her knees together, and when her father cursed and hit her again, she welcomed it, for it snapped her out of that creeping faint.

Eochaid stalked back to his chair and gripped it, his knuckles white. Maeve licked the cut on her lip, grateful to have a different pain to focus on.

"What did you do with it?" Diarmait demanded.

Maeve turned her sore cheek toward him. "I burned it. There was not much to it." Though he rutted like a beast, he was repulsed by her swelling body, and had not seen her naked for some time. He would not realize how far along she was.

"She is young." Eochaid's brows lowered, spiky and red over his blue eyes. "There will be more sons."

Diarmait glowered, heaving himself to his feet. He went to

lumber out of the hall, but stopped by Maeve and grasped her bruised chin. His eyes narrowed. "You gave me a filly that had not been broken, Eochaid," he grunted. "I can't have her running every time she balks, or our oath will be untied. See that she is broken now, before you give her back."

Eochaid watched him go, frowning. The Connacht king's hand was still flexing, as if he longed to take his fury out on Maeve properly. But he only growled to her, "The women will put you to bed to be healed by the druids. You must be nursed back to strength."

Strong enough to bear more sons to Diarmait of Mumu, he meant. Maeve bent her head as her father passed, as if she was giving in. When he'd gone, she lifted it again, holding her cloak over her aching belly. *They won't get more from me,* she vowed, her eyes on the fire. *My son and I will go somewhere no one can find us.*

For days the wrath of her father and Diarmait confined Maeve to bed. She was held there by chanting druids and frightened maids, and also the guards who lounged outside the women's lodge. When she hobbled to the waste pit, they followed. When she went to the temple of Bríd to burn an offering, they followed. She didn't know where her horse was.

Her breasts ached and leaked, and she shoved a fist in her mouth at night so the maids sleeping around her bed would not hear her weep. Fear for the child and for Brenna made her retch, until she was dosed with more bitter brews.

One thing she knew about warriors was that eventually they would feast, and then they would drink. Maeve played contrite, crying on Diarmait's shoulder and begging him to forgive her moment of madness. She even knelt to kiss her father's hand, keeping her desperation hidden behind bright, hard eyes.

Soon they stopped watching her, and on the night before riding home to Mumu, Eochaid held a feast. Maeve bribed the maids with Diarmait's jewels, and dressed in her old riding gear, slipped from the king's hall and fled along dark paths from Cruachan on foot.

The cave called her.

Clouds darkened the night sky...she could barely see anything. A hush fell over the Connacht hills as she drew near. The hawthorns were silent, no wind in their leaves.

⛤

No.

Dread surfaced from the depths that enveloped the adult Maeve as, deep in Ulaid territory, she was pulled down into the river of spirit, of memory, by Ruán's anam. She couldn't see his silver flame anymore. The blackness, the emptiness, was seeping into her. *I won't go there.*

A throb of warmth came that somehow held Ruán's essence. *Let it drown you, or you will die.*

That did not make any sense.

The blackness of that long-ago night in the cave was filling her nose, her mouth...pouring in to stop her heart. And then the agony hit her, and her present-day body arched on the pebbles by an Ulaid stream.

⛤

The cave near Cruachan was a gash in the earth, the trees and hill faintly picked out by the moon, which had risen behind the clouds. There was no glimpse of a lamp flame within.

Maeve trapped her breath in her throat and slithered down the tunnel to where the cave flattened out. A cold reached up that came from the very bowels of the earth.

"Mistress...?" Brenna whimpered.

"I am here." Maeve groped along the wall toward this poor woman who had sat in the darkness and cold alone, for her. Brenna was too weak to shiver as Maeve hugged her, the pulse in her wrist faint.

Maeve was already reaching for the child when Brenna's whisper halted her. "Forgive me. The milk...gone. So...so cold..."

The blackness had only been held at bay by Maeve's frantic heartbeat, the force of her desperation that everything would be well because she willed it so. Now it rushed upon her, overwhelmed her.

The babe's skin was icy, the dome of his head fitting her palms. Though her hand braced his back, as she drew him close his limbs fell from the swaddling. His neck sagged over her wrist.

All strength bled from her and she sank down in the dark.

By the Ulaid stream, Maeve's heart was dying now.

I did it. I killed him. The poison of the past was drowning her.

Ruán's voice wove through her awareness. *Feel it all, a stór, or you cannot find what you are beyond.*

I killed him. It bore her down, and Maeve lost the last sense of Ruán's brightness. The agony sucked her under, took all life... breath... light.

She shuddered back into her body. She was sprawled on the bank of the stream on hands and knees, slipping on fallen leaves. Water streamed from her hair, the tendrils swirling in the mud. Her mouth opened and a cry she had never voiced came from the depths of her, and was at last emptied into the earth, the Mother.

The ancient black waters gushed from Maeve—from her eyes, mouth, and nose. Everything she had buried in that cave she retched from her throat and belly. She wept into the earth beneath her then, caught in a paroxysm she could not escape.

Levarcham scrabbled over to Maeve, her hands hovering, unsure.

Blindly, Maeve groped for her, and Levarcham caught her fist and drew Maeve to her breast. The druid cradled her as the agony drew Maeve into a ball, her face buried in Levarcham's cloak.

Maeve bore that pain like a terrible birthing, and it took with it the last hours of the night.

Cúchulainn woke in the dark. With no one to tend it, the fire was nearly out and the cold wind numbed his scabbed cheeks and swollen hands.

He rolled on his back, pain shooting through every muscle. The wound on his hip gnawed inward. The cuts all over him stung, like nips of sharp teeth. Beneath that, he was so exhausted he was not sure he could move again.

Worst of all were the stabs in his heart, *jabbing* like Ferdia's dagger. There was no way to raise a shield to that. He sighed, putting a hand over his breastbone and looking up at the stars. Were they the soul-fires of the gods, as people said? One of them was very bright, the morning star that seemed to follow him as he wandered Erin.

Cúchulainn dared to gaze at it. He thought of the rumor, so precious he had never dared admit it to his own heart. His mother Dectire, Conor's sister, was not wed when she became pregnant with him. Her mind had gone, and she never told anyone who his real father was. The druids knew, though.

They said it was Lugh, the many-skilled—the bright god of light and sun, wisdom and valor.

Utterly alone, at that moment a glimmer of the boy emerged in Cúchulainn. He realized his face was wet. *Father.* The plea that came could never be formed into words, it was only a swelling of feeling. *Help me.* There was no one to bathe his wounds or sing healing songs over him. No one to feed him something warm, to bring strength back into spent limbs.

His hand remained over his heart, as if he could pretend it was Emer's. He had sent her away, though, told her to lead their people to safety. There was no one.

Cúchulainn at last fell into a desolate sleep.

The night passed strangely, as he swung between dreams and moments where he nearly surfaced. He was sometimes conscious of the hollow of cold grass beneath him, or the stars above, but he never woke properly. Nevertheless, he slowly became aware of a warmth in his limbs. The darkness was pushed back, the starlight kindling into gold.

Sun-gold.

He was aware of someone standing watch nearby, like a lone tree guarding the bank. Afraid, he tried to drag himself awake, but only sank further into sleep until he knew nothing more.

When Cúchulainn woke at dawn he was no longer aching. He gazed down at his hands, pulled up the hems of his torn trews. The spear-cuts were almost closed, as if they had enjoyed days of healing. His hand went to the wound Ferdia had inflicted in his side. It had crusted over and no longer gnawed. When he got to his feet, he felt as if he'd drunk a draft of clear water.

It was light, and it filled him as the sun grew in strength and spilled over the hills.

"I felt Her," Levarcham at last whispered into Maeve's brow, near dawn.

The awe in her voice penetrated Maeve's fog of exhaustion, her mind barely conscious.

The druid was still slumped beneath Maeve, cradling her. "I felt the Goddess with you, Maeve, the light behind the world. She held you ... and one other was there also, a bright flame. And me. It is not yours to bear alone anymore." Levarcham gripped the back of her head. "Can you not see the light, even now?"

Light ... silver ... *Ruán*. He came to her. He called her *a stór*. Beloved.

With a catch in her breath, Maeve opened her swollen eyes. Her face was a mask of dried salt that cracked as she touched it. She blinked, turning her cheek in Levarcham's lap.

Dawn was coming. The world was hushed, a soft gray, and there was a lightening in the east. The trees dripped dew. Only then did she realize the pain in her womb was gone. She placed a hand over that gentle swell. Heat radiated from within, and Maeve gazed down in wonder. To her, it glowed, though she could see nothing with her eyes. *This* babe was safe, still rooted within.

She sat up, curving her hands over her belly. Instantly, a fierce heat swept her—and this time it was her own fire, pouring through with a greater force than she had ever experienced. It was brilliant now, not red and wrathful.

A silver flame.

Maeve let it surge through her, tilting back her chin. The Source of the Mother joined that light, drawn from the land, the airs and waters. *She knew it.* It was as if it had filled her many times in ages past, but she had forgotten its ecstasy.

This was what she truly was—a cradle, not a shield.

Unknowing, she had been yearning for it only because she sensed its faint echo from before-lives. She did not hate the sídhe... she was not numb to the gods. She *hungered* for that radiance and grace. And now she would find a way to hold not just her people with this force, but her child. She would keep this one safe, pour everything into him until he grew tall, and ran, and laughed.

Her gaze lifted to Levarcham. The druid's eyes were once more luminous.

Maeve looked higher, to the sliver of red showing over the dark hills. Levarcham helped her up, and Maeve held on to a birch sapling as she straightened. The silver flame spread out from her core, filling her limbs.

This ecstasy was what Ruán had touched—she had seen it in his face. A longing seized her to part the veils with him, and be enveloped by it always. But there was more to do first. "I have to find a way to end this. Enough death has been done. Erin needs... *life.*"

Her heart racing, Maeve approached the stream. Was he still there in the ripples? She uncurled a hand to beckon him back, but she couldn't feel him anymore. *Ruán...*

Levarcham's cry shattered the dawn. Maeve spun about to

see the druid with her hand over her mouth, pointing across the stream.

The mist was turning gold, but on the western bank, not the eastern. Levarcham stumbled forward as that light grew so bright that Maeve had to shade her eyes. That fiery brilliance...was it Ruán?

No.

Maeve saw a glimmer on the water. For a heartbeat it shimmered in and out of mist, as insubstantial as the vapor. An arched neck, fluted wings...a swan.

Then it was gone, and in the flood of light that spilled through the woods a maiden appeared. Maeve could not see her clearly. Her slender limbs were wound with the pale branches, her golden hair the streamers of mist. Her heart-shaped face was the most beautiful Maeve had seen, but her green eyes bore a wild glint, as of an untamed creature.

Levarcham fell to her knees, burying her face in her hands. Her shoulders shook.

That wildness in the maiden softened when she looked at Levarcham. "There is no parting, no loss, Mother, I told you. The spirit comes to rest for only a brief time in the body, but it is always free to fly, and always alive."

She did not look solid, but her voice resonated through Maeve's chest. *Garvan,* she thought in wonder. One day she would see him again.

Levarcham raised her face, hands clasped beneath her chin. "Fledgling."

"Let go the bitterness, for that bars your way, and then you will see me in everything."

Levarcham drew a sharp breath. "So I can die and come to you—"

"Not yet." The maiden smiled, and there was a glimpse of a human girl in that flash of joy. "The light of the Great Goddess belongs to all. You must birth it for others in Thisworld before you come to Her in mine. And too many have died in my name. I want it to end. I want you to *live*."

Levarcham wrapped her arms about her waist, her head bowed.

Deirdre of the Ulaid turned that luminous face toward Maeve. "To you, raven queen, I bear a message."

Maeve swallowed, nodding. For a moment sorrow flitted across the girl's glowing eyes, dimming their sheen.

"You are the Mother now, so see to all your children." Deirdre raised a slender arm, unfurling it like a wing toward the north. "Conor comes, and he is seeking you."

CHAPTER 37

To Cúchulainn, Ferdia looked worse this day.

In the dawn light it was apparent his wounds had been cleaned, his forearms bandaged, and the scratches on his face salved. No matter how many druids had worked on him, though, Ferdia's skin was gray, his face and once-proud shoulders sagging.

Ferdia and Cúchulainn stared at each other. They had exhausted the chariot, horse, spear, and sling feats. If they repeated them this day, or if one surrendered, all the warriors of Erin would accuse them of cowardice, and betrayal of their lords and oaths.

Can I do that for him? Cúchulainn again asked himself. He rubbed the sore lump in his throat, scraping the stubble with raw fingers. In battle, he would not hesitate to throw himself before a blade to save Ferdia's life—but *give up* for that?

Cúchulainn was defending the Ulaid, and if he surrendered for one man, he would have his people's blood on his hands. But there was more to it than that. The flow of Source that heightened his strength and senses was a gift from the gods. If he betrayed it, they might deny him his place on the Blessed Isles. And he knew what the bards would sing, and what the people of Erin would remember ever after of Cúchulainn.

Coward. Traitor. *Defeated.*

If, the gods willing, he ever had sons, that was all they would hear. Emer would know he was not the man she held in her arms. His golden name, sung to the gods, breathed into Erin's air, would turn to lead. He would no longer be *him*—and what would be left for Emer or Ferdia to love?

Cúchulainn's blood beat out that dirge as he studied Ferdia's haunted face. He tried a last, desperate throw. "I cannot surrender because I have women to guard, Ferdia—*children*. If not, I would humble myself to you. But you have no one to guard. You can save us both."

Ferdia gritted his teeth. "I would lose the only scraps I have left—my name, my pride." It came as a whisper, his sureness ebbing, and then his eyes flared with a last defiance. "I cannot leave this world with nothing, reviled and scorned." He shook his head, his brow crumpling. "I would no longer be Ferdia mac Daman. I would no longer be *me*, and what would be left for you to love?"

The jaws of the trap snapped shut.

Cúchulainn forced his lips to move. "Why don't we wake these men up?" he croaked. He cocked a brow. "The Salmon Leap?" It had come down to swords, at last.

Ferdia's mouth turned up and he rubbed his bloodshot eyes. "One of us has to cross the river for that." He glanced behind him at the throng of spectators who had tumbled early from their beds, their restless mutters a rising wind. "It is safer for you if I come to that side."

"It is better for you if I cross to yours," Cúchulainn returned. He could at least give Ferdia that.

Ferdia's smile trembled. "Salmon Leap, then. I remember when Naisi and I did it, that day at Emain Macha before he met Deirdre."

"I remember. I will prepare."

Cúchulainn gathered together his discarded weapons, the fallen spears, unbroken sling-stones, daggers, axes, and swords. He piled them up on the banks of the stream where he could get to them. They shone rose and gold in the rising sun, and for once that dancing glitter did not make his heart sing, only weep.

Ferdia was slicing the sinew bindings from spear-tips, piling up the blunt shafts. Cúchulainn waded into the stream, and as he crossed the ford he drew in the silvery glints of the water, his body a fountain for Source. When he stepped out the other side, the muttering of the warriors broke into louder rumblings of excitement. The sun flashed off their helmets and swords as they raced to rouse others from their camp.

Soon the drumming and banging of shields began again, an urgency for death forced into Cúchulainn against his will.

Ferdia approached, holding two spears with intact points. "Whoever makes the longest throw can choose whether to leap or defend." His voice was matter of fact.

Now that Cúchulainn stood close, all he could think about was grabbing his friend around the shoulders, feeling his strength at his side. The longing overcame him, but he crushed it. Ferdia spoke so because it was unbearable not to.

They lined up and threw the spears into the rising sun.

Ferdia's landed a breath in front of the Hound's, both points buried in the pebbles of the lakeshore. The sheet of water beyond was as bright as a flame. "I will jump," Ferdia said. His pained glance went to the warriors baying for blood on the red hillslope above.

Cúchulainn's chest cramped. The man who jumped the Salmon Leap was more vulnerable than the one who stayed on the ground. The leap was the spectacular move, though, a way to show off. *What have they seen of you, Ferdia, that makes you so ashamed?* But the Hound only nodded. He could see that Ferdia's sanity could only cling to pride now.

It was difficult to leap in either horn or iron armor, but Ferdia's was in segments, and Cúchulainn's mail-shirt had been made by the finest smith in Erin and was pliable.

The Hound retreated and stood with arms away from his blades. When undertaking the Salmon Leap as a duel, the defender had to keep his feet in one place and his hands off his weapons until the leaper left the ground.

Ferdia balanced the spear-shaft over his shoulder. "Manannán give me strength," he called.

"Lugh give me speed," Cúchulainn returned.

The pounding of the war-drums quickened, joined by the shriek of horns. The audience got to their feet and cheered, excited to see the famed Salmon Leap with their own eyes.

Ferdia poised on his toes as the roar grew, punctuated by those galloping heartbeats. His stare fixed on Cúchulainn. Together, their blood coursed.

Cúchulainn was keeping the Source reined in, struggling against being taken over in case he harmed Ferdia. He let its flame pour along his limbs but did not allow it to flood his heart or push his mind out of the way. He was so distracted by the agony in his friend's eyes he therefore did not see the ripple go through the silver around them.

Ferdia took off without warning.

Racing, he shoved the butt of the spear into the ground, bent the shaft, and twisted his body high in a vault. Looking up, Cúchulainn was blinded by the sun and caught out by the unexpected angle of Ferdia's body as he tumbled down.

Cúchulainn's muscles were a heartbeat behind where they should have been, his reflexes blunted by pain. Ferdia came over his head even as Cúchulainn was still turning.

When the leaper was more skilled, he stabbed his enemy before the other spun about. A good defender could skewer the leaper as he hit the ground. There was no way to accomplish either feat without committing to a deadly blow.

Both men were instantly lost to training, to instinct. Ferdia's blade was heading for Cúchulainn's throat as Cúchulainn was grinding around on his heel, stabbing toward Ferdia's groin.

Neither sword met flesh. Perfectly matched, they clanged together.

A shout flew from Cúchulainn's lips, shock at Ferdia's speed and his own failing. Ferdia gasped at the impact of their swords, the tendons in his neck standing out. With senseless eyes, Ferdia slashed again, growling, his mind lost to his heart's pain.

Cúchulainn was too stunned to react, and Ferdia's blade opened a seam across his hand. The Hound's first sword-blood.

The Source flared in Cúchulainn, and he saw only an enemy outlined in silver fire, every movement trailing an afterburn. He cried out again, and combat began in earnest.

Back and forth they traded blows. Thrust, block, spin away, lunge in. Swords were bent and thrown aside, fresh ones caught up. Blades locked, they grappled against each other and broke apart, and one after the other launched fiercer assaults, raining down blows.

Ferdia fell first, grappling among the littered weapons and at the last moment blocking Cúchulainn's downward swipe with a broken spear. While his friend was off balance from the lunge, Ferdia grabbed another sword off the ground and, jumping up, ran at Cúchulainn.

Cúchulainn stumbled back, scrabbling for the grip of a shield and bringing it up just as Ferdia's sword buried itself in the wood. Cúchulainn tossed the shield away, wrenching Ferdia's blade from his hands. They grasped new weapons and fell upon each other again.

Their flesh was caught by sword-edges and shattered wood. Blood streaked their faces and mixed with sweat and flecks of saliva, and where it poured from arm wounds it made their hilts slippery. "Drink," Cúchulainn gasped at last.

Side by side they staggered to the water, drinking and washing the blood from their fingers. By unspoken agreement they did not clean their faces. It was easier to fight a nameless enemy, eyes white within a mask of gore.

Squatting on his heels, Ferdia looked into the tumbling water. "When I'm dead," he said hoarsely, "take my head and put the skull by your hearth so my shade can find you at Samhain. We will always be one then, until you come to my camp on the other side of the veils. I want our names to be forever joined."

"They are already." Cúchulainn swayed on his feet. He hawked up saliva and blood and spat them out. "And you will not die."

Ferdia straightened, wincing. "Lugh's balls, what are you doing to me, then?"

Cúchulainn blinked, reaching out and at last clutching Ferdia's shoulder. "Trying to clobber some sense into you."

Ferdia snorted, the shoulder bones beneath Cúchulainn's hand shuddering. For a heartbeat they were together.

Then Ferdia's face spasmed, and grief roared up in his eyes and sense fled again.

He knocked Cúchulainn's arm away and staggered, groping for a sword. As he was beaten back by the next attack, Cúchulainn glanced at the climbing sun. *Hurry*, he said to the remains of the Red Branch, willing them to shake off their sickness. *Come and make this a battle, so Ferdia and I can fight and be spared.*

In weariness, blows became more desperate. Ferdia landed a cut along the edge of Cúchulainn's mail-shirt again, nearly piercing his belly. Cúchulainn swiped the back of Ferdia's leg— a wound that would have crippled another man. Perhaps madness blocked Ferdia's pain, for though blood filled his boot, he did not break stride.

Eventually the pain blurred even the love in Cúchulainn's heart. Ferdia's bloody face became that of every savage who had ever run screaming at him, trying to sever his pulse. The urge for survival swamped everything.

Ferdia also glanced at the sun, and Cúchulainn thought he saw a shadow cross his eyes. Then Ferdia sucked in a great breath and threw himself on Cúchulainn in the fiercest assault yet.

Their blades became a blur of flashing steel, the air filled with the whiz and bite of iron. Cúchulainn was at last forced to let go into the frenzy, his gestures flowing into the deadly dance, divorced from his mind.

They staggered into the ford, water spraying up. Sun shafted through the droplets, enveloping them in bright mist and shutting out everything else. Consumed by flame, Cúchulainn knew when he cut Ferdia's arm, when his sword snapped the taut flesh at Ferdia's side. Tears ran down his face as he struck away Ferdia's weapon and stabbed him in the thigh. "Don't do this!" he bellowed.

Ferdia's empty eyes stared through him, though, and his manic smile curdled Cúchulainn's blood as he bore down upon him once more. With a leap, Ferdia drove Cúchulainn back over a rock until the Hound stumbled and fell in the shallow water.

Cúchulainn was aware of Ferdia scrabbling at his waist again, and thought he reached for another sword. The silver fire roared up and the Hound groped desperately among his discarded weapons at the water's edge, looking for anything to break through Ferdia's madness. *Anything.*

A shaft came to hand. Cúchulainn grasped it and went to throw.

Ferdia staggered back, his smile flaring, and the shining plates of his armor fell away—he had been cutting them free. With a furious yell, Cúchulainn tried to check his thrust, but he had already loosed the spear. It flashed past his eyes toward Ferdia's undefended body.

Bronze and iron…

Cúchulainn bellowed again. He had grabbed the gae bolga.

Never had that vicious weapon been flung at such close quarters, and the Source had given Cúchulainn the strength of many. The barbed spear flew true, and with a sickening thud sank deep into Ferdia's belly. He fell to his knees, his gray eyes wide.

Cúchulainn scrambled over to his friend. *Push it through...all the way through and bind him and he will live.*

The sinew on the spear had tangled with Ferdia's weapons, though, and the current of the stream dragged the gae bolga even as Cúchulainn reached him. With a deadly snick the tangled barbs sprang out, lodging in Ferdia's innards. Sprawled in the stream, he whimpered, white-faced.

Cúchulainn clasped his friend in his arms, and his tortured cry rebounded off the hillslopes and far across the shining lake. The baying of the men faded away, and there was silence.

A cloak of red fanned through the water behind Ferdia. His helmet had fallen off, and his black hair trailed through Cúchulainn's fingers like river-weed. Cúchulainn cradled Ferdia's face, his other hand trying to hold the gaping wound closed. Blood poured from the runnels carved along the gae bolga's shaft. When Cúchulainn accidentally nudged it, Ferdia cried out and Cúchulainn let go, his hands flexing uselessly. He could not look at the wound again.

All was hushed; they were alone in sunlit mist among the trees.

Ferdia smiled, blood trickling from his mouth, his breaths growing shallow. "At last...a way out..."

Cúchulainn's shoulders heaved and he shook his head.

"Use your sword," Ferdia whispered, beginning to shudder. "A good end."

It was what warriors vowed to do, but for once Cúchulainn's oaths deserted him. "*No.*" He ground his cheek into Ferdia's wet hair. "Hold on—we will cut the gae bolga. There are druids here..."

"Cú..." Ferdia's breath bubbled and his head stirred. Could that be a gasp, a laugh? "This time...I will be first."

Numbness was creeping over Cúchulainn from the freezing water. He rocked Ferdia, lips pressed to his brow. "I've seen my death, Fer." For the first time, Cúchulainn whispered his secret. "I am tied to a tall stone and there are men around me with swords. I've seen it, but I don't know when it will happen."

Ferdia's cracked lips parted in a sweet smile. "I will come then...for you."

Cúchulainn crushed him to his breast, that desperate grip saying everything for him. It took some time before Ferdia's neck sank back upon Cúchulainn's wrist.

Ferdia's eyes still gleamed, but now they were glassy. His body settled into Cúchulainn's arms. At last Cúchulainn found a voice. "Take care of you as you would of me." For once there was no answering smile.

The sun of a new day was soaring above him, heartless and bright. But for Cúchulainn all light was extinguished, and darkness claimed him.

⸻

Wielding her healer's authority, Levarcham used the well-being of the unborn child to force Maeve to rest and drink more strengthening brews before she tried to walk. One part of Maeve was ablaze, desperate to discover Conor's whereabouts. The other was utterly exhausted.

"You will not be able to triumph against anyone if you collapse before them," Levarcham warned. "And you have scouts on the lookout." Though the veils had only parted for a glimpse, that silver light shone from the druid now with a quiet force that matched Maeve's fire.

They made their way back from the west side of the hills as the light climbed the sky. But Maeve was basking in a deeper glow: the spirits of the child and Ruán, woven together. *He came for me.* She was sure of it. She would not lose this babe—she would not lose *any more.*

Maeve and Levarcham reached the camp not long after highsun. It was deserted but for the warriors on watch, the rest of the men at the river.

Maeve's heightened senses transformed the camp into a colorful weave of bright threads. The smells of ash, meat, dung, and blood.

A wash of gold and brown from the trees. Banners flapping on the tents. The dull gleam of tarnished metal.

She heard the distressed breathing of a man before she saw him.

The warrior rushed up to her, very young and white-faced. "My lady!" As he touched his chest and brow he shivered.

Maeve was still floating on the strange sensation that her spirit was now vast and glowing. It expanded far from her body like the flow of an ocean, encompassing the earth and streams, the trees and hills. It was hard to remember that a small part of her was a queen. With a great effort, she drew herself back, focusing her senses down to this body, this mind.

The man was afraid to speak to her.

Maeve gripped his shoulder, her voice welling with power. "Tell me."

He gulped. "Ferdia mac Daman died not long after dawn. My lord Fraech ... he was so angry he caught up weapons and went to face the Hound himself! But the Hound was in a great rage and struck him down, and Lord Fraech collapsed. Morand charged in to challenge Cúchulainn instead, but then we saw Lord Fraech stir. He was only wounded—he lives, though he lies on the field and we cannot get near him."

Maeve's relief chilled when the boy's eyes dropped. "*What else?*"

He screwed up his face as if expecting a blow. "When the Lady Finnabair thought him slain she screamed and tried to run to him. The men would not let her ... so she broke from them and fled. Away. Up the great hill."

Maeve jolted back fully into her body. "And no one went after her?"

The youth's head drooped. "Some were trying to get to Lord Fraech and were beaten back by the Hound, others argued over who would go next. We thought her gone back to camp ... to you. Men set after her, but she is so fleet she disappeared and ..." He trailed off.

"The scouts?"

"They've gone out already, lady."

Maeve dismissed him and turned. Levarcham gripped her cold hands, searching her face.

"There is nothing you can do now, friend." Maeve did not see her, only Finn. "Put forth your arts to save the wounded, and prepare for Fraech, if he lives."

As Levarcham hurried away, Maeve summoned all of her willpower. She must blaze again, for Finn.

She swooped through the camp, belting on swords and daggers and gathering the remaining scouts. Finally, she summoned a troop of the fleet-footed Galeóin spearmen that had come with Ailill. A large force of warriors would only reveal their presence—and Finn's—to an enemy lurking in the hills.

Maeve could feel him now, a darkness gathering beyond the ridge. Conor.

She and her men struck out west. Scouts used birdcalls to each other, and soon the bleak cries of ravens echoed over the bare hills as the trackers cast great circles looking for Finn.

The sun was falling down the sky when they met in the blue shadows of a cold wood.

"We found her trail," a scout told Maeve. He was clad in deerskins, the mottled hides blending him into the forest. "She was running, breaking branches and bracken with no thought to hide." His eyes fell away from Maeve. "The Ulaid have her. She stumbled into their scouts and they took her with them to a camp nearby."

Maeve stared into the shadowed woods. "I thought there were no Ulaid nearby but Cúchulainn."

"There were not yesterday," another scout piped up. "A warband came before dawn along hidden valleys from Emain Macha. They know the land better than us. It is not a great number—two score at most."

"Who?"

The man scratched his beard, puzzled. "Boys wielding swords like clubs, their armor too big for them."

The man in deerskin nodded. "It is an odd sight—a chariot sheathed in gold but drawn by cart-horses, and one tent only, with a red banner, the poles gold-tipped. And...a shield outside. A white shield."

Maeve took a step to a birch tree and held its trunk, head down. She knew that white shield. It was called Ocean, made of whalebone and bleached sealskin, with patterns picked out in sea-pearl.

A shield fit for a king.

CHAPTER 38

The fighters accompanying Conor were clearly no better at keeping watch than wielding swords. Though they camped upon a low knoll among leafless trunks, Maeve and her men were able to crawl unseen up behind a higher hill nearby and come down a gully on the other side, giving them a good vantage point.

Maeve crouched there in a hawthorn thicket clustered with red berries. The scouts were in brown hides and feathers. The Galeóin bore their lances in back-carriers, the shafts sticking up like bare saplings.

To the Ulaid they would look part of the forest itself.

They peered at the figures moving among the makeshift shelters of branches on the knoll. There were no banners bearing the gold tree, or proud rows of spears and shields. "They do not look like Red Branch, or strut about like Red Branch." Maeve tucked her hair behind her ears, squinting. "It seems Conor has come with a ragtag bunch of...boys, yes. He must be mad." She sat back on her haunches, her fingers on her brow.

Her war-band could easily destroy this pitiful troop of youths.

Then she dropped her hand. Her pulse kept hammering a different song, over and over.

Conor has Finn.

The eyes of the scouts slid toward her, and she read in them the bitter truth. Finn bore jeweled brooches, a fine cloak and gold torc. Though Conor could not know her, he would be thrilled to snare a noble girl as a bargaining tool. However, Maeve knew if she launched an attack and it descended into battle, Conor would no longer need to bargain. He would kill Finn.

If she was even alive.

Maeve's palm crept over her breast. *Yes, she was alive.* "We cannot attack them." She closed her eyes, trying to conjure the brilliant idea no one else would think of.

Behind her eyelids, though, she saw only Finn's terrified face. And then her own at sixteen, tears streaming among the stones of the sídhe. *I will not lose her again.*

The flame propelled Maeve to her feet.

If she diverted fighters from Cúchulainn, the Hound might break away and save Conor, or mount some defense of Emain Macha, or rally more Ulaid men. Enough men had died. *Enough. There is only me.*

She must somehow get to Finn's side—but that would put her in danger, too. Maeve's hand moved to her belly. How could she choose between her children...?

Another throb of warmth came from the one she carried. She heard its song, this babe of the sídhe, that she and it were one, and any and all paths would carry them both to light.

In her life, she had been maiden, seducer, warrior, and queen. There was only one path left to her.

"Go back to our men," she told the scouts. "Tell them Conor's war-band is approaching the lake, and if it comes closer they must prepare for battle." She beckoned to the leader of the Galeóin. "You and your men will help me, though only from afar." The Galeóin looked surprised, but nodded his dark head.

One of the scouts broke in. "But...my queen...you cannot face them alone!"

Maeve glanced at him, though she did not really see him. "I am her mother."

Something in her voice silenced the warriors, and they only stared at her with awe.

"If Fraech dies and I do not return, Fintan is in charge. He must get the others back to Tiernan at Cruachan."

The scouts bowed and crept away, disappearing into the dusk.

Maeve sank down with the Galeóin leader. "I can get in, but I cannot get out as easily." She pulled some of the thorns and berries in the thicket aside. "Before the light fades, mark Conor's tent, there. Assuming I can get to Finn, I still have Conor's warriors to break through on our escape. That is where you come in. Wait until the moon is this far above the horizon," she held up her hand, "and then start throwing spears at the *fringes* of camp. By then I will either be dead or with Finn in Conor's tent." She bared her teeth. "So avoid the center, for I'd rather you did not kill us."

The black-haired Galeóin leader eyed her with concern. "But...there are no fires, lady. There will be nothing to aim for in the dark."

"You have light for a time yet." She cocked her head. "The tales say your spears are part of your souls. Before it is loosed, you know by the tilt of the shaft and spring in your hand exactly where a lance will fall." Her eyes were alight with that challenge.

The Galeóin bowed his head, the gull feathers in his braids falling over his lean face. "It is true."

"Count up to twenty and then stop throwing. They will be too busy screaming to bother with us then—if we are still alive."

The Galeóin shuffled over to murmur her orders to his men.

Maeve sat cross-legged, hands uncurled to the sky, and watched the Ulaid camp fade into darkness. She kept her eyes on the last gleam of sun as it caught the gold of Conor's tent, and a tremor went through her.

Will he recognize my stamp on her face? And if he does, what will he do?

What creature can creep silently through darkness?

Maeve tried to summon the anam of such a beast, but it was beyond her for now to melt into wilderness. The ceaseless flame that joined her to Finn burned all else away.

On hands and knees she crept through icy streams and tangled bracken, grazing her palms when they slipped on wet stones. The ground rose, and she took her bearings from the ash tree beside Conor's tent, black against the stars. Now she was on sheep-bitten turf, and then among the trees.

There were no horses or hounds to betray her. Conor's warband was restless, unable to hear anything beyond their own clumsy feet and fearful mutters. There were guards by his tent-flap, however.

Maeve realized she should circle the knoll and come upon it from the north, for on that side his tent was unguarded. Foolishly, Conor's men faced only east and south, terrified of the enemy over the hills.

It took an age. She kept having to pause to feel the ground for sticks that would crack and stones that would shift. She pressed to her belly whenever someone stirred nearby, holding her breath until she could avoid the huddles of whispering men.

Conor had allowed them no fires, blessing her with darkness.

At last Maeve approached the only sliver of light, which leaked from beneath Conor's tent. Hidden among the ferns, she studied the faint lamplit outlines that showed through the bleached hide. One paced back and forth, man-shaped. There was a solid pile that did not move—packs or baskets. She could see nothing else.

She dug a stone from the mud, unsheathing her dagger with her other hand. Taking a breath, she flung the stone so it bounced off a tree on the fringes of the camp.

The clatter set off exclamations at the front of Conor's tent. Under cover of that noise, Maeve slit the leather near what she thought was the baggage and crawled inside. Her heart was racing so fast she could hear nothing else, and only had her eyes to guide her.

She glimpsed Conor by a lamp, his ear cocked to the noise outside—a huddle of red hair at his feet. Though Maeve immediately sank behind a bundle of furs, Conor's head snapped toward her, as if his senses had been honed for her alone.

There was no time.

Like a cat, Maeve tensed legs and arms and sprang over the pile of baggage, her dagger outstretched. Finn's cry came, cut off to a gasp. Checking herself, Maeve twisted in midair and landed with arms out. Her hackles went up.

Conor had Finn by her hair, his own blade at her throat.

The girl's eyes rolled, and she clawed at Conor's veined hands. She'd been stripped to her knee-length shift. Pale linen, unbound hair, white skin ... she was dressed as a sacrifice.

Maeve tried to quell her fury, to focus on the Ulaid king.

Conor was a withered man now, his long, pale hair an uncombed straggle, his skin waxy. The gleam of the lamp revealed opaque eyes devoid of human sense.

His chuckle was the rustle of dry leaves. "I *thought* I'd caught the chick—the very image of the raven herself."

Maeve eyed his hand. He'd pushed the dagger in a little under Finn's ear, and a trickle of blood marred the girl's fair skin. Finn's eyes creased, tears running down her cheeks.

The Ulaid king did not miss the hatred that leaped into Maeve's face, and his lip curled, exposing yellowed teeth. "Did you think I would cower, waiting for you to destroy me? Did you think *you* had at last bettered *me*?" He laughed. "I will cleanse this world of you, she-wolf, and the bards will sing that by my hand the foul witch of Connacht met her end." His mouth was flecked with spittle. "And no one will say I lacked the courage, or the strength, or the *blessings of the gods*."

Maeve let his crazed words wash over her, sizing up his pressure on the dagger. Unconsciously, she clenched a fist, tensed a leg. Conor saw and pressed harder.

Finn gurgled in pain.

Maeve thrust that sound away lest she also go mad. "It is me you want. Let her go, and you can have me." *Just get his hands off her and onto me.* She never thought she would ever pray for that.

The tangled hanks of Conor's hair stirred as he shook his head. "I know your wiles. Now you will throw your daggers and sword in the corner by the door—don't think I am not already tasting the slide of this blade into her flesh."

Maeve's sight narrowed, the rush of blood driving all logic away. She fumbled at her belt, dropping scabbards and then reaching to release the sword she'd strapped down her spine. They clanked as she threw them down.

Conor cocked his head. "Take off everything," he hissed.

Maeve quelled the sickness in her throat, dragging off armor, kilt, tunic, and trews. If he wanted *that*, she didn't care. She would do anything. Holding his eyes, she unbound the blade from her thigh and the one from her ankle, slashed the breast-band into shreds, and her breechclout, and kicked off her boots. She was entirely naked.

She tilted her chin. Conor had wanted something of her once, enjoyed some spark of pleasure, even if he had been thinking of Deirdre all along.

His gaze as it slid over her was not full of desire, however. Conor's nostrils flared as he glanced at her breasts, and when that gaze dropped to the cleft between her legs, his stringy throat bobbed with revulsion.

Maeve heard the faint rush in the air before he did. Someone screamed outside, and Conor's head jerked toward it. Whizzing spears, the clatter of shafts, the thunk of points. More shrieks and shouts. The Galeóin.

Conor's eyes widened, his hand at Finn's throat trembling.

Hands on her hips, Maeve thrust her breasts at him. "Come,

husband. Try once more to satisfy me, as you never could before." She smiled. "Me or Deirdre."

Something in him snapped, and with a bellow, Conor thrust Finn so hard she thudded head first into the tent-post, sprawling limp on the ground. Maeve's attention went to her daughter.

Her distraction was a costly mistake.

Conor threw himself upon her before Maeve could raise her arms, bearing her on her back to the ground. The impact winded her, and as the weight of a man crushed her once more, his gray hair in her mouth, an old part of Maeve froze.

Ros Ruadh, grinding her into nothing.

Diarmait of Mumu holding her down.

Her father striking all breath from her.

Maeve was paralyzed just long enough for Conor to get his hands about her throat. The Ulaid king was withered, but he was tall and had been well-formed in youth. The strength of madness was in his grip, shocking Maeve back to herself.

She would die, she thought clearly, as his claws crushed her windpipe. But she would still take him with her, and give Finn a chance. She growled in her chest, writhing and twisting so she could knee him, and scratching any skin she could reach. She smelled blood, and hooked her nails on the vein in his neck, digging into flesh.

Conor's glassy eyes did not flicker as he struggled to strangle her.

And then Maeve was floating, a tunnel of darkness closing in. *I should be stronger, faster. Duck…dive…leap and spin…* She choked, her kicks growing weaker.

Maeve, Innel yelled. *Get off Father's horse or I'll break your arm myself! You're not strong enough…Father will have your head. Maeve, he's taking off—Maeve!*

Maeve drifted. *I'm not strong enough. I'm not enough.* A feeble flame still joined her to Finn—she could see the girl's face—but Maeve could no longer feel that fire in her limbs. *Ruán…hold me… I won't ask again…please…*

Faintly, she heard a scream.

Conor shuddered.

Maeve was caught in the vibration of what felt like blows, each one shivering through his body on top of her and down into her own muscles. Something hot spattered her face. The limpet grip on Maeve's throat slackened.

Sucking up the air, Maeve shoved Conor with all of her remaining strength. He rolled off, heavy and limp. Panting, Maeve stared down at the puddle of blood on the grass that spread from beneath Conor's body. He was gurgling, his horrified gaze fixed on the roof of the tent.

The lamplight was still spinning about her, but Maeve rubbed her throat and skewed around on her haunches.

Finn was on her knees behind Conor, her hair covering her face. Rivulets of bright red tangled with the copper strands, flowing down her shift to her knees. Scarlet blood splashing pale linen. Maeve could not look away from the dripping dagger in Finn's hands.

Finn stared only at Conor, her breast fluttering like that of a bird.

The King of the Ulaid was clawing at his own throat now, his chest, gasping as he drowned in blood. His eyes were wide and white, then red as the veins burst. At last he slowed and stopped struggling and was still, his limbs twisted.

Nostrils flaring, Finn lifted glazed eyes to her mother. There was a purple bruise on her brow. "I listen to everything you say ... everything, Mamaí." Vacantly, she plucked at her leg with bloody fingers. "They took the blade on my belt, but you said bind a little one at the top of my thigh."

Maeve crawled over and took her icy hands. "I remember." She had said that only in passing, almost in jest. "What a brave girl you are, my Finn. Brave and clever."

Finn went white, shaking so hard Maeve thought she might faint. "I listen ... to everything."

Wiping Conor's blood from her own face, Maeve got up, grabbing a fur cloak from Conor's cot-bed and laying it around Finn's shoulders. Then she chafed Finn's cheeks to bring the color back. "Come, focus on my face. *Fraech is alive.*"

Finn's blue eyes flickered, and the pupils contracted and awareness came back. "Alive?"

Maeve kissed her brow. "Yes, so we must get back to him. Hurry."

Maeve swiftly dressed and armed herself, and found Finn's tunic and trews. While the girl struggled to draw them on, Maeve poured the oil from the lamp around Conor's body then tossed the flaming wick on top.

The fire burst alight, and they hurried to the tent flap. Maeve paused to listen. The spears had stopped falling—there were only the cries and shouts of men now, and the drumming of feet. Maeve withdrew her sword, and putting Finn behind her, they crept out.

The guards around the tent had disappeared into the black night. Chaos reigned. Young men ran back and forth through the ghostly trees, yelling at each other and hauling at weeping, bloodied comrades. Others gathered into huddles, bracing their swords at the darkness and spooking at every noise.

They barely gave Maeve and Finn a glance. Maeve ripped Conor's shield from its post and hefted it. As she and Finn stumbled down the slope, behind them Conor's tent caught alight, the flames crackling. Seeing that, a knot of warriors cried out and swung around to block their way.

Wheezing, Maeve brandished her sword, her throat still aching. "Even now my army approaches...but our only enemy was your king, and he is dead!"

The whites of their eyes turned red in the firelight, the flames contorting their faces with writhing shadows.

"You are free of his madness. Go back to Emain Macha and we will spare you. Harm us, and my men will storm this hill."

Confused, the youths drew back, and Maeve swung her sword and strode through them, drawing Finn along and trying to protect her with the shield. Her skin crawled, her back tensing in anticipation of a spear-thrust. Whatever had happened at Emain Macha, though, Conor's makeshift war-band now crumbled, many throwing down weapons and racing off into the dark.

Maeve kept going until the night swallowed her and Finn, finding her way back to the Galeóin. Together they trekked over the hills in the moonlight, until Finn's strength deserted her and at last Maeve let her sink down among the bracken.

The Galeóin squatted on the slope above, their spears fencing the skyline.

Her arm aching, Maeve tossed aside the shield and gathered Finn in her lap, rocking her as the girl wept. The wind lifted Maeve's hair as she stared into the dark with empty eyes.

All at once she crushed her cheek to Finn's brow. "I lied to you, and will bear it no longer."

Finn's sobs faded.

"It was not because you were betrothed that I never returned. It was because I lost another babe, and could not face that pain again. *I could be a mother no more.*" Maeve's bruised throat closed up.

Finn was silent for a moment, then wiped her face and took Maeve's hand with wet fingers. "But you did come for me, Mamaí. Last night, you came for me."

When Maeve, Finn, and the Laigin spearmen climbed the bracken shoulder of the great hill, Levarcham was waiting for them, crouched on an ancient cairn of tumbled stones. In the shadows, the druid was as gray as the rocks on which she sat, dew on her cloak of seal-fur, her face pale.

A cold wind bent the bronze grasses as Maeve and Finn approached, Finn plodding beneath Maeve's arm. Just then the sun crept over the brow of the mount and Levarcham rose and it caught her hair.

The Galeóin trotted on ahead, and Maeve unbound Conor's

shield from her back and threw it at the druid's feet. Levarcham's glance flew between the shield and the blood staining Finn's untucked shift.

"Conor is dead," Maeve croaked.

Levarcham's silver eyes flared.

Maeve's smile was bleak. "No, not me." She turned and touched Finn's cheek.

Levarcham limped up to the dazed girl and took hold of her fists, uncurling them to expose the smears of dried blood on her palms. "He must die by the hand of Woman," the druid murmured to herself. She searched Finn's face, making the girl's mouth tremble. "You are a woman now," Levarcham said. "A brave warrior. The Goddess chose you to set us free, and for that I thank you." And the druid awkwardly lowered herself to kneel before Finn, and bowed her head over the girl's hands in blessing.

They were caught there as the sun poured down the grassy hillside, sweeping away the last shadows.

When Finn helped Levarcham rise, the girl's cheeks were once more stained with color. Finn rubbed her eyes with the back of her hand, blinking. "Fraech...?"

"Cúchulainn let him be taken from the field, and I have put forth all my efforts to salve him. He will live."

After an intake of breath, life flooded Finn's limbs. Without a backward glance, she bounded up the slope and streaked toward the camp like a young deer.

"Cúchulainn let him go because he himself is crumbling," Levarcham said to Maeve as they climbed the hill. "It is the loss of Ferdia that has at last struck the blow."

They crested the shoulder of the mount and the rays of sunrise flooded Maeve. She gazed down the slopes of dewy heather and wet, brown ferns that glittered all the way to the shining lake. The sun set the far bracken slopes on fire. On the still air she could hear the clash of arms. Cúchulainn. She had brought him here, and now she alone held him here.

The heat soaked into her, melting all the horrors of the night. And so her heart unfolded once more, vast and filled with light.

"What you felt by the stream with the child, when the gods touched you." Levarcham was also gazing down the slope, shading her eyes. "It made anything possible." She turned, and her eyes were glowing, the wrinkles in her haggard face softened by dawn. "Anything *is* possible."

Maeve's breath rushed out. *Conor is dead. We are free.*

Enough blood had been spilled in these hills. If she was to be a mother of the land, then she must heal the land. Maeve closed her eyes, spread her arms and let the sun pour through. When she opened her eyes, Levarcham was gone.

You would bend fate to your will. Ferdia's words.

And Deirdre. *See to all your children.*

Cradle them in light.

Maeve turned and climbed higher, coming over the crest of the hill above the ford. She followed the sound of trickling water to the rill that tumbled down the slope, squatted and combed its current through her fingers. *Come to me.* She summoned the memory of being filled again, of flowing out into Source. Unfocusing her eyes, she watched the sun-glints blur into a stream of silver that rushed up her arm.

It sheathed her in another form, a shimmering outline.

Ruán's gift to her, twice over. For the third time, Maeve summoned it for herself.

She stood.

Now *she* held an echo of the sleek otter, able to glide through water both swift and silent. Maeve looked up at the fringe of stunted birches and bent rowans. They swayed like flickering flames. She slid into the rill, her muscles fluid. She did not feel the cold or the sword along her thigh.

She was more than human Maeve now—she was a creature of bright water.

She wove between the rocks in the stream, through the ferns.

No one below saw her, for the roars of the men went on. When she next flickered back to awareness, the stream was rushing in threads of foam to the ford below.

Maeve gazed in wonder. She saw two worlds at once. There were the shapes she knew, rocks, trees, and people, but their solid forms were now ghostly. Brighter and more real were the streams of sparks that made them, swirling and flaring. The trees and men were fire-blooms, the water silver filaments, the air a wash of light.

She looked down, and her breath rushed out. The Hound of the Ulaid had always been dark in her mind, even when she glimpsed his flame on the raid. He was a death-wielder to her, forged of the same blackness as Conor.

Now Cúchulainn's brilliance was blinding.

Maeve had watched stars fall, the only things she had ever seen as bright as he was now. A towering flame, incandescent.

Summoning the otter essence, she melted back into the stream and poured down the slope, gliding around rocks. Her own woman-shape broke into ripples, curls of water and glinting light. Cúchulainn's fire remained bent upon his latest opponent as they both fought in the shallow ford.

Only when she was closer did Maeve see that, as before, Cúchulainn's soul-fire was also rent with streaks of blood-red and black despair. He bellowed and struck at his enemy's blade in such a rage he seemed blind to all else.

Maeve smoothed the boulders with her body, and slunk along the stream-bed.

Ahead, the struggling fighters sent up plumes of water. Cúchulainn stood on a band of gravel in the middle of the stream, flanked fore and aft by deeper pools. He was smashing blows upon the hapless Connacht warrior, who was up to his knees in one of the channels, his shield and helmet dented, arms running with blood.

Maeve glided around a boulder into the pool behind Cúchu-lainn. She pulled herself along the stream-bed, palms cupping the pebbles. Her chin flowed below the surface, her eyes above. She chanted a summoning inside. *I am only sunlight on rippling water.*

Cúchulainn was oblivious.

Maeve coiled up, otterwise. At that moment, perhaps the sun glinted off her sword, for the eyes of the Connacht warrior flicked toward her.

Cúchulainn immediately pounced on him, grabbing the man by his tunic and tilting his sword to stab it into his neck.

In one fluid movement Maeve rose from the pool behind Cúchulainn, and now her wrist was about *his* throat, her sword pressed below his ear. Water streamed from her body.

"I have you," she whispered.

At last someone had gotten past his guard and laid cold metal against his erratic pulse. Cúchulainn's relief came in a wave. *At last.* An end had come to darkness.

His sword was still poised beneath the jawbone of the Connacht warrior, who was struggling to find a footing in the deeper water.

"Let him go."

It penetrated Cúchulainn that it was a woman's voice. Against all odds, he had been bested—*by a woman.* The delight of old coursed through him, to witness such skill in anyone, such bravery. *Brilliantly done.* In disbelief, there was only one thing he could do.

He laughed.

He'd been drowning in blood, the taint sickening. Triumph had long since turned to slaughter, and glory had fallen into the stink of piss and bowels carved open. *And Ferdia.* Cúchulainn's wheeze faded. A gift of the gods, this must be. They laid a hand on his brow now and said, *We are pleased...rest your grief...*

Cúchulainn's awareness still wavered between Thisworld and

the Source. For the first time in his life he perceived behind him a spirit that flamed with a wildfire equal to his own.

"Maeve," he said.

"The very one. Drop him, and throw your sword away."

A tremor ran over him. *If I turn and attack her, the warriors will rush me and I cannot fight them all.* Cúchulainn's mind and body ached. He was so tired of blood. He blinked as sweat ran in his eyes. Ferdia...where was Ferdia? "Are you replacing this challenger?"

"On my honor as a queen."

Honor. He still had that.

Cúchulainn shoved the Connacht warrior away, and the youth groped for the bank and fell upon it, gasping, his face purple. "Go," Maeve barked at him, and the boy scrabbled away.

Only then did Cúchulainn realize the lakeshore was at last hushed. He heard the faint cry of geese, their wings a glimmer over ruffled water. Maeve's dagger pressed his neck, her chest and thighs molded to his back like a lover's embrace. Her murmur tickled his ear. "Your sword."

Cúchulainn smiled to himself. "My fate is to die young, anyway. What power can you wield over me?"

"You care for the Ulaid, for your wife and people. You care for Emain Macha and the Red Branch. Die like this, and they face only ruin. Listen to me, and you can change their fates."

The Hound's neck prickled. He detected something strange in her voice.

His soul was torn: to follow Ferdia through the veils, or stay with Emer and fulfill love and duty. Did Maeve sense that, too?

Listen to me.

The words floated from Maeve's unconscious. The great hero Cúchulainn was at last in her hands. All the tangled paths of the past had led to this—a death blow.

And yet she was filled not with old pain and fear, but Ruán's voice. *Come to know your own heart so you can understand others. That is what will win you freedom.*

Maeve was still. The faint murmurs of the war-band fell into silence. The wind on her cheek and the icy cold of the stream faded. She was for once the eye of the storm, not its tempest.

She closed her eyes, dropped her chin so it almost touched Cúchulainn's shoulder. The glow inside her grew and spilled out, overflowing into the radiance of Source. *I want only life—for me, for him, and all of them.*

As she surrendered, something in Cúchulainn was also released, the tattered bonds of desperation and duty at last snapping. He sighed, and the light flooded between them and took away the last of sight and sound.

Maeve had felt the Goddess move in her now—the unformed seeds She nurtured in darkness, the moon-tides of oceans that birthed life. She had always cast Cúchulainn as the blade in Conor's hand, part of his twisted darkness.

Clasped to him now, Maeve knew that she had been wrong.

The world swung them in an ancient dance about each other, for if she was the moon, then he was the sun. Brilliant flame and brightness...the fire that makes the seeds of the Goddess grow. The thirst to build, forge, and strengthen. The wielder of the blade that guards the fields and flocks, that shelters the young.

A man is also sacred.

She could not kill the God, now that she had been the Goddess.

"The name Cúchulainn stands for honor," she whispered, "but the betrayals of men have riven you. So will you claim your true name again? For I offer you peace, Hound of Cullen."

His emotions flared around them. "You lie."

"Yesterday Conor took my daughter and would have slaughtered her like a deer. Instead, he tried to kill me when I was unarmed. My child pierced his lung with a dagger. Nessa's son is dead."

Maeve felt the leap of Cúchulainn's heart in her own breast.

"What bound Conor to you is gone also. I have seen Deirdre with my own eyes. She and Naisi are free, and now we can be free." Maeve let out a shuddering breath. "My darkness brought us here, and Conor and I trapped you. *We* killed Ferdia."

To her astonishment, Maeve felt a tear drop onto her forearm. Her voice broke. "Now Conor is dead, and I am reborn. You can be, too. Throw down your sword and let the kingdoms of Erin be strong together."

Neither of them moved, Cúchulainn's breathing labored. Maeve realized what she had to do. "So this is the only way you will trust me."

And she released her hold.

CHAPTER 39

C úchulainn spun about, dazzled by the sun above him.
   "The remains of Conor's war-band are nearby, Hound. Send your own man to seek the truth."

The light shimmered, and Thisworld resolved itself about Cúchulainn. He saw a cloud of red hair, and a beautiful and harrowing face streaked with blood and dirt about her eyes, the rest of her skin washed clean by the stream.

"I will not surrender," Cúchulainn croaked, swaying on his feet.

"Me neither. Our men must believe in our strength if we are to save Erin." A wry smile touched Maeve's mouth, but her eyes were a luminous blue.

The flame, thought Cúchulainn.

"At Emain Macha, Hound, I saw when an end had to be made of a duel at sundown, and neither man would back down. I saw what you did."

Cúchulainn filled his lungs, taking in life as if for the first time. "So be it."

Maeve threw down her dagger and unsheathed her sword, and both of them flowed into the same dance at the same moment, as if one person. Maeve spun and lifted her sword—Cúchulainn carved the air with his own weapon. Their blades met over their heads with a ring.

Maeve's arm curved over Cúchulainn's head. His stance matched hers. They made a frame, and inside it they stared at each other as if into a mirror. The silver Source was glowing in her face. "Well met, Hound," Maeve murmured.

"And you, Maeve of Connacht."

"Maeve of Erin."

For a long moment they stood in the middle of the stream, between their two realms, gazes locked.

"Though they cost me dearly," Maeve murmured, "your deeds these past days will be remembered and honored forever."

Dazzled, Cúchulainn let all his breath out.

They dropped their arms as one, and each stepped back until they reached their opposing bank. Cúchulainn sheathed his sword.

Maeve's eyes were drawn to Ferdia's body, lying behind him in the shadows of the trees. She touched a fist to her brow. "I will send Ulaid-men to you. Then we will speak again."

The ranks of Maeve's warriors were a shining sea that parted, waves whispering as she slowly walked through them.

She had somehow bested Cúchulainn. The men were not sure what had happened. Even so, many went down on one knee before her, or bowed their heads and touched their chests with respect.

Maeve stopped. Her body vibrated with a deep song that seemed to resonate through the air about her and the ground beneath her feet. "An end is come of this fight. An end, for now, of death. Conor mac Nessa, our enemy, was slain by Finnabair, daughter of Connacht and Laigin, and the Red Branch is broken. While there is *no surrender*, the great Hound and I seek peace, for all our sakes."

The whispering was broken by crests of exclamation and wonder and, as one, the flames of men that had been dim, worn down by death, now flared anew.

Maeve approached Cormac and searched his face. The pallor of despair had masked his youth, but it was lifting now as he absorbed her words. The stamp of Conor's proud bones could perhaps radiate nobility from now on, and wisdom.

"The Ulaid will need a king," she said, resting a hand on his shoulder. "But I think Cúchulainn needs only his hearth and his wife."

Cormac nodded, dazed. He looked not at her eyes but around her, as if he glimpsed the remnants of that light. "It is well done, lady. I will go to the Hound myself."

She smiled. "I will send him food and knit-bone salve for his wounds." Clapping on his helmet, Cormac bounded down the slope like a boy.

Finn. Maeve needed to feel her warmth, see Fraech alive with her own eyes.

She turned her back on her warriors, all muttering in wonder and relief. As she floated along the track toward the camp, lightheaded, for a moment a shadow darkened her heart.

Maeve halted, her unfocused eyes on the trees. They bent in a cold wind from the west, and above their canopies of brown and gold, great gray clouds scudded by. It was no more than that, she realized. A cloud shadow. The wind. She was back in Thisworld now, the land gripped by leaf-fall.

With an effort of will she shook off her trance, pulling herself firmly back into this body, this place, this time.

Her men needed her.

Maeve sent swift riders to the Gates of Macha—a man of Connacht and one of the Ulaid to halt the fighting there.

Before sunset, meanwhile, the Ulaid messenger that Cormac and Cúchulainn charged with seeking news of Conor returned to them. Cúchulainn listened to the scout's report of Conor's death, staring into the burnished light on the lake.

Cormac slumped on a rock, the tension going from him, and taking off his helmet, he scratched his sweat-streaked hair and looked up at the sky.

Cúchulainn nodded and walked to Ferdia's body. The Hound had wrapped his friend in furs and set his chariot horses to guard him. Now he squatted beside Ferdia, his head low on his own breast.

After a time he took a bundle of cloth from his chariot and approached the stream, his gaze intense on the water, as if there was no one around. Heedless of the Connacht warriors, he began to strip off his armor. He threw down his tarnished helmet, unbuckled his mail-shirt, and laid aside his blades. Finally, he peeled off his boots, his filthy, torn tunic, blood-encrusted trews, and the leather breechclout warriors wore into battle.

Cúchulainn was pale and naked now, and even from a distance Maeve could see the red weals that marred his body.

Striding proud, the great Hound of the Ulaid waded into the deepest pool and plunged in. He stayed underwater for many heartbeats. Maeve could just see him turning and scouring himself with silt from the stream-bed.

Washing away all the deaths.

At last he emerged, his fair hair dripping, and just as carefully dressed himself in the clean clothes he had put by. Trews of checked wool. A tunic of blue. He left the helmet and mail-shirt on the ground, and strapping on his sword, crossed to Maeve's side of the water.

She met him there.

The Hound was chilled and wet, hair plastered to his brow. His eyes were red-rimmed, though as calm as a bright sea. "Peace cannot last forever. Warriors must win renown and gold from their kings, or they will not be there to fight when needed."

Maeve nodded. "If we are lucky, peace will last as long as our oaths are remembered. That still gives the Ulaid time to rebuild, time for us all to heal. For in the light of Source, I sensed that the battles to come are not of Erin's making. She will need the strength of all her children to endure that darkness."

Cúchulainn stared into her eyes. The Source they had shared still flowed between them. "Then let us forge peace now, whatever comes after."

Maeve's shoulders lowered, and her hand fell from its customary grip on her sword-hilt. "The oaths should be marked with a sacrifice to the gods. I have already sent riders to drive Finnbennnach, the royal bull of Connacht, to us."

Cúchulainn blinked, his mouth quirking. "So your bull has been that close to our border all this time?"

"I hid him some time ago, in case a Hound came sniffing. You Red Branch were always casting too far from home."

Cúchulainn smiled, dragging a hand through his hair to squeeze the water out.

Maeve sobered. "What will you give in return?"

Cúchulainn gestured to the north. His hands were webbed with cuts. "The Donn Cuailgne is our finest bull. He was Conor's, and is quartered not too far. Let us make a great feast of both beasts, send their blood to the gods, and then Ulaid- and Connach-men alike can share their meat as a mark of peace."

A few nights later, druids of Connacht, Laigin, and Mumu reverently slit the throats of the White Bull of Connacht and the Brown Bull of the Ulaid, and laid their bodies to sleep.

On the smoke of their livers, the prayers of the warriors were lifted to the gods. Their blood was mixed with mead, and brought strength to men who were wounded and drawn. Finally, they were roasted on spits of oak saplings, the meat shared among every warrior gathered from the four kingdoms.

The flames of those bonfires were seen far across the dark land.

The druids painted the white bull's blood on the brows of Cúchulainn and Cormac, and the essence of the brown bull marked Maeve. Their oaths to each other's kingdoms were thereby painted on their bodies, and recited thrice over by the bards.

Cúchulainn sat and let the raucous celebrations swirl about him, taking ale for the first time in weeks. Something about his stillness kept everyone at arm's length, even the Ulaid warriors, and at last he was able to slip away.

On the edge of the camp, he took hold of the Gray of Macha and the Black of Sainglu, harnessed to his chariot, and led them up and around the shoulders of the great hill through the heather. In the back of the chariot lay Ferdia, strapped securely to the wicker.

The horses were steady-footed, and labored as if they knew what burden they bore. High up, where Ferdia could see far across Erin, Cúchulainn gathered heather stems and rowan-wood and built a great pyre. On it he laid his friend. The stiffness had gone from Ferdia's body now, and ignoring the faint, sickly scent, Cúchulainn uncovered him.

The Hound had bound the great wound and dressed his sword-brother in his own finery, and now Ferdia merely looked asleep, young and pale in the moonlight.

Cúchulainn had given one of his most precious possessions to Naisi before he died, a dagger with a crystal hilt. There was only one thing left to give Ferdia. The Hound unbent his Red Branch arm-ring—the first time it had left his body. That Red Branch lived no more, even if he did create another. He bound it next to Ferdia's own armband and kissed his cold brow. "Keep it for me until I come to you."

Then Cúchulainn lit the fire and sat on a rock to watch it

burn. The flames roared and streamed away, higher than any pyre he had ever seen. *His spirit was so bright… and thus it leaves us.*

As Ferdia burned, Cúchulainn curled his arms about his knees, glassy-eyed. He had given everything for the Ulaid, but the power of the Champion, that divine flame of battle Source, had also driven the gae bolga through Ferdia's body.

Cúchulainn sucked in a breath as if surfacing from a long dive. He got to his feet. The twisting flames of the pyre were orange now, no longer bright silver. The sky was merely dark and cloud-blown. And he was just cold, gooseflesh spreading over his neck.

The Hound laughed for the third time that day. He was a man after all. Only a man.

Late in the night, once Ferdia's body was consumed, Cúchulainn led his horses and empty chariot across the rocky summit, away from the din and fires of the war-camp below. One thought alone quickened his step, a desire as old as the hills themselves.

Emer.

Behind him Ferdia's flames reached for the other realms. But Cúchulainn knew nothing but the earth beneath his sore feet now, and the cutting wind on his cheek. Every muscle ached, and he was glad.

He came off the mountain and disappeared into the woods, heading north to his wife and home.

Maeve stood alone, gazing up.

It was hard to see beyond the bonfires, but she thought she glimpsed another flame in the hills. She walked out into darkness, drinking in the mist above the nearby stream. As their senses had been joined, she understood now that Cúchulainn was gone.

A shiver took her over.

For days her mind, heart, and body had been consumed with

the needs of the many—the fates of thousands in her hands. She had been focused on Finn, Conor, and then Cúchulainn. She had exhausted herself to convince her men this peace was right, dealing with those who argued against it, calming the concerns of others. The ritual of the bulls, the carousing of the men...they had drained everything from her.

Now, for the first time, Maeve was alone. She was only now able to feel the pulse of her own body, her own heart.

Her heart...

It was thumping out of kilter, and had been for some time. The shadow she glimpsed, that strange chill...it came from *inside her*, not outside.

At last she could feel the needs of the one. Her legs buckled.

Ruán.

Already armed and cloaked, Maeve raced to the horse-lines beside the baggage carts. The guards on watch started forward, then saluted with their spears.

She dug saddle and tack from the cart beside Meallán, fumbling as she untied him and threw his bridle over his head. "Go to the princess Finn and the lord Fraech," she ordered the guards. She had to bite her tongue to steady herself. "Tell them I am safe, but had to go to someone who needs me. I will rejoin the warband as soon as I can."

Climbing a dead stump, she leaped to Meallán's back. He shied, and Maeve had to fight to hold him, wheeling him about. "Do you understand?" she demanded.

The young warriors nodded, wide-eyed. "Aye, lady."

Maeve had to pick her way along a stream heading west, the trees blocking the moonlight. Once on the cart-road the warband had followed, however, the light spilled over the track, making night as day, and she let Meallán break into a canter.

Panic was making it hard to think; that sense of wrongness

was suffocating. She pulled Meallán up at the edge of a marsh. Panting, Maeve cradled her belly and sent her awareness inside. The child's spirit was a stronger flame now, pulsing in time with her blood. *Reach for him*, she cried to it, willing herself to surrender into the same sensation she experienced by the stream that dawn a few days before.

The threads of her own soul wove through the glimmering waters and radiant air of Erin, the sparks of living things.

The tiny life inside her flared, and Maeve caught a glimpse of her land as if she hovered above it. It was a vast cloth of many colors, the courses of the rivers marked out in silver filaments. A place at the core of that bright web was torn to her, all the light quenched. A dark rent.

Her eyes flew open.

Ruán, by a river…? The great watercourse that spilled through the Connacht lakes on its way to the sea.

Sinand. A river guarded by the sídhe.

Delirious now, Ruán struck out at the dogs that must be gnawing his leg. His fingers swung through empty air.

He collapsed on his side, flickering back into consciousness for a moment. He was burning up, slick with sweat. His tongue stuck to his mouth. Something dripped down his face and he licked it, but it was only salt.

I failed…blind again…

He curled fingers under his chin, trying to burrow away from the pain. An otter…Maeve. Before the agony drew him back to his body, he felt her lift from despair. He remembered a glow inside her, and his wonder at its warmth. That must be the flame of her spirit. She would save people with it now. He didn't fail.

So it was done. The rush of power had consumed what was left of him. The river would take him into the ocean and the arms of the Mother Goddess. He thought he heard Her whisper at last in the burbling of the water through the reeds.

Come to me…

Ruán startled awake again. Beads of sweat ran into his mouth. "Where are you?" he slurred. The sídhe had always been with him when he was in pain. He just had to sleep, that was all, and then he would dream of them again.

A druid chant rose to his tongue. His death-song:

The sky take me…the earth cradle me…the waters welcome me.

CHAPTER 40

T he world had become only shadow and light.

Even in the day, Erin remained dark to Maeve now, etched with silver only where Source ran through the creatures, trees, and water. She withdrew from her body's sight until there was nothing but the streaming of that Other sense.

She met the banks of the River Sinand after two sleepless days and two nights of travel. Another day came, bleak and gray, a nightmare of gathering darkness in her heart.

On the crest of a hill, Maeve pulled up her weary stallion. She was driving Meallán onward with a frantic mind, as if her fear could thrust the veils apart. But when she succumbed to panic, she lost the trail of bright threads. Where along Sinand's course was he?

The answer came unbidden. Ruán was of the wild, caught between Thisworld and the Other. So was their child, restless inside her. Animals also sensed the song of the sídhe through the veils.

Meallán. Trust the wild itself. Trust the sídhe. She had to finally let go.

Maeve closed her eyes and exhaled. She dropped her reins, holding out her arms to the wind. Meallán stood for a moment, used to her directing him, his ears twitching back toward her.

Show me. Maeve drew an image of Ruán in her heart: his face, his voice. She pictured him standing at Meallán's head, murmuring.

Meallán's ears pricked forward again, and with a snort he began to walk. Maeve grabbed his mane and clung on, her legs loose across his back, her belly warm against his flank.

At daybreak Maeve knew she was close. At last, along a hidden bend in the river, she threw herself from Meallán's saddle. She landed hard, jarring herself back into her body.

Her eyes were drawn to what looked like a fallen tree washed up on the banks, its bark bleached white. *Ruán.*

Heedless of her own safety, she skidded down the riverbank through a fringe of mossy alder trees, stumbling over stumps embedded in the wet earth and reeds. Below, Ruán's stillness was unearthly, his arms flung wide, his hair encrusted with mud.

Maeve fell to her knees at his side, and at first could not even unclench her fists to touch him. She glanced up. A place on the bank above had given way, and he had brought down a slip of soil and sticks. There were furrows all around him in the mud, delved by his hands. A sliver of bone on his thigh showed through torn trews. By its smell, that wound had turned.

Bending over, Maeve could see no movement in his chest. "No." It was a growl. She grabbed his wrist. His filthy skin burned, but there was a slight flutter of a pulse, hard to feel amid the storm of her own heart.

Maeve filled her flask from the river, though when she prized his chapped lips open, most of it ran back out. "Ruán." For the first time ever, she dragged up his blindfold, exposing his ruined eyes. His eyelids had fused over sunken wounds, the hollows knotted and red. She smoothed his temples, gripped by a senseless instinct to kill the person who had harmed him, to throw herself over and protect him with her body, though it happened long ago.

All of him, at last. *Beautiful to her.*

Maeve gazed down, cursing her helplessness. She could do little to heal his leg wound, for she did not know how. A breath leaked from Ruán's lips, as something ebbed from him.

Maeve clutched him and breathed her own life into his mouth. "Ruán, you will wake now and you will live." She thumped his chest. "Wake now! *You will wake now...*" Her voice cracked and she could not go on.

His skin was pale beneath the dried mud, his lips bloodless.

Maeve bowed her chin to her chest. She could see nothing now, tears blurring his face as if he was already receding from her. She caught that thought in her breast. *No.* She wiped her wet face. There must be a way to force her own strength into him.

She got beneath Ruán, her legs on either side as she rested him against her, clasping his matted head to her breast. She kissed his brow. "I am here now, *mo chroí.*" *My heart.* Why did she not say it when he could hear her? "All that you told me, I felt. I saw the light of the sídhe. I made peace with the Ulaid." She rocked him. "There is a baby, *a stór.* Come back for the child, Ru ... for me ..."

Her words slid into a senseless crooning. She gazed at the sunlight on the river, the ripples sending up splashes of light. *Help me.* Maeve ground it through numb lips, pleading at last with the sídhe.

She sought in her heart for everything she knew. When the otter came, and when she fought Cúchulainn, she had melted the boundaries of her body into the water, releasing her spirit.

Her hands shaking, Maeve got on her knees and eased Ruán over the mud another hand-span into the shallows. There she lay back down, cradling him.

Seek the goddess of life, the Great Mother, in a river.

Become a river...

She let herself sink into the mud beneath them, her head tangled in reeds. The water closed over Ruán except for his face, cooling his fever.

Maeve sank. The river murmured.

She brushed Ruán's scarred eyes, and it came to her that nothing mattered, not beauty nor ugliness. *We wear mantles of flesh, but they are not what we are…We are light…*

Maeve breathed out along Ruán's cheek. And because there was nothing left to give but her love—because at last her whole being was bent upon him—she slipped from her shell and there was no struggle at all.

The cold of the river faded. Maeve lost all sense of her body, and drifted toward a veil of brightness. A moment of terror came, for that unknown.

But he was there somewhere, and she needed him.

Maeve stood naked and waist-deep in a broad river—swifter and darker than the real Sinand on whose bank her body lay. The deep green water curled about her, sinuous and alive, tugging at her flesh and slapping white-edged waves over nearby rocks.

She reached out her hands, and upwellings rose to the surface as if to meet her palms, gurgling with bubbles. Her hair streamed through the water like river-weed. Though she was spirit, she had clothed herself in a memory of her body, and her heart beat faster as her toes sank into silt and she felt it sloping away into unknown depths.

Maeve looked down. Her skin was not cold anymore. It glowed from within, and the same luminescence was coming from all around her, flowing from the water and radiating from the air. The trees on the riverbanks were spires of silver.

That wash of light seemed endless…timeless. It made her thoughts slip away. She began to forget. Why was she here…? She was the river itself; she would stream away now and be Maeve no more. She took a step, fingers out. The curls of water reached back, beckoning her in.

A movement caught her attention, and she lifted her head.

Someone stood on the opposite bank, a naked child of almost three years old. His hair was as russet as a stag's coat, and his eyes looked straight into hers. They were Maeve's own, dark blue and intense for one so young.

They held the solemnity of an older soul. *Her babe to come.* Then his eyes filled with an urgency that rooted her there, and he raised his arm and pointed upstream.

Maeve turned.

Drifting down the middle of the river came a long narrow boat with a curved prow. The rails were carved into curling wave-crests, the prow painted with spirals. Two maidens clad in deer-skins paddled the boat. They were small, with feathers wound through their dark hair, but their heads were proud and limbs graceful as they drew the boat through the water with a flowing rhythm.

The maidens showed no recognition of Maeve, paid her no attention.

Maeve peered into the boat, and a shock of ripples passed through the water from her flesh.

Ruán lay at rest on a bier, his hands folded over his breast. His hair was tangled on bracken, the red twining with green fronds. His face was unmarked, his eyes whole but closed as if in a peaceful sleep. It was not his body slipping away, then, but—

"Stop!" Maeve tried to reach out, but her foot slid on the riverbed and she nearly plunged in before scrabbling upright.

The Otherworld maidens appeared not to hear, the wind drawing back their unbound hair. Downstream they headed, toward the ocean, into the arms of the goddess waiting to claim him.

A darker surge filled Maeve. *I will not allow it.*

Without hesitating, she launched herself into the depths, flail-ing toward the boat. The water choked her as it closed over her face, but she would not let that vessel pass. From the corner of her eye she glimpsed the child, leaping along the riverbank to keep up with her as she swam closer to the boat.

With the last of her strength, Maeve caught its side. Her feet found purchase on a sandbank and she dragged on the prow. Ruán lay there just out of reach.

Still the maidens paid her no mind, their faces turned away. Maeve struggled to her feet in the shallows, the water streaming from her. She blinked as she held the vessel against the current, gasping, "He is not for you yet—*let him go.*"

There was no flicker of acknowledgment that she existed from the sídhe, though they did stop paddling, as if waiting for something.

Maeve gripped the rail and leaned over it. "He was coming to help me, to find peace for Erin. He did this for the people—he deserves life!" She glanced at Ruán. His skin was bright now, his lips no longer cracked, but full and blush-red. "I...need him. I give myself to him, and him alone...I will never fail him again, *never*..." It poured from her in broken gulps, and she could not stop that torrent. "*We* deserve this life!"

Only then did the sídhe maiden at the prow turn her graceful head. Maeve gazed into her eyes and it was like plunging through a night sky. They were dark and full of stars, opening onto worlds vast and deep.

Maeve lost her footing on the riverbed, clutching the side of the boat. Terror swept her, that if she did not remember who she was she might fall into that glory and be consumed. With every scrap of strength she possessed, she held that starry gaze with her own. Her courage would not fail now—not for him.

The sídhe-maiden smiled. "So, battle queen. Have you come to bargain with us at last?"

Maeve's speech failed her.

"Here we are." Despite her merry smile, the maiden's voice welled up from immense depths. She waved at the sleeping Ruán. "But if we do restore to you a life together, what will you do with it?"

Maeve swallowed, licking her dry lips. "Anything you want me to. What is your bargain?"

The maiden at the stern dipped her paddle in, and the river

current died and it became still as a pool, the boat rocking from side to side. The veils of light hung in the breathless air.

The sídhe-maiden at the prow rested her dripping oar between Maeve and Ruán. "So you still think us tricksters, always trying to trap you? That game would have palled many ages ago!" A rippling laugh. The sídhe swished her hand through the glowing air as one would water, watching it swirl into spirals.

Then those dazzling eyes staked Maeve to the spot. "We are not your lords—we serve the Source. We are the bridge for that light, so that it may flow between the Otherworld and Thisworld." Slowly, like an unfurling bird-wing, the sídhe reached out her arm and pressed her white finger to Maeve's brow.

A brief pain pierced Maeve's mind, but understanding came with it.

A bridge for the Source. They gathered it, summoned it, and poured it forth. Of course. The sídhe were known as the guardians of the animals, plants, and sacred springs, which were filled with Source. Source was the flame Cúchulainn summoned in battle, and the essence of the otter that saved her life. It lay behind everything in Thisworld.

"Though brethren to you, we do find humans hard to reach." A smile flickered about the sídhe's mouth.

Unaccountably, Maeve's skin grew hot.

"And so . . . we now seek a bridge *in Thisworld*, between the sídhe and your own people in turn. To safeguard the life of Erin."

A shiver passed over Maeve from head to feet. "I will do whatever you want. You can take anything you want of me . . ."

"Ah, you always see a fight brewing, don't you, sister?"

For the first time, Maeve felt cold, a flicker of fear arising that she would be called to arms once more. The longing to stay here with Ruán was all that existed in her now. "No," she realized, and that utterance rippled out through the radiant air. "I am no warrior. I am no battle queen. I will not send men to war, or rule their wills, or trap them . . . or *be* trapped."

She had now glimpsed what lay on the other side of pain and

sorrowed memories, what the light of the world truly was. She had felt, through her body, what her power could become, even if she did not know how. A cradle, not a shield.

Maeve's eyes did not waver before the sídhe. "You cannot take anything you want of me. But I will give of what I am, for him."

The maiden's smile flowered. "The task of which I speak is more arduous than ruling a kingdom, make no mistake. It is a challenge of spirit, demanding surrender to the rivers of Source—and thereby belongs only to the bravest of souls." She looked hard at Maeve and then glanced at Ruán. "He has at last found the God of the land in him, and so a bridge he will be, in some life. We could take him now to learn more of this."

"*No.*" Frantic, Maeve peered at Ruán's face. She thought he was glowing brighter, losing the outline of familiar features. She went to clutch his hand, but a subtle movement of the oar stopped her.

Maeve's gaze flew back to the sídhe.

The maiden was no longer smiling. "For him to claim his fate in this body requires the power of you both now, God and Goddess, Father and Mother, for all of Erin." With an intense stare, the sídhe reached out her hand to Maeve. "So will you claim yours?"

You have felt it already, little sister, when you flew with him above the hills. That joy can be yours, even in this mantle of flesh, if you still have the courage of your heart.

Maeve's heart gave its answer in a rush, without any thought at all. She reached out to clasp the hand of the sídhe.

A dizzying storm caught her up, a tempest that blinded all her senses. When it set her down, she knew she saw a future—one that might, or might not, come to be.

Maeve walked a sacred path by a vast lake. There was singing on the air, voices she knew to be sídhe as well as human. She immediately sensed the great upwelling of Source that was being gathered here, as of an immense spring of light.

The joy of belonging spread through every part of Maeve. As she walked, it tingled through her hands and radiated from the crown of her head.

By the lakeshore, a spring of water gushed from a hollow of reeds. There was Erna, her step graceful as she glided among the sick who came to seek healing from the Source-light.

Set back in the trees was a hut, humble and thatch-roofed. Yet proud men came to its door, ducking beneath the lintel with swords at their waists and their eyes troubled. And they hearkened to a seer, a priestess with frosted hair and gray eyes, who bent the streams of Source to illuminate what was to come.

A man waded through the reeds that fringed the lake. He had a net slung over his shoulder like any other fisherman, his blind face lifted to the sun. Maeve saw that much of the radiance of this place flowed from him, for Other lights swirled around him, and they were the ones who sang. The veils through which he walked made his body so bright he appeared to the people who came here as sunlight on water.

And still there was her great task.

As Maeve trod the spiral paths, she gathered the threads of Source and held them within the vessel of her body. And when people came for healing and told their stories, and summoned memories; when bards recited tales; and the glimpses of Otherworld knowing grew from a stream into a flood—so Maeve, Levarcham, Erna, and all the others who had chosen to serve wove those threads into the very fabric of Thisworld.

The voice of the sídhe drew her back. "For even when the wind blows over those empty shores, the knowing we weave into the land now will arise in those who come after, and some will hear Erin's song of what was, and can be again."

Maeve blinked as if waking. The river washed around her thighs, the light shimmering. The child on the banks was gone, but her hand was over her belly, and it was full.

Tiernan's dream. It was not Macha who gathered the Source, it was meant to be her. The destiny she always longed for—to protect the people, to be something greater, to be a *mother of the land*—it had only ever been an echo of this.

Within the rush of that thrill, Maeve felt a presence greater even than the sídhe wordlessly ask for her allegiance: She who was not Bríd, Macha, or Danu; Nemain or the Morrígan; but all goddesses as one.

The Great Mother, who wanted to claim her as Her vessel.

Maeve bowed her chin, hardly able to speak. "I give myself to this fate." She gazed at the luminous sídhe, and beheld at last the beauty she had never felt she deserved. "I give myself to you."

The sídhe's grin was swift. "Then perhaps you may be worthy of him after all."

Sure now, Maeve waded to Ruán, and this time the sídhe made no move to stop her. As fluid as the water, Maeve leaned over the boat and wound her hand about his neck. Drawing his lips to hers, she breathed that glimpse of glory into him.

At last she broke the kiss, leaving her mouth above his. "Ru, there is a baby."

His eyes opened, as brilliant green as the river.

CHAPTER 41

SUN-SEASON

The little group stood beside two riders on the marshy shores of the great lake in the far north of Connacht. Late afternoon sun poured over them from the west, the water an expanse of gold etched with ripples. The bright-tipped reeds murmured and dipped, that stirring spreading back to the trees that fringed the shore and up the slopes of the hills that sheltered them.

Beside Ruán squatted a statue he had hewn from the trunk of a dead oak tree. It bore the simple carvings of two faces, one on either side, with large eyes, long noses, and enigmatic mouths.

"Is that to scare people *away?*" Finn asked.

Fraech frowned. "Finn!"

Ruán only chuckled, and lifting Dáire from his shoulders, bent down beside the wooden pillar. The little boy squirmed from his arms, toddling a few steps and falling over on his face. He sat up, too stunned to cry, his mouth and eyes round. Erna and Levarcham laughed.

"Ruán spent many nights working on that," Maeve explained to her daughter, with a smile.

The carvings were a male figure looking out across the lake, and a female looking to the hills. They were meant to show the god and goddess of the land in harmony—a marker to point people the way to the healing spring.

Ruán answered Finn, tracing the lines in the oak. "It is supposed to be your mother and me. Does she look grumpy enough?"

Finn grinned. "Oh, aye."

Dáire tottered to the statue and clumsily patted the male carving. Ruán curved an arm about his son, and Dáire turned to his father's face instead, his chubby fingers gentling when he touched the blindfold. "See." Ruán's voice was husky. "It must be a good likeness."

Maeve bent and kissed Ruán's brow, then scooped her ruddy-haired son up, making him squeal. "You must go," she said to Fraech, hanging Dáire over her shoulder. "I want you to camp long before dark—before the ground gets damp."

"Oh, Mother." Finn rolled her eyes.

Fraech was holding his horse by the bridle. His royal guards waited for them farther down the shore. "She shouldn't even be riding." Since Finn's belly began to swell, that frown had become permanently drawn on Fraech's brow. "I told her we could pack a cart with cushions and rugs, but—"

"I'm not a sack of barley!" Finn retorted. She tossed her head, and with a subtle tug of her reins made Nél prance, pawing elaborately with one hoof.

Fraech glanced at Maeve with a dark expression as he hauled himself into his saddle. "Speaking of likenesses..."

"Oh, no, don't blame me." Maeve leaned up to kiss Finn and then held Dáire out for his sister's hug, which made him squirm and shriek.

Maeve propped her son on her hip, and when Finn's gaze locked with hers, she took the girl's fingers. "It will not be long," she murmured. "We will be with you at Cruachan for Lughnasa, and you will come back with us for the birth." Maeve allowed the deep welling of peace within her to flow from her flesh into her daughter's hand.

As that warmth poured forth, it brought color back to Finn's cheeks, and the fear in her eyes softened. "Yes, Mamaí."

Maeve kissed Finn's fingers. "Erna will bring you through safely. She has the most skilled hands in Erin, they say." She grinned at the dark-haired druid. "Well...the men all say."

Erna flushed and gave a little bow toward Finn. "I will be at your service, lady. There is no safer place in Erin, I promise."

With a last flurry of farewells, the King and Queen of Connacht rode away southward, down the shore of the great lake toward Cruachan.

Maeve watched Finn kick her horse into a gallop, streaking away with Fraech hard on her heels. His shouts floated back to them on the wind.

"Poor man," Maeve remarked.

Ruán was still smoothing the carved hollows on his statue, picking out shreds of wood he had missed. "I will do one for you," he said to Levarcham as he straightened. "For outside your hut."

Levarcham snorted as they all turned back. Ahead, the little scatter of thatch roofs glowed in the lowering sun, and the smoke of cookfires curled into the purple shadows that stretched over the ground. There was a haze over the spring, glimmers of silver dancing like dragonflies.

"Make me look like an ugly crone, my boy," Levarcham said, "and you might find your supply of honey-cakes suddenly drying up."

Ruán grinned. "I can only imagine what your voice brings to mind, Lady Levarcham."

Maeve glanced at him. Without distraction, and buoyed by the powers of the sídhe, he could see, at times. It was a secret, though, between them. Ruán sensed her thought and turned his head a little, so she caught the gentle curve of his mouth.

Her fingers could not hold back from curling in the hair at Ruán's nape, touching his sun-browned skin in answer.

"Maeve, you will explain to your man I am not ancient yet."

The last of the golden light was pooling on the shores of the lake. It had been a warm day, and a slick of sweat ran down Maeve's back beneath the thin linen tunic.

Abruptly, Ruán's head was drawn toward the water. He spun on his heel and then plucked his son from Maeve's arms. "Will you take him back for us?" He swung Dáire toward Erna.

Startled, Erna grabbed the babe. "Of course! Come, little one." Erna placed Dáire on the ground, and she and Levarcham each took one of his hands.

Ruán pulled on Maeve's fingers, his voice dropping. "*You* come with me, *ceara*," he breathed.

Maeve paused, breaking his hold and glancing over her shoulder as Ruán continued toward the water. Bent to one side, Levarcham was shuffling in time with Dáire's dawdle, Erna nodding gravely as he babbled. The setting sun wreathed the three of them in gold.

The sense of the life of this place rushed through Maeve and overflowed.

Light on her feet, she ran after Ruán, throwing her arms about his neck and nearly bowling him over.

He chuckled and turned, catching her around the waist. "It is not suppertime yet." His kiss was fierce at first, a hand in the small of her back drawing them together. Then his fingers cradled her cheeks and his lips softened until Maeve forgot everything else. The moment she sank against him, though, he backed away, tugging her along.

Laughing, they raced to the water's edge, Ruán's damaged leg breaking his stride. He did not pause but flung himself through the shallows, wading out from shore until it was deep enough, then diving in headfirst.

Holding her breath, Maeve walked in more slowly, the lake floating her tunic around her. She watched Ruán streak along underwater, sleek and cloaked in ripples, his hair streaming behind him. Despite the cold, she had to smile at his delight in that freedom of his body, the glee that filled him when no one else was watching.

Ruán flipped over beneath the surface, his skin gleaming like an otter-pelt. His hands reached out for her ankles as they always did, ready to yank her in.

No ... *she must jump.*

A gust of wind broke the sunlight into dancing sparks that blinded her. Before Ruán could reach her, she took a great breath and flung herself into that flood of brilliance.

As she sank through the shimmering veils, the bubbles from Ruán's laugh tickled her skin.

Maeve put her head back, eyes closed. She floated in light.

The story of Deirdre of the Sorrows and
Naisi and the Sons of Usnech is told in
The Swan Maiden.

NOTE ON MYTHOLOGY
AND HISTORY

The Raven Queen mixes Irish myths with Iron Age history and my invention. It is about the famous Irish queen Maeve (also Medb, or Meadbh).

Unlike Deirdre of the Sorrows—the subject of my previous novel, The Swan Maiden—Maeve does not appear in one coherent tale that I could follow. This novel is therefore a "reimagination," not a retelling: I used scraps of the stories about her, then invented the rest to fit my own tale and the Maeve I wanted to bring to life.

However, readers like to know which parts are which, so I will try to give a summary of what is taken from other sources versus my own storytelling.

MYTH

Stories of Maeve of Connacht are part of the group of old Irish tales called the "Ulster Cycle," the most famous of which is the "Táin Bó Cúailnge," or simply "The Táin," translated in English as "The Cattle Raid of Cooley." The classic version of this tale is The Táin, by Thomas Kinsella (Oxford University Press, 1969); there is also a new translation of The Táin by Ciaran Carson (2008). In addition, there are versions all over the Internet.

The Ulster Cycle revolves around the exploits of King Conor and his Red Branch warriors, including the famous Irish hero Cúchulainn.

Maeve appears mainly in "The Táin" but also crops up in other tales, some of which contradict each other in terms of timeline and events. Her name—"she who intoxicates"—is related to "mead," a sacred alcoholic drink. In the tales she is married to many kings, and so some scholars propose that Maeve might originally have been a goddess. The stories might therefore retain an echo of kings being ritually wed to the land by pledging themselves with sacred mead to "the goddess" Maeve and vowing to protect her and thereby their territory.

In later tales, however, Maeve is portrayed as a very human and ruthless warrior-queen: sexually voracious, bloodthirsty, and power-hungry. But the context is important here.

The early peoples of Ireland were not literate, and the tales were passed on by word alone. Nothing was written down until after the coming of Christianity in the fifth century, but the earliest surviving manuscripts were made in medieval monasteries much later than that.

Some therefore see Maeve's unflattering portrayals as simply attempts by a new religion to replace the old religion, as well as a negative attitude toward pagan goddesses and a fear of women's sexual freedom. They see in the stories a medieval attempt to "downgrade" Maeve from a goddess to a sinful woman: someone who could then be derided and belittled.

I wanted to resurrect the powerful Maeve, and imagine what it was about her that could have inspired such censure.

In the ancient tales, she was married to various kings, including Conor of Ulster, from whom she did run away. She did marry Ros Ruadh of Laigin, and later, Ailill of Laigin. She did become Queen of Connacht in her own right.

The story about Macha Mong Ruad and how she found Emain Macha is a genuine myth. I could not ignore the opportunity to connect Maeve to Macha. Both were red-haired warrior-queens;

Maeve was—possibly—a goddess in origin; and Macha is portrayed as a goddess of the land and of battle and death, as well as sometimes assuming human form. The similarities were startling, and gave weight to my portrayal of why the people of Connacht might choose a queen over a king.

In the myths, Maeve is strongly associated with cats. Cats are not native to Ireland, so my original idea was to associate her with otters instead, since they have some of the same "catlike" grace. I eventually decided to also give Maeve a cat that originally came from Egypt.

Finnabair was indeed Maeve's daughter in myth, but I made up their early estrangement. In "The Táin," Finn's great love is the young warrior Fraech; however, I made Fraech of royal kin and Maeve's war-leader so he could be king at the end of the book.

"The Táin" describes the war between Maeve of Connacht and Conor of Ulster over two famous bulls—the white bull Finnbennach and the brown bull Donn Cuailnge. It starts when Maeve and Ailill are comparing each other's wealth, and Maeve realizes that Ailill has Finnbennach but she does not own a bull of equal stature, so she goes to war with Conor to steal his bull.

I came up with quite different reasons for the war; however, I did retain a thread about the sacred bulls.

Central to "The Táin" is the defection of a large number of Red Branch warriors, led by Fergus mac Roy, from the Ulster side to the Connacht side, due to Conor's treatment of Deirdre and Naisi (portrayed in *The Swan Maiden*).

Ferdia and Cúchulainn are shown in the myths as best friends, foster brothers, and soul mates. Cúchulainn was King Conor's nephew, and did stay with the king when the other Red Branch defected to Maeve. Ferdia, however, could not serve Conor any longer and went with Fergus. This device leaves Ferdia and Cúchulainn—the two greatest warriors of Erin—on opposite sides, and heading for a heartbreaking and inevitable showdown.

The myth of the goddess Macha includes an episode where

the Red Branch warriors heartlessly force her to race the king's horses. She ends up giving birth to twins on the racetrack in great travail. She curses the men of Ulster, that in their time of greatest need they, too, will be struck down by the "pangs." It is these so-called birth pangs that incapacitate the Red Branch in "The Táin" and allow Maeve's army to attack.

In the original myth, Cúchulainn does not suffer the pangs, which is why he is forced to defend Ulster alone at the ford while the other Red Branch are bedridden.

I decided on a nonmystical reason for the pangs—the special Alban ale that Conor gives his new Red Branch warriors at the feast is contaminated with the ergot fungus, which grows on barley and causes illness, hallucinations, burning in the limbs, and eventually death if enough is imbibed.

This is why I made Ferdia originally teetotal, and Cúchulainn a drinker. After Conor's actions part Ferdia and Cúchulainn, Cúchulainn stops drinking out of respect for his friend. This prevents Cúchulainn from imbibing Conor's ale, which is when he throws the cup against the roof pillar. He is therefore able to go on to defend his kingdom in single combat.

Maeve was said to have had a voracious sexual appetite, including bedding Fergus mac Roy. Ailill therefore did grow jealous of Fergus, and he did kill him, though in the tales this takes place after the events of "The Táin" and in a different manner.

In the myth, Cúchulainn does hold the ford by himself and challenges the Connacht army to single combat. Days of fighting ensue, but Ferdia will not at first fight his friend. Maeve does offer Finn to him, and in the myth, this eventually makes him fight, whereas I have it that he decides he would rather die at Cúchulainn's hand than live as he is.

Ferdia and Cúchulainn fight for days, and eventually Cúchulainn uses the gae bolga on his friend, slaying Ferdia. This heartbreaking series of events is one of the most famous duels in the ancient world. It has been portrayed in many stories, in painting, and in song. To me, it encapsulates the tragedy of the Celts.

Honor—which the Celts revered above all else—weaves a fateful trap that destroys one of the "great loves" of Irish myth.

In "The Táin," Maeve is eventually incapacitated by a "gush of blood," which is often translated as menstruation—a possible attempt by medieval scribes to scupper Maeve's power by inflicting a female "weakness" upon her. I changed this to a possible miscarriage. At this point the two sides do make peace, neither actually "winning"; though the suggestion is that Connacht surrenders.

Maeve besting Cúchulainn is my own invention, as is Conor's death at Finn's hand (he does not die then in the original). Cúchulainn does outlive "The Táin," but in a later myth is attacked by a group of enemies. Wounded, he straps himself to a standing stone in order to fight to the bitter end, and is eventually slain. A poignant statue portraying his death—the crow goddess hovering over him—can be found outside the main post office in Dublin, Ireland.

The lake sanctuary at the end is sited on Lough Erne, a large two-part lake in County Fermanagh. In myth it is named after "Erna," a handmaiden of Maeve's. It is scattered with many small islands. One of them is Boa Island, where a tiny cemetery contains two enigmatic and undatable stone statues. The largest statue bears a face on each side, one "male" and one "female." The smaller figure is of an old woman. This is the first place I went to when I researched this book, though it relates to the end.

I like to think that memories of Ruán's wood carvings eventually made their way into stone, just as Maeve and Ruán also made their way into local myth, and then into some now-forgotten memory.

HISTORY/ARCHAEOLOGY

I have set Maeve's tale in the Irish Iron Age, in the first century BC.

Thomas Kinsella takes his translation of The Táin from the twelfth-century AD Book of Leinster, although the language of the prose is eighth century, and the verse sections sixth century. Back further, we disappear into the mists of time.

That is why there was once a belief that the Ulster Cycle preserved a "window" into the Iron Age in Ireland in the last few centuries BC. Modern scholars don't like this idea, and think these stories merely reflect the medieval period in which they were written down.

Since they were transcribed by Christian monks, no one knows how faithfully these tales of Celtic pagans have been copied and whether the bias of the writers means that events were changed or even left out.

However, many of the aspects of these tales—feasting, cattle raiding, boastfulness and courage of warriors, single combat of champions, taking of enemy heads, riding in chariots—tie in with what Roman writers observed firsthand about the Celts, as well as archaeology in France and Britain.

I have therefore grounded the story in the archaeology of Ireland, Britain, and Gaul, and the writings of the Romans about the Celts, with regard to weapons, dress, food, and houses.

This has been mixed in with the original myths. For example, Iron Age swords found in Ireland are not very big, yet those in the myths are described as large hacking swords—the sort in use when the stories were written down in medieval times. Chariots are also described in the tales. They have never been found in Ireland, but are known from Iron Age graves in England, France, and Switzerland, and there are wooden trackways in Ireland made for wheeled vehicles.

Conor's fort at Emain Macha has been identified as present-day Navan Fort in Armagh. Excavations have shown that a large roofed building (my "temple of Macha") was destroyed in a great burning in about 95 BC. I used this for the idea of Conor burning the temple down in a fit of madness.

These excavations also found the skull of a Barbary Ape, which was native to North Africa, buried at Emain Macha. This suggests that Irish kings of this period did enjoy trade links with the Mediterranean, and probably had a little access to wine, tableware, furniture, oils, and other luxury items from Greece, Rome, Egypt, and the Near East.

Other archaeological finds back up some elements of the myths. Great cauldrons, drinking vessels, and pits of animal bones suggest that large-scale feasting was a vital part of Celtic life.

Cattle were obviously important, evidenced by sacred deposits of cow bones as well as depictions of cattle in art. The mass of decorated bridle bits and rings for reins show that nobles were riding around on horses, showing off their wealth.

Jewelry is of highly skilled workmanship, and the amount of gold, other metals, and enamel found in Iron Age excavations fits in with the boastful and showy warrior culture described in the Irish myths.

The four festivals of Imbolc, Beltaine, Lughnasa, and Samhain appear in the myths, and they are also named in a bronze "calendar" found in Coligny in France dating to this very period.

Evidence from Irish bog bodies suggests that warriors stiffened their hair with a paste made from pine resin and herbs imported from the Continent. Many bog bodies show evidence of ritual death, often a triple death of strangulation, stabbing, and drowning.

Iron Age trackways have indeed been found in Ireland. Stretches of oak planks form extensive road networks that could have carried chariots and great carts across the vast expanses of wetlands.

PLACES

King Conor's fort of Emain Macha has been identified as the present-day site of Navan Fort, near Armagh. There is a wonderful museum there all about the Ulster Cycle of tales.

Queen Maeve's stronghold of Cruachan has been identified as Rathcroghan near Tulsk, Roscommon. Dun Ailinne in Laigin is the name of the modern site (though this is a ritual site, not a residential fort), and the Hill of Uisneach is supposedly sacred because it is in the center of Ireland.

The Aran Islands (the "Stone Islands") are off the west coast of Galway. The largest island, Inishmór, is the site of Dún Aengus, an enormous stone fort perched on the western edge of the cliffs.

The Sinand is the River Shannon, which connects many of the lakes and bogs to the east of Cruachan.

There is a statue of Cúchulainn carrying a dead Ferdia at Ardee, which lays claim to being the site of the battle at the ford (its name comes from Áth Fhirdia, the Ford of Ferdia). However, I sited the fight beneath the slopes of Slieve Gullion, Sliabh gCuillinn in the Irish, which means "Cullen's Hill" and is related to Cúchulainn in the old myths.

The little cave where Maeve has her baby is called the Cave of the Cats and is beneath the ground near Tulsk—go to the museum in Tulsk and ask for directions. A stone was found in this cave that in old ogham writing mentioned the names of both Maeve and Fraech.

On the coast of County Sligo stands Cnoc na Rí, the Hill of the King (Knocknarea in English). At its foot is the Carrowmore cemetery of passage graves. Such ancient stone tombs were seen by Irish people of the past few centuries as the dwelling places of the sídhe, the "people of the mounds."

Maeve is supposed to be buried beneath the great cairn on the top of Cnoc na Rí. She is reputed to be standing up in all her war regalia—facing the north, and her great enemy, Conor of Ulster.

ABOUT THE AUTHOR

JULES WATSON was born in Western Australia to English parents. After gaining degrees in archaeology and public relations, she worked as a freelance writer in both Australia and England. Jules and her Scottish husband divided their time between the UK and Australia before finally settling in the wild highlands of Scotland. She is the author of the Dalriada trilogy—*The White Mare, The Dawn Stag,* and *The Song of the North* (U.S. title)—a series of historical epics set in ancient Scotland about the wars between the Celts and the invading Romans. *Kirkus Reviews* named *The White Mare* in the top ten Science Fiction / Fantasy releases of 2005, and *The Song of the North* was featured as a "Hot Read" in the April 2008 *Kirkus* special Science Fiction / Fantasy edition.

www.juleswatson.com